DEAD
TIME

DEAD TIME

A HANK FALLON WESTERN

WILLIAM W. JOHNSTONE

and J. A. Johnstone

PINNACLE BOOKS
Kensington Publishing Corp.
www.kensingtonbooks.com

PINNACLE BOOKS are published by

Kensington Publishing Corp.
119 West 40th Street
New York, NY 10018

PUBLISHER'S NOTE
Following the death of William W. Johnstone, the Johnstone family is working with a carefully selected writer to organize and complete Mr. Johnstone's outlines and many unfinished manuscripts to create additional novels in all of his series like The Last Gunfighter, Mountain Man, and Eagles, among others. This novel was inspired by Mr. Johnstone's superb storytelling.

All Kensington titles, imprints, and distributed lines are available at special quantity discounts for bulk purchases for sales promotions, premiums, fund-raising, educational, or institutional use. Special book excerpts or customized printings can also be created to fit specific needs. For details, write or phone the office of the Kensington sales manager: Kensington Publishing Corp., 119 West 40th Street, New York, NY 10018, attn: Sales Department; phone 1-800-221-2647.

PINNACLE BOOKS, the Pinnacle logo, and the WWJ steer head logo are Reg. U.S. Pat. & TM Off.

ISBN-13: 978-0-7860-4384-2
ISBN-10: 0-7860-4384-9

First printing: February 2020

10 9 8 7 6 5 4 3 2 1

Printed in the United States of America

Electronic edition:

ISBN-13: 978-0-7860-4385-9 (e-book)
ISBN-10: 0-7860-4385-7 (e-book)

CHAPTER ONE

The lousy coffee he had managed to drink for breakfast started rising from his gut when he stepped out of the prison wagon and saw "The Walls."

Harry Fallon forced the coffee back down. He had seen prisons before—too damned many, thanks to Sean MacGregor, president of the American Detective Agency in Chicago, Illinois—but sight of the Texas State Penitentiary in Huntsville did something to his nerves.

Buck up, he told himself. *This is no different than Yuma or Jefferson City. And behind those walls, you're going to find the man or men who sent you to Joliet, that murdered . . .*

Fallon shuddered.

"She sure has a way of doin' that to a feller," the deputy marshal drawled as he stepped up on Fallon's right. "Another feller once tol' me that 'The Walls ain't no place to be.'" The lawman snorted, laughed, and spit chewing tobacco onto the cobblestone path cut into the spring grass and pine needles.

The Walls. One hundred thousand square feet surrounded by a foreboding wall of red brick, fifteen feet high and three feet thick. And inside . . . hell on earth.

"Ready, Fallon?"

"Alexander," Fallon told the lawman in a tight, hard whisper. "Harry Alexander."

The deputy cursed softly. "Sorry," he whispered. "I knowed that. Just ain't good at this private detective business."

"Just don't slip once we're inside."

"Right."

"Let's go."

The chains hobbling his legs and wrists rattled as Fallon walked to the gate, where beefy guards waited to welcome the latest inmate to The Walls.

Those red bricks, the stories went, got their coloring from the blood of every inmate to be sentenced to the prison since it had first opened in 1848.

"Warden," the deputy said, removing his hat, as he stepped inside the dark office behind Fallon, whose manacles had been removed in the anteroom inside the gate. Another prison official shut the door behind Fallon and the deputy.

"Superintendent," the warden corrected. "According to the *Rules, Regulations and By-laws for the Government and Discipline of the Texas State Penitentiaries, at Huntsville and Rusk, Texas.*" He nodded at a four-shelf bookshelf to his left. One shelf held a Bible. The top shelf held what Fallon figured had to be *Rules, Regulations and By-laws* . . . The rest of the case was empty.

Fallon hoped the prison library had more books.

"Besides, I detest that vulgar word, *warden*. And Warden Walter Wilkinson has far too much alliteration."

The deputy stared in complete confusion. *Alliteration* would not be in his vocabulary, but Fallon considered him to be a good man . . . as long as he didn't forget to use Fallon's alias.

Walter Wilkinson, warden—personally, Fallon never cared much for the word *superintendent*—at the Texas State Pen, looked pretty much like every other warden Harry Fallon had known. Sweaty, pale, beady eyes, balding—in fact, Wilkinson was completely bald—whose handshake would be flabby had he dared lower himself to shake hands with a prisoner. Fallon already had the man pegged. A politician, he went to church to keep up appearances, took part in all the fairs, attended the meeting of men of power once a month, and used the underground tunnel that led from the hall to some classy brothel. He took bribes frequently, but not from prisoners. Prisoners didn't have enough clout or influence, let alone money.

"You've been a naughty, naughty young man." Wilkinson shook his head and muttered, "Tsk-tsk." He did not look up but kept right on reading the file the American Detective Agency and the Texas attorney general had prepared. "A life sentence." Wilkinson tsk-tsked again. "Well, you'll be happy to know that when your life is over, we have a very fine graveyard for you."

He had a nasal voice, a heavy gut from too many mashed potatoes and port beer, and thick, dark, unruly eyebrows that contrasted with a bald head glistening from sweat. "I suppose you're innocent, too."

Fallon said, "Why should I be different than anyone else here?"

The warden looked up. His eyes considered Fallon for a long time before he stepped back toward the window, leaned against the sill, and brought the tips of his fingers together.

"Actually," he said, "we have one prisoner who says he's guilty. You'll meet him eventually . . . if you live that long. The first night usually drives the weak ones to kill themselves. But . . ."

The fingertips parted, and the warden shoved his hands into the deep pockets on his striped woolen trousers. ". . . I don't think you're weak, Harry Alexander." He said the name as though he knew it was an alias, but, in this part of the United States, people were always choosing whatever name they wanted, and that wasn't because they were outlaws or running away from someone, or something. Before he pinned on that badge in Fort Smith, Arkansas, Harry Fallon had cowboyed and hunted buffalo, and he had known cowboys and skinners who changed their names with the seasons, sometimes on a whim or bet. Just to freshen things up.

The warden nodded to the assistant who had been quietly standing near the door and the deputy marshal who had escorted Fallon the one hundred and fifty or sixty miles from Austin to Huntsville. Once the assistant signed a receipt and handed it to the deputy, the lawman looked at Fallon, nodded, thanked the warden, and opened the door. The assistant closed the heavy door behind the departing lawman, and Fallon slowly, discretely, let out a long breath.

So far, so good.

The man in the dark uniform spoke in a dreary monotone, as though by rote.

Fallon would be issued a uniform, of white and brown stripes. This being summer—it was actually spring, but spring usually seemed like a figment of one's imagination in Texas—Fallon would be given shoes, pants, shirt, and hat. Socks, drawers, and a jacket would be provided in winter.

"If he's still alive," the warden said, sniffed, and searched for a handkerchief in his coat pocket.

"You may keep any drawers, undershirts, socks, or handkerchiefs that you brought," the assistant said, "or may receive any through friends, or purchase them but only after receiving permission from Superintendent Wilkinson, the assistant superintendent, or the sergeant."

Fallon learned about the bedding he would receive, how to handle mess call—once again, no prisoners could speak while eating—bathing (once a week), privileges (like Fallon would ever be granted any of those), visitations, punishments, and work details.

"Start him out tomorrow in the mill," the warden said.

The assistant went on. Fallon had heard it all before. Maybe one time, Fallon thought, he might hear it coming from someone who cared. *Wouldn't that be something!*

"Questions?" the warden asked.

"No, sir," Fallon answered.

"Peter." The warden had found his handkerchief and wiped his nose. Spring, Fallon realized. Hay fever. Fallon grinned. It was good to see a man like Walter

Wilkinson suffer. Fallon had never been allergic to anything, though he wished he were allergic to prisons.

"Get him . . ." The warden sneezed. "Outfitted. Show him . . ." Another violent sneeze that almost doubled over the lout. This was only March. Wait till all the cedars started doing their damage, the wild-flowers started blooming, and the winds picked up. "His cell. Then . . ." This time, the sneeze provoked a vile oath from the warden. "Turn him over to Sergeant Drexel."

The assistant chuckled. "Barney loves breaking in the fresh fish."

Every muscle in Fallon's body tightened. He had been inside The Walls for no more than thirty minutes, and everything—all the planning they had spent— could be jeopardized. Fallon had mentioned the possible risk, but the Texas attorney general and Sean MacGregor had waved off his concerns.

"What would you say the chances are of you actually running into someone you know in Huntsville?" MacGregor had asked. "As a deputy marshal for Judge Parker in Arkansas and the Indian Nations, the men you sent to prison went to the Detroit House of Corrections."

"I ran into them in Joliet," Fallon had reminded the Scot. "And in Yuma. And in Jefferson City."

"But Huntsville's Texas," MacGregor had scoffed.

"I cowboyed in Texas," Fallon had reminded him. "A lot of men I chased out of the Nations rode south to Texas."

The attorney general hadn't bought that argument, either.

"The chances are slight," Malcolm Maxwell had said. "And it's a risk you'll have to take."

Fallon had corrected him. "You mean it's a risk I'll have to take."

"If you want out, Fallon," MacGregor had said, "say the word." He had spoken that so smugly, condescendingly, that Fallon had found himself grinding his teeth. "Say it, Fallon. There's always room for you at Joliet. Just remember, this isn't just a chance to bring justice to a madman. To help your country. But more than that, this is your chance, your only chance, to right your name. To avenge the murders of your wife and daughter."

Now, thinking about that meeting, Fallon saw their faces then. His wife, Renee, so young, so beautiful. His daughter, Rachel, a sweetheart of a baby . . . who would be approaching young womanhood had she not . . .

Fallon shuddered.

The warden laughed, and the images before Fallon, those recurring, haunting memories, stopped instantly, bringing Fallon back into the office of the superintendent of The Walls.

"It happens all the time, doesn't it, Steve?"

The assistant chuckled softly.

"The Walls have a way of sending a chill up your spine. Especially when you know that you'll be here for the rest of your scum-sucking, miserable life." The warden sneezed again. "No. No. Not a life. You don't have a life anymore. You have an existence, and maybe that's only a figure of speech. Get him out—" Another violent sneeze rocked the warden, and the assistant, Steve, opened the door and nodded for Fallon to follow.

Barney Drexel, Fallon kept thinking as he picked up

his clothing, exchanging his denim pants, cotton shirt, and boots for the scratchy, ill-fitting summer uniform of white and brown stripes, rough shoes, and a cap that had to be one size too small. At least he had socks, relatively clean, and summer underpants. Those shoes would cripple a man without socks.

Barney Drexel.

Fallon hadn't thought of him since Judge Parker had fired the lout back in Fort Smith maybe twelve years back. Drexel had pinned on a badge after Parker had just been appointed as the only federal judge serving western Arkansas and the Indian Territory. Drexel had brought in most of the men he went after dead, but Fallon had also killed his share. The rule of outlaws in the Indian Nations was: die game. Certainly, it beat hanging on the scaffolds outside of the old army building that now held the jail and the judge's courtroom. Even if, sometimes, you'd get to hang with your friends. Judge Parker's gallows could hold up to six doomed men at a time.

Drexel should have wound up on those gallows himself. He shot another deputy marshal dead while both were off duty in a saloon on Garrison Avenue. Put four .45 caliber slugs into Deputy Marshal Flint Logan's stomach, and another in the back of Logan's head while he lay in a pool of his own blood on the saloon's sawdust-covered floor. He would have put another bullet in Logan's corpse but the Colt misfired the last chamber.

That shooting had not surprised Fallon. Drexel had always been a brute and a bully, and too often went for his Colt or Winchester. What saved Drexel from the gallows was the fact that Flint Logan's reputation also smelled like a coyote's carcass, and witnesses couldn't, or wouldn't, say that Drexel drew first. The argument seemed to be over a prostitute, but she couldn't be found after the shooting. The U.S. marshal, U.S. attorney, and Judge Parker agreed that they had rid the U.S. Marshals Service of two bad apples. Flint Logan was dead. Barney Drexel was told not to show his face in Arkansas or the Indian Nations again.

So Drexel had wound up as a sergeant of guards in Huntsville.

Such was Harry Fallon's luck.

He made it through the prison doctor's evaluation in rapid time.

"You seem to attract a lot of bullets, sir," the bony, white-haired old-timer said.

"And knives," Fallon told him. "Clubs. Broken bottles. Fists. Hatchets. Fingernails."

"I've performed autopsies on bodies with fewer scars. Take a deep breath. Exhale." The doctor lowered the stethoscope. "You're in remarkable condition for what should be a corpse. Have a peppermint stick, Mr. Alexander. And welcome to The Walls."

Now he had been turned over to a guard, a redheaded man with a thick mustache and blackened teeth. As the guard escorted Fallon across the prison yard toward Sergeant Barney Drexel, Fallon kept thinking that maybe, just maybe, after all these years Drexel wouldn't recognize him. A dozen years had passed, and ten of those years had been hard, brutally hard on Harry Fallon. The Illinois State Prison at Joliet certainly had earned its reputation for aging a man.

"Sergeant Drexel," the black-toothed guard said. "Fresh fish for ya."

Big, ugly, bearded Barney Drexel turned around and rapped a big stick into the palm of his beefy left hand.

Barney Drexel looked the same.

Fallon muttered a curse under his breath, but he was saved by another savage curse.

His escort stopped, and stepped aside.

Fallon turned toward the curse and saw a man in the uniform of a Huntsville inmate running hard.

"You turncoat yellowbelly," the man said as his lowered shoulder caught Fallon's middle.

CHAPTER TWO

Josh Ryker.

Fallon recognized him just before the wiry onetime cowboy knocked the breath out of him. Landing hard on his back, Fallon managed to bring his knees up, and then he kept rolling, somersaulting, sending Ryker sailing toward Sergeant Barney Drexel and the other guards and inmates gathered around the whipping post.

Josh Ryker. The last person Fallon expected to find in Huntsville. Who else could be here? Not that it mattered. What had Fallon expected the American Detective Agency to do? Go through a list of every inmate housed in the state pen and see if Fallon recognized the names? Hell, half the men Fallon had arrested in the Indian Nations and Arkansas had been using aliases.

Fallon rolled to his side, pushed himself up on elbows and knees, trying to get his lungs to work again. He heard cheers, curses, and shouts coming from inmates who now provided a wide arena for the fight. Maybe some of the guards were cheering, too. Fallon also saw Josh Ryker running toward him.

Fallon let him come. At the last second, he dived to his right, lifted his left leg high, and managed to trip Ryker. The man cursed as he went sailing into a wall of men in brown-and-white or black-and-white uniforms. The prisoners shoved Ryker back into the circle. He fell onto his back, spread-eagled, and slowly came up, shaking the cobwebs out of his head.

By then, Fallon had pushed himself to his feet. He stood waiting.

"Go get him!" an inmate shouted.

"Kill him!"

"Stomp his head into the dirt!"

Fallon shook his own head. He wasn't moving. He was still trying to remember how to breathe.

And the spectators in prison uniforms and guard uniforms weren't all cheering for the fresh fish.

"Ryker, you's a-fightin' like a Baptist deacon's wife!"

"Get off yer ass, ya puny sack of snake turds, an' kill dis new meat!"

Ryker came to his feet, turned, staggered, straightened, and began moving cautiously, ready now. He probably expected Fallon to be the young green pup he had been back during their cowboying days, back when they had first arrived in Fort Smith. Ryker was the older of the two, the one who could outdrink, outfight, and outride anyone he ever met. Fallon had been the tagalong kid still in his teens and wet behind the ears.

Now Ryker knew that fifteen years had hardened his onetime pard.

He doesn't know the half of it, Fallon thought as he brought his arms up, fists clenched, and began countering Ryker's feints as he drew closer. *Ten years in Joliet for a crime I didn't commit. The riots. The knifings.*

The weeks in solitary and the whippings just so the guards could let everyone know who bossed the prison. And then, pardoned by the governor, only to find myself back in prison—this time working for the American Detective Agency. Yeah, that'll harden a man until his skin and fists are like iron, and his soul and heart even harder than that. Yuma in Arizona Territory, known, rightfully so, as The Hellhole. Jefferson City in Missouri, called the "bloodiest forty-seven acres in America." And now inside these god-awful Walls in eastern Texas!

Yeah, Fallon wasn't that kid Ryker had punched longhorns with in Texas, Indian Territory, and Kansas. Wasn't that puppy dog who had followed Ryker to Fort Smith to gamble.

Ryker swung a right. An easy punch to avoid. Fallon felt it pass over his head, and he came up quickly, bending his head so that the back of his skull caught Ryker's jaw. He heard the crunch of teeth and saw Ryker fall backward. Fallon straightened, shaking off the pain in his head, and raised his right foot. He slammed the ill-fitting shoe down toward Ryker's bleeding face, but Josh Ryker wasn't the same youthful cowboy Fallon had ridden with from Dodge City to Fort Smith all those years ago.

Yes, Ryker had learned a few things, too. He grabbed Fallon's foot, twisted it, and sent Fallon spinning into the ground. Now Fallon rolled into the feet and legs of the prisoners who had formed a circle to watch the brawl. They kicked him, hissed at him, and rolled him back toward Ryker.

Fallon turned and rose off the ground, just in time to feel Ryker's kick that caught him in the left shoulder and drove him into the dust and sand. Fallon brought his legs up again, catching the diving Ryker, and once again sent the cowboy sailing. Again, Fallon rose quickly, rubbing his shoulder, already feeling the beginnings of a big, painful bruise. But his collarbone hadn't been broken.

"Quarter pound of tobbacy says the fresh fish takes that little punk."

"Bet."

"I'll let you see that tintype of that whore I met in San Angelo if Ryker loses this fight."

"I've seen that picture. And never want to see it again. Give me nightmares, it did."

Eighteen months, Fallon remembered. That had been Ryker's sentence. The scenes replayed in Fallon's head.

They had been drunk, Fallon and Ryker, not an unusual state for those two young fools. Pretty much cleaned out by Fort Smith's gamblers, they had been shooting out the streetlamps the first time, only to be stopped by a man that Fallon guessed to be a preacher. The stranger turned out to be Judge Isaac Parker. Fallon should have learned then that Ryker wasn't the type of saddle pal you wanted to be with. For a moment, Fallon thought Ryker would murder the judge, and maybe he would have had a lawman not come along then. Fifty dollars or fifty days. Ryker had to sell his horse and saddle to get them out of the Fort Smith calaboose, then lost most of what he had left over in a craps game. And decided to steal a saddle on display at a saddle shop.

Fallon had tried to stop Ryker. Ryker wasn't one to be stopped. They had fought. Ryker had won. And then another lawman came around, and after an insane and intense few seconds, Fallon had stopped his pard from murdering the lawman in cold blood. The lawman whose life Fallon had saved was a deputy U.S. marshal for Judge Parker's court. When Fallon had been brought to the judge's office, there had been no plea deal, nothing like that. The judge and the U.S. marshal, after hearing how Fallon had saved a deputy's life, offered Fallon a job.

"It's not a gift," Judge Parker had warned him.

And it most certainly wasn't. Fallon had moved up from driving a prison wagon for deputy marshals to becoming a federal deputy himself, one of the youngest, and best, in Parker's court. Till that all came crumbling down.

Josh Ryker had spent eighteen months at the Detroit House of Corrections for assault on a federal lawman. He could've gotten more had the state pressed for charges of breaking and entering, attempted burglary, and unlawful discharge of a firearm.

Well, Fallon thought as the convicts and guards cursed and cheered, he couldn't really blame Ryker. From the look of the inmate, life had never turned out the way the gambling, foolhardy cowboy had thought it would. Detroit was the first step. Now he was in Huntsville.

Why don't the guards stop this?

Fallon threw a punch, ducked another, as the cheers and the curses grew louder. The dust blinded him.

He answered his own question. *They wouldn't have stopped it in Joliet, Yuma, or Jeff City. They wouldn't have stopped it in the dungeon in Fort Smith where men awaited trial. Unless it got out of hand. Huntsville's no different.*

His nose was bleeding. So were his lips. His back hurt and shoulder throbbed. He swung, missed, ducked, swung again, connected, felt a punch that almost took off his right ear, and responded with one that Ryker deflected.

Ryker brought his prison shoes down hard on Fallon's right foot. Fallon wrapped his arm around Ryker's neck and drew it close. He tried to flatten Ryker's nose, but Ryker caught the wrist and held it tight, trying to twist it off. The men grunted, squirmed, attempted to break free, but neither man was willing to give.

"Hell, they ain't doin' nothin' but waltzin'," a Texas accent drawled. Fallon didn't know if that came from a guard or an inmate.

"*No más. No más,*" a Mexican prisoner shouted.

Ryker tried to spit in Fallon's face. His breath stank of bad tobacco and worse coffee. He was missing several teeth. Scars cut through his once-handsome face, but, well, after all those years of hard time, Fallon wasn't going to win any beauty contests himself.

"Been waitin' . . ." Ryker heaved. "A long time . . . for this."

Fallon said nothing. Ryker's grip was so tight on his wrist, he felt his hand growing numb. They weaved this way and that. The shouts and curses sounded all around them, but by now the dust was so thick, the sweat stinging his eyes, Fallon couldn't see much beyond Ryker's bloody, sweaty, grimacing face.

"I read . . . about . . . your . . . kid and wife," Ryker said. His eyes gleamed. He laughed.

Which was all Fallon needed.

"You're a softhearted kid, Hank," a deputy marshal once told him in Fort Smith. *"Too nice for this job, I often*

think. But when you get riled, it's like I don't even know who you are no more."

Josh Ryker now saw what Fallon was like when he was riled.

Fallon's knee came up, caught Ryker hard in the groin. The grip relaxed, and Fallon broke free and slammed his flattened palm against Ryker's throat. The inmate's eyes bulged as he tried to breathe. Had Fallon hit harder, Ryker would be dying, but Fallon had not lost all control. He had just lost his temper.

He slammed a right into Ryker's jaw, buried a left into the man's gut. When Ryker doubled over, Fallon brought up his knee again, catching the man in the mouth, smashing his lips, knocking out two more teeth. Fallon reached with his left, grabbed Ryker's shirt, hoping to pull him up and keep pounding his face until it was nothing but an unrecognizable pulp. But the cotton ripped, and Ryker fell into the dust. He was lying still when Fallon landed on top of him. He swung a left, a right, again, again, and again.

Then he felt the stick of a guard against his skull, and Fallon rolled off the now-unconscious Ryker.

Fallon saw stars first, then dust, and finally a burly, bearded face just above him.

CHAPTER THREE

It was a face that Fallon recognized, but this time, it was a welcome sight.

Aaron Holderman, another ex-convict Fallon had once put away but now an operative for the American Detective Agency, waved the nightstick over Fallon, then bent down and jerked Fallon to his feet.

"Drexel," Fallon managed in a strained whisper, "knows me."

At first, Fallon couldn't tell if Holderman, not the keenest mind in the detective business, heard him or understood him, and if he did hear and understand, Fallon realized, he might not have cared one whit. Fallon had never trusted Holderman—for too many damned good reasons to count—but this time, in this operation, Fallon had no other choice.

Holderman heard Fallon, however, for he balled his massive right hand into a fist and slammed it into Fallon's face, breaking the nose, sending blood gushing from both nostrils.

The big brute roared, "Take that, you son of a—!"

"Holderman," said another voice. "That's enough."

Through the pain, the ringing in his ears, Fallon knew that new voice, too. Barney Drexel.

"Get up," Holderman said, and Fallon felt himself being jerked to his feet. Blood continued gushing, and Holderman brought his left hand up and smeared the blood all over Fallon's face.

When Sean MacGregor and his son Dan had started explaining the plan to Fallon back in Chicago, Fallon wasn't sure it would ever work. He especially didn't like the thought of Aaron Holderman being sent into Huntsville undercover, taking on the role of a prison guard. Fallon had worked with Holderman in Yuma and Jefferson City. Even if Fallon trusted the big lout, Fallon certainly didn't think that Holderman was smart enough to pull off the job of a prison guard.

Now Fallon realized he had been wrong. Aaron Holderman might not be the brightest man Fallon had ever known—that's why they had told him to use his own name; he'd never remember his alias—but he had played everything perfectly.

Holderman shoved Fallon toward Sergeant Barney Drexel.

"Watch it, you damned fool," Barney bellowed at Holderman. "I don't want to get blood on my uniform. Damn, what a bloody mess." Drexel chuckled. "Who's the fresh fish?"

The guard who had escorted Fallon into the prison yard produced the paper. "Harry Alexander," Drexel read. "Life sentence." He crumpled the paper and tossed it back to the guard. "Well, Mr. Harry Alexander. You might as well know how things work at Huntsville since you'll be here maybe a long time, maybe a few days. Till the end of your pathetic life."

Fallon lowered his head, letting the blood pool in

the dust between his miserable prison shoes. *God bless Aaron Holderman,* he thought. *Any chance Drexel would have recognized me ended when that big galoot broke my nose.*

At the very least, Holderman had bought Fallon some more time.

That time was about to grow.

"Fighting is not allowed in Huntsville. We don't even have a boxing club for prisoners. But we'll give you some time to think about all you've done wrong here today, and maybe by that time, your nose will have stopped bleeding."

He stepped back, glanced at Ryker, and shook his head again.

"A dozen lashes for Ryker," Barney Drexel ordered. "As soon as he wakes up. Then get him to the hospital, give that ol' sawbones something to do. A dozen days for the fresh fish. What's his name again?"

"Alexander. Harry Alexander."

"Introduce Harry Alexander to the sweatbox. Let's make it an even two weeks, though. He's got fourteen days to think about all the things he shouldn't have done. Meditate on how you got here, fresh fish."

Fallon felt strong hands grab his upper arms. Still weak, in agony, his feet dragged over the dust, even over Josh Ryker's legs, as he came to another dungeon. The heavy iron door was opened by two men, and Fallon felt himself hurtled into the box. He saw the slop bucket, a blanket, and a jar of water. Hitting the floor hard, he rolled over just before the iron door slammed shut, putting Fallon into a black void.

Solitary confinement. The black box. Sweatbox. For two damned weeks.

He had plenty of time to think now. In the darkness,

in the tight confines of the sweatbox, Fallon could think. He thought a lot. There was much he could remember, some he wanted to, some he had to, some he hated to recall.

Like sitting in that foul-smelling, dark-as-night office on the top floor of that brownstone building in Chicago.

"Have you ever been to Huntsville?" Sean MacGregor had asked. He puffed on the cigar. His hair, what he had left, was mostly orange but the silver was rapidly gaining ground, and his eyes were a dead green. That was about the only color you could find in MacGregor's office except for Fallon's clothes. Everything around Fallon appeared to be brown, and once again, the curtains were closed. Only a little light came from the lamp and trickled through cracks in the curtains.

"Illinois?" Fallon asked. "Or Alabama?"

The little man slowly removed the cigar from his mouth and set the repugnant stogie on the ashtray. His eyes narrowed, and he answered angrily, "Texas."

Sean MacGregor knew that Harry Fallon knew that his boss meant Texas. And Fallon knew he knew.

"Oh," Fallon said. "Didn't Jesse James rob some bank or train or paymaster in Huntsville, Alabama?"

"Jesse James is dead. Frank James is retired and an outstanding shoe salesman or race starter or something along those lines."

Fallon nodded, and that movement hurt.

"No," Fallon got around to answering. "Huntsville's over in East Texas, in what they call the Piney Woods. When I drove cattle, the trails were farther west."

"You know what's in Huntsville, Texas, don't you?"

The aches started to intensify. Fallon had just gotten out of the prison in Jefferson City, Missouri. Before that, Sean MacGregor had sent him to Yuma Territorial Prison in the hell on earth that was southern Arizona Territory. Fallon had thought that assignment was something like some gin-guzzling writer of dime novels would plot.

Get arrested. Sent to The Hellhole. Befriend, or at the least, join up with that crazed killer Monk Quinn, who had robbed a Southern Pacific train of some two hundred thousand bucks' worth of gold bullion. Escape the prison with Quinn, follow him into Mexico, find that stolen gold, and return it—along with Quinn and his companions, dead, hopefully, but alive if there was no preventing that. Let the American Detective Agency—make that, Sean MacGregor— enjoy the glory, and the rewards, of a successful operation.

The Jefferson City assignment had seemed equally asinine.

Go back to another prison—that ninth circle of hell called the Missouri State Penitentiary—once again as a convicted felon. Get friendly with another inmate, a pregnant young woman who happens to be married to a bank-robbing scoundrel trying to better everything the James-Younger, Dalton, and Reno gangs ever did, and find out where he's hiding his stolen loot. Of course, no one could have foreseen a riot breaking out and Fallon barely getting out of there alive.

Sean MacGregor had angrily repeated his question.

"I don't suppose," Fallon answered, "that you mean Sam Houston's grave."

"Don't be a fool!"

Fallon turned, not showing his surprise that the comment came from neither Aaron Holderman nor Sean MacGregor, but the agency president's son, Dan, who sat next to big, bruising Holderman in the dark office.

"This is serious," Dan MacGregor said.

Fallon looked back at the elde ——————
prison," he said.

The tiny man nodded his ch ———

A sigh slowly escaped, and ——————
chair. It could have been wor ————
House of Corrections, for instan ————
prisoners would love to send a ———————
meet his Maker. Or back to Joliet, which the MacGregors and
Holderman had often threatened, to return Fallon "for the
duration of your sentence."

He had been paroled from Joliet after saving some lives
during a violent, ugly riot. According to what he had been
told, Fallon was supposed to attend church services on Sundays (the minister was to report to the parole board and the
Joliet warden that Fallon had attended). He was not to drink
intoxicating spirits. He could not gamble in public venues or
private ones. He was not supposed to associate with known
gamblers or any former convict (which always made Fallon
look at Aaron Holderman, whom Fallon had sent to prison).
He was supposed to be working at Werner's Wheelwright in
Chicago and staying at Mrs. Ketchum's Boarding House
near Lake Michigan. Those had been the nonnegotiable conditions of this parole.

Fallon had never met Mr. Werner or spent one night in
Mrs. Ketchum's Boarding House. No one had served him
with an arrest warrant yet—probably because Fallon had
been doing time in the worst prisons in America.

And now he was going back to one.

He had worked with buffalo hunters, buffalo skinners,
cowboys, and even deputy United States marshals who had
been well acquainted with the state pen, The Walls, in the
heavily forested city of Huntsville, Texas. They all said the
same thing.

will put the fear of God into the most ardent

ght," Fallon said. "Let's hear it."

Inside the sweatbox, sweat—the box had been aptly named—burned his cuts, blinded his eyes—not that he had anything to see—and soaked his clothes. He reached over blindly for the ladle, dipped it inside the pitcher, and brought out tepid water. He drank, wanted more, but understood that more would likely sicken him, and the sweatbox would just make the odor of his vomit more . . . hell . . . nauseating.

He returned the ladle and began fingering the slices of bread scattered about his sides.

When he had first entered Joliet, an old trusty had warned him not to eat the bread if he ever wound up in solitary confinement. *"That'll just make you more and more thirsty. Man don't need bread. Well, a man in solitary don't need bread. Lessen they keep you in for an eternity. Then you ain't got no choice, buts to eats it. So just drinks the water, suh, lessen you just ain't got no other choice."*

He counted. One. Two. Three. Four. Five. His hands kept patting. Five. *That's it?* He cursed, and found another flintlike thin slice.

Six.

Six days. Six days on water.

Oh, they gave him bread. But it had to be at least a week old, hard as the iron walls in the sweatbox. But moldy, too. Fallon's teeth had been loosened from surviving innumerable scrapes in Yuma and Jefferson City, let alone Joliet, and his gums were prone to bleeding. Live off the food you got in prison, then in the deserts of Mexico, and Fallon figured he was maybe two jumps ahead of scurvy. His teeth couldn't handle what passed for bread here.

He swore, gagged at the stench from the slop bucket, and heard the sounds from above. This time, it wasn't the screams from a prisoner as he was whipped by one of the brutes that called themselves guards. It wasn't the pounding of fists as one inmate wailed another. It was laughter.

A guard was telling a joke to prisoners as they exercised by throwing a ball around. Laughter. That would drive even the hardest man insane, and Fallon knew. That's why they were doing it.

Breaking in the fresh fish. Seeing just how tough he was.

Fallon's hands worked again, finding the rock-hard slices of stale, repulsive bread. He hoped, prayed, that he had miscounted.

Five . . . Six . . .

He hadn't. Six days.

Six days, he thought. Two weeks. How many days are in a week? God. I can't . . . Seven.

He sighed. He felt like crying. He had eight more days. Eight more days. He couldn't make it. He'd . . .

No. He remembered. He steeled himself, clenched both hands into tight fists. Damn right he would make it. He had a reason.

He remembered again. He had to. Had to get his mind away from where he was, take him back weeks, months, even years later. He had to recall everything. Had to remember that he was Harry Alexander now, not Harry Fallon. He had to remember. No matter how much the memories might hurt.

CHAPTER FOUR

"*Have you ever heard of Josiah Jonathan Justice?*" Dan MacGregor had asked.

They had left Sean MacGregor in his darkness and crossed the hallway to a smaller, brighter office. That's where Fallon first met Malcolm Maxwell, attorney general for the state of Texas.

Fallon's head shook, which left him cringing, the pain reminding him of how he had barely gotten out of the state pen in Missouri alive—and now he was going back to another brutal prison.

"Cotton magnate," Maxwell, a slim, balding man, said in a Texas accent. "Sugarcane, too. He is based in Natchitoches, Louisiana, though he's from the city of Houston, Texas, originally, and lives there—if you believe this—part-time to escape the heat of Louisiana." The Texan had an engaging grin. "But his operations spread from Pensacola, Florida, to Corpus Christi, Texas. And he's not limited to farming on his plantations. He has some cattle ranches in South Texas. Part interest in a shipping line that's based in Corpus Christi."

Fallon waited. The last time he had checked, there was no law against growing cotton or sugarcane, or diversifying into other businesses.

"Filthy rich," Dan MacGregor said.

Which wasn't against the law, either.

"He commanded his own regiment during the War Between the States," the attorney general continued. "Justice's Legion. Supplied his own artillery. You might have heard of them."

Fallon hadn't.

"Unlike a lot of Southerners, the war didn't hurt him. After the surrender, he went back into business, using sharecroppers instead of slaves, paying them a pittance."

Fallon sipped coffee, set the cup on a tray resting on a side table, and looked at the younger MacGregor and the Texas official.

"So why am I going to Huntsville?"

"Colonel Justice has found labor that's even cheaper than former slaves," the attorney general said. "Have you heard of leasing?"

"Leasing what?"

"Inmates," Malcolm Maxwell answered.

Fallon cocked his head.

"It's similar to what you experienced in Joliet and even Jefferson City," Dan MacGregor explained.

Fallon had been put inside the broom factory at Jefferson City, though he didn't think anything he tried to make would have satisfied his mother when it came to sweeping, and he had done various jobs inside the Illinois state pen.

"With one exception," MacGregor continued. "The inmates aren't working within the prison walls."

"According to state law," the attorney general said, "with consent of the penitentiary board and the superintendent, inmates can be hired out. It's a winner in theory. The state gets money from the factories or railroads or plantation owners and farmers. The prisoners learn a trade. The person hiring the inmates gets cheap—real cheap—labor."

"*You want me to get hired by Justice,*" Fallon said.

"*Exactly,*" the attorney general said. "*You fill the bill of what Justice has been hiring. You're a Southerner, from Arkansas.*"

"*Missouri,*" Fallon corrected. "*Gads Hill. Which leaned more blue than gray.*"

"*That's Harry Fallon,*" MacGregor said with a smile. "*You'll be Harry Alexander. Fought with the irregulars between Little Rock and the Missouri border, those that hid out in the Devil's Den.*"

"*And you'll be entering Huntsville with a life sentence,*" Maxwell said.

"*Surely they don't allow men with life sentences to be leased out to anyone,*" Fallon said.

Both men nodded. The attorney general picked up a small book, flipped through a few pages, and adjusted his spectacles as he read: "'. . . *no convict shall be hired out or sent to an outside camp who was convicted of rape for a greater term than ten years, or who has a particularly bad reputation for lawlessness, or whom the penitentiary physician may pronounce physically unable to perform the labor required of him.*'"

"*The life sentence means you're one bad hombre, and that's what Justice is looking for. But your sentence shall be reduced to ten years,*" MacGregor said. "*The files on you in the prison superintendent's office will say you have been an exemplary inmate.*"

"*Like many other prisoners who have had a remarkable turnaround,*" Malcolm Maxwell said, removed his spectacles, and began cleaning them with a handkerchief as he rolled his eyes.

* * *

Fallon woke, the light blinding him, and felt the slop bucket being removed, the water pitcher being refilled, and the slice of bread being dropped onto his shirt.

"He's still breathin', boss," the trusty said as he dropped a new, empty slop bucket in the corner.

"That's a quarter pound of tobacco you owe me," the guard said.

The door slammed shut. Blackness returned. Fallon picked up the bread, placed it at his side, and counted the slices again. Eight.

How long can a man survive without food? A month would be on the top end, maybe longer, depending on his condition physically and mentally. A week on the low end. As long as he had water. Fallon reached for the pitcher and drank.

A voice from outside, in the daylight, glorious daylight, reached him.

"Conners. Superintendent Wilkinson wants to see you."

Conners? The name meant nothing to Fallon. Inmate? Maybe. Guard. Perhaps. Wilkinson. Oh, yes, he knew Wilkinson.

Warden—*superintendent* was too classy a title for a man like Warren Wilkinson—at The Walls. A former executive with the National Pinkerton Detective Agency. That's why Sean MacGregor had taken the case. That little man would do anything to discredit his major rival in the private investigation business.

He thought back.

Pensacola, Florida, was sweltering, and this was what most people called spring. Fallon had gotten used to the

Midwest climate of Joliet, even though the past months had found him in Arizona Territory, Mexico, and hot and humid Missouri.

"Remember, Master Hank," the old black man had said. "I know that machete is big and you probably be used to swinging it, but you don't swing nothin' on no sugarcane, suh. You gots to saw it. Real gentle. Close to the ground."

The shoot fell, and Fallon picked it up and laid it into the wheelbarrow, then mopped his brow with the sleeve of his shirt.

"That's right, suh. You gettin' it now real fine, Master Hank. Iffen they put you somewheres else, you remembers what to do?"

"Strip the cane," Fallon said. He was dying for a drink of water. "No leaves. Just the green shoot. Use my hands. Maybe a knife."

"Like that?" The big man grinned as he pointed at the machete.

"No. Something smaller."

"Right. Now, this ain't the best time to be doin' no harvestin'."

"Fall," Fallon said. "But in Louisiana and other places, you can get a couple of growing seasons."

"Right. Then you can cuts the shoots into smaller sizes. It's right good eatin', Master Hank. Right good. So we wouldn't be harvestin' this here cane except that's what the boss man says."

Fallon rose, leaving the machete on the ground, and rubbed his aching back. Why couldn't Mr. Justice have gone into some other kind of business? Something less painful. Like breaking wild mustangs. Or wrestling wild boars or even grizzly bears.

"So how you knows when da cane be ready to get harvested, Master Hank?"

Fallon again wiped away sweat. "The leaves will be . . ."
The heat and the sun baked his brain, and he had to think,
but the old Negro was patient. "Dry. Maybe yellow."

"That's good, Master Hank. You gonna be a top hand
come next harvest time. Iffen this job they's teachin' you for
don't pan out, you come on back down here to Pensacola. I'll
let my boss man know how good you is. Then maybe we go
fishin'. You like grouper? Nothin' better, Master Hank, than
fried grouper on my missus's bread."

Fallon hoped that meant his lesson was over, but the black
man was one thorough teacher.

"What else can you tell me 'bout how to say when it's time
to start sawin' down cane, Master Hank?"

Groaning, Fallon lowered himself into the muddy ground,
picked up the machete, and tapped the side of the blade softly
against a growing cane. "The sound," he answered. "If it's
ready, it'll sound different."

"That's right good. Sound like metal agin metal. Ain't
makin' that sound now, on account that it ain't time to do no
harvestin'. And there's one other way, ain't there?"

Fallon nodded. He made the motion of cutting sideways
into a shoot. "It'll shine . . . glisten . . ."

"That's right. You's real smart, Master Hank. That shine
comes from the sugar. Sweet it is. Now you come on back to
my shack. I bets my missus has some cane syrup that we can
pour over your flapjacks."

Eleven. Fallon sucked in a deep breath and slowly
exhaled. Eleven days. He had been sentenced to a
dozen . . . He groaned, remembering again. Barney
Drexel had originally given Fallon twelve days, but
extended it to a full two weeks. This was day twelve,
though. Fallon thought he might just live through it.

But he had lived through the sugarcane plantation in Florida. He had marched across the cotton fields in Mobile, Alabama.

And he had met with Malcolm Maxwell one more time in New Orleans.

"I know this undercover, spy business isn't your cup of tea," the Texas attorney general had said.

They were in the politician's berth on a stern-wheeler, the Texan, Fallon, Dan MacGregor, and Aaron Holderman.

"You haven't told me what you think Justice is doing," Fallon said.

"We wanted to see if you could pass muster in the sugarcane fields first," Dan MacGregor said.

"From what Dan says," Malcolm Maxwell said, *"you'll have no trouble getting a job."*

Fallon did not laugh.

The silence caused the Texan to clear his throat. "We don't know exactly what Justice is doing. But we fear it could be devastating to Texas and our country."

"I'm really not interested in Texas or my country," Fallon said, and stared hard at Dan MacGregor. *"All I want is the man or men who killed my wife and daughter. And put me in Joliet for something I didn't do."*

"You killed him already, Fallon," Holderman said. *"In Jeff City."*

Fallon knew that. A few officials at the Missouri pen had come up with a brilliant plan. Murder for hire. And the murderers were inmates at Jefferson City. They'd go out through an old escape tunnel, kill some politician, or . . . Fallon frowned with bitterness and clenched his fists . . . a young wife and a little girl. That killer had been a man known at the Missouri state pen as The Mole. But Fallon couldn't hate

*him because the murderer had become a shell of a man, and
when he died, he probably did not even remember killing any
mother and child. And The Mole had saved Fallon's life.*

"The man who sent The Mole to do it," Fallon snapped.
"That's who I want."

"We think it's probably someone working at The Walls,"
Dan MacGregor said.

"You think?"

"It's complicated, Fallon," the attorney general told Fallon.
"We don't know what Justice has planned, but he's using inmates at The Walls to help him."

"Cutting sugarcane. Picking cotton." Fallon rolled his eyes.

"No," the attorney general said. "Robbery. Murder. Treason."

Fallon sank back into the settee. He sipped the potent
chicory folks called coffee in this part of Louisiana.

"Six months ago, an army caravan was robbed on the way
to Fort Clark," Dan MacGregor explained. Springfield rifles,
Colt revolvers, and ammunition were stolen and taken into
Mexico. Where they disappeared. The bandits were dressed as
Mexicans. That close to the border, it made sense, and Mexico
is always in turmoil. So is the north side of the Rio Grande.
But an officer said he recognized one of the bandits and that
he was not Mexican. His name was Cole Hansen."

Maxwell paused.

"I've heard the name," Fallon said. "Texas hard case."

"Who was serving a ten-year sentence at the time of the
robbery. Six more years to go. At The Walls."

Fallon waited.

Dan MacGregor answered. "The commanding general for
the Department of Texas laughed down the captain's report.
Superintendent Wilkinson then announced that Cole
Hansen had died of pneumonia at the prison hospital four
days before the robbery."

"So your captain was mistaken," Fallon said, though he didn't believe it.

"I believe," the attorney general said, "that if we dug up that pine box in the prison cemetery, we'd find an empty pine box."

"Dig it up," Fallon said.

"That would tip our hand," MacGregor said.

"You don't have a hand," Fallon told him. "At least, not a winning hand."

"That's why we've thrown you into the deck." Dan Mac-Gregor grinned.

"Wilkinson has ties with the Missouri State Penitentiary," the Texas attorney general said.

Fallon stiffened.

"That doesn't mean he had your wife and daughter killed, Hank," MacGregor pointed out.

"But he's a mighty big suspect," Aaron Holderman said, and spit tobacco juice into a fancy cuspidor.

"Shut up," MacGregor said.

"Wilkinson also has ties with the Pinkertons," Malcolm Maxwell said. "That's why the Pinkertons would not take this case."

"And it's why Sean MacGregor did," Fallon said. He had wondered why the Texan hadn't gone to the Pinkertons. Now he knew. He drank more strong coffee, found a pastry on a silver dish, took the pastry, and bit into it. Once he had swallowed, he crossed his legs.

"So your rich man Justice is getting richer by robbing guns from the army. Probably selling them to some revolutionary down in Mexico, or even the Mexican government."

"Josiah Justice is ruthless and ambitious and just damned evil," Maxwell said. "But we don't think he's doing all this for money."

"Then what?" Fallon asked.

"To start another Civil War," MacGregor answered. "Here. In the South."

When that finally sank in, Fallon said, "That's insane."

"Which also describes Josiah Jonathan Justice to a tee," Attorney General Malcolm Maxwell said.

Insane. The darkness. The heat. The wretchedness of his own body. That could also drive someone mad.

Fallon counted the bread slices again. Twelve . . . Thirteen . . . Fourteen . . .

No. His eyes widened in the darkness.

Fifteen . . . Sixteen . . . Seventeen.

It couldn't be. He was supposed to be in this furnace for only two weeks. Fourteen days. He counted again. Seventeen. He wanted to reach up and bang on the iron door, but he lacked the strength.

They'd forgotten him. The damned fools had forgotten him. Or they were trying to break him.

He reached for the pitcher and knew it was empty before he ever got it to his mouth.

No. They weren't trying to break him. And they hadn't forgotten him. They were trying to kill him.

CHAPTER FIVE

Two days later, the door opened. Fallon covered his eyes with both arms and tried to turn his head from the intense light.

"Son of a gun," a guard drawled. "He's alive."

"Son of a gun," a trusty echoed. "Reckon that's a half pound of chewing tobacco you owe me, Mort."

"Hell." Fallon heard the sound of feet beside him, joints popping as prisoners helped him up. The guard snorted, then laughed.

"Well, Alexander," the guard said, "I guess we just plumb forgot about you. Get him to the infirmary."

The prison doctor looked more like a skeleton this time, and his hair seemed even whiter. He looked up from his desk as the guards led Fallon inside. Slowly, he removed his glasses and let recognition come.

"More scars, Mr. Alexander?" he said as he groaned and pushed himself out of the hard-backed chair.

The doctor walked slowly to Fallon but stopped and kept his distance. Fallon understood why. The doctor should smell Fallon's wretchedness from Fallon's point of view, and scent.

"Who set your nose?" he asked after a moment.

"I did."

The doctor nodded and looked at the lead guard. "Get him to the bathhouse. Let him bathe as long as it takes. Give him some coffee, but nothing to eat. When he's clean, get him a clean, decent uniform. Then bring him back here as soon as you can."

Grumbling, one of the guards nudged Fallon's shoulder and muttered an order than sounded like, "Come on."

Once Fallon reached the doorway, the doctor added one more instruction.

"Make sure he's not in worse condition when he gets back here."

By the time he had his third tub of water, Fallon didn't hurt so much. He didn't consider himself completely clean, but no one stayed completely clean in a prison.

The new uniform didn't fit any worse than his first one, but now he had no underdrawers and he had to bribe one of the guards for a clean pair of socks. That was fine. Fallon neither smoked nor chewed tobacco, so his quarter-pound allotment wouldn't have done him any good.

When he found himself back inside the infirmary, the doctor dismissed the two guards and went to work.

"Not the first time your nose was broken," the ancient cadaver of a man said.

"Not the first time I had to set it myself, either," Fallon said.

The doctor checked his records. "You've been here a little more than two weeks and already in the sweatbox." His bony head shook. "How long were you in that contraption?"

"Since I walked out of here the first time."

The doctor stepped back and sat on the stool across from Fallon. He tapped Fallon's knee with a small hammer.

"That sweatbox didn't alter your reflexes."

He let the old man do his work, and when the doctor settled back behind his desk and told Fallon to put his shirt back on, Fallon asked, "How long have you been here?"

"Six years," the doctor said without looking up. "Feels like sixty."

Six years. He wouldn't know the history of the warden, not personally. He hadn't been in Huntsville long enough to know about Justice, either, and Fallon couldn't just go about asking him direct questions.

"Am I in good health?" Fallon asked.

"You're walking and breathing and talking." The doctor looked up.

"Fit for duty?"

"You'll enjoy working in the mill," the doctor said. "It's better than two weeks in solitary."

"Seventeen days," Fallon corrected. "And I'd rather be doing something other than working in some damned factory."

"Your record says you're from Louisiana."

Fallon nodded. "Born there. Cotton and cane. When I was in my teens, my folks moved to Arkansas. Corn and more corn. But I also have some experience with . . . trains." He winked.

The old man shook his head sadly. "Repairing track

is different than robbing trains, young man. And if you're thinking about getting leased out to some farming operation, think again, Mr. Alexander. You're in for life. Lifers don't get outside until they're dead."

"My wife's working on that with our lawyer," Fallon said. Those words caused his stomach to constrict. *My wife.* The image of Renee locked in his mind. His eyes closed.

"Well, I wish her luck. Stay out of solitary. It's no place to be."

"Nor is Huntsville."

"Agreed."

The doctor jotted a few notes, set the charts on his desk, and leaned back in his chair before he called for the guards.

My wife. Fallon had wondered how it would feel when he finally had to say that. He hadn't realized how hard it would be, though, or the memories it would resurrect. Renee had been dead for years. He had no wife. And someone in this prison was likely responsible for that.

Quickly, he forgot about that, and as the guards led him into the yard, he saw Sergeant Barney Drexel walking toward him. The doctor had put some white cotton and bandages over Fallon's nose and the cut over his right eye. The left eye remained blackened, and the swelling hadn't gone down in his lips.

A prisoner walked alongside the prison guard, and both men stopped a few feet in front of Fallon and the guards.

"I guess it's time," the sergeant told one of the

guards, who giggled. "Take him to The Judge. See what sentence he gets."

Fallon stiffened. "I just finished better than two weeks in that sweatbox," he said. "I've been sentenced, and I damned well served my time and then some."

"Well," the ragtag convict standing next to Drexel said. "You see, fresh fish, that was the free people that sentenced you. Now you gotta face our trial. You got to go before The Judge."

As the old trusty led Fallon away, two bigger, younger prisoners joined them, walking on either side of Fallon as the older inmate fell behind them. The two new convicts were big men, hair shaved down to nothing but stubble, with muscles bulging against the ill-fitting striped uniforms. A line of prisoners parted, creating an opening, and Fallon and his guards passed through into a field where inmates kicked a ball to one another. Exercise. Others smoked tobacco; a few chewed tobacco.

Fallon kept walking, guided by the hulking men on either side of him. He saw The Judge. Well, he figured it had to be The Judge. That was the man sitting in a rocking chair in the shade next to the redbrick wall. Fallon noticed the guard towers where the guards looked well past the man in the rocking chair and the men approaching him.

"Stop," the con on Fallon's right said.

Fallon obeyed.

The circle tightened. One small prisoner fanned The Judge with a book. The volume of *Blackstone's Commentaries* seemed a bit heavy to be using as a fan.

The man stopped fanning and handed the book

to the dark-haired man, who kept right on rocking in his chair.

"Hear ye, hear ye," the convict who had been fanning The Judge said. "All those with business before this court, step forward and ye shall be heard."

The men who had been kicking the ball stopped their exercise. The circle of men in black-and-white-or brown-and-white-striped uniforms stopped their whispers, crushed out their smokes, or removed the chaws of tobacco.

"The Right Honorable John Wesley Hardin presiding."

John Wesley Hardin, the most notorious killer in Texas, raised his head and let his cold eyes lock on Fallon. *Hardin was The Judge?* Although The Judge remained sitting in the rocking chair, Fallon guessed Hardin to be no taller than five foot ten, and weighing perhaps 160 pounds. The Judge wore no robe and looked nothing like Judge Isaac Parker. Hardin's uniform was like Fallon's, brown-and-white stripes rather than black-and-white, his hair close-cropped but not as tightly shorn as the two brutes still standing beside Fallon. His face remained bronzed by the sun. He folded his hands and rested his head against them.

The would-be bailiff said, "Harry Alexander of Arkansas and Louisiana. Sentenced to life for robbing a damned Yankee paymaster."

"That's a crime?" Hardin said, and the surrounding throng roared with laughter.

"He's charged with assaulting Josh Ryker," the bailiff said.

"Who swore out the complaint?" The Judge asked.

"I did."

A blond-headed convict with a pockmarked face and missing his left ear stepped out of the wall of striped uniforms. "Larry Purvis, Your Honor."

Hardin's eyes rolled. "Of course," he said. "Ryker's concubine."

"I ain't no such," the inmate said in a nasal voice, and he kept talking until The Judge turned and gave him an icy stare. Larry Purvis swallowed and dropped his head. "My apologies, Judge Hardin," he said timidly.

"Why isn't Ryker making the complaint?" Hardin asked.

"That's just it, Judge," Purvis said. "Two days after that little set-to, Ryker got hisself transferred to Rusk. They just come up and grabbed him and took him to the warden's office. And nobody knows why or nothing. He didn't even get to tell nobody good-bye."

Holderman, Fallon thought. Holderman had to come through, sent word to Dan MacGregor or someone outside. The American Detective Agency and the Texas attorney general had gotten Josh Ryker sent to another Texas prison—for Fallon's safety. At least, that's what they must have thought. Only Fallon wished they had left Ryker alone. This would just arouse suspicion, and that doubt crept into The Judge's gray eyes.

"How about it, Alexander?" Hardin said. "Why did Ryker get sprung from The Walls and sent to Rusk?"

Fallon cleared his throat. "I wouldn't know, Your Honor. I've spent the past seventeen days in the sweat-box."

A murmur swept through the wall of prisoners.

The Judge sat up a little straighter in his rocking chair.

"Seventeen?"

"Yes, sir," a trusty said. "I was there. Sergeant Hard Arse give Ryker a dozen lashes, put this fresh fish in the hole for twelve days, then said make it fourteen. Which he conveniently turned into seventeen. Only reason they opened the hatch to let him out is on account they figured him dead."

"That's hearsay, Mr. McCord," Hardin said.

The trusty nodded. "Apologies to the court, Your Honor."

Hardin's head shook. "Seventeen days. Hell, they only gave me five when they learned about that escape we had planned all those years ago. You must be a hard case, Mr. Alexander."

"I was just defending myself, Your Honor."

"Not very well," Hardin said, and his grin sent a ripple of laughter among the spectators.

Fallon shrugged.

"The fight got broke up," Larry Purvis said. "That new guard, Holderman, come up and broke the fish's nose."

"Figures," Hardin said. "Ryker wouldn't have enough strength, or guts, to do that. Who started the fight?"

"He did." Purvis pointed at Fallon.

"That ain't true," the trusty, McCord, said. "Ryker called the fish a turncoat lowlife. Just charged right into the fish. It was a pretty good fight, Your Honor. Ryker started off pretty good, but at the end, it was him lying in the dirt not knowing what day or month it was."

Hardin brought his hands out from behind his

head, spread his fingers, brought the tips together and leaned forward. "'Turncoat lowlife' . . . not a compliment, Mr. Alexander. Turncoat lowlifes told the guards about our planned break. Put me behind in solitary for five days."

"Consider the source," Fallon said.

Hardin lowered his hands. "Well put." He opened the *Commentaries*, turned a page, closed the book, and studied Fallon for the longest time.

"But the charge, for the time being, is not being a turncoat bastard but of assault and battery. Do you wish to enter a plea?"

"Not guilty," Fallon said.

"A wise choice." The Judge cleared his throat.

Fallon guessed Hardin had to be around forty years old now. When had he been convicted of shooting down that sheriff and sent to prison? Fallon hadn't been riding for Judge Parker's court for that long when he had read about Hardin in the newspapers. Fifteen years ago? Sixteen? Longer than even Fallon had served in Joliet. Of course, John Wesley Hardin had killed that lawman. Fallon had been framed. And most people in Texas and across the West would have said that John Wesley Hardin, who might have killed forty men, deserved to hang. But here he sat, playing judge and, apparently, jury, trying fellow inmates.

"But a witness says that Josh Ryker started the fight, so Mr. Alexander was merely defending himself. The charge is dismissed with prejudice. Purvis. You must pay court costs. Cigarettes and some of your home-made brew delivered to my clerk by noon Friday of next week. Mr. Alexander, you are free to go, but you will sit at my table at supper tonight. McCord, see to that. This court is now adjourned."

The men spread out. Fallon found himself swept away from The Judge, known outside The Walls as the man-killing John Wesley Hardin. A few men slapped Fallon's back and shoulders, but most stared in silence and suspicion. Transferring Josh Ryker had been a tactical error. Fallon looked around for Holderman, but the big man was nowhere to be found.

Then the men surrounding Fallon disappeared, and Fallon knew why. Two guards were making a bee-line toward him. They stopped. So did Fallon.

"You got a visitor," the smaller of the two guards said. "Your wife's here to see you."

CHAPTER SIX

"Your wife's here to see you."

He never heard that in Joliet.

Fallon saw Renee again. Standing in the middle of the exercise yard at The Walls, staring at two ugly prison guards, he saw his beautiful wife. He was back in Van Buren, Arkansas, and Renee was crying.

"It's not funny anymore, Ted," Fallon had snapped at the deputy marshal standing just inside the door to the place he and Renee had rented in Van Buren. Fallon swung back to his wife. "It's all right, honey. Don't . . ." Now Rachel, his daughter, only two years old, was crying.

"Ted!" Fallon whirled back at the deputy. "See what you've done? I don't know what the hell made you think . . ."

Fallon stopped. Ted Merritt had his right hand on the butt of his holstered Remington, and behind him, Fallon now saw four other deputies, armed with revolvers, some with rifles, one holding a Greener shotgun with the barrels sawed off. None of them even cracked a smile.

"You're serious," Fallon whispered.

His daughter wailed. Renee sobbed as she tried to get the toddler to stop crying.

Fallon looked at the writ Ted Merritt held in his left hand.

"You're under arrest, Hank," Merritt said, and Fallon swore he saw tears welling in the deputy's eyes. "Don't make this any harder."

Fallon felt as though someone had punched him in the stomach, but he remained upright. Slowly, he reached for his hat and called back to Renee. "Find Chris," he said. "Tell him what's happened."

Chris Ehrlander was a lawyer. Judge Parker had recommended him, but Fallon never thought he would be asking Ehrlander to represent him. Parker had suggested that Fallon study for the bar. Read law with a good attorney. Become a lawyer. "You'd make a good one," Judge Parker had said as they walked to the corner to catch the omnibus for home. "You have a wife, son. Riding down outlaws in the Indian Nations is no job for a married man. Especially not for a married man with a child."

"I guess I'm lucky in one regard," Fallon later told Chris Ehrlander.

"How's that?" his lawyer and friend had said.

"Judge Parker told the solicitor he didn't have enough evidence to try me for murder." A deputy marshal had been shot dead. A peace officer with the Creek Nation had been wounded, too. "So it's not a rope I'm facing."

Ehrlander shook his head sadly.

"If you get sentenced to Detroit, you'll wish you'd hanged," the lawyer said, and Fallon knew he wasn't joking.

But Judge Parker later intervened. After Fallon had been convicted, the judge had somehow made arrangements to get Fallon sent to the Illinois State Penitentiary in Joliet and not the Detroit House of Corrections.

"Lucky again," Fallon had said stiffly in the stifling court-house.

"You are lucky beyond belief," his lawyer had whispered. "Look behind you."

And he saw his wife. He saw his daughter.

"Good-lookin' wench ya got thar, Alexander," the guard in the anteroom said. He rapped the heavy stick against the palm of his hand. "No contact whatsoever. Ya don't kiss 'er. Ya don't hold 'er hands. If she passes anything to ya, I knock yer head off an' yer back in the sweatbox. An' she don't never come to see ya agin. Understand?"

"Yes, boss," Fallon said, keeping his head down, staring at his miserable shoes.

"Visitation be a privilege. Ya gets that? The superintendent says yes or no. I don't know why he said yes to a scumbag like ya. Well, maybe I do. Most mothers an' aunts an' sisters an' nuns an' wives who comes here looks like the back side of a heifer. Yers don't."

He pulled a watch out of his pants pocket. "Fifteen minutes. Startin' now."

Fallon stared at the watch. He saw his dead wife again.

"A watch," the Swiss man had said, "is not a hammer, sir. It should be treated with respect, and gentle hands."

Fallon nodded. "The whiskey runner I was arresting in the Winding Stair Mountains didn't know that. Can you fix it?"

The watchmaker sighed. Fallon never could remember the old man's hands, and the way his hands shook, how he still had to squint behind the very thick lenses of his spectacles, gave Fallon pause about trusting the old silver watch to the ancient Swiss watchmaker.

"Miss DeSmet."

Renee DeSmet came out of the back room, and Fallon forgot all about the old man. She had black hair that gleamed in the small office that sounded of hundreds of clocks and watches ticking. That noise had pricked every nerve in Fallon's body. Now he forgot all about it.

The old man slid the busted watch to the woman, whose blue eyes shone as she grabbed tweezers and a magnifying lens.

Fallon did not move. He just watched as the old watchmaker told the beautiful woman what to do. They spoke in French. Fallon scarcely breathed.

When it was over, the Swiss man looked up. He muttered something in his own language, then squinted behind his thick eyeglasses. "You are still here?"

Fallon must have nodded.

The old man looked at the nearest clocks.

"You wait two hours and sixteen minutes for . . . this cheap watch?"

Renee DeSmet laughed.

He had walked her back to the boardinghouse.

At some point, Fallon realized he had seen her before. But he had been so dumbstruck, he did not even realize where until she stopped at the boardinghouse in Van Buren.

"This is where I live," she told him.

"Oh." He was sad the walk had ended, even if they had barely said five words to each other on the trip out of Fort Smith.

She opened the door, and he grimaced that he had somehow forgotten to open the damned door for her.

Once Renee DeSmet stepped inside, she looked back. "Aren't you coming in, too?"

Fallon straightened and stepped back. His lips parted and he thought he might have even blushed when he recognized the sign above the door.

MA TALLEY'S HOUSE
Rooms For God-Fearing People
☞ Good Food: 15¢ Boarders, 25¢ Visitors

"Oh yeah, I . . ." He entered The widow Rita Talley's two-story boardinghouse. He lived here, too, in fact, three doors down from Renee DeSmet.

That's how it started.

He walked her to work, even though, as a former working cowhand, he hated walking, but he made himself do it, even boarding his horse at a Fort Smith livery. They didn't talk a whole lot that first week, even at the widow's dining room table over breakfast and supper. He learned that her grandparents came from France, that they had settled first in New Orleans, then followed the river to Memphis, Tennessee, and later St. Louis. Renee DeSmet had answered an advertisement and taken a job with the watchmaker in Fort Smith.

Renee didn't like the gun Fallon wore. She certainly didn't care much for him risking his life as a federal lawman, but she must have liked him. Three months later, she had agreed to be his wife. A month and a half after that, they were married and living in a rented apartment in Van Buren but with a shorter commute to the watchmaker's shop and the district court in Fort Smith.

Most deputies hated having to appear in court. It surprised Fallon, who had spent time on cattle trails and hunting buffalo in the wide-open countries of Texas and Kansas, how much the legal system fascinated him. He learned from prosecutors and the defense attorneys, and he respected both sides. The average deputy marshal for Judge Parker's court thought every defense attorney belonged on the gallows. Not Fallon.

After Renee became pregnant and gave birth to Rachel, six pounds of everything adorable in the universe, Fallon started reading with Chris Ehrlander.

Renee liked that a lot. She even liked Ehrlander. Then she had a baby, and when Fallon held the tiny, pink-skinned six-pound loaf wrapped in swaddling cloth, Fallon felt his life change.

"You're livin' the dream," a jailer told him after he had deposited four criminals and one corpse at the courthouse. "Gonna be a rich lawyer. With a beautiful wife and even prettier baby gal. And not have to get shot at or stabbed or kicked or whipped no more."

And then . . .

The door opened. Fallon heard the guard say:

"It'd be a shame for that pretty girl to see me bash yer head in. Remember that. The clock's tickin'."

Fallon walked into the room to see his new wife.

CHAPTER SEVEN

She sat at the table, wringing her hands, wearing a dress of pink gingham, and a white bonnet covering her blond hair, pinned up in the back into a bun. She wore eyeglasses. Her eyesight was better than Fallon's.

"Hello, honey," he said, and sat into the uncomfortable chair across from her.

"Harry." Christina Whitney had been smiling, but when she saw Fallon, she paled, her lips flattened, and her eyes soon hardened. "What happened?"

Fallon shrugged. "It's nothing."

"All right."

She had to know. Aaron Holderman would have gotten word that he had busted Fallon's nose, that Josh Ryker had recognized him, even that Barney Drexel might remember Fallon. Christina was putting on an act for the eavesdropping guards. She could have made a fine actress, if she had not become a detective for Sean MacGregor's Chicago-based outfit.

"Would you like me to tell the Reverend Ulysses anything?" she asked.

That was one of the codes. In the eyes of Sean Mac-Gregor, and probably even MacGregor's son, Dan, and

certainly Aaron Holderman, Christina Whitney was a
minor player in this spy business, but Fallon would
never rate her that way. She held the affidavit signed
by Texas Attorney General Malcolm Maxwell. If Fallon
said he wanted to see the Reverend Ulysses or get word
to the preacher, Christina would produce the affidavit
and get Fallon the hell out of Huntsville before it was
too late.

"No," Fallon said.

"Are you sure?"

"You pray for me, honey."

It felt strange. Fallon was no actor. He could count
on one hand the times he had been inside an opera
house to watch some stage production. Christina
Whitney? She was good at it. They had spent months
together in Chicago, Florida, Louisiana, Alabama,
and Texas, she trying to teach him how to be a thespian because his life could depend on it. Fallon had
offered to teach her how to shoot, but he soon
learned that she was more than fair with a rifle, revolver, and even a shotgun. The woman could take
care of herself.

The best thing of all: not one thing about her reminded him of Renee.

He even liked her, which he could not say about
most members of the American Detective Agency.

Fallon touched his bandaged nose. "I met a man
my first day here," he told her. "Josh Ryker."

"Did he do that to you?" Christina asked.

"He tried to, but the nose is courtesy of a guard. I
ought to thank him."

She shook her head and sighed.

"Don't worry about Ryker," he told her. "They put
me in solitary for seventeen days after my brawl.

Prison rules, you see. And I guess they transferred Ryker to another prison." He laughed without humor. "To protect me, maybe."

"I see."

"I wish they hadn't done that. I could make things hard on Ryker."

Meaning: *that might make things more difficult for me.*

"Yes." She agreed. So she had nothing to do with the transfer of Josh Ryker to Rusk.

"But it's spilt milk now."

Meaning: *Don't correct that mistake. That would just complicate more things if Ryker suddenly got sent back to The Walls.*

"I met another man here," he told her. "John Wesley Hardin."

She sat up.

He smiled. "So you've heard of him, too."

"Who hasn't?"

"That's a fact. What do you know about him?"

Her head shook. "What every Christian knows. That he's a notorious killer. Should have hanged. He was a rough sort, but I've heard that he has lately been studying for the bar. Can you believe that? He wants to become a lawyer."

Now Fallon wished he knew how a man like Booth or a woman like Lillie Langtry did that acting thing. Because he thought again of Renee, and Rachel, and him studying for the bar in Arkansas. He thought of the life that might have been.

Christina reached out for his hand, but stopped when one of the guards pounded the wall with his billy club.

The hand withdrew, and she kept on talking. "John Wesley Hardin's an unreconstructed rebel."

She said it loud enough that the guards didn't have to strain their ears.

"Nothing wrong with that," Fallon said. "I've been called one, too. And I've never denied it."

"That's why you're here," she snapped. "We could still be back home. Or in Louisiana, maybe Alabama. Everyone said you knew sugarcane and cotton better than anyone in the county. You were good at anything once you set your mind to it."

"That's enough." He tried to sound angry at her, tried to remember how he had acted when Renee had made him angry. "I . . ."

This was all for the benefit of the guards. "Do you know how hard it is for me to be outside, and all my friends, all the neighbors, everyone knows that you're in prison? For life."

"You're supposed to be working with that lawyer. You know I don't deserve a life sentence."

They had gone over that exchange countless times in Chicago and the hideaway shack in Childress, Texas—too far for anyone with connections to The Walls to learn about. Fallon thought he sounded halfway convincing.

"I am working on it."

Their shoulders sagged simultaneously.

"I'm sorry," they both said at the same time.

"I know it's stressful," he told her.

"I know it's hard on you, too."

"Maybe I'll get out of here."

"I'll wait for you."

"Time's up," one of the guards said, but Fallon didn't believe fifteen minutes had passed.

"Anything else?" Christina stood.

"Yeah. I'm supping tonight with Hardin."

She looked shocked, and that probably wasn't an act.

"Be careful," she told him.

"He should be careful around me," he said.

He backed away from the chair and table and was heading for the door. A redheaded guard walked past him to Christina, and as Fallon reached the wall, he heard the brute say, "I gotta search ya, sweetie."

Fallon spun, but the other guard clamped both massive clawlike hands on his shoulders and pulled him into an embrace.

"Most wives that come into this place don't look nothin' like your sweetie pie," the guard holding Fallon whispered.

"Don't touch me," Christina said, and her voice trembled. "Please," she begged.

The redhead reached for her blouse.

Then he was doubled over, vomiting, clutching his groin with both hands, sinking to the floor as Christina walked past him.

The man holding Fallon laughed heartily.

"You got spunk, missy," he told her as she slipped through the open door. Fallon heard her banging on the other door, which slid open, and closed as Christina Whitney walked away.

The guard shoved Fallon toward the table, which Fallon had to catch to keep from falling.

"When Warren's done pukin' his guts out and makin' sure ain't none of his valuables is ruptured beyond repair," the foul-breathed guard said, "clean up his mess. Then find Blackbeard the Pirate and have him get you to the mill. Time you earned your keep, Mr. Harry Alexander."

The guard laughed. The other one groaned.

"How long were you in the sweatbox?" Hardin asked.

Fallon stared at his supper: biscuits, broiled beef, soup, dried apples sweetened with molasses. He sat at a table alone with John Wesley Hardin. The other inmates sat eight to a table, eating rancid bacon and corn bread that was stale two days back.

Fallon looked up, chewing on his apples. He glanced at the guards.

"You can talk at my table," Hardin said. "I'm John Wesley Hardin." The killer laughed and turned to the nearest guard. "Isn't that right, Johnson?"

The guard glared, but said nothing.

Fallon knew the prison rules. You did not talk in the dining room. There were signals with utensils or hands that meant more coffee, another piece of bread, a second helping of vegetables—whenever they actually served vegetables—but Hardin got special treatment.

"I asked you a question, Alexander," the killer said.

Fallon swallowed. "Seventeen days."

"Drexel's doing?"

"Yes, sir."

"Don't *sir* me, Alexander. I ain't *boss*, I ain't *sir*, I'm Wes."

"All right," Fallon said.

"Seventeen days." Hardin's head shook and he

sipped coffee out of his tin cup. His coffee had been sweetened from a pitcher of goat's milk. Every other prisoner drank their coffee black, and their coffee was lukewarm at best, usually cold. Hardin's steamed.

"Seventeen days?" Hardin asked again. "Are you sure?"

"Yes," Fallon answered, and added, "Wes."

That made the gunman smile.

"A man can go out of sorts when he's in the sweat-box. Loses track of time. Five days might feel like seventeen."

"I counted the slices of bread," Fallon said. "Seventeen. I counted them more than once."

"Not your first time in stir," Hardin said after he whistled his admiration at Fallon's answer, and toughness.

Fallon shrugged. "First time in Texas," he said softly. "Under this name."

Again, Wes Hardin grinned. He turned again, looked up at the guard, and said, "Johnson, do you know the maximum number of days a prisoner can be confined in a dark cell?"

The guard glared, but did not answer.

"Seven days, Johnson." Hardin sipped his coffee and set the cup on a napkin. "Not seventeen. No more than seven days, at one time." He glanced at Fallon. "They didn't let you out, say, break things up, give you one day to clean up, then put you back in the box?"

"They opened the lid to see if I were still alive. Sometimes they gave me a new slop bucket. They refilled the pitcher, until they conveniently forgot about me for three days. And they tossed in a slice of bread that was harder than the iron door."

"Well, Harry Alexander. That'll come in handy for us."

"Us?"

Hardin raised his right hand toward the guard named Johnson. The cold-blooded killer snapped his finger, and Johnson, that hard frown turning into a hate-filled grimace, stepped forward as Hardin lifted his coffee cup. The guard produced a flask, twisted the pewter cap off, and splashed a finger or two of amber liquid into the coffee. Hardin nodded, and the guard moved toward Fallon's coffee, but Fallon covered his cup with his left hand. "No thanks," he told Johnson.

Johnson moved back, made sure no one was looking, and took a fast swallow of whiskey before tightening the lid and slipping the flask back into the rear pocket of his pants.

"No liquor?" Hardin asked.

"You don't want to see me drunk."

"I'm not sure I trust someone who doesn't drink," Hardin said.

"Then I'm likely the only person in The Walls you don't trust."

Hardin laughed, drank some more of his sweetened coffee, and leaned back.

"Do you have an attorney?" he asked.

"My wife found one," he said.

That caused Hardin's eyes to close. The laughter left his face. The hands came back to the table, now balled into fists.

"You got a wife?" Hardin asked.

Fallon nodded.

"Pretty, too," Johnson said. "And heller with her knees. Ask Perkinson."

Hardin's face did not relax. "Shut up," he told Johnson. He looked coldly now at Fallon. "I had a wife, too." Bitterness filled his cold eyes. "She died." The killer's head shook. "Jane. That was my wife's name."

Mine was named Renee, Fallon thought.

"Went to her Maker a year ago November."

There might have been a kinship, but Fallon wasn't going to let a murderer like Hardin know about Renee. Still, he knew how Hardin must have felt. To hear that your wife had died, that you could not go to her funeral, because you were behind bars.

"She was a fine Christian woman," Hardin said.

So was Renee, Fallon thought.

"Consumption killed her."

At least she wasn't murdered, along with her daughter.

Hardin lifted the tin cup, drank more whiskey-flavored coffee, and sighed. "I'm going to do some checking on you first, Alexander. I'll let you know if I decide to take your case. If I do, there's a good chance I can get that sentence reduced. How would twenty years sound to you? Rather than life?"

"Ten would be better," Fallon said, adding, "Wes," with a smile.

Hardin laughed again, putting the memory of his dead wife behind him. He drank more coffee and wiped his lips with a napkin. "I'm sure it would."

"What'll it cost me?" Fallon asked.

"Don't worry. You'll pay me, all right. But it'll be reasonable."

He snapped his fingers.

"Johnson," Hardin called out. "What's for dessert?"

CHAPTER EIGHT

For a week, he had been pretty much left alone, which reminded him of those ordinary days at Joliet. You fell into the routine. Up for the head count. Marched to the toilet facilities. To breakfast. To work. Keep your head down. Never look a guard in the eye. Do your job. Don't talk. Dinner. Supper. Back to the cell. Lights out. He proved passable at the mill. They had tried him at some of the more complicated jobs, then sent him to menial work.

Dan MacGregor had told him that the American Detective Agency and the Texas attorney general were going to take their time on this case—at least, for the time being, until they could find out just what it was that Justice had in mind. Well, they certainly had spent enough time training Fallon and everyone else. How many weeks had they spent in the South? How many times had they pored over *Rules, Regulations and By-Laws for the Government and Discipline of the Texas State Penitentiaries, at Huntsville and Rusk, Texas*?

So, Fallon wondered, how long would it be before he got out of that stinking mill? Or had the American

Detective Agency and Texas attorney general forgotten all about him?

It was Sunday. He had attended church services in silence, as usual, and now wandered around the exercise yard. He had not seen Hardin since supper that night. Fallon did not see him now. Nor had he seen much of Sergeant Barney Drexel, but that was about to change.

"Alexander!"

Fallon tensed, stopped, lifted his eyes to see the sergeant standing by the whipping post.

"Get over here, boy!" the guard shouted. "I got a job for you!"

The sadistic jackass laughed, and Fallon saw another inmate, shirt stripped off, tied to the post, waiting for his punishment.

Somehow, Fallon managed to force down the bile that climbed up his throat.

"Pronto, Alexander!"

Fallon jogged over and stopped a few feet in front of Barney Drexel. His head remained lowered, and he touched the bandage that the prison doctor had put over his nose a few days ago.

"Yes, boss?" Fallon said in his quietest voice.

"Look at me, boy."

Fallon raised his head. The bandage hid some of his features, and the bruises had not completely healed.

"You remind me of somebody, Alexander."

"Who's that, boss?" Fallon asked meekly.

"That's the trouble. I don't know. Where is it you hail from?"

"Arkansas, boss. But I grew up in Louisiana."

"Used to work in Arkansas, boy. Ever been to Fort Smith?"

Fallon hesitated. "Can't recollect, boss," he said, and watched the grin widen on the big man's face.

"I bet you can't. Federal court was there."

"That sounds right, boss."

"Where did you live in Arkansas?"

He didn't like talking this much. "Farm up north a ways."

"You wore the gray?"

"Yes, boss."

"Bit young for that, weren't you?"

"Old enough to hold a Colt, boss."

"Somebody told me that you rode with those guerrillas that hid out in the Devil's Den."

"I heard the same thing, boss."

Drexel laughed. "I like a man who curbs his tongue, Alexander." He tossed the blacksnake whip into the dirt before Fallon's feet. "Pick it up."

Fallon stared at the whip. It was ugly, eight feet of black leather that resembled a snake.

"Pick it up, I said."

Bending, but now keeping his eyes on Drexel, Fallon found the handle with his left hand, and he rose. The butt of the blacksnake was about an inch in diameter, heavy, too. Likely the leather had been braided over a heavy shot load. That made the whip two types of weapon. The narrow, sharp, painful whip at the top, and a heavy blackjack style of club at the butt.

"Reginald has been a naughty boy, Alexander." Drexel nodded at the man lashed to the post. "You're gonna whip him."

"No, boss," Fallon said, trying to sound as though he were pleading.

"Eight lashes."

"No, boss."

"Boy," Drexel said. "Reginald here was a traitor to the South, to Texas, to all that you were fighting for all those years ago. He didn't wear the gray. He backed the blue. You ought to enjoy laying eight lashes on his back."

"No, boss."

Drexel straightened. Fire burned in his dark pupils. "That's an order, Alexander."

Fallon wet his lips. "I can't do it, sir."

"You will."

"No, boss. Rules say so."

That stumped the sergeant. He tilted his head and even took a step back. "What the hell?"

"Prison rules, boss," Fallon said. "Convicts can't punish another convict."

"What?"

"It's in the rules, boss. That's what it says." Actually, it said: *No convict shall be made in any manner to punish another convict.*

Fallon remembered other rules and regulations regarding the whipping of prisoners, too. First of all, the blacksnake whip was prohibited. Lashings were to be made using a leather strap, two feet long and maybe two and a half inches wide, affixed to a wooden handle. There were other rules, too, but Fallon knew better than to tell Drexel everything he had learned about The Walls.

Drexel removed his cap, scratched his head, returned the cap, and grinned. "You've been spending a fair amount of time at the library, haven't you, boy?"

"Yes, boss."

"You ought to be reading the Bible, boy, and not prison regulations."

Fallon kept quiet.

"But you're going to lay eight lashes on this cur's back. Now."

Fallon lowered his head, shook it, and whispered, "No, boss. I can't do that."

"Well, one of you dogs are going to whip him. Holderman!"

Aaron Holderman stepped up to Drexel.

"Give me that whip."

Fallon's eyes lifted to see Aaron Holderman raise his beefy left hand toward the sergeant. Holderman held a whip, too, almost an exact match to the one in Fallon's hand. Drexel had anticipated this. Maybe not an inmate citing prison rules, but certainly refusing to whip another convict.

"Give it to the greaser," Drexel ordered, and Aaron Holderman, not even glancing in Fallon's direction, walked about forty paces and held out the blacksnake to a burly Mexican, maybe six foot two and better than two hundred pounds. The convict took the whip, and Holderman spun on his heel and returned to the whipping post.

"The winner," Drexel announced, "gets to whip Reginald. And gets the day off tomorrow from his assigned duties and an extra quarter pound of tobacco. The loser gets the day off, too, but he'll either be in the sweatbox or in the infirmary."

Dully, Fallon realized that the guards and the prisoners had backed away from Fallon and the Mexican inmate, forming a circle that included the whipping post where the man named Reginald remained lashed.

Fallon glanced at the closest guard tower. The guard was watching, smoking a cigar, rifle butted on the floor.

Fallon realized his mistake. He never should have taken his eyes off the Mexican. The grunt caught his attention, and he felt the blacksnake bite into his britches just above the ankles, wrap around his legs. The Mexican grunted again, and the whip jerked Fallon off his feet.

Fallon rolled, freeing himself from the whip. He came up, felt his legs give way, dropping him to his knees. The Mexican was gathering the whip. Realizing that he still held the blacksnake in his right hand, Fallon reached out and back, letting out the leather, and grunted as he sent the whip toward the Mexican.

It fell lamely to the ground, not even coming close to the big man.

Fallon came up, moved forward and to his left, as the Mexican sent the whip again. This time, the lash failed to find Fallon's body.

Stopping, Fallon tried again. He missed again.

He cursed himself. All those years riding for the federal court. He had been in fights involving guns, rifles, shotguns, knives, hatchets, pitchforks, fists, knees, claws, a ball-peen hammer, chairs, tables, bottles, a single tree twice, firewood, a tree branch, hats . . . He had even thrown cow pies at one felon when they had both shot their pistols dry and missed when they had thrown their empty revolvers at each other. All those brawls, but never once had he ever used a whip in a fight.

His left arm came up, just in time to prevent the whip from possibly taking out one or both of Fallon's eyes. It bit into his forearm, slicing the sleeve like a

dressmaker's scissors. Grimacing, Fallon felt and
smelled the blood running out of his arm. But he
dropped his own whip and grabbed the taut end of
the Mexican's blacksnake with his right hand, wrapped
the leather around his hand once, and charged forward.

The movement surprised the prisoner. The Mexican had expected Fallon to move backward, and had
leaned back. Now he fell on his back, his head striking
the ground hard, and he released his grip on his
whip.

Fallon yanked hard, pulling the whip farther from
the Mexican. He let it go and kept running. Part of the
sheared sleeve fell toward his wrist. His lungs burned.
The Mexican lurched for the handle of his whip,
stopped, looked up, and felt Fallon's shoe smash into
his jaw.

"Hombre," another Mexican inmate yelled. He
shouted insults or encouragement in his native tongue.
Some cheered for Fallon. Others booed. Most watched
in silence.

Fallon tried to kick the Mexican again, but the big
man reacted quickly, caught Fallon's right foot with
both hands, twisted, grunted, and rolled, sending
Fallon flying. He hit against the whipping post, the
body of Reginald cushioning the collision.

Fallon caught his breath, tried to bite down the
pain, heard Reginald heaving. He slid around, blinking the grime and dust and sweat from his eyes, and
heard the whistle of air as the Mexican let the deadly
end of the blacksnake sail again.

For a big man, the Mexican moved fast. Fallon fell
away. Reginald screamed as the whip caught his bare
side and back. As the Mexican tried to gather up the

whip again, Fallon leaped, fell on this stomach, and gripped the whip with both hands.

He rolled over, came up on his knees, and this time jerked the whip toward him. The Mexican had expected Fallon to keep moving toward him, as Fallon had the first time. The big man fell to his knees, but did not let go of the whip. Instead, he jerked backward, and Fallon fell on his face, dropping the whip.

He came up quickly, sucked in a lungful of hot air, and saw the end of his whip before him. Leaping, he grabbed the butt, felt the Mexican's whip lash his back, still sore from the whipping Drexel had given him weeks earlier. Fallon did not stop, though, gathering his legs underneath him, he pushed himself forward, then stopped, turned, and swung his arm, sending the whip toward his assailant.

To Fallon's surprise, the whip wrapped around the Mexican's right arm. That had been pure luck, but in a fight like this, luck needed to be on somebody's side.

The big man screamed. Fallon saw the blood staining his striped uniform. The Mexican dropped his own whip, and Fallon tried to pull his free from the big man's arm. But the Mexican grabbed the leather and jerked Fallon forward.

Fallon kept right on coming. He collided with the prisoner, smelled the blood, sweat, and rancid breath. His head butted against the Mexican's nose, but missed, catching more of the man's cheekbone. Still holding the whip, Fallon pulled his right arm away, then slammed the heavy end of the whip. The handle smashed against the Mexican's temple—probably would have killed a smaller, not-so-tough man—and the Mexican whispered something in Spanish and sank to his knees.

Fallon thought about bringing the weighted handle of the blacksnake down on the Mexican's skull, to make sure the man was out cold, but he just didn't have enough strength. He sank to his knees, and there Fallon and the Mexican were, heads bent over, breathing heavily, blinded by pain and sweat, wondering how long they would be able to stay conscious.

CHAPTER NINE

"What is the meaning of this?"

The voice sounded distant, even though somehow Fallon realized it came from nearby. The voice also sounded oddly familiar, though Fallon could not quite place it. Maybe he was dreaming. He reached up, gripped the Mexican's shoulder, and used that as leverage to look up. It took a while for anything, anyone, to come into focus.

The first thing Fallon saw clearly was the Mexican, whose glassy eyes shone. The man heaved, bled, and spit out a busted tooth. Then he grinned.

"Amigo," he said hoarsely, "you fight well."

Fallon hadn't known the man could speak English until then.

Fallon tried to nod, but the pain prevented that, and all nodding would have done was spray blood dripping from his nostrils across both men's shirts.

"You do . . . too."

"I said, what is going on here?" The voice sounded through the dust, and Fallon and the Mexican used each other to push themselves to their feet. They didn't stand steadily. In fact, a slight breeze would have knocked both men down, but moments later they were surrounded and found themselves being helped by other inmates toward Barney Drexel, other guards, the lashed prisoner named Reginald, and a familiar-looking man in a gray suit and bowler hat.

"Sergeant Drexel, I presume, you will answer me," the man said, "and you will answer me now. What is the meaning of this?"

"Who are you to be giving me orders, mister?" Drexel demanded.

"Byron Roberts," the man said. "Inspector of penitentiaries."

The man, Fallon suddenly understood, was not Byron Roberts, inspector of penitentiaries. He was Dan MacGregor, vice president of the American Detective Agency out of Chicago, Illinois. MacGregor, son of Sean MacGregor, withdrew some sort of identification and showed it to the sergeant, who frowned.

"What happened to Horton?" Drexel asked.

"He's down with the grippe," MacGregor replied. "What's the meaning of this?" A slim finger pointed at Fallon and the Mexican.

"Exercise." Drexel's smile was chilling.

"And this?" MacGregor nodded at Reginald.

Drexel wasn't smart enough, or any fast thinker, to come up with a quick reply for that one, and the evil smile turned into a frown.

"Must I remind you of the statutes, sir? That convicts are to be treated with humanity. That whipping of an inmate requires an application to the inspector's office, explaining the need for such a drastic measure, of the specifics spelled out as to what is appropriate for whipping a prisoner, that such punishment is to be administered by the underkeeper, overseen by the prison superintendent or his assistant superintendent . . ."

The more MacGregor went on, the redder Drexel's face turned. Fallon quickly glanced at the closest prisoners and felt pleased to see many of them smiling as MacGregor dressed down the cold-blooded snake of a man. Even some of the guards appeared more than pleased at the sergeant's comeuppance.

". . . You do know, Sergeant, that I have the authority to investigate any illegal punishment and can have you suspended or even discharged for such repulsive, illegal, and immoral actions."

MacGregor had to catch his breath. "Remove me? You'd need Superintendent Wilkinson's approval for that, Mr. Inspector, sir."

The cockiness returned to Drexel's face.

"Do you think he'd defend you, Sergeant, after the governor, attorney general, and every newspaper reporter hammered this prison like Grant hammered Johnston at Pittsburg Landing?"

Drexel clenched his fists.

"Now answer me, Sergeant. Under whose authority were you going to punish this man?" Before the beast could answer, MacGregor ordered that Reginald be taken down, his shirt returned, and that he be escorted to the infirmary immediately and given water to drink, a sip of brandy if the doctor deemed it appropriate.

Reginald looked a whole lot happier. Drexel didn't.

"He wasn't going to be whipped, sir. We just wanted to make him think he would be." Drexel had managed to come up with a lie. "I wouldn't give him brandy, sir. Because we think he's been running illegal spirits to some of our . . . guests of honor."

Reginald's happiness faded.

"You have proof of this?" MacGregor asked.

"Suspicions, sir. Right, Hartley?"

A diminutive, pockmarked prisoner shivered. "Yes," he said, his voice weak and cracking with fear. "I mean. Some of us thought so."

"I see," MacGregor said, and nodded at two guards besides Reginald to follow his instructions.

"And these two men?" MacGregor continued after the guards had escorted Reginald through the throng. "All that's missing are the Romans, the Christians, and the lions."

"This was a game, sir." Drexel's grin returned.

"A game."

"Prisoners' game. You don't think we'd allow two murdering scum of the earth to whip each other in a regular brawl, do you, Mr. Prison Inspector? That might lead to a riot. Wouldn't take much for those cur dogs to turn those blacksnakes on us."

"A game?" MacGregor repeated.

"They play rough inside The Walls, sir."

"We shall see about this." MacGregor spun on his heel, snapped his fingers, and nodded at Fallon and the Mexican. "You two men. Follow me. You." Now MacGregor spun, pointing—seemingly randomly—at Aaron Holderman. "Take us to . . . the visiting room." He looked back at Drexel. "If I hear one complaint, substantiated or not, Sergeant, your head will roll, sir."

The visiting room no longer smelled like Christina Whitney's shampoo and perfume. It smelled of stale cigarettes and the foulness of a prisoner's uniform. The Mexican sat at the table. Fallon leaned against

the wall. MacGregor removed his hat and reintro-
duced himself as the inspector of prisons.

"I need you men to tell me exactly what happened
out there," MacGregor said. "Why were you two armed
with long, lethal whips? What was the purpose of your
fight? Why was the other inmate lashed to the whipping post?"

MacGregor focused on the Mexican. Fallon didn't
even know the man's name.

"Amigo," he said, placating, with not a trace of a
Spanish accent. MacGregor grinned. "What was going
on outside?"

The Mexican's face remained expressionless.

"Tell me," MacGregor pleaded. "The truth. Why
were you fighting with whips? Why did the guards do
nothing?"

"*No sabe,*" the Mexican said.

"What?" MacGregor took a step back, as though he
had not expected such an answer. "Please. Help me.
Help yourself. Help your other inmates. The purpose
of a prison is to rehabilitate, not to condemn. But I
need your help. What were you two doing out there,
armed with whips?"

The Mexican had barely moved. "*No sabe,*" he said
again.

MacGregor's jaw hung open. He watched the Mexican drip blood onto the visiting room floor.

Finally, MacGregor took a step back, pointed at the
big man, and then jerked his thumb toward the door.
"Get out of here, you horse's ass. Now. I try to help
you and this is what I get!" He backed to the door,
slammed his boot heel against it, and yelled, "Guard!"

Holderman jerked open the door.

"Get this damned fool out of there. Get him to the infirmary. Have the physician patch him up. Then put him in his cell."

"All right, Capt'n," Holderman said. "Come along, fella." The nightstick popped against Holderman's palm. "Don't try nothing, though. What about the other one, Capt'n?"

"We'll see if he's a bit more cooperative."

The bleeding Mexican ducked underneath the doorway, and Holderman slammed the door shut.

"Sit down," MacGregor said to Fallon, and motioned at the table and chairs.

When both men were sitting, the detective pulled out the makings and laid them on the table's top. He nodded, and Fallon helped himself to cigarette paper and tobacco.

"What can you tell me about what was going on outside?"

Fallon rolled the cigarette, licked it, and stuck it in his mouth, waiting expectantly.

"I'll give you a light when you answer some questions," MacGregor said. "What was going on out there?"

"*No sabe,*" Fallon answered.

MacGregor's fist pounded against the table. He stamped one foot on the floor. He cursed long, loud, and vilely. Fallon had a hard time keeping his face blank. Never would he be able to match the thespian talents of Christina Whitney or Dan MacGregor. Hell, even Aaron Holderman was better at this than Fallon.

Fallon started to rise as if to leave, but MacGregor sharply told him to sit down. Fallon obeyed, sighed, and listened as MacGregor—or rather Byron Roberts, inspector of prisons—pleaded with him again to answer a few questions.

"*No sabe,*" was Fallon's answer.

MacGregor's head shook.

A brief silence passed between the two men. They heard nothing, but neither man had any doubts that somewhere in an adjoining room, Barney Drexel or one of his men, either guard or convict, was hearing everything said inside the visiting room. It would not have surprised either to learn that somewhere a spy was watching them through a peephole. Visiting rooms in prisons had never been known as something sacred like a Catholic's confessional or a bachelor's privy. Visiting rooms at prisons were no place to tell someone a secret.

"Are you all right?" MacGregor asked.

"*No sabe.*" His hands rested on the table. His left thumb moved once.

"Can I get you anything?"

"*No sabe.*" The right thumb moved twice.

"Mr. Alexander, let's be reasonable about this. You're in this prison for life, but that life can be very short. Because I have friends who are preparing a case against you in the state of Arkansas. The War of the Rebellion is long over, and while our government executed only one Confederate official—that butcher at Andersonville—men can still be tried for treason. Or the butchering of an army patrol on the road to Lucas Town, Arkansas. Murdering them merely because they wore the blue—when in fact most of them were too young to have done any fighting during that late war. There shall not be another Civil War, sir. Remember that."

Fallon stared at him blankly.

"You have skills, sir." He had been given a folder containing Fallon's and the Mexican's records. "Experienced in agriculture, sugarcane. There are work programs for inmates. I see that your lawyer is working on getting that sentence drastically reduced." He closed the folder. "That might not happen if the parole board learned of what is being investigated in Lucas Town, Arkansas."

The paused lengthened.

Fallon said, "*No sabe.*"

Then he leaned back in his chair, rocking on the hind legs, as MacGregor cursed and slammed his fists on the table and screamed until another guard opened the door.

"Get this unreconstructed piece of rebel trash out of my sight!" MacGregor bellowed. "Tell your sergeant, this Drexel ape, that he has trained his wards quite well. They become mute. Damned fools. But tell Drexel and Superintendent Wilkinson that if it takes me half a lifetime, I shall get to the bottom of this. I will be back in two weeks. Maybe by then this . . ." He paused to glance down at the papers . . . "Mr. Alexander will have found his tongue."

"*No sabe,*" Fallon said, and walked through the door.

"Guess you ought to get to the infirmary, too," the guard said, and called for a trusty. Then he reached inside his pocket. "You need a light?"

"Nah." Fallon removed the cigarette. "I'll save it for after supper. My tobacco rations all went to paying off the guards and trusties."

The guard grinned.

A white-haired convict named Todd arrived, and

the guard instructed him to take the prisoner to the infirmary.

Fallon kept a good hold on the cigarette as he walked alongside the old man. *"Half a lifetime,"* Mac-Gregor said. *"In two weeks."* Meaning MacGregor would return in one week, not two. Fallon would wait until he was in his cell—so far, he had the room to himself, but at The Walls, that would not last much longer— so he would read MacGregor's instructions written on the inside of the cigarette paper then. Before destroying it . . . since Fallon did not smoke.

CHAPTER TEN

What troubled Fallon the most was something else Dan MacGregor had said in the visiting room. *"There shall not be another Civil War, sir. Remember that."*

Another Civil War? Could the investigators outside The Walls have more information that proved that was Josiah Jonathan Justice's motive?

It sounded extreme and Fallon did not want to believe anything like that could be possible. Besides, he needed to focus on something more important to him. If the warden, Drexel, and others were using prisoners leased to Justice to commit crimes, similar to the long-running operation he had cracked in Jefferson City, then chances were Fallon would find the man who ordered the murder of his wife and daughter.

The following Sunday after church, he went to the library, found a copy of Dumas—*The Count of Monte Cristo* had been the most-read novel among inmates at every prison Fallon had been in—and sat at a table. After opening the novel, he slipped a pamphlet-sized book inside the thick volume of Dumas and turned to the pages that began explaining Texas penitentiary regulations: *Article XX: Labor of Convicts.* That didn't have what he wanted, so he thumbed back to *Article XV: Outside Labor and Hirers of the Same.*

He had gone over the regulations with Dan MacGregor and Christina Whitney over several nights in Mobile, Alabama, and New Orleans, Louisiana, but mostly what they had discussed was what to expect in the camps once Fallon had been assigned to one. And how Fallon had to make sure he got assigned to the right camp.

Now Fallon found what he wanted:

> *There shall be appointed, as required by these rules, for each outside force of convicts, one Sergeant, two Camp Guards, and Day Guards, as follows: For every six convicts in force, one Day Guard, and for any fraction of six, over three, one Guard . . .*

He considered this. The warden—superintendent or whatever hifalutin title he went by—might be involved in the conspiracy, or at least his assistant was. Most likely the sergeant would have to know about the robberies and other crimes being committed, and some of the guards would as well.

Frowning, Fallon swore underneath his breath. He was missing something, something vital, something so damned obvious but a fact that he just could not put his finger on. Somebody else had to be part of this plan. It was different in Jefferson City. Prisoners were put into a punishment cell where they left the state penitentiary through a tunnel, killed their target, returned to the prison—the perfect crime. How could an inmate murder some stranger when he was already behind the iron bars of a state penitentiary?

That was Missouri. In Texas, though, the prisoners were leased to a farm, factory, or railroad. That meant someone on the outside had to be part of this . . . Justice, the sugarcane and cotton magnate? Maybe. A strong possibility. But there had to be someone else. Only . . . who?

Footsteps echoed in the spartan library, and Fallon looked up, slowly closing the copy of *The Count of Monte Cristo* over the pamphlet of prison regulations. He smiled as the Mexican with the whip walked over, stopping beside the table.

"Hello No Sabe," Fallon said. He was ready, though, to turn the table over, rise, pick up the chair, and smash it over the big man's head.

"What are you reading, Lash?" The accent was there, but he spoke perfect English.

Fallon nodded at the book. "*The Count of Monte Cristo* by Alexandre Dumas."

The Mexican nodded. "What is it about?"

"A Frenchman gets sent to prison. Unjustly. He breaks out. Gets revenge."

"You trying to learn how he broke out? Use it for yourself?"

Fallon's head shook. "Hell, no. It took the guy in this book way too long—we're talking *years*—to escape."

The Mexican laughed.

"You want to read it?" Fallon asked.

"No. I don't read."

"You speak good English for a Mexican who doesn't read."

"I read Spanish," he said. "And I speak Spanish much better than your ugly language."

Fallon had no response to that, but the Mexican did not believe in silence.

"The Judge wants to see you," he said. "Now. Let's go."

"Let me put the books away," Fallon said, and quickly picked up the novel, turned, and discreetly dropped both books into a box marked TO BE RESHELVED. He nudged two dime novels to cover the prison pamphlet and left Dumas beside *Uncle Tom's Cabin*, which he doubted if anyone in Texas had read.

"You didn't want to keep the book till you finished it?" the Mexican said.

"I've read it before."

"Hmmm." The Mexican considered that. "I have never read anything twice. It would be like killing the same man twice."

"Never thought of it that way," Fallon said as he followed the big man out of the library.

John Wesley Hardin sat in the shade, another prisoner fanning him, while The Walls' most famous resident drummed his fingers on the well-worn leather cover of *Blackstone*. The Judge was holding court again.

"Here's Alexander, Judge, sir," the Mexican said.

"Gracias, Juanito," Hardin said.

Well, now Fallon knew the big Mexican's name.

The Mexican nodded at Fallon, who started toward the Judge's bench, which was a rocking chair likely fetched from the prison's infirmary.

"Good luck, Lash."

"*Gracias, no sabe.*"

The Mexican named Juanito chuckled as he moved to his right and took his place in the front row of a line of prisoners three rows deep.

"Harry Alexander," Hardin said before tilting his head at a shaking, pale, pockmarked kid still in his teens, who sat in the dirt, legs crossed, his face covered with bruises and dirt, tears carving paths through the dirt. "Meet Eugene Gray. Your client."

"My client?" Fallon stopped and faced Hardin again.

"By order of this court."

Fallon nodded. "All right."

"You got ten minutes to confer with your client. My docket's full and the asses will be shipping us off to evening worship in eighty-three minutes."

Fallon squatted in the dust beside the sobbing boy.

"You . . ." The kid had trouble speaking, and Fallon had trouble staring at the snot that poured out of the frightened inmate's nostrils. "You . . . you . . . my . . . a-a-a-tor-ney?"

"Yeah." The word hung on Fallon's tongue like a brick.

The boy went off into a stuttering and dizzying account of what had happened. Fallon understood only half of it, but that was enough for him to hold out his hand and slowly, politely ask the boy to stop for a few minutes.

"Son . . ." He smiled, or tried to smile. "First off, what's your name?"

"Gene. I mean Eugene. Eugene Gray. Folks call me Gene, though. I mean, folks that know me."

"I see." Well, that was the name The Judge had said. "So . . . here's the deal, Gene. My name's Alexander.

Harry Alexander. This isn't a legal court of law. This one is for the prisoners. I'm a prisoner. The Judge is a prisoner. Just like you. So there's no need to tell me what got you behind these redbrick walls, Gene. I can't represent you in that regard. That's for your attorney who's on the outside. What I need to know is just why you're being tried before your peers. Can you tell me that?"

The kid sobbed, shook his head, and blurted out, "That's the awfullest part of it all, Mr. Harry. I don't know what they say I done. But I know I didn't do nothing."

Fallon looked up at Hardin.

"His mate found four rations of tobacco underneath his bunk," Hardin said. "He hasn't been in The Walls long enough to have that many."

"Stolen?" Fallon asked.

"That's the charge," The Judge said.

"Who made it?"

"His cellmate, Big Dan McAllister."

Fallon looked back at Gene Gray, then faced Hardin again. "What kind of tobacco?"

"Smoking. All of it was smoking."

Another nod, and Fallon slid closer to the kid. "You heard that, Gene?"

"Yes, sir."

"Did you steal any rations?"

"No, sir. I give mine away. I don't smoke. Don't even chew."

"Who'd you give yours to?"

"Big Dan."

"Very good."

Behind him the inmate who had been fanning

Hardin jumped to his feet and said, "Hear ye, hear ye, this court is now in session. The Right Honorable John Wesley Hardin presiding. All rise."

"Hear ye, hear ye," the convict who had been fanning The Judge said. "All those with business before this court, step forward and ye shall be heard."

Rising to his feet, Fallon motioned for the kid to stand and whispered, "One more question, kid. What are you in for?"

"Rape," Gene Gray said.

Fallon swore underneath his breath.

"We'll skip the formalities," Hardin said after striking a match and lighting a cigarette. "No opening statements. The defendant is Eugene Gray. He is charged with stealing tobacco rations from Zeke Montgomery, Black Jim, Crow Jeffreys, and Frenchy Caron. McAllister, call your first witness."

Big Dan McAllister wasn't that big in height, but his head was enormous and his hands looked like anvils. He told Zeke Montgomery to take the stand.

Hardin said, "No need to swear him in, Bailiff. Zeke's an anarchist and an atheist."

Once the laughter died down, McAllister asked, "Tell us what happened last ration day."

Zeke Montgomery said he had gotten his tobacco allotment and placed it on his bunk, but then had to run to the privy. When he returned, the tobacco was gone, but was later found in the cell manned by Big Dan McAllister and Gene the Rapist.

"Objection," Fallon said.

"Overruled. The defendant is in here for raping. Two women. One of them fourteen years old."

"Which has no bearing on this case."

The Judge glared. "I said overruled."

"Exception."

Hardin leaned back and fanned himself. "Noted," he said, but did not look away as McAllister finished his examination.

"Your witness, Counselor."

Fallon did not bother standing. He asked, "Where's the stolen tobacco?"

"What?" Zeke Montgomery countered.

"The tobacco. The evidence. Where is it? It hasn't been admitted as evidence by the prosecutor. Do you have it?"

Montgomery looked blankly. "No," he eventually answered.

"Then where is it?"

Montgomery scratched his head.

"Answer the question," Hardin ordered.

"Well, Judge, sir . . ." The convict wet his lips. "I smoked it."

The spectators laughed.

"All of it?" Fallon asked.

"Well, it's been three weeks. I got a . . . habit."

Fallon leaned back. "No more questions."

Before McAllister called Black Jim to take the stand, the big-headed man with giant hands rushed to the first line and retrieved pouches from three men. The second of those was Black Jim.

"Is this your pouch of tobacco?" McAllister asked Black Jim after he had been sworn in.

"That's right. The rapist took it."

Fallon did not bother objecting this time. He listened to the idiotic questions and stupid answers before McAllister passed the witness.

Fallon stood this time, walked to Hardin, and took

the black man's tobacco pouch, a well-used pouch of grimy cotton, once yellow, now faded and dirtied into a brownish tan.

"Since Counselor didn't bother doing this, Judge, I'll offer it into evidence."

"Objections?" Hardin asked.

"Huh?" Big Dan McAllister said.

The crowd laughed again.

"It's admitted, Mr. Alexander. Proceed."

"So you're saying the rapist stole your tobacco. Right?"

"That's what I said," Black Jim answered.

"That's how you recognized it," Fallon said. "I mean, you found your pouch, right?"

The man stopped, looked at McAllister, then at The Judge.

"Well, no. I had my pouch with me. Still had plenty."

"I see. What did the stolen ration look like?"

"It's a Bull Durham bag," Frenchy Caron said. At least, Fallon assumed the thin man with dark hair was Frenchy Caron. He spoke with a French accent. French. Not Cajun. "Show him, Big Dan."

"Hell," Hardin said, and flicked his cigarette into the dust. "Go ahead and bring up Frenchy's pouch and Crow's."

Both were Bull Durham pouches, nothing fancy like the first one. Fallon walked over to The Judge and Big Dan McAllister and looked at the pouches.

"I bet you have a pouch nicer than this, Judge," Fallon said.

Hardin smiled and brought out his pouch, a self-closing container of green rubber that felt and looked like velvet.

Fallon walked to the line of prisoners, but called

out to The Judge, the prosecutor, and the witnesses, "No more questions. Go ahead, Big Dan, call your next witness. Don't mind me. I'm listening." He moved through the line of prisoners, but he was lying. He didn't listen to anything the witness had to say.

He did call out, "No questions," after Frenchy Caron had finished his testimony, and was walking back toward Gene Gray while McAllister questioned Crow Jeffreys.

"Your witness, Rape Lover," McAllister said.

Fallon picked up the tobacco pouches of Frenchy Caron and Crow Jeffreys, smiled at the judge, and dropped seven Bull Durham pouches on the ground between Jeffreys's shoes.

"Which bag's yours?" he asked.

"What?"

"Which bag is yours?"

"They's all Bull Durham sacks," the man protested.

"But you discovered yours in the defendant's cell, didn't you?"

"Well, yeah, well, it was McAllister . . . but . . ."

"Which one is yours?"

"Your Honor!" Big Dan erupted. "This ain't right."

"Four pouches of Bull Durham tobacco were found in the cell," Fallon said.

"But mine was stole," Crow Jeffreys said. "Mine was . . . Well . . ."

"Can you tell which one is yours here?"

"No. I mean." His shoulders sagged. "Ought to have writ my name or initials on it. Just never learnt my letters."

"You could've made your mark," The Judge said.

Crow Jeffreys shook his head. "Never learnt how to do that, neither."

"Your Honor," Dan McAllister was yelling as he charged toward The Judge, Fallon, and the witness. "Four pouches were stolen and found in this rapist's cell and . . ."

"Can you identify which of these pouches were found in the defendant's bunk and which ones I borrowed from our spectators?"

"Absolutely!" Big Dan McAllister bent to his knees and looked at the pouches.

"And then can your witnesses pick out the same ones?" Fallon said.

Big Dan froze. One pouch slipped out of his hand. The hand disappeared behind Big Dan's back. When it reappeared, it held a small but lethal three-cornered file. Big Dan McAllister swore as he leaped up and slashed at Fallon's stomach.

CHAPTER ELEVEN

He leaped back, feeling the rush of air as the cell-made blade missed his prison shirt by mere inches, though Fallon doubted if it would have cut any flesh. Fallon knew that luck had smiled down on him for he had not even seen the sharpened file; it looked that small in the man's meaty right hand.

Big Dan turned, made a backhanded slice with the small black blade, but the three-cornered file never came close to Fallon's body. The murderer of three family members on a farm stopped, turned, and bent his knees. Crouching, he grinned, moving the blade back and forth. Fallon moved with him in a semicircle, waiting, trying to read something in the man's beady eyes that seemed too close to his nose. The nose, Fallon thought, had been busted countless times. That made Fallon's own nose itch.

The circle of prison-yard courtroom walls of inmates closed in. Men cheered. Once again, the guards ignored the melee.

"Stick him deep, Big Dan!"

"Slit his throat!"

"C'mon, Alexander. Make that big cuss eat dirt."

Fallon had come far in the weeks he had been inside The Walls. Not everyone cheered against him these days.

"You going to dance?" Hardin's voice called out. "Or fight?"

Some of the prisoners laughed. A few kept shouting encouragement or obscenities.

Big Dan McAllister straightened, raised his right hand over his head, and charged, muttering a Confederate war cry that led to other prisoners mimicking the rebel yell.

The killer's left hand swung out, away from his body.

Instinctively, Fallon guessed Big Dan's intentions. Use that left arm to wrap around Fallon's body, bring him into a death grip, then stab, stab, stab. McAllister wasn't that big, except for his head and fists, but Fallon wasn't going to risk getting too close to the killer. So Fallon dropped to his back, arched over, brought up his legs, and caught McAllister at the waist. Fallon kept moving backward, pushed his legs hard, and sent McAllister sailing.

Fallon rolled over, to his knees, watched McAllister land with a thud, sending dust rising, causing the nearest spectators to stumble back. Seizing his moment, Fallon came up to his feet and charged. He didn't have far to run. Big Dan McAllister came up, his lungs heaving, but still held on to the file. Someone shouted a warning, and McAllister turned his head, just enough so that Fallon's foot only grazed the cauliflower ear instead of flattening the nose and knocking some teeth down his windpipe.

The file came hard. Fallon cursed, spun, felt the blade slice his side, a burning wound, but more of an irritant than deadly. Still, Fallon lost his footing and stumbled into the wall of prisoners. Immediately he was flung back toward McAllister.

Seeing the deadly blade coming down, Fallon raised his left arm and somehow managed to stop McAllister from stabbing him. The monstrous left hand came up, though, and clamped on Fallon's throat. The palm pressed against his throat. Fallon brought his knee up, slammed into Big Dan's groin. The man grunted, released his hold, allowing Fallon to pull away. The hand came back. Fallon turned his head, saw the three-cornered file coming at him again. He stepped hard on McAllister's left foot, heard the bones breaking, because McAllister's feet were more in line with the rest of his body and not his oversized head and hands.

That gave Fallon just enough time to pull free, and he let himself fall to the dirt as fast as he could. The file kept coming, and drilled its small blade into the center of Big Dan McAllister's thigh.

"Awwweeeeeee!" Big Dan cried out in a voice like a young girl's.

He tried to pull out the knife, the wooden handle was already slippery from the blood, and his big fingers just couldn't find a grip on the small handle. McAllister limped around, grunting, panting, and pawing at the small weapon.

Fallon rose, moved in, sent an uppercut that cracked Big Dan's jaw. The man staggered back. *Big head*, Fallon thought, *big hands, no brain, glass jaw.*

His left connected, another right, then he drilled a quick succession of three short but powerful punches into the man's ribs. One cracked. Fallon came up with his left. Blood sprayed from McAllister's lips into Fallon's face, causing him to blink away the coppery-smelling wetness. He hit again. Again. Once more, and was going in for as hard of a blow as he had ever punched, but missed.

That carried Fallon again into the crowd, who turned him around. One of them managed a glancing blow off his kidneys, and then he felt himself pushed back into the center of the ever-shrinking ring.

Fallon stumbled and felt his knees being ripped by the pebbles and sand in the yard. He expected to feel McAllister's retaliation, but just heard the buzzing and humming in his head, his heavy breathing, and curses, laughter, and cheers from the prisoners.

Then came the screeching of the whistle.

"Move! Move! Move!"

"Out of the way, you cur dawgs, or it's into the sweatbox for a week!"

The guards, Fallon knew. They must have decided that enough was enough.

Fallon brushed away sweat, blood, and sand from his forehead. His vision cleared long enough to find Big Dan McAllister, still trying to push himself up, still collapsing, and groaning, but determined to make himself get back up. Fallon respected that. There was no quit in the man, even though one of his legs just wouldn't cooperate. Eventually, McAllister might have managed to stand, but one of the prison guards planted a foot against the center of the killer's back and pushed hard. Another guard swung his nightstick and Fallon grimaced at the crack it made against McAllister's head.

McAllister groaned and fell limp into the dirt.

Prisoners cursed. Guards bellowed.

Someone helped Fallon to his feet.

"Get that mutant to the doctor," Sergeant Barney Drexel said. "What was the meaning of this?"

"Boxing match," John Wesley Hardin answered.

"There's a weapon in this turd's thigh, Sarge," a guard said.

"Explain that, Hardin," Drexel demanded.

"Some fool must have hid it in the dirt, Sergeant," Hardin said. "Good thing we had boxing for our exercise and entertainment. Else one of us might have found that little sticker and done one of you some harm."

Fallon was shoved toward Drexel. Again, the sand, sweat, blood, and bruises on his face helped disguise Fallon's appearance.

"Here's the other one, Sarge."

Barney Drexel glowered, shook his head, and spat in the sand.

"You seem to be in the center of things again, boy."

"Keeping in condition, sir," Fallon managed to say.

"Get out of my sight."

"Should I take him to the infirmary, Sarge?"

"No. Maybe he'll die from bleeding from his insides."

"Clear out!" another guard began yelling. "Clear out. File in your groups and be prepared to return to your cells. Exercise is suspended for all you scum for the next three days."

The inmates answered with hisses. Fallon just found a handkerchief and started wiping his face.

* * *

"What made you so sure the inmates would have nothing but Bull Durham sacks of tobacco?" Hardin asked that evening.

They sat at Hardin's private dining table again, but eating the same fare the rest of the prisoners were being fed: bacon, stale bread, bad coffee.

They had finished their supper. Fallon sipped coffee. Hardin rolled a cigarette.

"You want to know how many personal tobacco pouches I've ever seen in a prison?" Fallon asked.

Hardin licked the papers and stuck the smoke in his mouth. "How many?"

Fallon nodded at the rubber velvet pouch near Hardin's empty tin plate. "Yours," Fallon said.

That got a chuckle and nod of approval from The Judge.

"Johnson," Hardin said.

The guard stepped forward, struck a match against his trouser leg, and lighted Hardin's smoke.

"You're a tough con, Alexander," Hardin said after blowing a smoke ring toward the ceiling. "You whup up on Ryker. You live through an unfathomable time in the sweatbox. Get past Juanito. And now Big Dan McAllister. Plus, you showed you're not just one more stupid fool to get himself incarcerated in The Walls. You know things. You're pretty smart."

"So are you," Fallon said.

"Why? Because I'm learning myself to be a lawyer? You've had lawyers. You know how smart most of those varmints are."

Fallon's head shook. "That's not what I meant."

Hardin removed the cigarette, blew smoke out of his nostrils, and waited.

"How long have you been here?"

"Since '78," Hardin answered.

"And you're still alive. You don't live that long in a place like this if you don't have brains."

The killer laughed again. Fallon waited, wondering if Hardin might say something. Hardin was The Judge inside The Walls. So whatever was going on outside The Walls, involving killers and guards, Hardin had to know about it. Get in good with The Judge, Fallon told himself, and you might get closer to the man or men who killed your family.

"Good night, Harry," Hardin said.

Johnson, the guard, stepped forward and gave a stern tip of his head at Fallon. "Let's go, Alexander," the man said.

"Sleep tight, Harry," Hardin called out as the guard escorted Fallon to his cell.

When Fallon stepped inside, he saw a man sitting on the top bunk. Fallon had been sleeping solo since he had gotten out of solitary. He had also been sleeping on the top bunk, because that made it harder for the roaches and spiders to get to you. But the newcomer had thrown Fallon's bedding onto the floor.

The door slammed shut behind Fallon, and locked.

CHAPTER TWELVE

He didn't know the convict's real name, though he had seen him at the mill and wandering around the exercise yard. And Fallon had heard other inmates talk about him. The called him The Weasel.

"I didn't ask to be here, Hank," he said from the bunk, smoking his cigarette, blowing smoke toward the dark ceiling. "They put some greaser in the cell with me and tossed me out." He spoke with a nasal whine. "Wasn't my idea. Just so you know."

Fallon had not moved. "Whose idea was it to take my bunk?"

The bony right hand removed the cigarette and flicked ash to the floor.

"It's seniority, Hank. I've been in The Walls for fourteen years. Eleven more to go and I get out of this dung heap.?"

"I've got seniority in this cell, Weasel. By, what, a month?"

The Weasel sat up. He started to take another drag on his cigarette, but stopped. Instead, still holding the smoke, he pointed at Fallon. "Listen here, Hank . . ."

"My friends call me Hank," Fallon said.

The Weasel's head tilted, uncertain, and then he looked through the iron bars at the darkened walkway. Fallon did not have to look. He knew every inmate in every cell in this wing stared at his cell. He also knew, as he had not heard the outer door open and shut, that the guard who had escorted Fallon to the cell was listening, if not watching, himself.

"All right." The Weasel tossed the cigarette to the floor, leaped down, and crushed it out with the heel of his shoe. "No need in getting mad, Alexander. I'll give you some slack, seeing as how you're still a fresh fish, don't know all the rules about how things work in The Walls. You take the top bunk. I just thought, as big as you are, it'd make more sense if I take the top one, you see."

"With my bedding and blanket," Fallon said.

"Well . . . it's . . . you know, part of that seniority I was talking about."

"Put my stuff back."

The Weasel drew in a deep breath, held it, and let it go, but turned around and carefully began returning Fallon's meager possessions to the top bunk. Then he sat down on the bottom bunk and said, "You satisfied?"

Fallon wondered how long The Weasel had spent rifling through Fallon's belongings. Not that he was worried. There was nothing here to give away Fallon's true identity. As far as anyone in The Walls knew, now that Josh Ryker was finishing his sentence in the prison in Rusk, Fallon was Harry Alexander, convicted of armed robbery, three counts; assault and battery, twelve counts; assault with intent to kill, five counts; and grand larceny (horse theft), two counts—which had netted him a life sentence.

All of the crimes had happened in the Panhandle
northwest of Amarillo and the once-thriving cattle
town of Tascosa. Which might as well have been part
of New Mexico Territory for all anyone in Austin, or
Huntsville, was concerned. That's why the American
Detective Agency and Texas attorney general had
made up the crimes and set them in that remote location. The chances of anyone following up on those
crimes were as remote as any settlement in the Panhandle.

Fallon moved past The Weasel and climbed into
his bunk.

"I scored two peppermint sticks from a guard," The
Weasel said. "Want one?"

Fallon didn't answer.

"Well, my teeth ain't so good, so like as not, I'll just
have one. So if you get a craving, you just let me know,
Hank . . . I mean . . . Mr. Alexander."

He heard the little man settle into his bunk.

"They say you done some farm work," The Weasel
said after a lengthy silence. "Cotton?"

In the growing darkness, Fallon smiled. So that's
why The Weasel had become Fallon's cellmate. The
interrogation. See how much this man knew.

Fallon didn't answer.

"My pappy raised cotton up in eastern Arkansas,
sort of northwest of Memphis. Good black-land dirt.
Good soil. Got some good harvests when we wasn't
flooded."

"I wouldn't know about that," Fallon said.

"But ain't you from Arkansas?"

"Not where anyone could grow cotton."

"Oh. So that cotton-picking story I heard about you
is just a cotton-picking lie?" He cackled at his own joke.

"I wouldn't say that," Fallon told him after the laughter faded.

"Oh." He heard another match strike and soon smelled smoke from The Weasel's cigarette. "Cotton's getting ten dollars a pound."

"Like hell," Fallon said. "I don't know what it's selling for, but if it's ten bucks I'll eat my shoe."

"Well, it was selling for . . ."

"I wouldn't know what it's selling for, Weasel. I picked the damn thing. I wasn't a speculator."

"Oh."

"Besides, I was better at cane."

"Cain? As in Abel?"

Fallon laughed. "As in sugar. Miserable work. Just like picking cotton. Maybe worse than picking cotton. Cotton you had to replant. The roots of a good cane could last many ratoons."

"Ra-toons?" The Weasel said.

"Cycles. Growing seasons. Cane can grow in six months in a sweatbox like Louisiana. It'd take maybe two years for it to grow eight, ten feet tall where I come from."

"Where's that, Harry?"

"None of your damned business."

"Ain't prying, Harry, no sir. I just like to learn things. What else can you tell me about sugarcane? Or cotton?"

"Not a damned thing. I'm through with that line of work. Hell, I'm through with every line of work I've known—gunning, killing, robbing, stealing, loving—it's all over now, Weasel. In case you didn't know, I'm here till I'm dead."

He smiled at his performance. He hadn't forgotten

Christina Whitney's coaching. Don't give away too much too soon. Peel the onion in layers.

"Harry, tell me . . ."

"Shut the hell up, Weasel," Fallon said. "Finish your smoke and go to sleep."

Fallon settled into his bunk, then he reached toward the wooden post, found the hollowed-out spot next to the damp, cold wall, and used his fingers to pry out what had once been a spoon. Carefully, he brought it up and folded his arm across his chest, gripping the weapon in his right hand.

It had been a spoon at the dining hall. But if a fellow had enough time and a cell by himself, he could scrape the spoon down on the floor and bars in his cell, then wrap the end with some rags he had found in a trash bin. It wasn't an Arkansas toothpick or one of Jim Bowie's blades, but in a place like The Walls, it would serve its purpose. The hiding place he had found. Credit for that belonged to a former resident of this cell.

Fallon closed his eyes. He could rest easier now, just in case The Weasel—he came by his nickname naturally—had been planted in here to do more than just learn a few things about Harry Alexander. In a place like Huntsville, any inmate who didn't have a shank or some other kind of weapon might not be a man for very long.

He caught a glimpse of Dan MacGregor—or should that be Inspector of Prisons Byron Roberts?—when he came back to The Walls, but there had been no communication that time. At least, not between MacGregor and Fallon. Probably MacGregor had managed a short exchange with Aaron Holderman, although they could have talked in secret beyond those redbrick walls. More than likely, MacGregor was trying to make his face known, so that no one would suspect him when he came in needing to find out, or pass on, some pertinent information.

Again, Fallon fell into the groove. Eat. Work. Eat. Work. Work. Work. Work.

He pictured Christina Whitney again and remembered something else she had told him.

"Ninety percent of detective work is boring as hell, Hank. Is it all right if I call you Hank? Thanks. Harry just doesn't fit you, but we don't have a say in our names, do we? I never liked Christina. Maybe that's why I like being a private detective. I can be someone else. So . . . I haven't talked so much in ages . . . where were we? Yes. It's boring. Sleep-inducing dullness. You sit on your heinie for ages, get little sleep, and just watch someone or someplace so that mundane gets a monopoly on your life."

Damn. He couldn't get her off his mind. He thought of her, pictured her face, in the mill, in the cell when The Weasel was babbling away. Even when John Wesley Hardin was talking to him.

He and Christina had spent much of the winter together, and now that he was in prison, he . . . well . . . missed her company, her smile, and her . . . damn it all to hell . . . beauty.

She looked nothing like Renee. He tried to remember his late wife. He tried to picture the face of The Mole, the psychopathic killer who had murdered her and Fallon's daughter.

He stood in line, waiting to be called in to breakfast with seven other inmates, including The Weasel, when a lanky guard with a potbelly came up to him and tapped him with his stick.

"Come along, Alexander. The warden wants you."

Fallon stared.

"Don't take all day, boy. You ain't the only one here who hasn't had his breakfast."

Fallon removed his hat, lowered his head, and waited for the warden's secretary to open the door. The squeamish little man announced that the prisoner was here as requested, a grunt served as the response, and the secretary pushed the door all the way open and nodded at Fallon and the guard to enter. Fallon stepped onto the Eastern-style rug and kept his head down, waiting.

The door closed. The warden clipped off the end of a cigar and fired it up.

"How long have you been in The Walls, Alexander?" the warden asked after his cigar was fired up to his liking.

Head still down, Fallon shrugged. "Six weeks. Don't rightly know, sir."

"That's a pretty good guess." The warden removed the cigar. "Six weeks. For a life sentence. And now this."

Fallon lifted his head. Walter Wilkinson, superintendent at The Walls unit, wasn't alone in the office. A tall man in a plaid suit, with a curled mustache, eyeglasses, stood next to the bookcase. He held a notepad and pencil in his hands. Reporter? Maybe. If he was, he did not identify himself as one, just nodded at Fallon and made a few scribbles on the pad with his pencil.

"I've had prisoners come inside The Walls and be taken out to the cemetery in six weeks, Alexander," the warden said, and the tall man began taking notes. Reporter, Fallon decided. "But never in all my years have I had one sentenced to a life sentence get that sentence reduced. Substantially."

The warden sighed, produced a thick yellow paper, and walked toward Fallon.

"The Lord looks over you, Alexander. Instead of dying inside The Walls, you can be out in ten years."

The reporter wrote. The warden handed the paper to Fallon, who took it and stared at the large, fancy cursive heading:

Commutation of Sentence

He saw the signature of the governor.

Governor? Fallon suddenly felt sick. Maybe this case was bigger than the attorney general, Christina Whitney, and Sean MacGregor ever imagined. Could this ring of killers go all the way up to the Texas governor's mansion?

CHAPTER THIRTEEN

"Congratulations, Mr. Alexander," the warden said. "Don't ruin this by doing something stupid and having additional years to those ten."

"I can do ten years easy," Fallon said, and he smiled. Hell, he had. And those last few months, with him damned near getting killed on multiple occasions in Yuma and Jefferson City, had felt like ten years, too. "Sir," he added.

The governor made a slight gesture toward the newspaper reporter, who moved easily toward Fallon.

"Might I have a few words with you, Mr. Alexander?" He handed Fallon a card.

MAJOR RUFUS K. CONLEY
❧
EDITOR / PUBLISHER
The Texas Times
Indianola, Texas

Fallon shrugged, but handed the card to the tall man. "I didn't think there was anything left of Indianola after those hurricanes." He had read about those in newspapers . . . the first one, from around 1875, he couldn't remember where; the second, in 1886, had been in the prison library at Joliet.

"There's a newspaper," Conley said with a smile. "For I refuse to believe that Indianola will not rise like the phoenix from the ashes, or, dare I say, mud and saltwater. A few businesses. Fishermen. Patriots. Men of the soil and sea with determination and spirit."

Fallon debated talking to a reporter, but decided he had to. Never had he met any prisoner who would decline an interview, a chance to state his case, declare his innocence, to a newspaper or magazine journalist. Most would give their eyeteeth for such a chance. Indianola was a long way from the Texas Panhandle. You could hardly find a place more far away, so the chances were remote that someone in the Texas Panhandle would see that newspaper and start saying that this crime this fellow committed . . . how come we've never heard of it? And it wasn't like a newspaper in a place like that coastal town would be sharing its news with papers farther north. What could the circulation be? Twenty? Fifty? A hundred at the most.

"How does it feel?" Conley asked.

"It hasn't set in yet," Fallon said.

"You are married?"

"Yes, sir."

"Children?"

His eyes teared unexpectedly. He blinked, coughed, and shook his head. That reaction had not been expected, but the reporter didn't seem to notice.

The rest of the answers were bland, noncommittal, but it wasn't like Mr. Rufus Conley was taking a whole lot of notes. Perhaps he was the kind of journalist who would make up his own facts to fit his own story.

When he was finished, Fallon thanked the newspaperman and accepted his handshake. For a man who pushed a pencil and maybe set type, he had a firm grip, and the hand was well callused. That's another thing that Fallon had not expected.

But as the man turned back toward the governor, now sitting at his desk, Fallon asked, "Mr. Editor, could I ask you a question or two?"

Turning, Conley studied Fallon and cautiously nodded.

Fallon held up the commutation paper. "Just who all has to say this here thing gets done?"

The journalist laughed, shoved his notebook into his jacket pocket, and said, "Well, the governor has the final say."

"Yeah. That I figured. But how did he find out about me? It wasn't like everything I did got writ up in all the papers. I mean, I wasn't Billy the Kid or the Daltons."

"Indeed." Conley's eyes brightened. "The men of the court where your trial was held have to agree that you deserve a reduction of sentence or outright pardon. Someone—in this case I take it, it was your wife, maybe your mother, father, your priest, your grandparents, a good friend with political clout . . ." He kept going, likely hoping for some kind of reaction that would lead to more questions, but Fallon gave away nothing—like there was anything to give away. "Anyway, someone writes a request, the proverbial story that leaves teenage girls and mothers sobbing. Anyway, once a majority of members from your trial have recommended commutation, in writing, it goes to the board in charge of pardons and paroles. Once they recommend it, it goes to the governor. Simple."

Fallon grinned. "How do I get a pardon?"

The newspaperman laughed. "Don't be greedy, my friend. I'm writing about this because it's rare that a life sentence gets reduced."

"Someone had the governor's ear," Fallon said with a grin. "I'd like to thank him."

"And plant a seed that a pardon is also in order?" Conley chuckled. "I admire your spirit. But I must be going." He walked back toward the warden's desk, and Fallon saw the guard approaching.

"All right," he said as he looked again at the paper in his hand. Maybe it was Malcolm Maxwell, the attorney general. But if it was someone else, Fallon needed to know.

He hadn't realized how many possible things could go wrong in an assignment like this. All those weeks of training, of learning about sugarcane and cotton and how to be a spy and detective, he hadn't had time to think of how one mistake, one item no one had considered, could get Harry Fallon killed.

The guard made himself grin. "Lucky day, eh, Alexander?"

"Yeah," Fallon said, doing his best to sound overjoyed and overwhelmed. He waved the commutation decree at the guard. "Ten years."

"That ain't what I meant, Alexander. Ya gots a visitor. That sweet-smellin', fine-lookin' petticoat of yourn. She be waitin' in the visitin' room."

Fallon tried to look amazed and excited.

He quickened his pace toward the office door, thanking the warden and the reporter. Once they were out in the hallway, alone, Fallon asked his escort: "You think I can find a privy?"

"Boy, I'd piss my pants if it meant I could see that bride ya gots."

"C'mon, boss. I gotta go."

The guard sighed. "Downstairs. I let ya piss on the superintendent's pot, I'll be emptyin' spittoons fer the rest of my career."

On the lower floor, the guard nodded at the dark room in the corner. Fallon thanked him and stepped into the indoor privy. Times were changing. He saw the cord he needed to pull to flush his stuff away. Sitting down, he withdrew the cigarette papers with his left hand while finding the pencil in his sock with his right. A sharpened pencil could be a dangerous weapon in a place like The Walls. He began writing quickly until the guard banged on the door.

"If ya don't hurry, Alexander, I'm gonna see yer petticoat myself."

Fallon returned both items, rose, pulled the cord, waiting a few seconds, and then stepped out of the toilet. He wiped his hands on his trousers.

"You're a pig," the guard said.

"A pig that'll be free in ten years."

"If ya lives that long. Let's go."

Christina Whitney leaped from the chair when Fallon entered the room. "Harry!" she exclaimed, clasping her heart. Tears of joy streamed down her cheeks. Damn, Fallon thought, she knew how to play her role.

"No touching," the boss of the visiting room said.

"You've been here before. Break the rules and you won't come back."

Fallon moved over to the chair, settling into it as Christina sat opposite him. She wore a yellow dress this time, with lace that accentuated her breasts. Fallon pulled out his cigarette papers and laid the pack on the table.

"Let me roll you one, honey," Christina said, and looked at the guard. "May I, sir?"

"Girl, I'd like to see you lick it. Go right ahead."

She gave the brute a glare and pulled the papers closer. Fallon spun around in the chair and frowned hard at the guard, even balled his hands into fists. He tried to look angry, but that was hard because the guard was staring right back at Fallon, instead of watching Christina Whitney's sleight of hand.

"Go ahead, punk," the guard said. "Ten years can get tacked onto your ten in no time. Might turn out to be a life sentence after all."

Fallon spun around in his chair.

Christina handed the rolled cigarette toward him. "See," she told the guard, "I didn't touch him."

"Good. You can touch me, baby. Just not your husband."

She frowned, blushed, fanned herself, and said, "Don't let him worry you, Harry. It's all right now. You'll be out in ten years."

"Ten years," Fallon snapped. "You shouldn't wait for me."

He stopped, turned his head. "*You shouldn't wait for me.*" They had gone over that line several times during their training. Fallon had said it countless times, but now it struck him. That's something he had never demanded of Renee. Hell, he had thought he would be freed at any moment, that the deputy marshals riding for Judge Parker would have learned the truth, caught the real robber, and sent him to Detroit while begging forgiveness from Harry Fallon. Maybe, eventually, he would have given up hope. Hell, he had. But only after they brought him news that Renee was dead. And so was Fallon's daughter.

"Harry . . ." Christina pleaded.

Fallon rose, trying to look hurt and angry, and headed for the door. The guard sounded about as happy as Christina sounded heartbroken.

"You damned fool," the guard muttered. "Best-looking petticoat to come in here in the past six and a half years, and you tell her to stop coming. Hell, Alexander, the only reason we let her in here is because of how pretty she is."

When Christina Whitney reached her room in the Sam Houston Hotel, she bolted the door, drew the shades, turned up the lantern, and pulled out the package of cigarette papers that she had swapped with Harry Fallon. She peeled out the first paper, bent low, and read Fallon's message:

Need names of parole board.
The Weasel, inmate, now my cellmate. His story?
Background on Rufus Conley, ed., Texas Times in Indianola.

She pressed the paper against the globe of the lantern until it lighted, then dropped the paper in the ashtray and watched it burn.

* * *

When Harry Fallon got his five-minute break in the mill, he moved toward the window and began rolling a cigarette in the paper Christina Whitney had exchanged with him.

$13,500 stolen from stagecoach strong box on Houston–Beaumont Pike last Saturday. Convict job? Be careful. Watch your back.

He read the last line again, found himself smiling, thinking of the operative as he brought the cigarette up and ran it under his nose, trying to catch the fragrance of the pretty woman. But all he could smell were odors of the mill. He licked the paper, put the smoke in his mouth, and found a match. Seconds later, he was taking long drags on the cigarette, hating the taste in his mouth, recalling Whitney's beautiful cursive penmanship.

Fallon made himself stop thinking about Christina. He tried to picture Renee and Rachel again.

"Alexander!"

Looking up, he saw the foreman waving at him. So much for a five-minute break. Fallon took two more quick drags on the cigarette, then dropped it into a puddle of water and riddled the cigarette, paper, and flakes of tobacco with the heel of his shoe.

He was walking back to his station at the carding machine when one of the inmates stopped him.

"Light?" the man said, a cigarette dangling from his lips—the last thing Harry Fallon remembered.

CHAPTER FOURTEEN

His eyes opened and immediately closed from the pain of the light. A million stampeding buffalo ran across the back of his head. Tentatively, Fallon brought his left hand up and found the cloth bandage that failed to hide the walnut-sized knot on his skull.

"Careful there, Mr. Alexander," the voice said softly. Fallon recognized the prison doctor's drawl.

Slowly, Fallon made himself sit up. When his eyes opened again, he made himself adjust to the light, which no one in his right mind would have considered bright. The shades were drawn tighter than a rawhide hatband, and the only light burning in the doctor's office was over at the old codger's table. The doctor himself sat in a chair, smoking a pipe, which he set on an ashtray, and slowly rose and ambled the eight feet to Fallon's bed.

The doctor removed Fallon's hand from the bandage and checked underneath the wrapping.

"Any dizziness?" he asked.

Fallon considered shaking his head, but decided against it and answered tightly, "No."

"Double vision?"

"No." To add *sir* would have hurt too much.

"You might have a concussion, but probably not. But you will have a headache for a while." The doctor stepped back.

Fallon stared at him. "What happened?"

The white-haired cadaverous man shrugged. "Jealousy. Someone heard about the commutation of your life sentence into a ten-year vacation. At least, that's the best guess of the warden and our illustrious guards."

Fallon chanced a nod of the head. It wasn't as awful as he had feared. "Who did it?"

The doctor shrugged. "Funny thing is that no one saw it. One bloke told Barney Drexel, our lovely sergeant, that you must have hit your head on one of the machines."

"That must've been what happened," Fallon said. He tried to remember the faces of the inmates by the carding machine. He could picture only blurs. The same happened when he wanted to summon up the face of the man who had asked for a light, but that was when the lights went out. His memory was usually excellent at recalling faces, the colors of horses, the clothing of men—such traits helped when you were a federal lawman. They also came in handy when you were serving a lengthy sentence at a hellhole like Joliet, Yuma, Jefferson City, and now Huntsville. But whatever had been used to slam against his skull had wiped out whatever he had noticed at the woolen mill.

He touched the knot on his head again.

"They're going to really hate you now, Alexander."

Fallon looked closely at the doctor, who had moved to his desk and was scribbling something on a yellow sheet of paper. With his back still to Fallon, the doctor said, "I'm detailing you for special duty, Mr. Alexander. Do a good job today and I might even be persuaded to recommend you for one of our outside camps."

Straightening, Fallon realized that his head didn't hurt so much anymore.

"How's that?"

The doctor kept writing. "Surely, Mr. Alexander, you are aware of the penitentiary's outside-labor programs."

Oh yes. Fallon probably knew more about that policy than the good doctor did for it had been drilled into his brain for weeks upon weeks with Christina Whitney, Dan MacGregor, Aaron Holderman, and the state's attorney general.

"Which camp?" Fallon asked.

The doctor did not answer that question. "Mind you," the doctor said as he ripped the paper from the pad, folded it, stuck it in the pocket of his white jacket, and turned to face Fallon. "I have no say in this matter. That's up to Superintendent Wilkinson and the penitentiary board. I'm just a paid sawbones, and not paid a whole lot."

The penitentiary board. Fallon pursed his lips. That's something else no one had considered during all the planning. The penitentiary board also had a say in who got released to farms. He had to remember— if this head would let him remember—to get word to Aaron Holderman to get the names of those board members as soon as possible. The American Detective Agency could assign some operatives to check out the character and trustworthiness of those board members along with those serving on the parole board.

"Well, I should thank you . . . Doctor . . . ?" He

looked into the doctor's eyes. In all their conversations, and visits to the prison infirmary, he had never learned the physician's name.

"Abel Crouch," the old man said. "That's Crouch with a *C*. Not Grouch with a *G*." He smiled.

"Thanks, Dr. Crouch," Fallon said.

The smile turned into a flat line of thin lips. "But your first trip beyond our red bricks shall not be fun." His white head nodded to the far corner.

When Fallon turned, he saw the coffin.

"You and our other pallbearers, rather, grave-diggers, shall be escorted by guards to Peckerwood Hill. There you shall inter another unfortunate colleague of yours whose head did not prove as hard as yours, Mr. Alexander."

"Who is it?" Fallon asked, though he doubted if he would know the dead man.

"Juanito Gomez," Doc Crouch answered. "During your short stay here, you added to his scars, and he added to yours. Luckily, you were here with me, sleeping a deep sleep, when poor Gomez hit his head against a rock or hammer or wall or nightstick."

Juanito. A bitter taste coated Fallon's tongue. The burly brute of a Mexican.

"Don't fret over that Mexican, Alexander," Doc Crouch said. "He wasn't getting out of here ever. Now he is. His suffering is over. He has a new life. A new land. A new adventure."

Shaking his head, Fallon let out a sigh.

Dr. Crouch moved to the office door, opened it, and called out something to the guards, but Fallon paid little attention. He eased his way off the bed.

Five inmates entered the infirmary from the hall-way. None were convicts that Fallon recognized. Two black men, one with white hair, the other completely bald. They were muscular but lean. A small Celestial man, eyes looking at his feet, way too small and brittle to be working a shovel and pickax to dig a grave or even carry the coffin of a man the size of the late Juanito Gomez. And two white men, one who coughed like a lunger and was so deathly pale that it struck Fallon that the next convict to be buried at Peckerwood Hill would be this young, dying man. The other white man was about Fallon's size and age, except he didn't have a bandage wrapped around his head.

Fallon decided to take his off, but Doc Crouch stopped him. "I wouldn't yet, Alexander. Leave it on for at least a day. Doctor's orders."

So Fallon grabbed his cap and watched the guards fill the doorway. Two of them, a graybeard and a red-head, both holding Winchester lever-action shotguns. The shotguns had thirty-inch barrels, twelve gauge, maybe ten. If the shells were filled with buckshot, those weapons would be a fine deterrent if any of the gravediggers had escape on their mind.

Out of the infirmary and into the hallway marched the prisoners, Fallon in the center on the right, each of the six pallbearers gripping one side of the coffin with one hand, except the Chinese con, who used both hands and shuffled his feet. Both guards followed the procession down the stairs and onto the prison ground.

Only a handful of inmates were outside in the yard of The Walls. They kept their distance but could not take their eyes off this cortege. Fallon could understand how they felt. He had seen enough men die in prison, had been made to dig more than one grave, and he remembered how he felt each time. It reminded you of your own mortality and the fear that no one would claim your body, that you would march to the gate of eternity in the one thing worse than a pauper's field. You'd rest till Judgment Day in a prison boneyard.

They went through the double doors and found themselves breathing free air with The Walls towering behind them, and a mule-drawn wagon in front. Two other guards, armed with Winchester rifles, waited.

After sliding the coffin onto the back of the rickety old vehicle, the prisoners began climbing into the back, finding a place to sit on either side of Juanito Gomez's shabby coffin. Apparently, they had performed burial duty before.

When Fallon started to climb into the wagon, a rough hand pulled him down and spun him around, irritating Fallon's already aching head. He stared into the dark face of Aaron Holderman.

"Just a minute, you!" the operative and ex-convict said. His breath stank of coffee and tobacco. Holderman's right hand ran along the bandage wrapping Fallon's head.

"For God's sake," the older guard said, "he ain't hidin' a file underneath Doc's wrappings."

"I don't trust this hombre," Holderman said. "He's gotten into nothin' but trouble since he come here."

Holderman's hand hurt. Fallon grimaced, even though his knees might buckle, but then he felt the big cur's free hand as it ran to Fallon's side and dropped something heavy into Fallon's trousers pocket.

"Watch your arse," Holderman whispered, and he shoved Fallon back toward the wagon. "Get in, Alexander!" Holderman snapped, raising his voice

and spitting at his side. "Dig the grave deep, boys."
Holderman backed away.

Fallon climbed into the wagon, his head still aching
from Holderman's rock-hard palm and fingers and
those nails that hadn't been clipped in weeks.

Shovels and picks just behind the driver's bench
clattered as the wagon pulled away, driven by another
guard who carried no weapon. The two men with
shotguns swung into waiting, saddled horses and followed, cradling the shotguns over their saddle horns.

Peckerwood Hill, the prison cemetery, lay about a
mile from The Walls, but that was a long mile.

The wagon loafed its noisy way to one of Huntsville's
main streets and eased through town. Fallon kept his
head down, but his eyes saw the passersby on the board-
walk as they paused, but only briefly, to stare, gawk, and
point while whispering to a companion or looking
stern-faced. No one showed pity. No one expressed
sympathy. Most funeral processions would have men
remove their hats, stop their horses or wagons, and
maybe even bow a head now and then. Fallon figured
that the residents had seen enough of these funerals so
they just went about their business. It wasn't like some
friend or relative had died. It was just another convict,
unfit for society, being carted off because nobody loved
him enough to take him home. Or maybe they just
couldn't afford a funeral, so they let the state of Texas
cover all the expenses.

Expenses. Fallon felt like spitting. A cheap coffin,
free gravediggers, and a cross to be put over the grave.

The wagon lurched, and the tools rattled, and
Fallon gently fingered his head. Then angered by the
callousness of everything, the lack of humanity, Fallon

pulled off his bandage, wadded it up, and tossed it beside the coffin.

Twenty-two acres stretched between Sycamore and Sixteenth streets that had been started as the prison cemetery by mistake, although a few years earlier the land had finally been deeded over to the state by some businessmen in town. Well, it wasn't like anyone was going to want to build a hotel or home on these acres anymore. This wasn't the hard-packed desert of Yuma. Fallon's feet sank deep into the grass and dead leaves as he and his men carried the tools to find a likely spot.

"Dig the grave first," the younger guard with the shotgun said. "Then we'll plant your pard."

It looked more like a swamp than a graveyard as the wagon stopped, the driver set the brake, and stepped down. The gravediggers would have to cut through the underbrush to get the final resting hole for Juanito Gomez started. Vines had already wrapped around some of the older wooden crosses. Others had rotted. Fallon doubted if anyone really knew where any prisoner had been buried or how many graves had been dug here in pushing forty years.

Fallon had a pickax. The other white inmate nodded at the ground. It was as good a place as any, Fallon decided, and lifted the pickax over his shoulder and head, and brought the tool into the damp earth.

CHAPTER FIFTEEN

Humidity had settled over Huntsville, and the pine trees and thick vegetation surrounding the cemetery made the air heavy. After fifteen minutes, Fallon's shirt stuck to his soaking, stinking skin. One of the black men spelled him, and Fallon stepped away from the hole in the ground and toward the pail of water the guards had brought. Quite generous of them, Fallon thought, as he watched the two armed prison employees and the wagon driver as they rested in the shade near the grave of some Indian who had committed suicide by jumping off the prison balcony decades ago.

Fallon reached inside his trousers pocket and pulled out the makings of a cigarette. If he kept this up, he might even develop a taste for smoking. He rolled the cigarette like he had been smoking for years, licked the paper, and offered the paper and makings to the Chinese, who stared up with ancient eyes and shook his head. Fallon returned the tobacco and paper to his pocket. This time, he felt the coldness of iron. He traced along the wooden grip, walnut perhaps, or maybe rosewood, which was inset in the metal frame, more rectangular than curved. The fingers came up to the metal. No hammer. Down the barrels, less than three and a half inches, slipping over the tiny blade of a sight, and then feeling the opening of the barrels. Four barrels. Finally, he came to the steel ring trigger. Leaving the sack of Bull Durham next to the derringer, Fallon found the book of matches and retrieved it to light his cigarette.

If you ride long enough for Judge Isaac Parker's court, you see just about every kind of gun sold on the frontier. Fallon did not have to see the derringer to know what it was. He could identify it by touch.

A Remington-Elliot .32. Four barrels. It wouldn't do Fallon much good from a distance, but up close it could do a heap of damage, and then leave Fallon with a weapon to crack over somebody's head—not that twelve ounces of blue steel was the same as a billy club.

He thought about the hideaway pistol Aaron Holderman had deposited in Fallon's trousers pocket. Never had Fallon trusted Holderman, who deserved no trust. So why had the detective given Fallon a derringer and a warning? Maybe it was because this was the American Detective Agency's biggest chance at fame and glory. Fallon couldn't guess. He took a few drags on the cigarette, then offered it to one of the black gravediggers before going back to work.

Once they cut through the roots, the digging got a little easier. Eventually, when the pail of water was all but empty, the older of the shotgun-wielding guards came over to inspect the progress.

"Looks deep enough to me," the guard said.

"It ain't near six feet deep yet, boss," said one of the black men.

The guard shrugged. "Muddy as this place is, soft as the ground gets, and as often as the damned boneyard floods, the coffin will sink. Gomez wasn't the littlest convict in The Walls."

No one felt like arguing with a guard with a ten-gauge repeating shotgun. They gathered their tools and lazily marched back to the wagon to exchange pickaxes and shovels for a heavy pine coffin.

Again, Fallon took a position in the center of the heavy coffin. The Chinese man grabbed the front with both hands, and the lunger brought up the rear with the two black men and the other white man on the other side. The coffin was heavy, heavier than expected. Juanito Gomez had been a leviathan, but Fallon did not think he weighed this much. They walked, leaving the three prison employees at the wagon.

When they reached the pit they had dug for the deceased, Fallon guessed why the guard had said to stop digging. There was no need to lower poor Juanito Gomez into the grave with heavy ropes. They just dropped the casket into the pit. It shuddered and sank a few inches into the soft ground. Maybe the guard had been right, Fallon thought. Maybe it would sink until it reached the six-foot mark. Or go all the way to hell.

The consumptive spit onto the coffin and glanced across the boneyard. "That's strange," he said in a dry, rasping voice.

"What?" asked the bald Negro.

"Ain't no preacher here," the man said, turned his head, and coughed.

"Maybe he wasn't no believer," said the other black man.

"Ashes to ashes," said the healthy white man. "Let's cover the greaser and get back inside The Walls."

"What's your damned hurry?" said the lunger.

"Because it's stinking hot out here."

Fallon grabbed a shovel, worked in a load of thickening sod, and dropped it into the hole.

"Won't take long to fill," said the older black man. "That's one good thing about it."

The lunger wiped his lips. "Still strange," he said. "Sixth time I've pulled this duty, and the superintendent always had a preacher come by. Once the sky pilot brought his daughter, and she sang something real sweet."

"I'll sing and preach if you just shut up and help us cover this peckerwood," said the other black inmate.

Despite the complaining, sweating, and lackadaisical work with shovels, the grave was soon covered. The lunger looked around once more for a parson, or maybe a sweet girl to sing a hymn or two, but the guards were heading for their horses, and the other employee was climbing into the wagon.

"Let's go!" called out the red-bearded guard.

Those were the last audible words over the next few minutes that felt like six lifetimes.

Hearing the first shot, Fallon instinctively dived to his left. He hit the ground, rolled over a grave, and came up behind a tree that offered shade to the nearest dead. By now, the gunfire sounded like a Gatling gun. Quickly he pulled the pepperbox .32 from his pocket, slipped his finger inside the trigger ring, and looked.

Fallon swore.

The guards lay dead, pinned underneath their horses, one of which kicked in agonizing death throes. The wagon had overturned on its side, the two wheels spinning in the air, while the old mule bolted back toward Huntsville. Fallon could make out a figure face-down in the high grass. That had to be the driver. The figure did not move at all. One of the black men was running toward the woods, leaping over graves, until a gunshot caught him in the small of his back, and he landed, wiping out three or four rotting crosses before rolling on his back and lying still.

The lunger and the Chinese man had showed the most sense. They had moved back to the grave of Juanito Gomez, taking advantage of the mound of dirt over the fresh grave, dirt that would not settle for quite a while or at least until the next thundershower. The other black man gripped a cross that he must have hoped would protect him from a bullet. It didn't. A bullet splintered the base of the cross and reduced the man's gleaming bald head into something that resembled a busted melon.

"C'mon!" a voice called from the brush at the far end of the grave. "Make a run for it and we'll get the hell out of here."

Fallon wasn't surprised when the other white inmate, the one about Fallon's size, stood up from his hiding place in the dirt and grass and bolted for the woods. The rifles opened up again and the man twisted and turned, blood spraying from his chest, thighs, arms, neck, back, and head in some obscene waltz before he collapsed in a heap and rested against a headstone made of metal.

"We got to get out of here!" a voice called from the woods.

"I don't think that was him!" another man said.

That's when Harry Fallon felt a sense of dread. Whoever was hiding in the woods, maybe, came to Peckerwood Hill to kill Harry Fallon.

He looked at the .32, useless for defense at this range. He hadn't even checked to see if the damned thing was loaded. Now he did, half expecting Aaron Holderman to have given him an empty derringer. No, all four barrels held cartridges, and Fallon pulled one out, circled it in his fingers. It felt right, looked right, and so he thumbed it back into the chamber and snapped the Remington-Elliot shut.

A bullet tore bark from the pine. Fallon leaned lower and barely turned his head toward the fresh grave and the Chinese man and lunger.

"Hey," he said in more of a whisper.

The lunger lay on his stomach, the Celestial on his back. Both men quaked in fear but they lifted their heads slightly toward Fallon's voice.

With his left hand, Fallon pointed.

The Chinese prisoner's eyes found the dead horses, the dead guards, and the overturned wagon.

"When I start shooting," Fallon said. "Make for the wagon."

The lunger coughed into the sod. "Huh? Shootin'? Shootin' what?"

Fallon did not answer. "On three," he said, and he slid to a standing position, pressing his back as hard as he could against the pine's trunk, making himself as small as he could.

"One."

He estimated the distance to the woods.

"Two."

To his surprise, he saw both the consumptive and

the Oriental seemingly prepare to leap and start running like hell.

"Three!"

The cadaverous man and the old Chinese man were running. Fallon swung around the tree, caught a flash of red and white plaid beyond the briars and brambles, saw the glint of sunlight on a rifle barrel. The derringer popped in his hand, and the plaid shirt disappeared.

"What the hell! That's a gun!"

"How in blazes . . . ?"

Fallon fired his second shot at that voice.

Then he took off after the two convicts in front of him, feeling his ill-fitting shoes kicking up dead pine needles, grass, and knocking over at least one ancient cross. The lunger and the Oriental moved with surprising quickness, but Fallon had learned years ago that when a man was being shot at, he had a tendency to summon up extraordinary speed and agility.

A rifle barked. Fallon felt the bullet whistle to his right. He started to run in a series of z's, then stopped, spun, dropped to his knee, and fired the pepperbox's third round.

Not one bullet has misfired. Aaron Holderman had not betrayed Fallon.

Of course, Fallon knew that those woods were well out of range for this little .32 peashooter. But the gunmen, these hired killers, low-down assassins, did not know what Fallon was firing, especially since the small caliber's pop was amplified among the trees and brush, and the echoes of gunfire made it hard for anyone to hear anything clearly.

One shot left. Fallon rose and took off running. Ahead of him, he saw the Chinese man dive behind the wagon, with those top wheels still spinning, and the lunger was next, though a spray of crimson spurted from his thigh, and he screamed and fell backward. Fallon turned, shot the last round from the pepper-box, and hurried for the wagon. A bullet tore through his pants leg, but caught no flesh. Another clipped a few strands of hair, and his hair had been cut incredibly short when he had first entered The Walls. Then he grabbed the lunger's outstretched arm and dragged him behind the wagon.

The Chinese inmate was starting to stand.

"Get down. Flat!"

Fallon fell without more instructions, and the Winchesters opened up from the woods.

CHAPTER SIXTEEN

The floor of the wagon splintered from at least a dozen rifle bullets. The lunger shrieked, and the Chinese convict buried his face in his hands. When the gunfire ceased, but the echoes still reverberated, Fallon came up onto his hands and knees. He looked toward the dead horses and murdered guards.

Shotguns, he thought. *I've got to get to those Winchesters.*

He drew in a breath. Then . . . a shadow fell upon him.

"Don't shoot!" came a distant cry from the thick woods. "It's Myrt."

Out of the corner of his eye, Fallon saw the figure of the driver of the wagon, the man he had presumed died in a hail of gunfire. No, the man had been playing possum, and now he had found one of the pickaxes—indeed the same one Fallon had used while digging the shallow grave for Juanito Gomez—raising it over his head and starting to bring it down.

"Wait!" the lunger yelled. "He's one of us."

Fallon knew the guard would pay no mind to the consumptive convict, for Fallon had heard that shout from the woods. Myrt was in on this ambush. He was part of the gang of murdering cutthroats, and now Fallon realized that most likely Fallon was the target. The guards . . . the other prisoners . . . they were just, well, in the way.

All of this went through Fallon's mind faster than a runaway buggy pulled by a frightened Thoroughbred on the Fourth of July.

He still gripped the .32, and now he brought it up quickly as he dived ahead and to his left, aiming it for just an instant at Myrt's grass-and-mud-stained shirt. That's all the chance Fallon had, and it was all the break he needed.

Myrt had not been counting shots. He had been too busy playing possum. Likely, he had never expected Fallon to have a gun, even a .32 that weighed less than a pound.

The guard gasped, flinched, and slammed the blade of the pickax deep into the graveyard sod. He lost his grip and stumbled, spinning like a boy's conical spinning top before it lost its speed and wobbled and wrecked. Which was pretty much what happened to Myrt. He fell to the dirt, rolled over, and sat up quickly, having recovered from his instant fright.

Fallon was sitting, too, bringing back his right hand. The guard looked around, trying to find a weapon, then seeing again the derringer in Fallon's hand. That hand was coming forward, over Fallon's head, and sending the empty Remington-Elliot at Myrt's head.

A grunt escaped Fallon's mouth as he heaved the hideaway pistol with all his might.

Myrt ducked, just enough and to his left. The somersaulting little gun caught the side of Myrt's left ear, tearing out a hunk, which brought the man's hand into a clasp over the bleeding ear. Myrt cursed.

Now Fallon heard the clanging of bells from a church. His first thought was stupid. *Someone's getting married?* Then he understood that those bells, clanging all across the bustling village of Huntsville, were not coming from one church, but several.

An alarm. By now Fallon could also hear the alarm from the prison.

The citizens and the men who ran The Walls had realized what was happening, or had at least guessed that something was amiss at Peckerwood Hill.

In the woods, the other assassins understood what was happening, too.

"Hear that? They'll be on us, soon!"

"We got to kill that skunk."

"You do it. I ain't going to prison in this hard-arse state."

Fallon started for the nearest dead horse and the nearest dead guard. He couldn't see a shotgun, but knew one had to be there. Maybe it was hidden in the grass. Maybe—

He didn't get far. Arms wrapped around his ankles, not catching a clear hold, but upending Fallon as he raced for the Winchester. Cursing Myrt as he fell, Fallon brought up his hands to break his fall. He landed with a thud, rolled over, and saw Myrt coming at him. Quickly, Fallon rolled onto his back, brought his legs up, knees bent, and then kicked out with both legs, the soles of his miserable shoes catching the turncoat in the center of his chest.

Myrt fell with a curse, groan, and crash. Fallon came up, ducked, trying to keep his head below the top of the overturned wagon. He dared not give one of those killers a clean shot. Myrt rose, too, swung blindly before he managed to learn exactly where Fallon was. The guard swung once, twice, grunting with every punch that missed. Fallon made a jab with his right, bounced back. Myrt kicked out, almost catching Fallon dead center in the groin. A bullet whined off the front wheel of the overturned wagon, sending it spinning again. Fallon quickly shot a glance toward the gate to the cemetery. Nothing. The lawmen of Huntsville and the guards at The Walls were taking their good sweet time.

Again, Myrt punched. This time his left glanced off Fallon's jaw. The man came in for the kill, but Fallon blocked his uppercut with his right forearm, then threw a punch that glanced off the man's ribs. They turned, Myrt charged, and Fallon leaped away, grabbing hold of Myrt's arm. Both of Fallon's hands gripped the arm just above the guard's wrist, and Fallon dug his feet into the slippery grass, feeling his heels dig into the mud, and he twisted his entire body and swung out with arms, hips, and practically his whole body.

Fallon grunted and fell to his knees after he released his hold on Myrt. Landing on his knees, again digging into the soft, sickening-smelling cemetery sod, Fallon pitched forward. Again he had to reach down to stop from slamming hard into the ground. He heard a scream and then a sickening sound.

"Oh my God!" The lunger coughed.

Fallon came up, sucked in a deep breath, blinked away the sweat, and then he saw Myrt still standing.

Only he wasn't standing. It was more like the guard

was leaning, somehow suspending his entire body at an unnatural angle.

Fallon's brain comprehended what had happened, and he shook his head, trying to clear his vision, trying to find some more energy. The lunger had rolled onto his hands and knees and was retching into the grass. The Chinese inmate merely watched with a face that showed no interest.

Myrt tilted toward the ground, his head bent low, blood seeping from his mouth. His arms hung down, the right one touching the grass. His legs were spread apart, and a yellow liquid was dribbling through his britches. The other end of the pickax, the blade that wasn't buried into the sod, protruded from Myrt's back, the rusty tool now the color of crimson. The crimson ran down the guard's uniform.

Then the weight of the corpse pulled the embedded tool out of the ground, and Myrt collapsed, dead, dead, dead.

Yet Fallon knew he had no time to spare. He heard footsteps running from the woods, so Fallon came up and moved for the horse, the guard, that damned lever-action shotgun—if only he could find the Winchester.

A rifle barked. Fallon caught a glimpse of the ground ahead of him and to his left being torn up from the bullet of a Winchester rifle. The next bullet went between Fallon's legs. He dived, hit the saddle of the dead horse, rolled over, and bounced up to his knees. Footsteps crashed behind him. Fallon looked to his right, to his left, ahead of him. The grass here was so high the shotgun could have been anywhere. Hell, it could have been under the dead horse. Or the guard could have thrown it ten or fifteen yards away once he had been riddled with bullets. Fallon looked behind him. Then he dived as the gunman rounded the edge of the wagon and snapped a shot from his hip.

Idiot, Fallon thought. All he had to do was take his time. Aim. Make sure of your shot.

The bullet went wide. Fallon went down. He rolled over the bloodstained body of the murdered guard. And there, right at the dead man's side, hidden by the tall grass, Fallon saw the Winchester.

All the while the murdering assassin brought up his Winchester, worked the lever, took two steps toward Fallon, and fired. Fallon felt the bullet burn his side. The man was already levering another round into the chamber when Fallon lifted the Winchester.

The man's finger touched the trigger. The hammer fell. The click caused the killer to curse.

Fallon butted the shotgun against his thigh, and his finger found the trigger.

Nothing.

As the guard fished out a shell from the bandolier that crossed his chest, Fallon cursed and worked the lever of the shotgun.

His mind flashed. An 1887 Winchester shotgun chambers five rounds, plus one in the chamber. But this weapon didn't have a shell in the chamber. Five rounds. Five chances. If the damned thing had any shells.

By then, the killer before him had slid a round into the rifle, an old Yellow Boy. He levered the rifle. Fallon brought the shotgun to his shoulder. This time when he fingered the trigger the weapon roared, the stock slammed hard against Fallon's shoulder. It would likely leave a bruise, for this was not a twelve-gauge, but a ten-gauge, and the shells had been loaded with buckshot.

The man never got to fire the Winchester. The blast reduced his chest to blood ribbons and sent him sailing into the other top wheel of the wagon. That wheel started spinning again as the killer landed dead in the grass. The Winchester dropped out of sight.

Fallon had time enough to blink. Then he was diving back toward the bloody carcass of the stinking horse, already drawing flies.

The other killer—if there were any more, Fallon knew he was a dead man—had come around. Fallon could see him despite the sweat now trying its best to blind him. The man held a rifle in his left hand, but his right gripped what looked like a Remington revolver. Smart. Use the rifle for long shots, the pistol for killing up close.

Fallon also saw the man's eyes. He saw those as clear as he had seen anything this day. The stark blue eyes widened in fear. A lever-action ten-gauge would put the fear of God into even the most callous killer. Probably even John Wesley Hardin would have paled at the sight.

The shotgun roared, and the man was diving, running, leaping behind the other dead horse. Fallon jacked the lever and sent another blast of buckshot that ruined what remained of the saddle of the dead horse.

The killer rolled a bit, came up, then dived toward the dead guard. Fallon's right arm jerked the lever down, then up. The assassin had dropped both his long gun and the Remington when he had seen Fallon's shotgun.

Instincts told Fallon to kill him. The man would

have murdered you without a second thought. These louts had already killed two prison guards and a handful of prisoners. For what? Nothing. But something deep down in Fallon's gut, in his soul, made his finger come off the trigger. Once, a lifetime ago, he had sworn to uphold the law. He had pinned on a badge. All those years in Joliet and he thought he had moved on far past that. But now?

Fallon swore. The unarmed killer came up, and for a second Fallon thought the man was lifting his hands high above his head. Only now Fallon saw that the killer had found the other guard's lever-action shotgun. And that gun was aimed directly at Fallon's chest. And the finger tightened against the trigger before Fallon could press down on the Winchester's trigger that he held.

The explosion roared across Peckerwood Hill.

CHAPTER SEVENTEEN

When his ears stopped ringing, when Fallon realized he wasn't knocking on hell's door, that he still stood, still held the ten-gauge against his aching shoulder, Fallon heard the earsplitting screams.

His vision cleared. The killer had brought both hands to his face, or what was left of his face. All Fallon could see was a grisly mix of bone, blood, and the grayish matter of brains. The man screamed, but it was no ordinary scream. Instead it was a gurgling curse of agony. One of the man's hands had been turned into a stump. A finger lay in the grass, twitching.

Dully, Fallon comprehended what had happened. The killer had jerked up the murdered guard's shotgun, but he had not noticed that the barrel had landed in the sod, and the sod had clogged the barrel. When he pulled the trigger, the shotgun's barrel had exploded, sending case-hardened metal and buckshot into the man's face.

There, Fallon thought, *but for the grace of God . . .*

Had Fallon gone to that horse, that guard, that fouled shotgun, that might have been Fallon dancing the sickening polka of a corpse.

Fallon looked at the Winchester in his own hand. Then he looked toward the woods. No one. If there had been more assassins, they had fled. No one was coming from town yet, either. So Fallon raised the shotgun again, braced it against his shoulder, and prepared to end the poor man's misery. Not that he deserved it, but that was going to be a long, agonizing way to die, and Fallon was already sick enough.

A shot boomed, and the gurgling screams stopped. The killer collapsed in a silent heap onto the bloody mass of the horse he and the others had gunned down.

Fallon looked to his right. The Chinese man held the Remington revolver that the killer had dropped. The Celestial turned to Fallon, nodded, and dropped the weapon into the grass.

"If I you," the man said in English, the first words he had spoken since Fallon had seen him. Indeed, Fallon had figured the man couldn't speak a word of English. "Me drop gun. And raise hands high. Real high. Like this."

The little man's hands reached skyward, and now Fallon heard hooves and curses and shouts. Without looking at the lawmen and prison guards racing toward the gate of Peckerwood Hill, Fallon lowered the hammer of the unfired ten-gauge and dropped the Winchester into the grass.

His hands were high above his head as he slowly turned around to face the rushing horde of men.

They placed the iron manacles on his wrists, but Fallon expected that. They shackled his ankles, too, with a chain connecting the lunger and the Oriental. They cursed. Two men vomited. They ran around the graveyard like ants, shouting more curses, while a few offered prayers for the dead. And more than one asked, "What the hell happened?"

Two newspaper reporters showed up, one from the local paper and another from Fort Worth who just happened to be in Huntsville, but the lead guard—who was not Barney Drexel—and a Huntsville policeman ran those two men back beyond the gate to the cemetery, where other peace officers formed a security line to keep the children, the ladies, and the gawking men from getting too close to the carnage.

Thirty minutes passed before the undertakers arrived, and it took another ten before Walter Wilkinson, superintendent at The Walls, Dr. Crouch, and Barney Drexel showed up. Major Rufus K. Conley, the journalist from Indianola, came with them—and the local law officers made no attempt to keep him out of Peckerwood Hill with the other newspapermen.

At least Fallon could be thankful for something. One of the guards standing watch over Fallon and the only two other surviving members of the grave-digging party, handed the prisoners a canteen. The water cooled his throat, quenched his thirst. Luckily, Fallon got the canteen after the Chinese man and before the lunger got his lips on the container.

Well, there was something else to be thankful about. Harry Fallon was still alive.

Dr. Crouch pronounced the dead men officially dead and came over to the tree where the prisoners were being kept. The old man knelt, his knees popping, and he shook his head. "Trouble follows you like a coyote follows a chicken," he said quietly.

Fallon shrugged.

The old man looked around, then handed the

nearest guard his black satchel and asked the young man to take it to the buggy that had brought the prison officials inside the cemetery. When the guard was out of earshot, the doctor glanced at the lunger and Celestial and began whispering to Fallon.

"Our dear superintendent and erudite journalist have come up with this story: Two men, possibly more, attempted to break out Henry Moses, who had been detailed to bury Juanito Gomez at the prison cemetery, Gomez having died of natural causes yesterday afternoon. His heart, you see."

Fallon did not know which prisoner was Henry Moses, and he did not really care.

"In the ensuing melee of gunfire, the two colored prisoners saw their chance to escape and joined the assault on the guards."

"You three prisoners, being obedient and God-fearing men . . ." He glanced at the Chinese man, shrugged, and went on. "You three did the right thing. You lay down and covered your heads, protecting yourselves as best as you could do."

"That ain't what happened at all, Doc," the lunger whispered. "It was this feller . . ." He nodded at Fallon. "And the Chink helped, too, at the end."

Doc Crouch paid him no mind.

"During the assault, three guards died in duty, but the last one standing, Todd Corey, managed to kill the last of the gang members attempting to free Henry Moses. Moses himself was killed in the gunfire, as were the two colored boys. If there were others involved in the attempted escape, they vamoosed."

"But . . ."

The doctor now glared at the lunger, who dropped his head and stared at the grass and mud.

"That's the story that will be printed in the Huntsville newspaper, in Fort Worth, in Indianola if the major deems it newsworthy that far away, and I dare say it will be picked up in papers from California to New York. Everybody loves a good prison escape yarn. We have dead heroes and martyrs and three more graves to dig here at Peckerwood Hill. I imagine the families of the deceased guards will take home their loved ones, and the outlaws will wind up in the potter's field of Huntsville."

The doctor paused, pursed his lips, studied the three prisoners briefly, and then looked directly at Fallon.

"What I'd like to know, Mr. Alexander, is what the hell really happened here?"

That was something Fallon wanted to know, too. While sitting here, nursing his wounds, he went through the ambush and everything that happened then, even before, and after.

Maybe it could have been an escape attempt that somehow had gone wrong. Really wrong. He even considered a theory that this had all been arranged to kill Fallon, that Justice and his cohorts had figured out that Fallon was working for a detective agency. But that would have been one extreme and sloppy way to kill off a detective. The gunfight had already brought out newspaper reporters. If you wanted to kill someone off in a prison, hell, there were hundreds of quieter ways. A knife between the ribs. An iron pipe against the skull. A kerosene bomb tossed inside the locked cell. They could have killed him in the prison mill. Pushed him off the balcony and called it a suicide, just like that old Indian that Fallon had heard about.

No, this had to be something different. Hell, the

theory Drexel and Wilkinson had concocted sounded as good as anything Fallon could come up with now. He touched his head, fingered the knot, and remembered the bandage.

"Mr. Alexander."

Fallon heard the doctor's voice, and now he remembered something else. The white-haired sawbones had told Fallon not to remove the bandage. Why? Medicinal purposes? Perhaps. Or had that been a way for the gunmen in the woods to identify Fallon. To kill him. Or to realize he was the one they didn't want to kill.

If he kept this thinking up, he'd wind up out of The Walls and into the nearest insane asylum.

"Alexander."

Fallon looked at Dr. Crouch and held the old man's gaze. He never looked away, but said clearly and definitely: "I wouldn't know, Doc. Once the shooting started, I dropped to the ground and covered my head and prayed to be delivered."

Their eyes held, but eventually Dr. Crouch looked away.

"Mr. Fat does not speak English," Crouch said as he looked at the Chinese prisoner. Fallon wanted to smile, but kept his face hard, though he enjoyed knowing how the Oriental had everyone in this prison fooled. "And Mr. Dupree . . . ?" He waited until the lunger looked up.

"Well," the doctor said.

"It's like he says," the weak man said, and dropped his head again to study the grass.

The doctor sighed, but not at the lunger's answer.

It was because now the superintendent came over, flanked by Barney Drexel.

"This will cause a lot of headaches for us," Wilkinson said as he put both hands on his hips. "Newspaper editors are already here. What did these men say they saw?"

"They say they saw nothing," Crouch answered.

The warden eyed Fallon. "Well?"

Fallon shook his head.

"That's good. We've got us a story and we're sticking to it. But don't think you're going to get your names in any newspapers. I'm telling the press that we are keeping the three surviving gravediggers' names a secret, fearing that friends of Moses, that black-hearted sidewinder, might retaliate. The Chink and the lunger are lucky. I'll transfer them to Rusk."

"What about him?" Dr. Crouch nodded at Fallon.

"He just got his sentence reduced. Lucky. We can get him out of The Walls to some farm." The warden looked at Fallon again, but this time his expression changed. "Hell, man," the warden said as he pointed at Fallon's side. "You're bleeding."

Fallon took a quick look at his side, where one of the bullets had grazed him. It wasn't anything more than a scratch, and the blood wasn't pouring, just trickling enough to stain the white part of his striped uniform.

"I'm always bleeding," Fallon said.

That got a laugh out of Barney Drexel.

"What are the chances of us getting these men out of The Walls before that damned nuisance of a prison inspector shows up again?" Wilkinson asked Drexel.

"None." Drexel's head tilted toward the gate. "He's

right outside the gate, behind the reporters. That dirtbag shows up at all the wrong times."

Drexel looked at the three inmates, chained together, dirty, sweaty, utterly exhausted. Once again, Fallon had lucked out. The chances of Drexel recognizing him in this condition, with his face covered with grime, sweat, gunpowder, and grass, were about the same as drawing into an inside straight in a poker game. "If you know what's good for you, you keep your mouth shut when that nosy piker asks you what all you saw," Drexel said, eyes narrow, tone forceful. "You saw nothing. You heard only gunfire and curses. If I hear that you told that snot-nosed arse anything other than that, it's to solitary for all of you." He grinned at the lunger. "And, Dupree, you know how long a lunger'll last after seven days in that sweatbox."

CHAPTER EIGHTEEN

Two days passed before the inspector of prisons met with Fallon. The inspector was, of course, Dan MacGregor.

MacGregor, once again using the cover of Inspector of Prisons Byron Roberts, met with the Chinese inmate briefly, then the lunger, and finally asked to see Harry Alexander. They met in the visiting room, MacGregor went through the usual introductions, explaining what he wanted, telling him that he should be honest in his answers, that no harm would come to him . . . the usual load of crap most prison inspectors thought to be truthful.

"What did you see?" he asked.

"Nothing," Fallon answered. "As soon as the shooting started, I hit the dirt."

"I see. So did Mr. Fat and Mr. Dupree."

"Probably why we're still alive and nobody else is."

MacGregor opened a folder and slid several photographs toward him. "Do you recognize any of these men?"

Fallon studied each image, photographs taken of

men lying on planks, bloodied from the fight at Peckerwood Hill, all of them looking very much dead. Yeah, Fallon knew those men, but not by name. Two of them he had killed.

"I know the guards," Fallon said, "but not by name."

"And the others?"

Fallon looked again. His head shook and he slid two photographs back toward MacGregor. "These gents must've been some of the cutthroats that took to shooting. The guards died bravely, I reckon, doing their jobs. These were just cold-blooded killers." He tapped the photograph of the man who had been driving the wagon, letting MacGregor know that the driver had been in on the . . . whatever it had been.

MacGregor jotted down some senseless nonsense on the pad and pushed the photograph back.

"I see."

Fallon leaned back in his chair, pushed the front legs off the floor, and rocked a bit, casually looking at the walls, the ceiling, trying to figure out where someone might be spying on them, listening to everything they had to say.

"You have no idea what this was all about?" MacGregor asked.

"Nope."

"Did you know the prisoner Henry Moses?"

"Nope."

"Did you see anything?"

Fallon laughed.

"Hear anything?"

"Gunshots."

"What else?"

Fallon shrugged. "Well," he said, "some fellow

yelled to someone to start running and then they'd hightail it for some other place."

"Did they mention a name?"

Fallon shook his head.

"Did you see anything?"

Fallon's head repeated the shake.

"Here." MacGregor tossed back the photographs. "Look at them again."

MacGregor pointed at the images. "None of the men killed trying to free Henry Moses have been identified by any of our country's leading detective agencies. The U.S. marshal, the city police chief, even three Texas Rangers have not been able to identify these assassins, and no one has claimed their bodies."

That meant something. It meant that the American Detective Agency could not identify the dead killers. Sean MacGregor's outfit might not be the Pinkerton National Detective Agency when it came to compiling hundreds and perhaps thousands of photographs of wanted felons, but Fallon had seen the files and files of likenesses in the Chicago headquarters of the American Detective Agency. Of course, the men had not been the sharpest outlaws Fallon had ever dealt with. Perhaps this had been their first criminal act. No wonder they were about to be buried in a pauper's graveyard. They weren't cut out for that line of work.

"They had no papers, very little money, and not one item that could identify them," MacGregor said, and he slowly pulled back his jacket, revealing a medal pinned on the inside of his coat. Fallon saw it. The gold was tarnished, and the once-colorful ribbon frayed and stained beyond recognition. Fallon shook his head. He wouldn't know what the Medal of Honor really looked like.

"Look at the photos again, Alexander. Please." He held up the folder that had kept the images, and Fallon read the writing:

Maximilian. Medal. Mercenaries

He pretended to pay no attention, but nodded as he sorted through the photos. Maximilian. Medal. Mercenaries. Now he knew what the medal was. Between 1865 and 1867, Emperor Maximilian of Mexico had recruited, and paid, a number of American fighters to travel south of the border and take up arms with the emperor's French forces against the Mexican rebels. Until the rebels took control of the country and wound up executing Maximilian.

Most of the mercenaries were former Confederate soldiers. One of the men who had taken part in the ambush had been carrying that medal.

Things started to add up. But Fallon was a long way from finding an answer.

"Are you sure those photos mean nothing to you, Alexander?" MacGregor asked in a whining, pleading voice.

"Nah."

Fallon found the image of the man who had run when called and was immediately gunned down. He tossed the photo toward MacGregor. "Nah. Like I said, I was hugging the ground."

"I see."

Fallon kept looking through the images. "I mean, Mr. Inspector, it's not like I could tell you who all died first, and last." Casually, while speaking, he began tossing the pictures back toward MacGregor, the dead guards first, then pausing to point a finger at the man who had been murdered while running for the woods, then the black men, and so forth, ending with the last man to be killed, the assassin who had been blown apart by Mr. Fat, the Chinese inmate.

"You're not much help," MacGregor said. Which meant Fallon had helped him a lot.

"You're sure you couldn't hear anything?"

"Let me see those pictures again."

They came back to Fallon, and he found the photo of the man who had been murdered. His head shook, he sighed, and he slid that photograph back to Mac-Gregor. "I don't think that was him," he said.

MacGregor wrote that down. He could probably figure out that after the convict had been murdered, one of his killers had said, "*I don't think that was him.*"

But what did that mean? Had they been trying to kill Fallon? Why? Nothing really made sense, no matter how many theories Fallon came up with.

The detective gathered the photographs, sighed, returned them to the folder, and said, "I'm going to run some names past you. Tell me if they mean anything to you."

He went through several names, none of which Fallon recognized.

"Nope," he said. "Never heard of them. Not a single one."

"You ought to get to know them," MacGregor said with a sarcastic smile. "Those are the names of the members of the board of parole."

Fallon shrugged. "Don't mean a thing to me."

"Want a smoke?" MacGregor passed a pouch of tobacco and some papers to Fallon.

"Thanks." He rolled two cigarettes, using the first paper, the one with writing on it, and sticking that one above his left ear. The other cigarette, he lighted as soon as he was finished.

"I said a smoke," MacGregor said.

"Figured you owed me two because of the time I've spent here helping you."

"I got more out of the Chinaman than I got from you, Alexander, and that Chink doesn't speak English." MacGregor doodled, found an eraser, and began erasing some lines from his notepad, plus what he had written about the medal on the folder. He shook his head, sighed, and rose. "You're a lost cause, Alexander. Just like the South."

"South ain't lost yet, Yank," Fallon said, and he stood.

MacGregor had made it to the door, which opened before the detective could even knock. Yes, Fallon figured, they were eavesdropping, maybe watching the entire interview. But that was all right. Because nothing had been said or done that would have given anything away. In fact, Fallon's head hurt from all this secret messaging and speaking in circles.

Despite all that training he had gone through, all the work, all the studying, all the learning of signals, even some Morse code—which he had yet to use— Fallon knew he wasn't cut out to be an operative. That just wasn't his strong suit, and, sadly, Harry Fallon knew what he was good at.

He had proved that again at Peckerwood Hill.

"You're a man of action, Deputy," a Creek Lighthorse policeman had told him back in the Indian Nations when they were tracking an outlaw named Davis Buscombe. *"That's all you know, my young friend. How to fight. How to kill. How to stay alive."*

The guard escorting him to the woolen mill let him make a stop at a privy. Inside, Fallon unwrapped the cigarette he had rolled and looked at MacGregor's message. It listed the names of those seated on the penitentiary board, but not one name triggered any memory in Fallon's mind. Another miss. Another wrong trail. This time, as he crumpled the paper and dropped it through the hole after the tobacco flakes and his own excrement, he remembered something Christina Whitney had told him.

"People think we detectives are always doing something exciting. They read too many dime novels. It's not like that at all. Ninety percent of the time, maybe even more, it's utter boredom. It's dull. It's the lousiest job in the world. Of course, sometimes, that other ten percent, or maybe even less, more than make up for the monotony."

Like a gunfight at a prison cemetery.

Fallon exited the toilet and saw another guard waiting for him.

"Today's your lucky day, Alexander," the new guard said. "You get out of more work. Superintendent Wilkinson wants to see you."

"Have a seat, Alexander." Warden Wilkinson sat behind his desk, head bent forward, and kept pushing the spectacles up with a finger as the glasses continued to slip down his nose as he read. "That'll be all, O'Brien. Wait outside."

The guard closed the door behind him, and Fallon settled into an uncomfortable chair. Just to do something, he gently touched the shrinking knot on his skull.

In a dull monotone, the warden found something

else to read, and he began reciting: "'The law gives the right, under certain restrictions, to hire out convicts, and to operate them outside the walls of the penitentiary.'" He looked up.

"Do you understand what that means, Alexander?"

"Yes, sir." Fallon's head bobbed and he felt his heart racing. He knew exactly what this meant. He was going to a camp. The only question was, which one?

"You meet the requirements, thanks to the recent commutation of your sentence to a mere ten years."

A mere ten years? Fallon had been in The Walls less than two months, and it had taken him every bit of luck, every muscle in his body, every instinct, and everything he had learned as a lawman in the Indian Nations and as an inmate in Illinois, Arizona, Missouri, and now Texas to have survived for that long.

"Dr. Crouch has pronounced you fit for physical labor, our board has given its unanimous consent, and as superintendent, I am in agreement that—perhaps because of how you handled yourself at the recent incident at our cemetery—that you should be given a chance to apply your skills outside of The Walls."

Would that be the skills he had worked on for weeks in Alabama, Louisiana, and Florida? Or the skills he had worked on in brawls in the prison yard and a bloody shootout at the cemetery?

"Do not let the thought of escape enter your head, Alexander. One mistake, one fight, one bad word, one wrong look, and you will be shackled and returned immediately here, and after a weeklong stay in solitary, you will be worked like you've never been worked before."

Fallon waited. *Where the hell are you sending me?* he wanted to say.

"The sergeants and the guards will assume all management, guarding, and discipline while you are outside in your job. Do not try anything, or you will feel as though every brick in this prison has dropped onto your body."

Where? Damn you. Where?

"Your clothes and bedding will be washed once a week. You will not be required to work when it is raining or on Sundays, unless the foreman believes it is absolutely necessary."

Just tell me where I'm going.

"You may not be subletted out to another operation without my consent, and if such consent is granted, you must be returned to your original place of hire before dark.

"You will work full-time, but not before dawn and not after dark.

"You will not work with any convicts serving time on the county level. You will work only with inmates from The Walls or our unit in Rusk."

WHERE?

"Your uniform will be the same as it is inside The Walls."

Fallon clenched fists in both hands.

"Do you have any questions?"

He relaxed, shook his head, tried to look patient and natural.

"Don't think this is some sort of vacation, Mr. Alexander. You're going from the hell of The Walls to what everyone calls *Hell on the Brazos.*"

CHAPTER NINETEEN

"When do I get out of here?" Fallon asked.

"Now."

Luckily for Fallon, the warden looked down and rang a bell, therefore he didn't see the reaction on Fallon's face. By the time Wilkinson had lifted his stare, he saw a convict beaming with pleasure that he would be walking out of this dung heap—instead of the shock, and maybe even a hint of fear, that Fallon had registered immediately. Yeah, Fallon agreed, he would never make it as an undercover private detective or some thespian treading the boards.

Two guards had entered upon hearing the superintendent's summons.

"Take him to . . . well . . ." Wilkinson looked at Fallon, turned up his nose, and said, "See that he gets a bath, shave, and a clean set of clothes. The usual gear for an inmate being hired out to a plantation."

"Does he need anything out of his cell?" one of the guards asked.

"No," the warden answered instantly, but then considered Fallon. "Do you?"

Fallon's head shook. The guards would likely search

Fallon's cell for anything that might give away his true identity. All they would find would be the weapon hidden in the post of his bunk, but, hell, if they looked hard enough, they would find that in every cell in The Walls . . . and the unit at Rusk . . . and any hard-time prison in these United States of America.

"Very good." The warden opened a drawer. "I'll have the papers at the front gate. Two guards will be waiting there to escort him to the train and deliver him to his new employer."

Fallon stood, nodded his thanks at Walter Wilkinson, and let the two guards take him away.

This was happening too fast. He would have no time to get word to MacGregor or the attorney general. His one hope would be to find Aaron Holderman, but the brute wasn't anywhere to be found. Fallon wet his lips, trying to think of something. Then he found himself standing face-to-face with John Wesley Hardin.

"Hell on the Brazos, eh?" the man-killer said with a grin.

Fallon gave a slight nod. "No different than The Walls, I expect."

"But you get to breathe free air."

"It's not really free."

Hardin rolled himself a cigarette. "Maybe. Maybe not. I'll miss having you appear in my court, Alexander. You made a fine lawyer."

The killer held out his hand. Fallon shook, and then Hardin was walking away, putting a cigarette in his lips and striking a match on his trousers to light the smoke.

"How did that snake know you was going to pick cotton or whatever the hell they'll have you doing?"

The exact question was going through my mind, too, Fallon thought, though he just shrugged off the guard's question and walked toward the bathhouse.

He gave himself a good scrubbing, though gently around the bullet scratch, the knot on his head, the other assorted cuts, scrapes, and sore spots, and let the prison barber trim his short hair and scrape away the beginnings of beard stubble. Then, after being outfitted with a new black-and-white-striped uniform and given a bag of necessaries and a blanket, he strolled toward the double doors that separated the prison from the outside.

Sergeant Barney Drexel met Fallon and his guards outside the iron door. A frail trusty, who looked old enough to be Methuselah's father, stood by the thick door and held the key.

"Try to escape, you'll be cut down," was all Drexel said, and he started to walk away.

"Come on," said the trusty.

Fallon stepped away from the guards but stopped when Drexel told him to. Fallon waited, head down, obedient, acting like every other convict inside The Walls.

"Look at me," Drexel said.

Fallon lifted his head.

The big cuss tilted his head one way, then the other, and his eyes narrowed.

"I swear I've seen you before," Drexel rasped after a moment.

Fallon shrugged. "I'd remember you."

The sergeant turned his head to spit tobacco juice, wiped his mouth on his shirtsleeve, and moved back a bit, as though distance would give him a better look.

"Ever been to Nacogdoches?" Drexel asked.

"No, boss."

"Fort Smith?"

"Time or two. Stayed out of that part of the state as long as I could, boss."

"Mexico?"

"No, boss."

"Natchez-Under-The-Hill?"

"No, boss."

"Your face brings someone to mind."

"Might be my pa. I got told I favored him, and he got around a lot more than I did. Rode with Quantrill."

Fallon's father had been a Unionist to the core.

"Quantrill was trash," Drexel said, and spit again. "Get him the hell out of my sight."

As Drexel walked away, Fallon stepped toward the trusty, thanked the guards, and hoped he wasn't sweating after the quick interrogation by the ex-lawman from Judge Parker's court.

"Don't you forget what Sergeant Barney told you," the old man whispered as his keys ground against the tumbler and turned the bolt. The door opened. The trusty nodded, and Fallon stepped inside, leaving the guards, Sergeant Barney Drexel, John Wesley Hardin, and a lot of Fallon's own blood inside The Walls. The door closed, leaving Fallon and the trusty in mostly darkness. The sound of the door being locked became amplified in the small room, and then Fallon felt more than saw the ancient man shuffling across the floor to the next door.

"The sentry box is just outside," the trusty said as the keys rattled on his chain while he found the right one for the next door. "Round building, just a few steps away."

"I remember," Fallon said.

"Yeah." The key began to grate. "Reckon you do. You got out for burial duty. And ain't been here long nohow."

"Feels long," Fallon said.

"Boy," the trusty said, "you don't know what long is. I got locked up in '53."

Fallon held his breath. The door pushed open.

The trusty pulled some papers from his trousers pocket and said, "Here's your bona fides, suh. Good luck."

Fallon thanked him and moved toward the opening, drawing in a deep breath of free air as he stepped out of the dark prison entranceway.

"Y'all come back now, y'hear," the old-timer said in a mocking voice, and closed the door, locking it behind him, after Fallon had stepped out.

The guard waited in the small, round sentry box, holding a repeating rifle in his hands and a perpetual scowl on his iron-hard face. He said nothing, barely moved, barely breathed.

Two other guards approached from the long road that led maybe a half mile to the street. Fallon waited for them, aware after about a minute that neither one of them was Aaron Holderman.

"Hell," he whispered to himself.

He handed the first guard the papers, who glanced at them, shoved them into the back pocket of his britches, and said, "Let's go."

Fallon resigned himself that he was about to be alone, on his own, but he had grown used to that. There had been no one to trust in Yuma. He felt pretty much alone in Missouri. Those years in Joliet had toughened him enough to make do on his own, because there was no one in prison that he could trust, or would trust, especially with his life.

They made it to the street, and one of the guards said, "The omnibus."

Fallon saw it and began walking to it. He saw the buggy across the street, saw the woman in the back, wearing a dress of yellow with purple stripes, and heard her call out, "Darling!"

Fallon stopped, took a step back toward the guards. He drew in a deep breath.

"Harry, dear!" Christina Whitney ran toward him, lifting the hems of her dress as her shoes clattered on the paved street.

"What the hell?" said the younger guard.

The other guard raised his rifle, a sawed-off Marlin.

"It's my wife," Fallon said.

The two guards, young, green, uncertain of what this unexpected reunion called for, took tentative steps back, and Fallon let the operative leap into his arms and kiss him full on the lips.

He heard the rifle cock, and Fallon immediately pushed Christina Whitney away. He turned to the guards and said, "It's all right. She's just . . . excited."

The guard refused to lower the rifle.

"I've been trying and trying to get inside, but that mean ol' warden, he just won't let me see you again," Christina said, sounding like a petulant teenager.

"I told you—"

She cut him off. "I am too young to be a divorcée, Harry Alexander. I shall not hear of it. No. No, sir!" She pouted.

"Ma'am," the guard without the rifle said. "We have a train to catch."

"A train. My goodness. Where on earth are you taking my husband?"

Both guards whispered curses.

"Honey," Fallon said, "let me state this for once and all."

"No." Christina sobbed. "No. No. No. No. I can't stand being away."

"Ma'am," the kid with the Marlin said, "you need to step aside. Right now."

She sighed.

Fallon said, "Do as they say, girl. They're letting me go out on a release program. Don't ruin this for me. You heard me, didn't you?"

"I heard you, Harry Alexander!" She stepped onto the street, put her hands on her hips. "I was just going to pay that mean old warden a visit when you happened to come out. I heard you, though. You're stating your case. I hear you plain and clear, Mr. Convict. Remember, I was the one who got your sentence reduced to ten years. And this is the thanks I get!" She wiped her eyes, looked at the two guards, and snapped, "You may have him, sirs."

Turning on her heels, she hurried back to the buggy, climbed in, said something to the Mexican driver, and the buggy carried her down the street.

"That's some pistol you got there, mister," the younger guard said.

"You married?" Fallon asked the boy.

"Nope."

"Good. Don't make the same mistake I did."

Both guards, even the one with the sawed-off rifle, chuckled, and they resumed their way to the omnibus.

Fallon breathed in deeply, and exhaled. Christina had gotten the message. He wondered how long she had been sitting in that buggy with the Mexican driver. He wondered if the driver had been hired by Christina or was also on the American Detective Agency's payroll.

But that didn't matter. She had gotten his message. *State* had been the key word. *State* meant that he was being sent to Texas. Hell on the Brazos. He'd be working on one of Colonel Justice's cotton plantations. They had gone over that for about a week until Fallon had gotten everything drilled inside his head.

State. Texas. Hell on the Brazos.

Look would have meant he was going to Louisiana. *Look, honey, you have to listen to me . . .* or something along those lines. *All right* was to be the trigger to let Christina, Dan MacGregor, or Aaron Holderman understand that he was bound for Alabama. *For Christ's sake* or *For the love of God*, something like that, would tell everyone he'd be in Florida. And if Justice had some operation, a secret one, in another state, or country, well . . . the detectives did not think that was a likely scenario.

At least Fallon could breathe a tad easier. Christina Whitney had his location. The omnibus reached the train station, and two men with muscles bulging against their muslin shirts stepped toward the guards. Both men wore twin holsters, butt forward, flaps snapped, but from the size of the duo, Fallon figured they rarely needed to draw iron. The lead guard from The Walls passed the papers to the bigger of the brutes, who signed a receipt, and the guards gave Fallon a curt nod, turned around, and left Fallon with the thugs.

"Get on the train," Fallon heard one man say in a

menacing whisper. "And don't say a word to anybody. You're deef and dumb. Savvy?"

Fallon nodded.

The smaller of the giants laughed. "He's got more of a brain than most of 'em."

"Uh-huh. Usually they answer, and I get to slap 'em hard and teach 'em what *deef* and *dumb* mean."

Fallon shrugged.

"Move."

This, Fallon thought with tired sarcasm, *should be a most enjoyable trip.*

CHAPTER TWENTY

It was a short, painless, fairly relaxing train ride for the first leg. Huntsville had a prison, a normal college, the grave of Texas legend Sam Houston, sawmills, and plenty of businesses, four stagecoach lines, but its only railroad was a short spur, all of eight miles, that connected the city with the Houston and Great Northern Railroad in Phelps.

Fallon stepped off the train, felt the iron claw of one of the guards grab him by the shoulder and shove him toward the ticket counter. Fallon remained mute. It wasn't a long train ride to Houston, he figured, but a man could get beaten senseless by the time the train pulled into the station.

At the counter, the smaller of the men stepped forward and showed his railroad pass.

"Three tickets," he said, "to Marshall."

Fallon tensed. Marshall lay north. Houston was south. Houston was the jumping-off spot to Josiah Justice's Hell on the Brazos empire.

The guard went on, "Then we'll take the train to Shreveport."

Shreveport. Louisiana.

Well, Hank, Fallon thought, *now you've got yourself into a real pickle. Welcome to hell.*

On the train ride north to Marshall he read a *Frank Leslie's Illustrated Newspaper* that someone had left on his seat. He sipped coffee and watched the woods pass by on the ride east to Shreveport, which felt so hot and sticky from the Red River that it made Huntsville feel more like Montana. There the guards showed another pass, and they waited a couple of hours before boarding a southbound Texas Pacific train that took them to Cypress, and from there, a smaller spur line rocked them gently through the swampy country into Natchitoches.

All totaled, it had taken them roughly twenty-nine hours, including time spent in the depot and a couple of delays, before Fallon found himself standing at the depot at Natchitoches. They waited some more outside the depot.

Fallon remained deaf, dumb, and tired.

Thirty minutes later, a farm wagon arrived, driven by a big-boned black man with two white men riding beside him. Fallon recognized the uniforms as that of the Huntsville guards. Alas, or maybe thankfully, neither of the guards was Aaron Holderman.

Face it, he told himself, *you're all alone now.*

"Give y'all any trouble?" said a mustached man with a patch over his right eye and an ugly scar over his left.

"Nope. Didn't raise no stink. Didn't say no word."

The other one added: "Lessen we asked him somethin'."

The man with the scar and patch came up to

Fallon and leaned forward until his nose was almost touching Fallon's face.

"That's good." His breath could stop a herd of stampeding buffalo. "You keep right on doin' that . . . What's his name?"

The guard had to pull out the paper. "Alexander. Harry Alexander. He's from Arkansas."

"The only good thing ever to come out of Arkansas," the man with the patch said, "was a whore I met in Vicksburg who called herself Alice. Said she hailed from Baring Cross." He grinned. "But it weren't no cross that that tramp bared."

The others giggled. Fallon remembered that he was still deaf and dumb.

By the time the wagon pulled away from the Natchitoches depot, the lanterns on the front had been lighted. By the time they reached Justice's plantation, supper had already been consumed, and Fallon was taken to the bunkhouse, where men snored, sweated, farted, and stank.

A wiry man, muscular, sweaty, and missing two fingers on his right hand, met Fallon at the door.

"Shhhhhh," he whispered. "Boys are sleepin'. I'm Cody. Don't know if that's my first name or last. See, I wasn't supposed to get born. Ya need somethin', you ask ol' Cody. What's yer name, kid?"

Kid? Fallon had ten years on the boy.

"Alexander. Harry Alexander."

"You'll bunk below me." Cody led the way, the boards creaking under his brogans, and Cody weighed less than a fart.

The guards closed the door behind them.

Fallon recalled something the warden at The Walls had read to him, something about having all bedding washed as well as all workers getting regular baths. Apparently, that looked good in black and white but wasn't always followed to the letter 315 miles, as the trains moved, away.

"What you want to know?" Cody asked, his voice a little less forced now that the guards had left the prisoners alone.

"How many prisoners?" Fallon asked.

"Thirty. Forty. Depends."

"Guards?"

"Twelve. Two sergeants. Two camp guards. The rest are day guards."

"And the work?"

Cody snorted. "Makes a white man wish the South hadn't lost the war, pard. Now I know why them slaves wanted to get their jubilee."

He was laughing, but it stopped instantly, and Fallon saw the towering figure before him.

"Who's the fresh fish?" the voice asked.

"Tom," Cody said, pleadingly, "you best take it easy, man. Sunday morning's comin' 'round, and you know how the Colonel want his Sundays to be quiet." Cody spun, probably grinned, though Fallon couldn't see that well in the darkened confines of the bunkhouse. "The Colonel, I ain't sure he's that God-fearing, but he don't like nothin' to bother him on a day of worship. Which suits us. We gets Sunday off. Nothin' to do but relax, maybe throw a ball around, pitch horseshoes. Gives us a day of rest of six days of nothin' but hell."

"I said," the monster called Tom repeated, "who's the fresh fish?"

"Harry Alexander," Fallon answered. "If it's any of your damned business."

A giant arm knocked Cody halfway across the room.

The snores stopped. Fallon could make out the squeaking of bed slats and sheets being tossed aside as the men sat up. A match flared. A candle was lighted, casting a golden glow that didn't brighten the room, but at least gave Fallon a chance to look into Tom's face.

Prisoners were required to be clean-shaven at The Walls. Apparently, the guards and Colonel Justice overlooked that rule when it came to convict labor at his Natchitoches plantation. Tom's beard was thick, likely filled with bugs, and came down to about where his heart would've been located. Had he ever gotten a heart.

"I'm makin' it my business, fish."

Fallon saw the thick, brutal fingers close up as Tom tightened his fist.

But big Tom never got a chance to bring that fist up. Fallon hit him in the jaw with a quick right, brought his left around almost instantly, and that punch sent the leviathan's head banging against the hard cedar post that held up the bunk beds. By the time Tom realized what was happening, Fallon had brought a knee into the man's groin, and then he reached out with both hands and pushed as hard as he could.

Tom stumbled onto the floor, breaking one of the floorboards.

He started cursing, but those were drowned out by the shouts of encouragement from the thirty-plus other prisoners now sitting in their beds.

Tom was wailing, trying to push himself back to his feet, but as he rose, his left leg went through the busted floor. The building—more dismal shack than any solid structure—was propped up by mortared bricks and a cypress tree stump, maybe a foot off the rotting, stinking Louisiana land. Tom gripped his leg, groaned, cursed, spat out blood, and tried to pull it back into the building.

Fallon glanced to his right, saw something on the floor, and he raced to it, grabbed the cold brass, turned, and emptied the spittoon's contents into Tom's ugly face.

The man screamed in rage, tasting the foulness of tobacco juice, spit, the well-chewed remnants of tobacco, and maybe fifteen dozen soggy nubs of cigarettes. He probably swallowed some of the juice, as well. Tom gagged, coughed, twisting his head this way and that like a dog shaking himself dry. He cursed and worked those big fists against his eyes, trying to paw away the wretchedness. When he looked up and his vision cleared, Fallon slammed the spittoon into the man's face. Cartilage broke. Blood spurted. The nose had been flattened, and down went the tough man, twisting, falling, one leg still stuck in the busted flooring.

He landed with a cry and an *oof*. Tom tried to push himself back up, but Fallon still held the spittoon. He lifted it over his head, waited until Tom's ugly head, the mane of hair now dripping with tobacco juice and blood, was above the flooring. He slammed the heavy brass onto the man's skull. His hands slipped from under him, and Tom's bloodied face crashed into the floor.

"That ain't fair!" A leathery figure leaped from a bunk to Fallon's right. Fallon heard the sound of a knife blade being unfolded. "You son of a whore!"

The figure came at Fallon, who saw the reflection of candlelight from the shiny blade.

"I'll skin you like a catfish," the man said, and added a few curses in his own language.

Fallon still held the spittoon, and he slammed it into the charging man's face. The man fell back against a bunk, and the bed kept him upright. But not for long. Fallon slammed the brass cuspidor again into the man's face. The blade fell to the floor. Fallon stepped closer, kicked the knife away, and brought the stinking vessel up. That caught the bottom of the attacker's jaw, wrenched his neck up, and Fallon slammed the heavy container against his head. This time the convict fell into a heap.

Turning, Fallon saw that the giant named Tom had managed to free himself from the flooring and shake some senses, some feeling, and a bit of consciousness back into his very being. He saw Fallon and roared like a grizzly as he charged.

This time Fallon let go of the spittoon. He sent it sailing like he was rolling tenpins, and that brass caught the big galoot's feet and sent him sailing onto the floor. No wood broke this time, but the man rolled over onto his back, cursed, and wound up lying between two bunks.

As he tried to push himself up, Fallon lunged forward and leaped. He caught hold of the top bunks and saw the occupants scurry back toward the wall, like children waking from a nightmare and pulling back the covers toward them in abject fear.

Fallon brought both legs down into Tom's face. The force drove the giant back, and Fallon let go, dropping his feet into the big man's gut. That cost

Fallon his own footing, and he slipped, landed on the floor, rolled over, jumped up, and looked at Tom.

Tom wasn't moving anymore. He was bleeding. And he was breathing. That was about it. Fallon turned around, made sure the man who had opened the knife remained out of the fight. No worries there. The man had regained consciousness, but he was whimpering and had pulled himself into a ball like a newborn baby.

Fallon sucked in the stinking air of the bunkhouse, held it, let it out. He made sure the knife remained on the floor. Fallon looked around and stared at shadowy faces.

"Anybody else want to take a hand?"

In answer, the front door of the shack was jerked open.

CHAPTER TWENTY-ONE

"Which one of you yellow-bellies thinks he can ruin my supper party?" a voice drawled.

Fallon saw the figure, like a white knight in the doorway. He saw the bright flash of flame and the roar of a cannon as a pistol—the loudest he had ever heard—sent a round that knocked out a good portion of the ceiling.

Torches flared behind the man. A guard—at least Fallon assumed it was a guard—ran up behind the man in white, and brought a lantern with him. Whoever had fired up the lantern shook it out, and by the time Fallon's eyes had adjusted to the new light, every one of the men in the bunks had pulled the covers up, a pillow—at least those fortunate enough to have a pillow—over his head. A few pretended to snore.

"Well?"

The man in white stared directly at Fallon.

Fallon figured he had no choice. He pointed at the man he had smashed to near oblivion with the empty spittoon, the man who still lay curled up in a ball and quivering on the floor.

"Him," Fallon said.

* * *

The man Fallon figured had to be none other than Josiah Jonathan Justice glanced at the man, then back at Fallon, and chuckled. "I dare say." His accent was a mix of sugar-thickened tea and cane syrup. His suit was white. It might have been from the yellowy glow of the lantern, but he looked bronzed from the sun, with a well-groomed white mustache and goatee, white hair, white sideburns. His shirt was white, underneath a white vest. Even the tie was white. The buttons—on shirt, jacket, and vest—were mother-of-pearl. The man's eyebrows were white and thick. Fallon figured everything about the man was white, except his heart. And his soul.

"Dave," Josiah Jonathan Justice said in that slow drawl. "Take this reprobate out to the whippin' post. Lash him to it."

"You want to whip him, Colonel? At this time at night?"

Justice sighed. "Did I say whip him, Dave? Heavens to Betsy, man, if we were to whip him at this time of night, we'd wake up my coonhounds, all the frogs and gators in the swamp, and half the population of Natchitoches. I said lash him to the post. We'll whip him in the mornin', boy. Now, get to it."

The man called Dave muttered something that might have been *Yes, sir*, and he snapped his fingers. Two men rushed inside, grabbed the whimpering man, and dragged him toward the door. When he began screaming, one of them stopped, stomped his head with a boot heel, which either knocked the pitiful man out or at least stunned him into silence. By the time he recovered or regained consciousness he would not be able to yell and wake all the animals and neighbors, for the second guard had stuffed a bandanna into his mouth and tied it around the back of his head.

The Colonel stepped aside to let them drag the poor convict to the whipping post.

"And what about that big monkey lyin' over yonder?" Colonel Justice pointed at the unconscious figure of Tom.

Fallon said, "I wouldn't know." He had not counted on his comment getting a poor fellow whipped, even though Fallon wasn't going to lose any sleep over that. The thug had intended to spill out Fallon's guts onto the floor.

"No?"

Fallon shook his head. "Maybe he likes to sleep on the floor. I've known some good old boys who did."

"You reckon?"

Fallon shrugged.

"And what about you? Why are you out of bed?"

Fallon nodded at the door. "I heard you knocking. Came to open the door."

Colonel Justice's grin widened.

"I don't recollect your face, son. You been hidin'?"

"Just arrived."

"I see. From Rusk?"

"Huntsville."

The man nodded. "The Walls, eh. You like it here?"

"From what I've seen."

The man grinned again. "I don't think you've seen a whole lot. This time of night. New moon an' all."

Fallon shrugged.

"You got a name, boy?"

"Alexander. Harry Alexander."

"Oh yes. Harry Alexander. They tol' me you was comin'. Needed a replacement. One of our ol' boys got hisself bit by a cottonmouth. You know about cottonmouths, Harry Alexander?"

"I do."

"Nasty snakes. Meaner than rattlers. Maybe not as deadly as copperheads. But mean, mean, mean old reptiles, cold-blooded as they come. Almost as cold-blooded as some Yankees I've known."

"I see."

"Then the poor lad, God bless 'im, fell into the swamp. A big ol' alligator come alon', and, well, gators got to eat, too, and maybe that gator, drownin' the po' lad, maybe that was a blessin', you see. Drownin' is a better way to die than all that p'is'n shuttin' down yer organs an' all. Don't you reckon?"

Fallon held out his palms in defeat. "I wouldn't know. Never drowned to death. Never died from snakebite."

"Do you like bourbon, Harry Alexander?" the cotton magnate asked. "I mean, Kentucky bourbon. Bona fide. Not Pennsylvania bourbon. We don't drink nothin' from Yankee land down here. Ain't that right, Dave?"

Dave had returned from lashing the unconscious man to the whipping post.

"That's right, Colonel. Right as rain."

"Well." Justice grinned. "Do you like bourbon?"

Fallon thought about lying, but instead his head shook.

"No? A strappin' young fella like you. You don't care for good Kentucky bourbon?"

"A promise"—Fallon had made—"to my dyin' mother."

The man cocked his head to one side, unsure what to make of Fallon's answer.

"Honest?" he said.

"I haven't touched an ardent spirit in more than ten years," Fallon said. Which was true. "God bless her soul." He hadn't tied on a good drunk since he had married, either, but he had sipped a bourbon, or a rye, or a beer before he had been arrested. But to drink now, after years of abstaining not by choice but by prison regulations, could compromise him. Fallon was on shaky footing all the time. Getting light-headed from whiskey could get a man like Fallon killed in a hurry.

"Well." The man bowed his head, shook it, and raised it. This time he pushed up the straw hat he wore. It was flat crowned, with a flat brim, and what looked to be a red satin band around the top. "That's admirable. I dare say, Mr. Alexander, that I don't meet too many workers from Rusk or Huntsville that I could say have admirable qualities."

"I've got some unadmirable qualities, too."

"I'm not sure *unadmirable* is a word, Mr. Alexander. But even if it's not, name one of them, if you don't mind."

Fallon shrugged. "I don't drink."

Now Colonel Justice laughed heartily, slapped his thigh, and nodded with pleasure. "You must join my dinner party, Mr. Alexander. Dave. Clean him up some. Give him a jacket to wear. Bring him over to the parlor in ten minutes."

Justice turned around, moved to the door, stopped,

and looked back. "And the rest of you low-down asses-dogs, stay asleep, and stay quiet, or you all might find yourselves bitten by water moccasins and et up by hungry gators."

The door closed behind him.

"Do you drink coffee, Mr. Alexander? Chicory. From New Orleans. Finest you'll find. Or did you promise your late ma that you'd abstain from that, as well?"

The Colonel sat in a rocking chair on the porch. The porch was screened in. On a night like this, hot, humid, still with mosquitoes and flies as thick as grasshoppers in a plague, a man needed a screened-in porch.

"Coffee's fine," Alexander said, and a moment later, a black man in a white jacket and crisp black pants came out of the main house with a china cup of steaming black coffee. Fallon thanked the old man and sipped the coffee.

"Benjamin," Colonel Justice called out, "have Grandma Tatum warm up a beignet for Mr. Alexander. You haven't had supper, have you, Mr. Alexander?" He did not wait for an answer. "But tell Grandma Tatum not to put on too much powdered sugar, for I dare say that Mr. Alexander promised his late mother that he wouldn't rot his teeth out with all them sweets. If y'all got some cracklin's left, warm some of those up, too. And maybe a bowl of gumbo. You like gumbo, Mr. Alexander?"

"We never got that in Arkansas," Fallon told him.

"It's real tasty, suh. Tasty, indeed. Spicy, too. But I

got to think a little hot action won't bother you too much. Am I right, Mr. Alexander?"

Fallon fanned himself. "It's a little hot in here."

"Bourbon would cool you off, suh."

"Like you said, Colonel, a little hot action won't bother me too much."

The man leaned in his wicker rocker and lighted a cigar. Fallon sipped the strong Louisiana coffee.

"Nice turnout for your dinner party," Fallon said.

"I think so," Justice said. "The sergeant brought me a copy of your record. Lucky, isn't it, that a life sentence got reduced to ten years? You wouldn't be here if that were not the case. Would you?"

"That's the way the warden explained it to me," Fallon said. The black man returned with a tray of food. He set it at a table to Fallon's right, and left.

"Sit, Mr. Alexander. Sit." The Colonel waved his cigar. "Eat. We'll have a nice little chat while you eat."

Once he was seated, Fallon spooned in a mouthful of the gumbo. He had never tasted anything like it. Spicy. Warm. Absolutely wonderful. Flavors assaulted his senses. *Hell*, he thought, maybe he should have taken up the Colonel's offer of Kentucky bourbon.

"From the record the warden sent along, Mr. Alexander, you have been a rather naughty, naughty man." He clucked his tongue and shuffled some papers before laying them on his lap.

Fallon shrugged. "Courts have one way of looking at things. I have another."

"You don't seem to like the Yankee government."

Fallon swallowed more gumbo and sipped coffee. "I probably wouldn't have cared for the Confederate government, either," he said. "On some things." He lifted the coffee. "Or the Creoles. Or the French."

The Colonel made himself smile.

"You got in some trouble in Arkansas."

Fallon pretended to ignore the statement. He tasted the sugary beignet.

"And a most dreadful act of violence in some place way up in the Panhandle of Texas."

"That's why I'm here, Colonel."

The white-haired gentleman laughed. "And I thought you came for the chicory coffee and our wonderful food."

Fallon kept eating and drinking.

"Don't you think the War Between the States is over?"

"Do you?"

"Whatever do you mean, Mr. Alexander?"

Fallon lifted the china cup and nodded at the wall behind the Colonel.

Justice turned around and looked at the flag. The Confederate battle jack.

"I carried that bravely with me for four years of the most dreadful fightin', Mr. Alexander," Justice said.

Fallon knew that a colonel of a legion was not carrying a battle flag into combat. He knew, not from experience, for he had been too young to serve in that war on either side, that the enemy seemed to enjoy shooting down flag bearers in battle. The Colonel would have been on a horse on a hill, watching men die. Some colonels fought alongside their men, of course, but Fallon didn't think Justice filled that bill.

"There's just one thing that troubles me, Mr. Alexander."

"What's that?"

"That all of these bad things you've done. How come I never heard of you . . . till now?"

CHAPTER TWENTY-TWO

"I didn't want anyone to hear of me," Fallon said with a shrug. "People heard of Jesse James. Of Quantrill. Bill Longley. Cullen Baker. And you know what?"

"What?"

"They're all dead."

"Cole Younger," Justice said, "isn't dead."

"Might as well be," Fallon said. "Rotting away as he is up in that prison in a damn Yankee state like Minnesota."

Justice smiled. "And John Wesley Hardin?"

"Hardin wasn't fighting the war. He might say he was, but he wasn't. He was fighting for himself."

"You might be right, Mr. Alexander, but The Judge does *judge* the men we select for . . . special duty on my farms." He yawned. "Finish your meal, sir. Have more coffee if you so desire. I must retire, for nights like this tend to exhaust me. But make sure you get plenty of rest. Sleep well in your new lodge, suh. You'll have a busy day tomorrow. After breakfast, I want you to whip that man who ruined my supper party. I want you to flay the skin off his sorry hide."

* * *

Fallon did not think Justice would listen to the argument he had presented to Sergeant Barney Drexel back at The Walls when the beast had ordered Fallon to whip another prisoner, so he gathered up the blacksnake after breakfast, as he was ordered, and walked to the whipping post.

All of the prisoners, the guards, and the regular workers for Justice's plantation had gathered outside, including women and children. Even a few hounds were brought out.

Entertainment for the masses after breakfast, Fallon figured, and drew in a deep breath.

He remembered his fight with Juanito Gomez with whips—after he had refused to whip a prisoner. He remembered how lousy he was at whip-fighting. A man has his limitations, Fallon knew, and he was glad that he had never mastered the art of using a whip. He would give these fine people a show, and he wouldn't be acting at all.

It didn't take long for Colonel Justice to grow tired of Fallon's weak attempts at whipping the prisoner being punished. Fallon did not come close to flaying off the poor soul's skin. He did manage to burn his own back and arm. He also tripped up a guard—which resulted in cackles, hoots, and howls from prisoners and the guards, except the one whose feet got jerked from underneath by an errant aiming of the blacksnake whip.

"Mr. Alexander, please cease and desist. You are no teamster, suh."

Fallon heaved, shook his head, and began curling

up the long whip. "Never said I was." He wiped sweat from his brow, let his lungs suck in air deeply, and blew it out in great gasps.

"I sure hope you are far better at cuttin' cane, Mr. Alexander, than you are with a whip, suh."

Fallon nodded. Inwardly, he thought: *So do I.*

"You want me to whip this cur?" the day sergeant asked.

To Fallon's relief, Justice shook his head. "No. No, I think not. Our workers, and your guards, are bemused. No sense in killin' their good spirits. Get them to the fields. Work 'em long and hard."

"And him?" The sergeant pointed at the prisoner who remained strapped to the post.

"Leave him. If he's still alive after your day in the fields, we'll call his punishment complete. If he's dead, well, the hogs like fresh meat this time o' year."

A guard gathered the whip, and the prisoners were marched to a shed to pick up all they needed for work in the cane fields. Forty minutes later, Fallon was in the fields.

Guards kept their distance, staying in the shade, shotguns and rifles ready, watching. Colonel Justice sent his own men, big black men in dungarees and well-used slouch hats, to make sure the workers knew what they were doing.

"You pretty good at this, boss."

Fallon looked up, wiped the sweat from his face, surprised to see that the big man kept nodding his head. The foreman wasn't joking.

"I mean, I can tell ya ain't been a-doin' this all yer life. But some of dese workers I gets . . . Jay-sus . . . they don't know nothin', hardly get no work done."

Fallon went back to work. "Why they're in prison," he said.

The big man let out a throaty laugh. "Yes, suh. Dat jes' might be da case.

"So whens sum o' dem white boys leaves, it ain't no big loss. No, suh. Not a-tall."

"Like the one who got snakebit and then eaten by a gator."

The man laughed uproariously. "Boss, you looks smart enough to know better'n believe ever'thin' ya hears in a place like this."

Fallon nodded.

"People dies here all da time. Natural causes, dey likes to say. Only things is . . . nots all of 'em is act'ly dead."

Fallon wet his lips, kept cutting through the cane, and waited.

"Wouldn't surprise me none a-tall to learns that you is dead when you ain't, neither. From da way I hears you handles yeself."

"I see."

"But da Col'nel, he's got hisself a good thing here. Don't know why he wants somethin' mo'. He had a fine time afore da Mas-sa-cree. Now he gots somethin' better."

"Massacre?" Fallon asked.

"Ya never hears of it?"

Fallon shook his head.

The foreman sighed, shook his head, and told Fallon all about it, but it wasn't the kind of massacre Fallon was expecting to learn about.

The way the black man told it, five-six-seven years

back, some Yankee boys came down and got the workers to assemble and form a union."

Fallon stopped long enough to stare up at his supervisor. "A labor union? In Louisiana?"

"I guess dat's what it was, suh."

Well, the hands harvesting the cane weren't exactly making much money. Barely living off what they could make. So right before November—what the foreman called "Grindin' Time," and from what Fallon had learned during his cane training back in Florida that was the crucial opening of a harvest season—the workers went on strike.

Fallon had never heard of this, but a strike in Louisiana wasn't likely to make the Illinois papers that he might get at Joliet, unless one of the Yankee organizers had hailed from the state.

"Dem po' boys didn't know what dey was a-doin'," the foreman said. "But da Col'nel, he knowed what to do."

Indeed. The way the foreman told it, Colonel Justice called upon the governor, who called upon the state militia—and not federal, Yankee, troops—to put an end to the strike. The militia arrived with a Gatling gun.

All of the strikers were evicted from their homes on the plantations. When they still refused to work, other workers were called in to replace them.

Well, the foreman went on, things got uglier and uglier. Out-of-work strikers made threats to burn the town, destroy the cane fields, kill the "scabs" who had been sent in to replace them. When two "scabs" were fired at with rifles one night—or at least when they said they were shot at—the militia, Colonel Justice, and some of his men retaliated. They gathered several strikers and brought them to the edge of a swamp.

"From what all I hears, the Col'nel, he tells 'em to swim and run or die right dere. That Gatlin' gun opens up. Dunno how many of our folks gots kilt, some says thirty, some says three hunnert. I wasn' there. Didn't come down till after, back when the strike done got busted up."

Fallon shook his head. "You didn't go to the law."

"Pshaw. You joshin' me, boss? Da law? White-man law? No justice for us, just Jus-tice. As in Col'nel Jus-tice." He laughed, but Fallon could tell the old man found nothing funny.

"And it's better now?" Fallon asked.

"For Col'nel Justice, sure." He pointed. "Afore dat strike, all dem workers got paid in what dey call *script*. Means da comp'ny pays you in paper dat you gots to spends at da comp'ny sto'. But now-days, da Col'nel gets his workers mostly from Texas. You criminals. Don't hardly pay y'all nothin'. And dats fine with me. 'Cause I ain't breakin' my back, jus' watchin' you fine gents break yours."

Fallon kept working. Working and sweating.

A few minutes later, the foreman sighed again. "Dat strike, it sure changed da Col'nel, though. He started doin' all sorts of things. Strange things. Bringin' in folks. Goin' down to Mexico. And sayin' some of ya pris'ners is dead when they ain't dead a-tall. Jus' shipped down to Mexico."

"Where in Mexico?" Fallon asked.

"Oh, ain't no tellin'. Or nobody's fool enough to tells me. Big country, I hear. I tried to get down there oncet, long times ago, back when I was just a field slave for some other white boss. But dey catched me. Got me a whippin', got sended backs to work."

He laughed. "Too bad I didn't have you whippin' me, boss. You ain't no good at that. So, suh. No good a-tall. But you ain't bad at cane, boss."

"I had a good teacher," Fallon told him.

"Yer daddy? My daddy taught me."

Fallon shook his head. "Not my dad. A man like you. A good man. A good teacher."

The Negro straightened.

Fallon kept working.

Things were starting to make sense now. That far-fetched guess that Colonel Justice might be trying to raise an army to restart the Civil War did not sound so insane after hearing the black foreman's story. The massacre would have been six or seven years ago. That fit the timeline the American Detective Agency had come up with.

The problem was that Fallon was alone. Mac-Gregor, Christina, and everyone else thought Fallon was in Justice's Hell on the Brazos, not in Louisiana. And he had no way of getting word to the detectives. He had no idea whom he could trust. Briefly, he considered asking the foreman, but he instantly rejected that idea. All that would likely do was get the black man killed. Thrown into the swamp. Shot down like a dog. No, Fallon wouldn't risk that. He'd have to find some other way.

They worked steadily. Few breaks. Just cutting cane till they could hardly straighten their backs. Finally, as the sun disappeared over the moss-covered trees off beyond the town of Natchitoches, the foremen told the men to stop working, to move to the cane-laden wagons, and get back to the compound.

Even the guards seemed half-dead, and Fallon understood why. Just sitting in that heat sucked the energy out of a person, and watching men harvest sugarcane wasn't the most exciting detail a man could have.

They filed back through the shed, lethargic, bitter, just wanting the chance to wash their faces and hands, get the stickiness of cane sugar off their bodies, and have a decent supper and good night of sleep. But they were dreaming. There would be no bath until Saturday night, the food they would get would taste like dung, and they would be up again before dawn for a breakfast of coffee and mush, and then march back to the fields of ripening cane.

The whipping post came into view. The prisoner had been taken down, not dead, for Fallon saw him in the corral, tending to the horses. That came as a relief.

Justice stood in front of his home, talking to a man in a derby hat and striped tan and green suit. A few other men stood near the Colonel, but it was the man in the derby who held Fallon's attention. The white-haired former rebel commander pointed at the feet-dragging men, laughed, and told the man in the suit, "Here come my boys, Chris. Look at 'em. Marchin' like John Bell Hood's Texans." He removed his hat and waved. "Welcome home, lads. Thanks for makin' me a richer man today."

He cackled.

The man in the derby turned, and Fallon made himself look away. He couldn't help himself, though. His right hand reached into his pocket and he gripped the handle of the knife he had been told to leave in the tray in the shed, but which he had managed to keep for himself.

It had been years, but Fallon recognized the face. And the name, the first name, which Justice had called out, fit. Fit perfectly. Right then, everything fit perfectly.

Harry Fallon felt, for the first time, that he was capable of cold-blooded murder. He wanted to charge, to draw the knife from his trousers, and cut that yellow dog's throat. No matter what would happen to him, he could exact his revenge—and maybe even stab Justice to death—before the dumb guards understood what was happening and opened fire. He'd be dead. But so would they.

The door opened. Fallon marched inside the awful shed. Went straight to his bunk. Sat down when ordered. And remained there after the guards did their head count, and moved back outside, locking the door shut.

Fallon remembered . . .

CHAPTER TWENTY-THREE

"Deputy Fallon, how old are you?"

It was 1877. Fallon couldn't remember the exact month, but spring, maybe early summer. He answered before the prosecuting attorney could object, and Fallon knew he would hear the federal solicitor berate him in the offices when the day's testimony was over.

The defense attorney was Chris Ehrlander, maybe only a few years older than Fallon. He wore a fine suit, a diamond pin in his cravat, and his hair had been slicked back so that not one strand fell out of place. From his spot on the witness stand, Fallon could see every woman in court staring at the handsome attorney, while Fallon sat sweating in his worn trail duds and his best coat and tie, both shabby and stained. The prosecutor would curse and gripe about that, as well.

"Your Honor," Ehrlander said with a charming smile at Judge Parker, "the solicitor implies that I am belittling Deputy Fallon because of his youth. By no means do I say that someone as young as Fallon lacks experience and therefore is not fit for the job. I commend Deputy Fallon. Why, everyone in Fort Smith has heard about how he ended the terrible reign of the notorious brigand Daniel K. Huntington—and when he was only supposed to be driving that jail on wheels."

Parker yawned. "Do you have a question for the witness, Mr. Ehrlander?"

The young attorney bowed at the judge, turned on his heel, and nodded at Fallon. "Have you ever been in jail, Deputy Fallon?"

The prosecutor shot up from his chair, hammered his fist on the table, and screamed, "Objection!"

"Overruled," Parker said.

"But," the district attorney pleaded, "Deputy Fallon is not on trial."

"Are you asking for an exception?" Parker asked.

The attorney sank into his seat. Everyone knew better than to challenge anything Judge Parker had decreed—at least, not while there were spectators and reporters in the gallery.

"Answer the question, Deputy Fallon," the judge instructed.

Of course, Judge Parker knew the answer. Judge Parker had been there when Fallon had been arrested, long before he ever took the oath to uphold the Constitution of the United States and laws of the state of Arkansas and the United States of America.

"Yes."

"More than once?" Ehrlander smiled, but it was a charming smile, more for the twelve good men looking bored and annoyed in the jury box. He didn't seem vindictive or cocky, though Fallon knew that a lawyer like this one had reason to be sure of himself.

"Three times or thereabouts," Fallon said.

"For what crimes?"

"Usually drunk and disorderly."

"I see. Was the defendant drunk when you arrested him?"

Fallon shrugged. "There was two kegs of rotgut in the camp, and only one had any liquor left in it. Maybe a quarter full. His eyes were glassy. His voice was slurred. And—"

Ehrlander held up his hand, and Fallon stopped talking.

"His eyes were glassy, you say. His voice was slurred. Was that before or after you bent the barrel of your revolver over my client's skull?"

"I didn't bend the barrel over Wright's skull, mister," Fallon said. *"Hard as that whiskey runner's head might be, it isn't going to bend the barrel of one of Sam Colt's equalizers."*

That got a reaction from the stone-faced jurors and the crowd. Even Ehrlander offered a mocking bow of appreciation.

"For such a young man, you have an admirable wit, Deputy Fallon," the lawyer said. *"But would you mind answering the question I put forth to you?"*

Fallon sighed. *"His back was to me as he reached for the rifle. I hit him on the head. Didn't knock him out. Just stunned him. So I guess that hurt I put on him could've made his eyes glassy and left his speech impaired. But his breath stank of whiskey. From my experience, he was drunk."*

"From your experience as a federal peace officer? Or from your experience as a man who has spent the night in jail on multiple occasions for being drunk and disorderly?"

The crowd laughed again. This time Judge Parker banged his gavel and warned them about outbursts in his courtroom.

"Both," Fallon said.

The judge had to bang away often before the crowd fell silent this time, but Fallon saw Judge Parker was grinning, too.

"A very fine parry, Hank," the lawyer said.

And that was probably the first time Fallon ever thought, and certainly the first time he ever said in public: *"Only my friends call me Hank."*

The examination resumed. Fallon had forgotten most of the sparring and the way Chris Ehrlander twisted Fallon's statements around, wrung them, strung them, repeated them, rephrased them, and pretty much twisted everything around *until Fallon himself had little idea what the jury must have been hearing.*

Even the district attorney appeared more than just a little frustrated and confused when he sprang out of his seat to try a redirect.

Well, it didn't surprise Fallon, or the prosecutor, and certainly not Judge Parker when the jury, after deliberating maybe six or seven minutes, came back into the courtroom and issued a verdict of not guilty.

What did surprise Fallon was that evening, when Chris Ehrlander showed up, smiled, and bought Fallon a draft beer. Fallon and a few other lawmen had gathered at the Cherokee Saloon to drink a beer or two and raise a ruckus about the injustice of having so many pettifogging lawyers earning a living in Fort Smith at the expense of federal lawmen who risked their lives . . . for nothing.

"No offense, Hank . . . I mean . . . Deputy Fallon." Ehrlander slid the mug toward Fallon. The other deputy marshals at the table stared. Fallon figured a couple of them had put their hands on the butts of their revolvers and were considering the wisdom of shooting this particular pettifogging lawyer dead.

"Good business for you," Fallon said. He stared at the drink.

The lawyer sipped his whiskey and looked over the thick tumbler.

"My client is not a wealthy man. It wasn't that profitable for me."

"It will be."

The attorney cocked his head. He grinned a little, curious, and asked, "How so?"

Fallon shrugged. "When I arrest him again for running whiskey in the Nations. He'll have to pay you again."

"And again," said Deke Benson.

"And again," said Bob Thornton.

"An' again," said Bass Reeves.

Ehrlander sipped. "You boys might be onto something."

"Unless we just shoot the man dead," Deke Benson said.

"Then you might find yourself in need of my services."

The lawmen drank in silence. Reeves was the first to leave. Benson and Thornton followed him after they'd downed their drinks, leaving Fallon alone with the grinning lawyer.

"Well," Ehrlander said after an uncomfortable silence. "Again. It wasn't personal. Just my job. You have my genuine respect for what you do. I just get paid to represent my clients to the best of my ability."

Fallon stared at his drink, didn't say anything, and sat there a long time after the attorney had pushed his way through the batwing doors and hailed a hack to carry him home.

"You all right, Hank?"

Looking up, surprised at the new voice, Fallon found the prosecuting attorney standing to his right. He was on his fifth or sixth rye whiskey by that time, and he had trouble standing up, so Fallon nodded at one of the vacant chairs.

The solicitor sank into the chair, spilled a finger of rye over his unbuttoned vest, wiped it off with his necktie, and shook his head. "He's one cocksure feller."

"No argument from me," Fallon said.

"And you know what really makes me hot underneath the collar?"

Fallon finished his beer, wondering if it was proper for him to be drinking the beer Chris Ehrlander had bought for him. He did not answer the solicitor, knowing that the lawyer, himself a pettifogging attorney who had come to Fort Smith to make his fortune, would answer no matter how Fallon responded.

"It's this: If I got myself arrested, if I needed a lawyer in

*this town, that's the jackal I'd want to defend me. And I'd
pay him anything he asked."*

It was also Chris Ehrlander that Judge Parker recommended to Fallon when the judge had told Fallon that he
might want to start studying law himself, that he had all it
took to be a good lawyer.

"Like Ehrlander?" Fallon had said with disgust.

"No. You'd never be the lawyer Chris is. But you'd be a fine
one, son—especially if you learned from Chris Ehrlander."

So Fallon had. He had spent evenings reading Blackstone with the young man. They had spent a few evenings
with Fallon's family. In front of Rachel and Renee, Chris
Ehrlander was as polite and kind as Judge Parker when the
judge wasn't sitting on the bench. He was charming. He
made both Rachel and Renee laugh, and sometimes, he left a
smile planted on Fallon's face.

Ehrlander always looked after Rachel and Renee when
Fallon was riding across Indian Territory, for weeks, sometimes months. Fallon's wife always had a nice story to say
about the lawyer whenever Fallon was back home, and the
damnedest thing about all of that was how Fallon never felt
jealous. Sometimes he even found himself thinking how nice
it was to have a friend like that quick-witted lawyer.

So when the walls came tumbling down on Harry Fallon,
when he found himself sent into that dungeon of a jail at
Fort Smith, awaiting to be tried for a crime he did not commit,
Chris Ehrlander was back in Fallon's corner.

The way it seemed—all these years later—how Fallon remembered it, anyway, was that Ehrlander had done his
best. But the evidence seemed to stack up against Fallon. The
witnesses said that Harry Fallon sure looked like the man
they had seen. He rode a horse like the one Fallon rode. The
weapons he used were like those Fallon was known to carry.
And the wallet he had dropped had Fallon's initials engraved

into the leather. Even Fallon had to admit on the stand that was his wallet, but he swore he had lost it . . . sometime. He couldn't recall when. He had it. Then, out in the Nations, he realized that he no longer had it.

To which Chris Ehrlander ranted and raved and said how everything that pointed to Harry Fallon's guilt was purely circumstantial. He urged the jury to acquit.

They didn't. Parker threw the book at Fallon.

Chris Ehrlander swore to Fallon that he would right this injustice, that Fallon would be freed. That Ehrlander would work until Fallon was free and back with his wife and daughter.

That stopped, though, as far as Fallon figured, when Ehrlander sent him the telegraph that said Rachel and Renee were . . .

CHAPTER TWENTY-FOUR

"Dead," Fallon said aloud in the darkened cesspool of a bunkhouse.

Dead. His wife and daughter were dead, and the man who had sworn to protect them, the lawyer who said he would never stop fighting for Fallon . . . here he was. Fighting for a plantation owner and cold-blooded killer. Fighting for a man with pockets much deeper than a dozen deputy marshals.

It all made sense now to Fallon. Chris Ehrlander could easily have slipped Fallon's wallet out of his coat pocket. Ehrlander's closing arguments and his cross-examinations, now that Fallon thought more clearly, didn't have that same savage attack as the attorney had used in other cases that Fallon had witnessed. And Ehrlander had always had this strange look in his eyes when he stared at Fallon's wife.

Fallon had just been too blinded by the man's charm and his ability with words, to see it all back then.

A lifetime in Joliet made a man see a whole lot differently, though, and Fallon saw Ehrlander for what he was.

"Snake in the grass," Fallon said with contempt. "I'm going to kill that cottonmouth snake."

He didn't remember sleeping, but knew he must have dozed for the clanging of the bell and pounding on the door caused him to open his eyes. His fists were clenched tightly, and he wondered if he had slept that way. Fallon swung his legs off the bunk as the guards opened the door and began yelling that daylight was being wasted—although the only light shining came from the torches and lanterns the men held.

The shoes slipped back on, he found his hat and slipped his right hand into the pocket of his trousers, feeling the reassuring handle of the knife he had stolen yesterday.

"C'mon," a guard shouted to the lollygaggers behind Fallon. "Get movin' or I'll ship your arses back to Huntsville."

A deal, Fallon thought, that most of the inmates would be glad to take. The Walls were tougher than hell, but this plantation was hell, pure hell, maybe even worse than hell.

Dawn had broken by the time they had finished the meager breakfast of hominy, hardtack, and coffee, and gotten the wagons harnessed and tools loaded for another day of misery in Justice's cane fields. Fallon stared at the whitewashed stone and wooden mansion that Justice called home. The buggy was gone. Fallon did not see the Colonel, but it likely was far too early in the morning for a man like Justice to be rising from bed. And Chris Ehrlander? Fallon figured he had driven back to . . . Natchitoches? Shreveport? Baton Rouge? New Orleans?

That information would have to wait. Fallon climbed into the back of the nearest wagon, made room for other hands, and before long they were on their way back to backbreaking labor.

"Work hard, boys!" the sergeant yelled at them as they moved into the fields. "Get as much done before the sun gets too hot. That's the way to cut cane."

No one listened to the guard, of course. Why should they? Maybe if they were working for themselves, maybe if they got paid a decent wage and were fed something fit to eat, they would work fast before the sun got too high, the temperature began to burn like a blast furnace, and the humidity thickened into a wet, stinking wall. But what was the point in working like an ant in the brief coolness when the guards would keep them in the fields through noon, the worst of the afternoon, and not bring them back to the stinking bunkhouse until after the sun was down?

He had a new supervisor this morning, but that suited Fallon well enough. The man's name was something French-sounding, but everyone called him Eyeballs because his spectacles were so big, his gray eyes appeared to be bulging out of their sockets. He also spoke in such a thick Cajun accent, few people could understand what he was saying. But that meant few people ever talked to him, asked him any questions, and from the brief time Fallon had seen him, he didn't like to talk to anyone, either. Fallon had heard that Eyeballs had eighteen months left to do on a seven-and-a-half-year sentence for some kind of disagreement at a livery stable in Marshall. If the stories were right, Eyeballs owned at least part of the livery, or he had worked there for a long time.

At the first break, Fallon saw Eyeballs's eyes appear to be straining underneath the lenses as Fallon rolled a cigarette. He looked up, as though noticing Eyeballs for the first time, shrugged, and handed him the smoke. That had been Fallon's plan all along, for all those years in Joliet had taught him the power of tobacco. When the big man was smoking, smiling, and leaning back with a contented look, Fallon tossed him the rest of the Bull Durham and the papers as well.

Eyeballs sat up straighter, and Fallon shrugged. "There's not much left anyway. And smoking just makes this kiln even hotter."

Eyeballs grabbed the makings, stuck them in his knapsack, and said something that sounded like *Smoking-cools-you-off*, but Fallon couldn't be certain of the translation.

On the second break, after Fallon had deposited a few armfuls of cut cane, he wiped his face and neck with his bandanna, which he had to wring out, and waited until Eyeballs had finished rolling another smoke.

"Careful," Fallon said, and winked. "Like I said. There ain't much tobacco left."

"Don't-use-much-flakes-in-my-smokes-you-see-so-I-get-more-out-of-a-sack-than-most-folks-do-so-you-don't-need-to-worry-about-me-do-you-want-one-I-can-roll-for-you-it-be-good-tobacco-not-Injun-stuff-I-usually-have-to-smoke-and-the-papers-mmmmmm-good-tasting-to-me-not-like-the-corn-husks-I-usually-have-to-use-myself."

Fallon had to run that through his mind three or

four times before he thought he understood most of what the Cajun had said.

"Keep it," Fallon said. "You use all the tobacco for yourself. It's too hot to smoke."

Eyeballs said something else. Fallon nodded. "I know. It's never too hot for you to smoke but it is for me." At least, he thought that was what Eyeballs had been saying.

Fallon removed his hat, fanned himself, and decided to take a chance. Maybe nobody talked to Eyeballs because they couldn't understand what all he was saying. Maybe Eyeballs was taciturn because no one talked to him. Perhaps he liked to talk.

"Did you see that buggy yesterday? The one in front of the Colonel's house?"

Eyeballs scowled.

"Fancy rig," Fallon said.

The Cajun removed the cigarette, blew out of his nostrils, and pointed a tobacco-stained finger at Fallon. He said something. Fallon tilted his head and wet his lips. Eyeballs repeated what he had said, a little slower, but still too hard for Fallon to make it out.

"No-steal-no-wagon."

Now Fallon smiled as his head shook. "Eyeballs, I'm not out to steal that buggy. I'm not looking to escape. Try that, they'll add to my sentence. I want to be the perfect prisoner."

The man's big head shook.

"You-come-here-it-be-no-time-before-you-escape-or-you-die-that-is-how-things-go-at-Colonel-Justice-farm-you-bet-and-I-know-it-always-happens-you-see-I-know-you-see."

Fallon rubbed his shoulders.

"Nice-buggy-though."

That much Fallon could translate. "That's what I thought. But I guess Colonel Justice can afford one that pricey."

"No-no-that-isn't-buggy-for-the-colonel-it-belong-to-his-secretary-his-partner."

Fallon apologized, but asked Eyeballs to repeat what he had just said. The Cajun obliged Fallon, spoke slower, tried to enunciate the words individually, and though that made it harder for Fallon to understand, he thought he got enough of it.

"His partner? I thought Justice owned all of this himself."

"He-does-he-does-not-partner-on-farm-but-in-town."

The guards were looking over from their seats in the shade. Fallon knew he'd have to get back to work, and he drank a ladle of hot water, nodded at Eyeballs, and returned to the cane.

At his midday break, he wasted no time.

"So that was Justice's partner's buggy?"

It took a while before Eyeballs remembered the earlier conversation. This time, his head just bobbed an affirmative.

"Well, Justice has good taste in buggies."

"Not-Justice-buggy-no-I-tell-you-it-belongs-to-his-partner-his-secreatary-his-attorney-and-it-not-that-fine-a-buggy-at-all-not-really-I-had-many-better-that-I-rent-out-in-Marshall-before-all-this-trouble-that-buggy-it-be-nice-but-you-can-buy-one-for-eighty-ninety-dollars-the-one-I-rent-in-Marshall-it-cost-me-one-hundred-and-seventy-five-dollars-Grade-A-buggy-Got-from-Columbus-Ohio-rent-to-new-brides-new-grooms-congressmen-governor-senator-railroad-presidents-big-deal-big-money."

"I see." Fallon saw. He just wasn't sure if he heard everything.

He filled the ladle and handed it to Eyeballs, who took it, drank greedily, and wiped his mouth. Talking that fast, and that harshly, had to work up a man's thirst.

"Well, who owns that buggy, then?"

"Big-lawyer-man-name-Charles-Chambliss-Christopher-some-name-like-that . . ." He stopped, and enunciated the last name. "Herr-land-der."

Fallon shrugged. He took the ladle. Drank more awful water himself, wiped his brow, dropped the ladle into the pail, ran his fingers through his hair, pulled the hat back on his head, and returned to the cane field.

He had not been mistaken. It was Chris Ehrlander.

There were other questions he thought about asking, but decided not to push his luck. Besides, if the guards saw that Eyeballs loved to talk so much, they might ask him questions themselves, and some of the guards were Louisiana natives. They wouldn't have so much trouble understanding everything the Cajun had to say.

The buggy was back when they were hauled back to the plantation's main compound, but Chris Ehrlander and Colonel Justice were nowhere to be seen. Which meant Ehrlander was in town, at least most likely, as Eyeballs had told Fallon. Fallon debated his chances of sneaking out of the bunkhouse, making his way to Justice's home, then cutting the murdering cur's throat. But only after Chris Ehrlander, that backstabbing, murdering swine, saw Fallon's face. Fallon wanted to make sure the pettifogging lawyer saw who was sending his soul to hell. Then, maybe, before the guards could cut down Fallon, he might be able to slice Justice's throat.

It was something to think about.

He woke that night with a start, sweating. The sweat wasn't that unusual because of the stifling temperatures in an overcrowded bunkhouse. But the dream? Fallon could not remember the last time he had dreamed, or at least remembered what he had been dreaming. But this one was so damned clear.

The problem was this: it hadn't been a dream. Not exactly. Dreams were exaggerations. They were made up. They weren't exactly history. But this one . . . it had been like . . . Fallon stopped to wipe away sweat— he had been transported back in time. He was reliving something that had happened, but it wasn't as though his entire life was passing before his eyes. It was just one brief moment.

They had sat in the café about five blocks from their home. The place served the most wretched chili Fallon had ever tasted, but the biscuits were pretty good and the pecan pie excellent. Fallon sat next to his little daughter, who was playing with her food more than eating it, while Chris Ehrlander sat next to Fallon, across from him, enjoying tea and supper.

"You can't blame me this time, Hank," Ehrlander said with a smile. "I wasn't representing Sean Crites."

Fallon smiled, though he was in what his wife always called ill *humor.*

"I'm not blaming him."

"Blaming the jury?" Ehrlander asked.

Fallon's wife frowned. She never cared much for when Fallon talked about work, especially in front of a daughter too young to understand.

Fallon shrugged. "It just gets under my skin. I risk my life. The court lets this vermin go."

"But this wasn't because of something you did, Hank," Ehrlander said. "It's because the jury didn't think he robbed that stagecoach. The evidence wasn't there. Was it?"

Fallon shook his head. He looked at his own plate and realized he had played with his food more than he had eaten anything. He was as bad as the precious little girl sitting next to him.

"Maybe," he said, and he lowered his voice into a whisper and leaned across the table, closer to the lawyer and Fallon's beautiful wife. "Maybe I should have just killed that low-down dog when I had my chance."

Ehrlander sat back, his face showing concern and shock, but it was Fallon's wife's response that had caused Fallon to wake up instantly.

"Yes, Hank, but what if the jury was right? What if Crites was an innocent man?"

CHAPTER TWENTY-FIVE

He hated himself. Because he couldn't go out in the dark now. Because he couldn't kill Chris Ehrlander in cold blood. That damned dream. It had been like . . . his wife . . . she had . . . been . . . talking to him from the dead. Only the troubling part was that his wife looked just like Renee, but the voice . . . the voice was Christina Whitney's.

This time, Fallon did not fall back asleep. He lay in his bunk, sometimes feeling the tears well in his eyes but never break from the dam. He stared at the dark ceiling until the guards came to bring them to the sugarcane fields one more time.

As he filed out of the bunkhouse, he glanced at the darkened windows of the Justice mansion, then moved into the washroom, the shelter where the cooks dished out the slop and poured the coffee, and, after making himself eat and drink, into the barn to hitch the wagons, check the tools, and prepare for another grueling day harvesting cane.

Once again, Fallon saw that the buggy was gone, but this time he watched Chris Ehrlander say good-bye to Colonel Justice and drive away toward Natchitoches.

Again, that worked in Fallon's favor. He couldn't kill the man, could not avenge the deaths of his wife and daughter, but the lawyer could not identify Fallon as a former deputy marshal. Even if he had—even if Ehrlander had somehow recognized Fallon from the distance—Fallon could come up with a quick response. Yeah, he had been a deputy, and he had gone to prison. So he had no love for the U.S. marshals or any lawmen after hard time in Joliet. And if you wanted to check a little bit more into Fallon's life since getting paroled out of Illinois, you could see that a man named Harry Fulton had spent some brief time in Yuma. He probably should leave Jefferson City out of it, though, unless they had found out about his time there, too.

It might work. It probably wouldn't, though, and Fallon would be supper for the gators in the swamps that surrounded Justice's plantation.

He was back at it, working again under the supervision of the Cajun named Eyeballs, sweating, working till his fingers and hands felt sticky with sugar, and wondering if the American Detective Agency's information was just plain wrong. Perhaps all Justice was guilty of was being a horse's ass and cheapskate who got practically free labor for his sugarcane.

As he carried an armload of cane to load into the wagon, Fallon saw another inmate standing beside the cart, wiping his brow. The big man, bald, with his left ear missing and the other ear with the texture of cauliflower, took a long time with that rag he was using to mop the sweat off his shining head. Too long. Guards typically jumped on a convict for not working.

The man's nose was misshapen, and as Fallon neared him, he noticed the scars on his face, the brutal hands that had been covered with tattoos. He was dark skinned, maybe six foot two and two hundred pounds. Fallon glanced at the guards, who fanned themselves in the shade. He looked at Eyeballs, but the Cajun was busy picking his fingernails.

Fallon nodded at the big man, dumped his load into the wagon, wiped his hands on his britches, and started back to the cane fields.

He heard the rush of air, then felt the wicked blow against his right shoulder and back—biting like a whip and definitely leaving a welt on his back. Fallon hit the ground, rolled over, and saw the big man flinging the busted stalk of cane into the dirt. The big man laughed and reached for another length of sugarcane.

"I don't like you," the big man said. "So I'm gonna kill you."

With sugarcane? Fallon thought as he came up to his feet.

Eyeballs was standing now, tilting his head, trying to figure out what was going on and what had started the commotion. The guards rose from their seats. One pointed. They stared, although one of the more experienced ones lifted his shotgun and began talking to the others.

The man took a few steps forward, toying with Fallon with the cane, maybe seven feet long. He waved it gently at Fallon's nose, crouched, then swung hard. Fallon jumped back and let the cane pass.

"Colonel-tar-your-hide-for-busting-up-cane-you-crazy-fool-you-get-us-all-in-trouble-or-dem-guards-gun-you-down-the-both-of-you-and-dump-you-in-swamp-as-supper-for-dem-hungry-gators-you-crazy-polecat," Eyeballs said, and backed away.

Now the big man lifted the cane over his shoulder

and came down quickly, downward, like some knight with a battle-ax or cavalryman slashing a saber. Fallon jumped to his left, feeling the cane whistle past him. The cane came up, moved toward Fallon, who ducked underneath it. Then the bald-headed man brought it lower, at Fallon's ankles, but Fallon leaped above it. He leaped to his right as the cane moved down again. To his left. Left again. Ducking as it came over his head and rolled over his back.

Fallon leaped back. The end of the stalk tugged at Fallon's sweat-soaked shirt. The big man laughed, brought the cane up, and slammed it down at Fallon, but this time it did not come close.

For a man that size, the big dog moved with surprising speed, but now he had to stop to wipe his eyes with his shirtsleeve, and his lungs heaved from the exertion.

Yet Fallon breathed hard, too, and took time to wipe sweat from his breath. Then he had to avoid another swipe of cane.

Out of the corner of his eye, Fallon saw that other hands had stopped working and gathered in groups to watch the show. Guards had rushed forward to make sure none of the noncombatants made an attempt to escape—not that anyone was likely to do that. Escape meant getting through the swamps. Besides, it was too hot to escape.

For that matter, it was too hot to fight.

The bald man swung again with the cane, angrily this time, and Fallon couldn't jump over or around this one. He lifted his left arm, felt the cane slam into it, and the cane broke, hung limply, like a busted sword, as the big man brought the cane back toward him. He looked at it, shrugged, and pitched it to the ground.

Fallon rubbed his forearm, which hurt like blazes.

"I've toyed with you enough," his attacker said, and pulled out a knife, a big blade, more machete than the small one Fallon had.

"Stop it there, Moeller," the sergeant yelled. "I said STOP!"

Moeller paid the guard no attention, even when the sergeant brought up a Winchester rifle and pulled back the hammer. "I don't want to kill you, Moeller."

"I have to kill this man," Moeller said to the guard as he approached Fallon, moving the knife left and right, grinning. "Then I go back to cutting cane."

The guard looked thunderstruck.

Fallon backed toward the wagon. The blade came slashing toward his belly, but Fallon moved, and the man slipped to one knee. Fallon saw his chance, turned, and bolted a few feet, then leaped into the back of the wagon filled with sugarcane. Moeller stood, stopped, and stared.

"Come down from there," he told Fallon.

Fallon held a length of cane in his right hand.

"Come and get me," Fallon told the man. He began carving one end of the cane with his knife.

"What are you doing?" Moeller asked. Then he saw the point Fallon had made at the end of the cane. "That won't do nothin'," he said.

"Won't it?" Fallon grinned.

Moeller hesitated, swallowed, and resumed his walk. When Moeller took his third step toward the wagon, Fallon threw his makeshift spear.

Moeller ducked, the stalk whistled over his head,

and when he started to straighten, smiling, even laughing at Fallon's weapon, he saw only the soles of Fallon's shoes as Fallon sailed off the wagon bed right behind his spear.

The feet caught Moeller in his face and chest. The knife went sailing into the marshy ground, and down went the bald man, spitting out teeth, blood, and vile curses.

Fallon hit the ground as he twisted around and extended his arms to break his fall. He sank into the muck that was earth, rolled over, bent his knees, and leaped up. Moeller was trying to rise, and he got his mangled head lifted as he groped for the knife, for anything. Fallon kicked him right underneath the chin, breaking the jaw, and Moeller went on his back.

The sergeant had lowered his rifle. He scratched his head. Two other guards rushed forward but the sergeant called out to them, "Might as well let them finish this."

Both guards stopped.

"Looks like Big Mo's already finished," one of them said.

But Fallon knew better.

Moeller was coming to his feet again, roaring like a wounded lion despite that broken jaw, summoning up all the strength he could. Fallon charged, leaped, twisting in the air, and letting his entire body catch the bleeding, mangled man's chest. Down they went, Fallon using his weight to drive the bald fighter deeper into the ground. He rolled over the bruiser's face, kept rolling, knocking over the cane spear, and coming up to his knees.

He had hoped that would have finished Moeller, taken the last ounce of strength from his muscle-bound body. But as Fallon caught his breath and blinked the sweat out of his eyes, he saw Moeller was already up. And fate had let him find the big knife he had dropped.

Moeller tried to laugh, but this time the broken jaw, busted teeth, and smashed lips refused to cooperate, so all he did was manage a gurgle or two. He charged with the knife, his feet making a squishing sound as they sank into the muck. Fallon found the cane, pulled it up, and charged himself as he rose to his feet. The point of the cane tip caught the big man in his stomach. The cane stalk broke, and Fallon tumbled to the ground, rolled up, and saw Moeller jerking the natural spear from his gut.

Blood spurted from the hole in the man's stomach. Somehow, Moeller refused to stop, sink, or even die. He spit out blood and froth, again tried to scream or curse or laugh. He had dropped the knife, but he stooped to pick it up and almost tilted forward when he tried to rise.

But there was no quit in this beast. Moeller did not fall. He did not lose consciousness. And he refused to die.

Fallon looked around. He saw the pail of water by Eyeballs's little camp. Fallon ran to it, grabbed the pail, and hurled it at the staggering man with the big knife. The water container slammed into Moeller's head, the handle slicing into his cheek and just above his left eye. The tin pail sprayed water onto the man's ruined face and caromed off and into the field. The blow staggered the beast, but still he came. Now

Fallon ran back to the wagon, where he had dropped the small knife. He found it just as Moeller's knife slashed down, ripping Fallon's shirt, cutting his back, not deep, but a painful wound.

Fallon swung around, saw Moeller lifting his hand, raising the big knife once more, starting to bring it down. Fallon rammed his own knife into the man's chest, driving it deep between the ribs, then sidestepping around as the big knife of Moeller's thudded into the wooden tailgate of the wagon.

Fallon stumbled, but managed to keep his feet. He whirled around, chest heaving, back burning from the wound and the sweat, and yet Moeller still stood.

Swearing, Fallon tried to catch his breath and wondered if anything could kill this beast named Moeller.

The guards provided an answer for Fallon.

"Hell. That's enough, boys. Put Moeller out of his misery."

The sergeant aimed his rifle.

The weapon spoke, and two other guards echoed the blast with their shotguns.

Fallon cringed as Moeller twisted from the bullet and the buckshot, sank to his knees, opened his mouth as best he could, and let out a silent scream as he fell into the cane field dead.

CHAPTER TWENTY-SIX

"How's your back?"

Fallon was trying to find a comfortable spot in the wicker chair on Colonel Justice's veranda. His back hurt. So did his arm and practically everywhere else on his body.

The man in the white suit laughed.

Fallon let him laugh. The Colonel had offered Fallon some brandy, but he had politely declined—even though he could have used the drink, if only for medicinal purposes.

"I bet the rest of your body doesn't feel a whole lot better," Colonel Justice said, his eyes beaming with delight, his face warmed by his own cocktail and the heat of a Louisiana evening.

"You'd win that bet."

Justice laughed again, found a cigar in a fancy wooden box on a small table, opened it, clipped the end of the cigar, and dipped it in his snifter before putting the Havana in his mouth and lighting it. He did not bother to offer a fine cigar to Fallon.

The medical treatment Fallon had received after his encounter in the cane fields with Moeller had not amounted to a whole hell of a lot. Eyeballs had rubbed some salve over the welts and cuts, but that seemed more like a mixture of bacon grease and grass than anything else, and then the Cajun had wrapped some rags over the wounds. There was no hospital at Justice's plantation, and nobody sent for a doctor. On the other hand, Fallon got better treatment than the bald prisoner, now dead.

A trusty had been sent to the plantation to fetch a mule, and Moeller's body had been tossed without any ceremony over the mule's back. Two guards carted the mule off, but did not take the path to the plantation. They took the body to the nearest swamp.

"Gators-ain't-no-dif'rent-than-us-critters-or-any-types-of-animals-mister," Eyeballs had said to Fallon as they watched the funeral train of a mule, a corpse, and two guards embittered by their latest assignment. "They-eats-good-tonight-though-ol'-Moeller-being-a-right-big-man-with-lots-a-meat-on-his-bone-so-don't-you-give-me-that-look-you-low-down-convict-because-I-rather-that-gator-or-crow-or-buzzard-be-eating-the-meat-off-ol'-Moeller's-bones-than-a-gnawing-on-mine-and-you-don't-wanna-say-it-but-you-know-it-be-how-you-feel-too-exactly."

Fallon hadn't answered Eyeballs's statement. He wasn't thinking about the treatment the dead man was receiving, for Fallon had no remorse over the death of a man who was bound and determined to kill Fallon. What Fallon wondered was why Moeller had been on the prod. Fallon hadn't said one word to the big, bald man since he had arrived in Natchitoches. Few other inmates had spoken to Moeller, either. What Fallon was thinking as the cortege made its way to the nearest swamp was that the guards had not notified the local sheriff. This had been a shooting, justifiable at least in Fallon's eyes as a former federal lawman, but there were things like jurisdiction that Justice and the guards from The Walls were overlooking. Not to mention the fact that even a brute like Moeller might have next of kin, and burial in Peckerwood Hill or the potter's field at Natchitoches or Justice's plantation was certainly more fitting than the disposing of a corpse in the croaking, foul-smelling bayous and swamps.

When Justice had his cigar to his liking, he removed it from his mouth, took another sip of brandy, and asked, "Are you sure you would not like some brandy? It's the best there is. From France."

Fallon shook his head.

The Colonel sighed. "Suit yourself." He puffed on the cigar. "What do you think is the matter with this country today, Mr. Alexander?"

Fallon shrugged. Which hurt his neck and his shoulder. "I imagine the prison system could use some reevaluation."

As Justice chuckled, sipped brandy, and smoked his cigar, Fallon glanced outside. Still no buggy. No sign of Chris Ehrlander returning.

"Are you not enjoying your accommodations and reapplying the skills you learned in cane fields?"

Fallon did not answer.

"I'll take that as a resounding no, suh." The cigar was placed in a silver ashtray. "Would you care to hear my assessment?"

"You are my host," Fallon said, "and this is better than the bunkhouse."

"I should hope so." The Colonel leaned back in his chair. "We remain a nation divided, and one that never should have been reunited. Reconstruction has been over, for, what, fifteen years or so? The coloreds are still inferior in all regards to the white race. The Yankees have learned that they might be able to produce iron and whatever, but it remains the South that feeds the nation. You look like you do not agree with me, Mr. Alexander."

Fallon sighed. "The West produces cattle. Even sheep these days. The Midwest grows wheat and other grains."

"You have a point. But my point is this: the South never should have lost the war."

"But we did."

"Yes. And do you know why?"

Fallon shook his head, waiting for the Colonel to finish puffing on the cigar, which he had picked up from his silver tray, again soaked the end in the brandy, and smoke, drank, rocked, and stared.

"It is," he drawled as he returned the cigar to the tray, "because our soldiers were boys. Untrained. They did not know how to fight."

"They fought well enough to die."

"And they died for a glorious cause. But these were sons of farmers, boys who had been brought up without proper training. And our leaders, our commanders, they knew not how to command or fight, themselves. That is what cost the South the war. Our generals sent boys charging at fortified positions. Our boys were too stupid to say no. We should have learned from the Indians."

Fallon cocked his head. "Indians?"

"Indeed. Those savage tribes teach their youth how to fight at an early age. And the Indians fought as those bushwhackers in Missouri and elsewhere. Slash. Hit. Kill. Run."

Fallon massaged his sore arm.

"You see my point, don't you, Mr. Alexander?"

"Well . . . the bushwhackers in Missouri are mostly dead now. The Indians are a defeated race."

"Because they were not properly trained, either, only slightly better than most of our soldiers in butternut and gray."

"So how do you train your soldiers, Colonel? How do you do that?"

The Colonel leaned forward and spoke in a savage whisper. "Exactly as I have been training you, suh."

Fallon blinked. He shook his head as if he had not heard Justice correctly, but the Colonel laughed and smoked his cigar again.

"You are a natural-born fighter, Harry Alexander. You have shown your worth, your ability. You have earned a place to ride to glory—but more than glory, to Southern victory!" He slammed his fist against the desk, laughed again, and tossed the cigar into the brass cuspidor.

"Training me?" Fallon said, trying to figure out what the Colonel meant. "You mean today's fight with Moeller?"

"Yes. But not just Moeller. I thought Moeller was a good man, but you showed me how weak and inferior he was. He was not fit to wear the new gray. He was a fool."

Fallon felt sick. He started sweating again.

"You chose your soldiers . . . like some gladiators in Rome?"

"No, confound it," Justice roared. "This was not a do-or-die deal. It was a test. But not the first test. Even a fool can win one poker hand, but over the course of a long evening, the professional will win, hands down, every time. You won . . . hands down . . . every time."

He shook his head. It was confusing. His head rose, and his eyes trained on Justice's. "The attack at the prison cemetery . . ." Fallon started.

"No. Well, yes. That was a test, at least it was supposed to have been a test, but not for you. I wasn't even aware of you until after that little incident. I arranged that attack to see how . . . well . . . the man did not pass, and he died. But then word came to me of how you handled yourself. Some other matters . . . well . . . I don't know what those men were thinking, but they—those leading the assault—did not follow orders, either. They died. You killed them. And you survived the test today. Plus, your record that I have seen says you still believe in our lost cause."

"I believe in the South, sir," Fallon said, and felt the bile in his stomach. The damned war had ended almost thirty years ago, and here Fallon sat on the veranda of a wealthy plantation that was owned by a raving lunatic.

"Do you want to fight for the South, Private Alexander?" Justice rose. "Do you want to avenge every Yankee transgression? Do you want wealth beyond your wildest dreams?"

"Yeah," Fallon said, and tried to look as crazy as Colonel Justice.

"Then you must join us."

Fallon looked skeptical.

"Well, that sounds mighty fine, Colonel, but I am still in prison. For ten years. And this little venture working for you can't last forever. I'll have to go back to The Walls. Unless I escape."

Justice laughed. "If you escape, Mr. Alexander, the

bounty hunters, the lawmen, the army, everyone will be looking for you. Bounty hunters even are not restricted by international boundaries. Say you made it to Mexico. They could track you down. Bring you back. Force you back inside The Walls."

Which, Fallon figured, would be better than serving a sentence at this god-awful plantation.

"I don't understand," Fallon said, but he was beginning to figure it all out. What he did not know was how Justice's insane scheme tied in with The Mole, the convict at Jefferson City who had murdered Fallon's precious family. But now he started thinking that if Colonel Justice planned to restart the Civil War, then . . . well . . . that was a much more pressing fight than avenging Rachel and Renee. That thought left Fallon's hands shaking. For years all he had dreamed of was getting out of Joliet and then finding the men who were responsible for ruining his life. Now he thought something different. It tore at his soul.

And where did Chris Ehrlander, that double-crossing lawyer, fit in?

"We are forming a new legion, a new country, a new army. In Mexico." Justice's voice rose. He sounded like a fanatic, like a monster. He even looked like one as he stood waving his arms, about to break into some Southern war song. "You can come with us. You can take part. We are on the brink of something great. We—I—a new confederation of Southern states— we need your help, suh. Can we count on you, Mr. Alexander?"

Fallon smiled. "And the money?"

Justice sank into his chair, laughing without control. "The money. You are a man after my own heart, Harry Alexander. Yes. There will be money. More money than you ever dreamed in your penny-ante career. Confound it, man, this is your chance. Are you with us?"

"I'm with you, Colonel," Fallon heard himself shout. "But I don't see how you get me out of Huntsville."

"Because, you dumb cockroach. Harry Alexander is DEAD!"

CHAPTER TWENTY-SEVEN

Fallon let the comment sink in while also making certain that Colonel Justice was not joking. Finally, understanding just how insane Justice must truly be, Fallon said: "I didn't know I was sick."

The Colonel laughed again, slapped his thigh, and shook his head. "You are a man filled with tremendous wit, Harry. Yet you have a head on your shoulders but more than that, you think fast on your feet."

"I'm alive," Fallon said, "even if I am dead."

"Which is why you've been invited to take part in the greatest rebellion, the greatest fight for independence, the world has ever seen."

"So I'm dead . . ." Fallon said, hoping that Justice would take it from there.

Which, after another gulp of brandy that had been made for sipping, Justice did.

"Harry Alexander died of natural causes—probably from the stress of living such a hard life—while working in the fields at my cotton operation in South Texas. 'Hell on the Brazos' as the jealous newspaper journalists like to call it. The heat, you see. He just keeled over dead. No one will think much about it. Another prisoner dies. Who is there to mourn for him? This is the perfect plan. With Harry Alexander dead, no sheriffs or marshals or bounty hunters will be looking for him. That is fine payment, do you not think?"

Fallon merely stared.

"But don't worry, Harry. You will be wealthy beyond your imagination once our rebellion, our war for independence resumed, is under way."

Money wasn't on Fallon's mind then. His stomach started twisting from a fear. He thought he was hiding it, but Justice noticed the stress on Fallon's face. Fallon tried to swallow, but couldn't.

"Yes, Harry, I know about your wife. From the reports I heard, she was quite a woman to look at. But I also heard that you told her you never wanted to see her again."

Images of Renee, of Rachel, and now of Christina Whitney raced through Fallon's mind and pulled at his conscience.

"You were wise to send her away. Now, if you still have feelings for her, you must pray that she does not desire to look upon your mortal remains. And if you hate her guts, just say the word. I can dispatch one of my most trusted associates to Huntsville."

Part of Fallon wanted to leap out of his chair and choke that cocky muttonhead to death, but something stopped him. He had a job to do. Fallon did not have to close his eyes to picture Christina again. He saw her clearly, and he heard her voice.

* * *

"Here's the one thing you have to understand, Harry," Christina Whitney had told him during their training in Alabama. *"The mission we are on is more important than me. You. Dan. Anybody. It's more important than Malcolm Maxwell or anyone else in the Texas government."*

They had been sitting in the hotel lobby, exhausted from their work.

"If I get killed, you keep doing your job. Remember that. What's at stake is bigger than our petty lives. We're talking about the lives of hundreds, thousands, of our fellow Americans. We're talking about the future of our country. Think about it, Harry. If Maxwell's theory turns out to be true, if there is some sort of treasonous rebellion in the works, if Texas zealots try to pull Texas out of the Union once again, do you think Spain will just sit back and watch? With ships and troops just a few miles from Florida in Cuba? My God, England might see an opportunity to get her colonies back. It'll be war, maybe the entire world at war. My life does not matter."

Fallon had said: "And if I get killed?"

Christina had shrugged. "I'll avenge you if I can," she said, and Fallon had smiled, but the smile faded when she quickly turned away. "But I'll miss you, Harry. I'll miss you a lot." With that, she had quickly risen from the chair and headed for the stairs that led to her room.

"She's out of my life, sir," Fallon told Justice as the vision, the memory, faded, and Fallon saw the white-coated old fool on the veranda at his home in Louisiana. "I don't think she'll bother us."

"Good, lad. Good. For my contacts say she checked out of the hotel where she was residing in Huntsville, fighting for your . . . parole or pardon!" Justice laughed. "And she gets your sentence reduced and you toss her out like bad milk. My God, Alexander, you are hard and cold—exactly the kind of man my army needs!"

Fallon saw his hands, balled into fists, were shaking.

"My associate was ordered to kill her only if absolutely necessary. I hope your wife has decided that she hates your guts."

Fallon nodded. "She does. Now."

"Then there's no need for concern. But if you change your mind, let me know where you were living, or where her mother lives, or where anyone you would like the world to be rid of lives."

Fallon wet his lips, struggled to relax his hands and keep from balling those fingers into fists again. Tried to tell himself that the mission was the most important thing.

"Who's your associate?" Fallon suddenly asked.

"Mr. Alexander," Justice answered with a frown. "You shall meet everyone in due time."

Justice wasn't going to give away the name, but Fallon knew who it was. Chris Ehrlander. Who had experience at seeing wives murdered in cold blood.

"Are we going to have a problem, Harry?"

Fallon made his head shake.

"Are you sure?"

"No problems, Colonel," Fallon said. "As long as we kill Yankees. As long as I get paid."

Justice laughed.

"A wise man." But Fallon knew that Justice had his doubts.

"You were laid to rest in the cemetery at my plantation. Hot as things are down there, much like here, well, it is usually not wise to open a casket after only a short while. I don't think we have anything to fear."

"So what happens next?" Fallon asked.

"In a few hours, a coach will arrive. You will take it. The destination is not important. You will be trained for the next battle that will lead to our destiny, our new nation. Then you go to our next camp for more training. Where these camps are is unimportant. What is important is this: Training is imperative. Execution is imperative. But what is most important is this: In a few months, we shall oust the Yankee tyrants from Texas. Texas first. Maybe Louisiana second. Or your home state of Arkansas. When the president and the blue-belly Congress understand that we will not be defeated this time, then peace will settle on our new nation."

Justice finished his drink.

Another question dogged Fallon. "What about the inmates here? They saw Harry Alexander fight here. Not die in your Hell on the Brazos."

"They know to keep their mouths shut," Justice said. "You died here. You died in Texas. No one really cares about another dead convict."

The only person in the coach with Fallon was a leathery gent in a frock coat and black hat, with a drooping gray mustache, who said not one word on the bouncing, jarring, miserable ride to wherever the hell they were going.

When they arrived—it could have been Texas, but it sure felt like the End of the Earth—Fallon was escorted to a Sibley tent. There he slept a good straight ten or twelve hours, only to be awakened by the earsplitting scream of a bugle.

He had never served in this man's, or any man's army, and it did not take him long to learn that he was not cut out to be a soldier. But he did what he was told, and he tried to figure out what the hell he could do to help the Texas attorney general, Christina—if she was still alive—and the American Detective Agency, his country, and himself. He sought out ways he could get word to the authorities, but dismissed every idea he came up with.

After two days, Fallon understood his situation.

By now, the American Detective Agency, the superintendent at The Walls, and everyone else—including Christina—thought he was dead, buried in some graveyard, never consecrated, in the region called Hell on the Brazos. He was alone. Completely alone.

After two weeks of intensive training, Fallon had figured out something.

His instructor, a hard-edged man who had lost some fingers on his left hand at Chancellorsville, knew that Fallon had figured it out, too.

"So what do ya think?" the old man said in a thick Texas drawl.

"We're taking a train," Fallon told him.

"We *are* takin' a train? Or we're *tryin'* to take a train?"

Fallon shrugged. "It's a good plan. But good plans don't always work."

"That's true."

"And while I'm fairly certain I can do what you have me doing . . . there's . . . well . . . this job might be a bit much for just one man."

"Who said there's just one man?"

Fallon let his head bob. "Shouldn't I know what the other man's doing?"

The Texan's head shook. "I don't think so. You just concern yourself with what we've been training you for. You swing into the express car, dynamite the safe, go to work."

"And while I'm working?" Fallon let the question die off.

"The other men training for this job do what they've been taught."

Fallon shook his head. "And if we manage to take this train?"

"Then the other men will show up and do what they've been trained to do."

Fallon chuckled. "You don't trust anyone, do you, Merle?"

Merle laughed. "Well, to answer that question, I guess the first thing you ought to know is my name ain't Merle."

Fallon grinned. "Since we're being honest, my name's not Alexander."

"Never figured it was, bub."

They worked five more hours, timing the fuse time and time again, seeing how it burned in the wind, in rain, in sand, when it was cloudy and when the sky was pure, pale, not blue. They tested matches to see which ones were the most reliable, how each brand fared in multiple conditions. Fallon had to guess that they had spent about ten dollars in matches alone. This team was thorough.

And every evening Fallon stood outside his Sibley tent and stared into the nothingness, and he tried to think of a way to let Dan MacGregor, or Attorney General Maxwell, or anyone know what was happening. The problem was that Fallon knew they would be robbing a train. But he did not know what they would be robbing from the train. The safe probably meant money, but express cars carried gold, silver, currency, bonds. He was being taught to blow open the door of an express car, if needed. Others were being trained to unload whatever they were stealing.

Maybe that was how Colonel Justice had commanded his legion back during the late War for Southern Independence, or as Fallon wanted to call it, the War of the Rebellion. Train his men for just one part of an operation. Like the blind leading the blind. No wonder the South had lost the war, if commanders like Colonel Justice outnumbered the minds of men like Robert E. Lee, Thomas "Stonewall" Jackson, and J. E. B. "Jeb" Stuart.

Two nights later, someone kicked his feet in the middle of the night. Fallon rolled, reaching for the Colt revolver he had been issued.

"Use the six-shooter later," his trainer, Merle, said. "On the enemy. We're moving out. Now. Get your gear and meet us at the corral. You got that, Alexander?"

"I got it," Fallon said. Once he was dressed, he stepped out of the Sibley and stared at the stars. There was no moon on this night, not yet anyway, and Fallon recalled a conversation he had had with the Texas attorney general—when they happened to be alone and not near the eavesdropping ears of Dan MacGregor, Aaron Holderman, or even the beautiful and charming Christina Whitney.

"Why hire a detective agency?" Fallon had asked.

Malcolm Maxwell had smiled. "You mean why the American Detective Agency and not the Pinkerton National Detective Agency? I think I've explained—"

Fallon was shaking his head. "I mean any detective agency."

Malcolm Maxwell tilted his head, curious, and not understanding.

"You have the Texas Rangers," Fallon said.

That the politician understood. "I see."

"The Rangers have a great reputation. I worked with a few now and then, and they take an oath."

"You took an oath, too," Maxwell had said.

Which caused Fallon to feel that blood rushing, the tension returning. "But I was innocent."

"And I believe you," Maxwell had said, "and I think the MacGregors believe you, as well, or they wouldn't have hired you. I know Miss Whitney believes in you. I can see it in her eyes."

Fallon had to steer Maxwell back to the question.

"The Rangers?" he reminded the attorney general.

Maxwell started to give a politician's answer, but he stopped. "I don't know for certain how high this conspiracy, this act of treason, reaches, Mr. Fallon. The Texas Rangers— at least some of them—might be part of it. I needed to bring in someone from the outside."

Which Fallon understood. He didn't know whom he could trust, and now he was completely alone. The camp buzzed with action. Men were excited. The new war was about to begin.

And Fallon still had no clue what was going to happen—or how he could do anything to stop it.

CHAPTER TWENTY-EIGHT

Fallon was a Missourian by birth. He had driven cattle up from Texas, but had never been much farther south than San Antonio. Since the American Detective Agency had sent this operation into motion, Fallon had seen Huntsville, Austin, a bit of Houston, and other parts of the sprawling state—not to mention parts of Louisiana, Alabama, a sliver of Mississippi, and the Panhandle of Florida. He didn't know where he was now, except that they were in Texas. He knew they had traveled too far to still be in Louisiana, and he knew they had traveled south and west.

Texas.

The training, once they had left Natchitoches, had been in the southeastern part of Texas, though. Swampy. Ticky. Humid. Snaky. More bugs than a man ought to see in his life. Not much different from Natchitoches, Louisiana. They had practiced for hours and for days and weeks on an abandoned railroad track in the thick forests, and the instructors had warned them.

"This won't be the same country where you'll bring glory to your first mission. Remember that. But it doesn't matter where you are as long as you do as you've been trained. Fail? Then you'll be in hell."

He thought about his conversation with Christina Whitney just before all the training, all the investigations, everything was all but over and Fallon was about to take that fateful trip to The Walls.

"Do you ever . . . ?" Fallon had paused. Christina looked up from her plate of stewed vegetables and roasted beef. ". . . Getting too involved?"

Her head tilted, and her eyes sparkled, and Fallon blushed. "What I mean . . ." he had started, and she laughed. It was a musical laugh, and her face radiated from the comedy. To Fallon's surprise, he laughed a little, too, and the blush faded, and his head shook. Yet he realized he also felt something, an attraction, or at least a feeling of comfort. Christina Whitney was an operative for the American Detective Agency, but she was also a woman, a good-looking, young woman, sure of herself, and nobody to trifle with. Yet Fallon had started feeling at ease when he was around her, and Fallon had not had any feeling like that since he had first been arrested a billion years ago for a crime he had not committed.

"I know what you mean," she said, and pushed the plate away. She reached for the cup of hot tea, lifted it off the table, but not to her lips. She stared at the steam rising over the lip.

"Damn Shakespeare," she said after a long while.

"How's that?" Fallon asked.

She sipped tea, set the cup back onto the saucer, and shrugged. "A thousand years ago, I was acting in a troupe in Hartford, Connecticut, home to Mark Twain, Harriet Beecher Stowe." She shook her head, and brushed the hair back behind her shoulders. "The Most Excellent and Lamentable Tragedy of Romeo and Juliet."

Fallon grinned. "You were Juliet."

She laughed. "No. And I wasn't Romeo, either, silly. I had the distinction of playing Capulet's wife." *She saw the blank expression on Fallon's face.* "Juliet's mother." *She affected an English accent, and her expression changed instantly.* "'Hold, take these keys, and fetch more spices, Nurse.'"

Fallon offered a shrug of defeat.

Christina laughed. "Two weeks later, the Traveling Thespians of Hartford brought our performance to Washington City. After that show, which attracted all of fifteen or maybe sixteen of the finest theater patrons in our nation's capital, someone knocked on the door to my room." *Her head shook.* "It was Sean MacGregor." *She let out a little sigh.* "I played Juliet's mother all too well. Mr. MacGregor said I had a higher calling than playing in second-rate theaters for an abysmal director."

She sipped tea.

"That's how you got into the detective business."

"There." *She gave him a wicked grin.* "You are a detective." *The expression changed, and she reached out and took his hand.* "I'm sorry, Harry. I didn't mean to be rude."

Yet the touch of her hand left Fallon's heart racing. He swallowed and tried to still those feelings that had not taken control of him in years.

"Call me Hank," *he told her.*

They took in a show that night in some slum of a theater called the Palacio. The Two Gentlemen of Verona. *Fallon couldn't make out most of what was being said, but Christina pointed out the flaws of the actors and actresses, which were many, and what they did right. Later, as they sat on the balcony of the hotel, Christina sipping a mint julep and*

Fallon nursing a cup of weak coffee, she said, "You asked me a question earlier tonight and I didn't answer you."

Fallon set his cup down. "I figured you figured it wasn't any of my business."

"Don't figure," she told him. "Get your answer."

"All right. Consider it asked again."

"It's a judgment call," she told him. "I'm paid, you're paid, to solve a crime, to break a case. You do whatever's necessary. And you have to ask yourself a question. No, you have to ask yourself a lot of questions: Do I have a way out? Is this going to get me killed? If it gets me killed, is the operation still salvageable? The operation comes first. So, yes, I do worry about getting too involved." She looked up at him, and their eyes locked.

"I'm not worried now, Hank."

Fallon could not look away. They were talking about something totally different now.

But that's when the waiter came over and asked if they would like to pay their bill or was there anything else that he could do for them.

Which Fallon interpreted as: We want to go home, so pay up, and get out.

He had walked her to the room she had on the third floor of the flea-bitten hotel—on the other side of town and a long way from Washington City and her long-ago career as an actress in New England and Washington and other strongholds of culture and civilization, even if she had been playing in second-rate theatrical troupes. She had opened the door, pushed it open, and stared at him.

Fallon felt his heart pounding, and he had utterly no clue what was going on.

"You're too good a man to be working for a snake like Sean MacGregor," Christina had told him.

"You're too good an actress . . ." he had started.

"No, I'm not." She shook her head. *"Maybe I am. But maybe this is my calling."*

"It's not mine."

"I know," she told him, and her eyes softened and Fallon could have sworn he saw tears welling. *"I know all about you. But here's what you have to remember, Harry. You know, I like Harry better than Hank. You look like a Harry."* She drew in a breath, let it out, and said, *"This operation is the most important case MacGregor has ever had. He doesn't deserve it. If the Texas politicians had any sense they'd have the Pinkertons working this, but that's Texas for you. It sounds corny, Harry, but there's truth in this. And it scares the living hell out of me. But our country is depending on us. We can't let America down."*

She had slipped inside her room, blew Fallon a kiss, and closed the door. The bolt had clicked, and Fallon had wished he had been drinking mint juleps and hot tea and not coffee as he found the stairs, walked down to his own floor, and opened the room he was sharing with a snoring Aaron Holderman.

The image of Christina Whitney faded. But Fallon kept remembering her words:

"Do I have a way out?"

Yeah, he thought. He could get up and run for his life. He could say to hell with Sean MacGregor. But, no, he understood that wasn't acceptable. There was no way out, not without jeopardizing the operation.

"Is this going to get me killed?"

Silently, a mirthless laugh came out of his throat. *Most likely*, he told himself. Yet that didn't matter.

What concerned him was how many innocent lives might be lost on this warm, moonless night.

"If it gets me killed, is the operation still salvageable?"

The answer to that one might have been what kept Fallon lying in the grass and briars next to the railroad tracks in the middle of the night and in the middle of nowhere. If he died taking part in this crazy train robbery, yeah, the operation would still be ongoing. Maybe Christina Whitney and even that idiot Aaron Holderman could reap rewards for the American Detective Agency. Or maybe Colonel Justice might see his insane dream come true, and a new flag rise over Texas and other states of the old Confederacy.

"The operation comes first."

Fallon heard the rumbling of an approaching train.

And he remembered, and pictured, Christina Whitney again.

He was getting on the stagecoach that would take him to The Walls, where he would become Harry Alexander, and just before the stage pulled into the dusty station in the middle of nowhere, Christina had rushed up to him and grabbed his hand.

"Play your part," she had whispered. "Be Harry Alexander. But the most important thing you need to remember is to be true to yourself. Do what you think is right. Do anything you can to stay alive." She started to pull away, seemingly embarrassed by her loss of control, but after a moment, she merely smiled, came up on her tiptoes, and kissed his cheek. "Good luck," she had told him, then kissed his cheek again,

*and, lifting the hems of her skirt, she had hurried back inside
the station.*

That memory seemed to restore his shaking confidence. Something else made his resolve hardened. He needed to stay alive, to kill the lowdown rats who had, not ruined his life—for that he could accept—but had killed a woman and a little girl who had never harmed anyone. The image of Chris Ehrlander came into his vision, then that of the demented Colonel Justice. He even pictured that bastard Sean MacGregor and his blackest of hearts.

He was about to take part in the biggest robbery the state of Texas had ever seen. All in the name of justice. And Fallon did not have a clue as to who would be helping him on this warm, dark night.

Drawing a deep breath, Fallon remembered everything he had been trained to do. Trained by men hired by Colonel Justice, not Judge Isaac Parker, not General Robert E. Lee. He wasn't sure what was going to happen, but his last moment of getting out of this insane mission had passed. Fallon was in it now.

To the hilt.

The train grinded to a stop at the watering station in the middle of nowhere, the sparks from the locking iron wheels lighting up the sky just inches above Fallon's head. The wheels screeched, and the coaches ground into a slow, painful stop.

They had covered a lot of ground from their training grounds in what was likely north and east of Houston, but they had moved at night, in coaches with the canvas windows drawn tight. Fallon figured they had started out west and turned south at some point.

When the coach stopped and they got out to stretch their legs, they were told to keep their mouths shut, do their business, and don't ask anything.

One man didn't. At the third stop, he asked the petite Spanish lady bringing him coffee, "What's this place called, señora?"

That's when Merle came up to him and shoved a bowie knife into the man's back, twisting the blade, pulling it out, and ramming the giant bowie between the screaming woman's breasts.

The driver shot the station boss as he ran from the mules he was hitching. Then he killed the dog. The boy who had been helping was shot as he tried to leap over the top post of the round pen.

"Anybody else feels like forgetting the rules of this man's army, now's the time to speak up," Merle said. "Speak up . . . and die. Cole!"

A grizzled volunteer stepped forward.

"Yeah?" No *yes*, no *sir*. The man looked tough.

"Now you know why you trained for two jobs, Hansen. You take over for Bronson. Savvy?"

"You bet."

Cole Hansen. Fallon remembered the name. The Texas hard case. The one who had been sentenced to a ten-year term at The Walls. Who had died of pneumonia in Huntsville—but whom a soldier had recognized taking part in the robbery of an army caravan on the way to Fort Clark four days after he was dead. Fallon hadn't believed it when he had first heard the story. But now . . .

"But first, torch the place," Merle ordered Hansen and the others. "Run off the stock. Make it look like Comanches are on the prod again." Merle cackled. "Twenty years after them bucks taken to the rez.

That'll put the fear of God in this country. Move. Damn it. Move. This operation runs like clockwork."

"Clockwork," Colonel Justice had told them. "But not like that joke goes about the man with the fifty-cent watch who's always busy. Busy because when he's not checking the time, he's winding his watch. Clock-work. This is a Swiss regulator, eighteen karats, fine-tuned. Do your job. For the glory of Texas, Louisiana, and the Southern Confederacy."

Men stepped out of the train. Fallon heard their shouts, their demands, farts, and curses. The arm from the water tank was lowered, and water began spraying, hissing, and more noise sounded from the train just a few feet from Fallon.

All this while Fallon counted backward from seventy-nine.

Seventy-nine. Not one more, not two less. Seventy-nine.

Seventy-nine-one-thousand . . . seventy-eight-one-thousand . . . seventy-seven-one-thousand . . .

He did not think how many nights had someone watched from the distance with a pocket watch and a notepad and timed this stop. He thought of nothing but numbers.

Thirty-two-one-thousand . . . thirty-one-one-thousand . . . thirty-one-thousand . . . twenty-nine-one thousand . . .

He wet his lips. The arm from the water tank was being raised.

He wondered if Justice had chosen this night be-cause of the new moon. There was no light. Someone was urinating before getting back aboard the train.

Another had struck a match. Fallon was aware just how heightened his hearing had become.

Seven-one-thousand . . . six-one-thousand . . .

The train hissed. The wheels screeched. The conductor waved his lantern and climbed into the back of the caboose.

Two-one-thousand . . .

The train began to roll forward.

Fallon rolled underneath the tracks, reached up, and grabbed the bar that ran along the undercarriage. His feet lifted as the train began to roll, and he braced his boots against a crossbar.

Insanity. Riding under a train for a quarter of a mile. That wasn't far, for a man riding in the smoking car, or on a horse, or on one of those popular velocipedes everyone was calling *bicycles* these days. But riding in the middle of a train, inches above the speeding tracks . . . well, that was totally different.

One slip, and Fallon could be cut in half, his entrails spreading across the crossties and iron rails to be feasted upon by buzzards and coyotes in the days to come.

The train whistle blew.

Fallon held on for dear life.

Then his left hand slipped off the iron bar.

CHAPTER TWENTY-NINE

The train's wheels began grinding again, sending sparks and earsplitting noise as Fallon's pores let out water that felt like gallons.

Fallon's hand bounced off gravel and the wood of a few crossties as the train ground to a halt at the trellis over some river that Justice and his instructors had never named.

"It's a river," the Colonel had said in his thick drawl and repulsive laugh. "That's all y'all need to know."

The hand came up, grabbed at the bar, missed, and fell back but Fallon somehow managed to stop from hitting the speeding ground beneath him.

Which did not mitigate the pain shooting from his knuckles, fingers, back of his hand, and even to his wrist. He didn't think any bones had been broken. The gloves he wore had helped. But he also felt blood seeping into the deerskin gloves. And the pain raced from his banged-up fingers all the way to his elbow.

Yet he still managed to keep hold of his life support. He did not lose his grip and fall beneath the passing iron wheels.

He wondered if others had lost their hold, and

their guts, and were lying hundreds of yards down the tracks. If someone had slipped, his screams would have been drowned out by that clicking sound of wheels on rails.

Now the train began to crawl, and Fallon let his boots drop. The heels bounced off the stones, dust, and iron-hard wood, and just before the Baldwin engine let out a belch of steam and stopped, Fallon had dropped to the ground.

He rolled to his right, over the rails, and down the embankment. Immediately, he sat up in the blackness of night.

Making out the lights from the locomotive, Fallon realized everything was working just as Colonel Justice had planned. Above hissing steam and groaning metal, he could hear the conductor on the other side of the tracks barking out orders. Fallon looked toward the front of the engine.

The train's cargo was so heavy it took two engines to pull the coaches, tinder, and caboose. But here, across this narrow but deep gorge, the bridge could not support the weight of two Baldwin engines. So the first engine had been uncoupled and in a few minutes would be crossing the seventy-six-yard expanse alone. Then the next engine would pull the tinder, cars, and caboose across the trellis to be rehitched to the lead locomotive.

Usually.

But not tonight.

Tonight belonged to Colonel Justice and his well-trained soldiers of the South.

* * *

"*We do not know exactly what Justice might have planned,*" Texas Attorney General Malcolm Maxwell had said. "*But the key to stopping him, if these rumors are true, means that we must cut off the head of the snake.*"

"*You mean . . . kill Justice?*" Dan MacGregor had exclaimed.

"*I mean destroy his camp,*" Maxwell had stated. "*Wherever it is.*"

Stopping this train heist would not accomplish anything, Fallon understood. So he had to remain Harry Alexander. He had to commit a crime.

As he came to his feet and hurried to the siding of the coach, Fallon suddenly felt an unnatural urge to laugh. Not that anything going on on this dark night was funny, for, indeed, Harry Fallon could soon be dead, but it suddenly struck Fallon. He had been sentenced to prison for a robbery he had never done. Now he was about to rob a train—as an operative for a national detective agency.

His banged-up left hand gripped the iron railing, then his right, and he pulled himself onto the platform and lowered himself in the shadows as the conductor passed along the other side of the tracks.

"Ain't that a beautiful sight, O'Halloran?" the conductor said.

Whoever O'Halloran was muttered a reply that was unintelligible.

Here was Fallon's chance—his only chance. Silently, he slid along the platform and pushed himself up. Gunfire erupted up and down the tracks, and Fallon leaped down onto the embankment.

The conductor turned, dropping his lantern and his pocket watch, and reached for a small pocket pistol tucked in his waistband. Fallon slammed the barrel of his revolver against the fat man's skull, and the conductor dropped into a heap.

Ten feet away, a man in what appeared to be blue-and white-striped trousers and a railroader's cap, let out a shriek of terror.

"Be dead," Fallon told him, and the .44 barked and spit out flame and smoke.

The man crumpled into a heap, and Fallon could see him shivering. He was not an actor, Fallon realized, when it came to playing a corpse. But by this time, the train had started backing down the tracks as the other engine had reached the far side of the gorge.

Fallon rushed to the unconscious conductor, grabbed the pocket pistol, then he was hurrying back, shoving his Colt into his holster and the conductor's pistol into his pocket, racing, lunging, and grabbing the railing to the coach with his left hand. The battered, bleeding hand refused to cooperate, slipped off. Fallon swore, picked up his speed, and made his right hand reach up. His fingers bounced off, and Fallon slipped, almost fell, but somehow grabbed the rail again.

Let the train go, Fallon told himself. *Stay here. Tell Maxwell, MacGregor, Christina what was happening.*

The fingers wrapped around the iron. Fallon's feet dragged.

No. That doesn't cut off the snake's head.

He knew he had to make it to Justice's camp. The toes of his boots were dragging along the gravel of the embankment when Fallon reached up with his left hand. This time, despite swelling and injuries, the muscles cooperated. With both hands now secured, Fallon pulled himself up. He reached the platform just as a ball of orange erupted on the other side of the gorge.

They had used nitroglycerine to blow the trellis to hell, and the explosion seemed deafening.

Fallon came up, tried to catch his breath.

The door opened, and Fallon drew the .44.

"What the hell . . ." said the man as he stepped out of the car. Fallon slammed the barrel of the revolver against the man's head, and he crumpled onto the platform. Then Fallon stepped inside.

He had been trained to blow open the door to the express car, then blow up the safe. But the unconscious man on the floor made things a little easier. Fallon was inside the car.

Two men started reaching for Winchester repeaters in a case. Fallon fired. The trim of the gun case splintered. One man stopped, turned, wet the front of his britches, and raised his hands high above his head. The second man grabbed a repeating rifle, and Fallon put a bullet through his right hand.

The man yelled, grabbed his mangled hand, and dropped to his knees as someone kicked open the other door.

"Down," Fallon said. "Both of you. Facedown on the floor. Don't lift your head. Do as I say or you're dead."

He caught his breath. The men did as they were told.

Now he watched the other man hurry from the door, gun in his right hand, and a black silk neckerchief pulled up over his mouth and nose. The mask could not hide his features, though, and Harry Fallon muttered a silent curse.

The masked man stopped, looked at the two shaking men lying facedown on the wooden floor. He laughed and aimed his cocked revolver at the wounded man.

"Never let a wounded bird suffer," the man said. "Or any other hurt critter."

"Let them be," Fallon said.

The masked man looked up, and his eyes burned with hatred.

"No witnesses," the outlaw said.

"And no posse coming after us," Fallon said.

"The hell are you talking about? Once we cross the border, no lawdogs can go into Mexico."

Fallon said, "Don't be a fool."

Now the man whirled away from the two prisoners and started to raise the pistol at Fallon.

"We're robbing this train. Add too many murders, and that'll intensify their pursuit."

The man looked skeptical.

Fallon said, "You've already given away too much. You told them where we're going."

"So they ought to die."

Fallon shook his head. "Leave them alone. This'll buy us some time."

"What?"

"They'll question all the survivors," Fallon said. "If there's no one alive to talk, they'll just keep on riding after us."

The man pulled down his bandanna.

"Come on," Fallon said. "Let's get that safe opened."

He moved quickly to the side of the car and knelt at the side of the big safe.

The man knelt beside him and pulled out his pocket watch.

"How much time do we have?" Fallon asked.

"Seventeen minutes."

Fallon nodded.

"You got the dynamite?" the man asked.

"Yeah."

"Well, use it, damn you!"

"Not yet." He came up and moved to the two prisoners. "Another reason not to kill these two dudes." Fallon kicked the ribs of the one with the mangled hand. "Roll over."

When the man hesitated, Fallon drew the revolver, eared back the hammer, and said, "I won't ask you again."

The frightened, pale man groaned as he lifted his head, but did not completely roll onto his back.

"My pard wants to blow the safe with dynamite," Fallon told him. "I'd rather open it another way. Like the combination."

"I . . . I . . . I . . . don . . . don't know."

Fallon waved the revolver. "I think you do."

The man's head shook.

"Then here's what is going to happen." Fallon lowered the hammer and slipped the pistol into the holster. "We'll blow up the safe. Open it the hard way. But if we do that, you're going to be sitting in front of the safe. With the dynamite right behind you. That'll keep my pard and me from possibly getting a chunk of wood or metal drilled into our innards. Leave us choking on blood and dying an ugly death. But . . ." Fallon shook his head. "It won't do a whole lot for your good looks. Or your buddy here." Fallon kicked the other guard's calf. "Because he'll be sitting right beside you. And we'll drag the fool who opened the door over, too. Make things safer for me and my pard."

"You . . . wouldn't . . ." cried the wounded man.

Fallon bent, jerked him up, and rammed his back against the safe.

"Wouldn't I?" Fallon said.

It was the other guard who spoke.

"Three passes left to seven. Right nineteen. Left twenty-one. Right seven. Left eleven."

Fallon nodded at his partner, who knelt at the dial and followed the guard's instructions. There was a loud click, and when Fallon pulled the lever, the door opened.

"Isn't that safer than using dynamite?" Fallon said as he knelt and looked inside the safe. "Nowhere near as noisy, either."

The other bandit was checking his watch again.

"Time?" Fallon asked.

"Thirteen minutes."

"I'll empty the mail sacks. We can use those to carry the loot." He stopped by the guard who had given away the combination.

"When we leave, we'll blow the safe," he said. "That way your commander will think we got the money the hard way. You'll be wise to remember that when they ask you about descriptions, what all we said, where we might be going, things like that. Because if we have to testify on our own behalf in a criminal trial . . . well . . ." Laughing, he made his way to the mail pouches and began emptying letters and packages from the first one.

I'm still Harry Alexander, he told himself, and wondered what Christina Whitney would say.

But that's when his partner in the express car, Barney Drexel, said, "I know who you are!"

CHAPTER THIRTY

Drexel had his gun out, cocked, and aimed at Fallon's chest. Fallon flung the mail sack he had just emptied and dived to his left while reaching for his own revolver. The roar of the cannon the prison guard held left Fallon's ears ringing as he hit the floor and the bullet thudded into the wall.

Rolling over, Fallon got his pistol out and cocked, but the mail sack had missed its mark. Drexel already had eared back the hammer of the big revolver and started aiming. That's when the train must have rounded a curve. The men running the locomotive at full throttle in reverse almost derailed the whole damned train. The turn sent Drexel tumbling. Fallon's revolver barked but the bullet splintered the wall, and then Fallon was trying to get to his feet as the train straightened.

One of the guards tried to get to his feet, slipped, dropped hard onto his knees. Drexel put a bullet through his chest, and the man slammed against the safe, shuddered, and slumped forward.

"Mother of God!" the other guard yelled, and began crawling on hands and knees to the door. Drexel's gun roared again and the guard screamed, fell, rolled onto his back, and tried to sit up. Drexel shot him again, this time in his forehead, and the bullet tore out the back of his skull and sprayed the floor with the dead man's brains.

Fallon fired. Drexel fired. Then Drexel hurled his empty pistol at Fallon.

"I'll kill you with my bare hands!" the enraged prison sergeant bellowed, and he charged at Fallon.

Fallon fired, but missed because Drexel slipped on the blood-slickened floor. The brute came up. Fallon squeezed the trigger and cursed when the gun jammed. Now it was Fallon's turn to throw the useless revolver at the guard, but Drexel ducked, and the pistol disappeared in the mail, packages, and dead bodies.

Drexel rose, laughing. Fallon sprang forward, kicked out, but the big man caught Fallon's foot, twisted, and spun him to the floor.

"You double-crossing little worm," Drexel said.

Fallon came up, stumbled into the wall, turned around. Drexel wiped his bloody hands on his trousers. "I'm going to kill you."

He could have tried the lie he had been working on, could have reminded Drexel that he had been a lawman a lifetime ago, but Drexel had to know about Fallon's stint in Joliet. He was after revenge. Revenge, Drexel's hatred, was all that mattered right now. He had forgotten Colonel Justice's promise of glory, riches, and a new, stronger, invincible Confederate States of America.

So Fallon slipped his hand into his coat pocket.

"What the hell are you two doing?"

Fallon and Drexel both turned toward the voice from the door. "Traitors!" Cole Hansen said. "Wanting to steal the Colonel's money for yourself."

Cole Hansen stepped forward when Fallon shot him in the belly. The derringer he had taken from the conductor fired both barrels, instead of just one, and Hansen was driven back, tripping over the legs of the guard who had foolishly opened the door, slamming against the wall, then twisting, staggering onto the outside platform and falling off the side.

The door bounced open and shut, open and shut, open and shut.

Drexel spun around, threw a mail sack at Fallon. Beating out the flames on his coat pocket, Fallon hurled the empty derringer at Drexel.

Fallon tried to find another weapon he could use, but nothing looked promising that was within reach, but Drexel was ready now, moving like a snake, his eyes savage. Fallon could try for a crowbar in the corner, but Drexel would have reached him before he could have gotten a good grip on the weapon.

Drexel made a feint. Fallon bit, and the guard laughed.

"You are yellow," Drexel said, snorted, and spat.

Fallon brought his arms up, weaving, making a few jabs that Drexel easily ducked. Then it was the guard's turn. He shot out a quick right that glanced off Fallon's ear just as he turned and brought up his left arm to block another blow from the big sergeant. Fallon tried an uppercut, but Drexel's head tilted back and to the right. Then the sergeant hammered a left into Fallon's ribs. A little harder, and Fallon figured that punch might have cracked if not broken two or three ribs. The man punched like a steel-driving hammer.

Drexel worked three quick jabs. Fallon ducked, buried his fist into Drexel's stomach. The man gasped, and Fallon tried a haymaker punch, putting all his strength into the blow, but the fist failed to connect and the momentum carried Fallon past the guard. Drexel whirled, delivered a wicked punch into Fallon's kidneys, and as Fallon groaned and spun around, another fist caught Fallon just above his right eye. Drexel charged, seeing his chance to finish this fight— and Harry Fallon—quickly, but his big feet tripped over one of the murdered guards' legs.

He fell to his knees. Fallon tried to kick him, but for a big man, Drexel moved fast and his reflexes had kept him alive for many years. The toe of Fallon's shoe clipped Drexel's ear, and Drexel dropped to the floor, rolled over the corpse, and he popped to his feet as Fallon regained his balance, turned, and waited.

The door at the front of the coach kept bouncing as the train rattled down the tracks.

Both men heaved. Fallon's hair was already matted with sweat. Drexel wiped his brow with his left sleeve while keeping his right arm up, the hand balled into a huge, powerful fist.

The train rounded another curve, but this time both men leaned with the movement of the speeding train. When they straightened, Drexel resumed his attack. He feinted with the left, then swung hard with the right, a roundabout throw, that Fallon ducked under and came up with a left that glanced off Drexel's arm. The men spun around. Drexel tried to kick, but Fallon twisted, and jabbed with his left. One. Two. Three. He hit nothing but air.

They turned again, and Drexel cursed and came at Fallon hard, spreading out his arms, and Fallon made the mistake of trying to flatten the palm of his hand against the Adam's apple in Drexel's throat. Smash it. Crush the larynx and leave Drexel sucking in air that would not come. Instead, his hand caught the side of Drexel's neck, and Fallon felt the huge hands wrap around Fallon's back. The man started to squeeze, but before he could get that bear hug, that death grip, Fallon managed to bring his left knee up and catch Drexel in the groin.

The big sergeant groaned, and the train twisted around another bend, sending both men stumbling against the cabinet on the wall filled with letters. Drexel's back slammed hard into the wooden corner, and he let out a sharp cry. The blow caused him to lessen his hold, and Fallon rammed his knee harder into the man's privates.

Drexel's breath stank and he sent spittle into Fallon's face, nose, eyes. But Drexel also completely lost his grip. The arms fell back to the sergeant's sides, and Fallon fell away, landed on empty sacks, rolled over, and threw another mail package at Drexel that missed, hit the wall, and clattered on the floor.

By now the express car looked like it had gone through a derailment.

Fallon pushed himself to his feet and leaped aside as Drexel kicked at him again, having recovered from blows that would have left most men writhing in agony on the floor.

Standing, heaving, trying to find some way to stop Barney Drexel, Fallon saw the man as he ran again, lowering his shoulder. Again, Fallon had no place to go. Drexel's shoulder caught him in the chest, and the man's legs kept churning like a powerful draft horse, pushing Fallon back, back, back and into the door at the end of the car. The door splintered open, but this time ripped off its hinges, and both men fell onto the platform.

Fallon's head struck the iron railing, stunning him, blurring his vision, but Drexel hit the bars harder, and the man fell backward, clasping his broken nose that poured blood. As Fallon came up to a seated position, shaking his head to clear his vision, the door to the next car opened.

"What the hell is goin' on? Cole, where are . . . ?" a voice thundered, followed by the blast of a revolver.

"Ugghh."

Drexel doubled over in the doorway, straightened, and began staggering toward the opposite end of the platform.

"My God! My God! Barney!" a voice cried. A figure leaped onto the platform. Fallon just saw a shadow, and the smoking gun in the right hand of the newcomer. The gun clattered on the platform as the man reached with both hands to grab the waistband of Drexel's britches, to keep him from toppling over the railing.

"I didn't know it was you, Barney!" the man cried as he pulled Drexel up. "I didn't mean . . ."

"Get . . . him . . ." Drexel gasped, and started to point.

The figure turned around. Drexel crumpled to the floor. Fallon reached for the gun, grabbed the butt, pulled it forward as the man stepped into the light.

Josh Ryker.

Then Josh Ryker saw Fallon. He let out a savage

curse, dived, and drove Fallon against the hard platform floor. Fallon's knuckles almost felt as if they had been crushed into particles like sand. But his left hand was free, and despite the pain he pounded a fist into Ryker's temple.

The Colt slid off the platform, disappearing in the night.

The convict, who was supposed to be serving time at the Rusk unit since his brawl on Fallon's first day at The Walls, groaned and rolled off. Fallon started to rise, but Ryker jumped back on top of him. Ryker punched Fallon's forehead with his right. Fallon grunted, watched Ryker draw back his fist to bring it down again, but as he did, Fallon twisted his head, and Ryker's fist slammed into the flooring. The sound of breaking fingers was drowned out by Ryker's cry of agony. As the man straightened, Fallon lashed out with his free hand, and the blow drove Ryker toward the open doorway of the express car.

Fallon scrambled to a seated position. Ryker shook off the pain, reached inside the open doorway, and found a piece of timber. He brought it out, raised it over his head . . .

Ducking low, Fallon rushed forward. The small two-by-four piece of pine rattled against the banister of the platform. Fallon spun around, and swung out with his right. It caught Ryker's mouth, busting the lips wide open and breaking several teeth, as the outlaw turned around. The two-by-four dropped onto the platform. Ryker spit out blood and gore and made a weak swing that missed Fallon and twisted Ryker. The momentum carried Ryker to the other side of the platform. He landed hard. Then he was gone, toppling over . . . underneath the wheels of the other cars and engines.

If he screamed, Fallon did not hear it. Fallon was backing up, watching the gut-shot Barney Drexel come at him with the pinewood that Ryker had dropped onto the flooring.

Drexel stepped into the light that shone from the express car. Fallon saw that the prison sergeant's eyes were glassy and his face a deathly white. His shirt and vest were soaked in blood from the bullet Josh Ryker had accidentally put in the killer's gut. Fallon took a step back as Drexel swung out with the two-by-four.

When Drexel swung, he slipped on his own blood that now slickened the platform. The piece of pine clattered on the railing as Drexel dropped it and staggered into the crossing that connected the two cars. His arms waved over his head as he tried to regain his balance. Fallon watched as the man danced and spun his arms like a windmill that was out of control.

One second Barney Drexel was standing there, his eyes showing fear—not of death, for he must have known that the bullet in his stomach was a mortal wound, but the terrifying feeling of how he was going to die.

Just like Josh Ryker had. And maybe Cole Hansen.

Barney Drexel also disappeared in the night . . . and the *clickety-clack* of the wheels silenced his final screams, too.

Chapter Thirty-one

Fallon stood alone on the platform, his chest heaving, his body aching, letting the whistling, chilling wind revive him. He gripped the metal railing with his left hand and dully realized that he was alone, except for one guard, one living guard, out cold on the floor in the express car.

First, he absently massaged his knuckles while staring into the night and at the occasional sparks that the iron wheels sent skyward. Fallon had no idea where they were going or where those men who had hijacked the locomotive planned on stopping the train.

It couldn't be long, Fallon thought. Chances were another engine would be screaming down the rails, and a collision would not help Colonel Justice's cause. What Fallon couldn't figure out, though, was why they would hijack an entire train just for the money in the express car.

Unless . . .

He wet his lips, swallowed what moisture he could summon up in his mouth, and slid to the crossing. Ryker had left the door open to the adjoining car, and

Fallon moved in that direction, careful not to slip on the blood.

When he stepped inside, he saw the dim glow of the lantern. No one was in this car. Fallon felt certain of that, because someone would have come out during the fight—although Josh Ryker had taken a long time before he summoned up enough nerve to see what had been keeping Cole Hansen so long.

After turning up the flame in the lantern, Fallon squinted until his eyes became used to the light.

"Damn," Fallon whispered.

Two guards lay dead in a corner, one with a bullet between his eyes, the other with his throat cut, but what prompted Fallon's curse weren't the corpses— he had seen far too many over the past several months to be bothered by more victims of violent deaths anymore—but the cargo being carried in this car.

Lining the wall to Fallon's left were wooden crates piled halfway to the ceiling, and stenciled into the sides on the boxes that Fallon could see were the words:

WINCHESTER REPEATING ARMS C^o
New Haven, Connecticut

Stacked on Fallon's right were other boxes, some smaller ones, a few long enough to hold dozens of rifles, but with different shipping labels: COLT'S PATENT FIRE ARMS MANUFACTURING COMPANY, HARTFORD, CONNECTICUT; REMINGTON ARMS COMPANY, BRIDGEPORT, CONNECTICUT; VOLCANIC REPEATING ARMS, NORWICH, CONNECTICUT; UNION METALLIC CARTRIDGE COMPANY, BRIDGEPORT, CONNECTICUT; MARLIN FIREARMS COMPANY, NEW HAVEN, CONNECTICUT; HOPKINS & ALLEN

ARMS COMPANY, NORWICH, CONNECTICUT; THE SHARPS
RIFLE COMPANY, BRIDGEPORT, CONNECTICUT. At the far
end kegs labeled GUNPOWDER reached all the way to
the ceiling in four rows.

Four giant boxes were labeled GATLING GUN COM-
PANY, ORTONVILLE, MICHIGAN.

If a man wanted to start a war . . .

Shaking off that thought, Fallon hurried to the
crates of Winchesters, but something else caught his
attention.

Stopping, Fallon knelt to pick up a newspaper. The
paper was folded, but Fallon saw that it came from the
Dallas Independent something-another. The crumpled
paper had been folded in half. It was the headline,
written in large, boldfaced capital letters, that made
Fallon stop.

TEXAS A.G.

Fallon turned the folded paper over and felt that
brutal punch to his stomach. The final word was:

ASSASSINATED!

He quickly started reading the story, scanning over
the date and the location, getting past the overblown
prose that talked about the mourning in the Texas
capital and the "biggest blow to America since the callous killing of President Lincoln almost one score and
two lustrums earlier . . ."

A Dallas newspaper lamenting the loss of Abra-
ham Lincoln. Certainly, the War Between the States
was over.

Malcolm Maxwell, the erudite and brave attorney general who had made justice for one and all, was brutally butchered—stabbed with knives and tomahawks, brained with clubs and pistol butts, and shot at least four times as the unsuspecting man was stepping out of Humphreys's Hotel to hail a hack and be driven back to work after meeting with high-level government officials in Austin's finest hotel.

Fallon's first thought was about himself. Malcolm Maxwell had the affidavit that explained that Harry Fallon, alias Harry Alexander, was not a criminal and was in fact working for the attorney general's office through the American Detective Agency of Chicago.

That didn't matter, though, he quickly told himself. A brave man, a good man, a man committed to justice just as the *Dallas Independent Daily Crier* had declared, had been savagely murdered.

But now Fallon knew just how completely alone he was. The operatives working with him thought he was at Hell on the Brazos. By now, they might think he had been killed. The highest-ranking government official who knew Fallon for what he truly was—and that he wasn't a wanted man—was dead. No one in his or her right mind would call Fallon a coward for trying to save his own skin and get away. He had done his job. He had done more than his share.

This wasn't his fight anyway.

"The hell it isn't," he said, and looked back at the newspaper.

An Austin policeman and a hotel employee had been injured while rushing to the defense of the attorney general, but both were expected to recover from their wounds and the Texas governor had praised the men for the valiant if in-vain efforts to save Malcolm Maxwell's life.

A Texas Ranger also came along, firing his Colt revolver at the cowardly assassins, one of whom returned fire but the Ranger, a man the *Independent Daily Crier* identified as Fred Bennett, ducked behind the solidly built corner of the hotel and escaped harm.

The Ranger, however, had seen enough to recognize one of the assassins.

Fallon read the name aloud. "Josh Ryker."

He looked back at the open doorway.

"Well, Mr. Maxwell," Fallon said softly, "I got one of your killers for you."

He skimmed through the rest of the newspaper article, turning the page to read the jump.

The two other assassins were killed by Ranger Bennett as they ran for their horses at a nearby hitching rail, but only Josh Ryker got away.

Ryker had spent time in and out of prisons over the past several years, the reporter stated, accurately, too, after spending much of his youth as a cowboy pushing cattle to the trail's ends in Kansas. He had been sentenced to twelve years at The Walls in Huntsville, but while being transferred to the Rusk unit, he had managed to escape. His reasons for joining in the brutal assassination were not known to the local police detectives investigating the foul crime or friends and colleagues of the late attorney general.

Fallon turned back to the front page to make sure he had read the date accurately. It all fit, Fallon decided. Josh Ryker would have had time to get from the road to Rusk to Austin, take part in the murder of the attorney general, and train for his role in the train heist.

It also meant—though Fallon had never doubted that for one second—that Josh Ryker's presence here proved that the murder of Malcolm Maxwell and the robbery of this train were connected. And the man behind the attorney general's assassination was Colonel Josiah Jonathan Justice.

"But who else?" Fallon asked, and finished reading the article. The attorney general left behind a grieving widow, active in the First Methodist Church of Austin, Texas, three daughters, a son, and two grandchildren. Funny, Fallon thought, he never figured Maxwell to have grandbabies. The man didn't look that old.

There were praises from Texas senators, Texas Rangers, a judge, the attorney general's barber, and descendants of Sam Houston. The deputy attorney general had been selected as Maxwell's interim replacement. Fallon read the name three times, but the new attorney general meant nothing to him.

He started to wad up the Dallas paper and throw it against the wall, but went back to the front page and skimmed over headlines and news items, wondering if there might be any mention of Harry Alexander, even an obituary that said he was dead. He didn't find anything, which he hadn't truly expected. He found nothing that might have anything to do with everything that was going on in Texas, and elsewhere, right now. Nothing about The Walls in Huntsville. Nothing about detectives. Nothing about Colonel Justice.

Now Fallon threw down the paper. He considered his options.

He had no options. He was aboard a runaway train and this whole damned operation kept spinning out of control.

Maybe the most important man in the operation— the man who had hired the American Detective Agency, or at the least had gotten the state to hire Sean MacGregor's operatives—was dead. Murdered. The Dallas newspaper had gotten it right. Assassinated.

"Justice," Fallon whispered, "you're a vile creature."

Yet he couldn't just squat here on the floor and do nothing but curse his luck.

Fallon had work to do, and he needed to do it fast.

Where to start? He looked at the crates. This wasn't just a holdup for the money next door in the express car. This armory had to be part of Justice's scheme.

That's why so many of Justice's soldiers had been trained as quartermasters—learning how to load, unload, balance weights, stuff like that.

He stood, moved toward the crates and crates of weapons. The Winchesters were first. Fallon didn't know exactly what to look for, but he decided to see where the guns were being shipped to. The army? It wasn't just some rich man out West who wanted a few guns to take his equally wealthy friends hunting.

On the smaller side of the boxes, facing the walkway between the rifle crates and the Gatling guns, he found an answer—although Fallon could not make a good guess as to what the answer meant. The closest Winchester box was being shipped to Ferguson's Hardware, Wilsonville, Texas. If the crate had been accurately labeled, this box held .44-40 caliber

Model 1873 Winchester rifles. The box above it, also filled with .44-40 rifles, was bound for Junior's Firearms, Carson Fork, Territory of New Mexico.

Fallon glanced at a few other crates, then quickly moved across the aisle to the closest crate containing a Gatling gun. He shot another quick look at the two dead guards and the one still unconscious. They weren't wearing army uniforms. The label on the crate said that the first Gatling gun was bound for Major R. C. Romero, Ejército Mexicano, but the destination was the Port of Indianola, Texas, where the weapons would be shipped to the Mexican Army in Vera Cruz. Fallon drew in a breath, let it out slowly. Indianola? He remembered the newspaper editor he had met from the *Texas Times* in Indianola. All right, there was nothing against the law for the Gatling Gun Company of Ortonville, Michigan, to sell a weapon to a foreign power. Gatlings had been sold not only to the United States, but Russia, England, France . . . and likely many other countries. Fallon looked at the other boxes from the Gatling Gun Company, and discovered all four crates were bound for Major R. K. Concepción. R. K. . . . R. K. . . . R. K. C. . . . R. K. C.? What did that stand for? Republic of Killer Confederates?

"Don't be joking at a time like this," Fallon told himself.

Fallon snapped his fingers, which he regretted briefly because it hurt his right hand. But he had been able to snap his fingers, despite the brutalized knuckles and all the punches he had thrown.

"Rufus K. Conley," he said aloud. "*R . . . K . . . C.*"

Rufus K. Conley, also a major, editor of the *Texas*

Times in Indianola. Coincidence? Fallon shook his head. He didn't think so.

"Wait a damned minute," Fallon whispered aloud, and he crossed the aisle. He found the crate of Winchesters—no, three crates—to be delivered to Lee's Mercantile, Indianola, Texas, and another bound for Pickett's Hardware & Sundries, Indianola, Texas. As he moved down the aisle and looked on the other side of the car, he found Colts bound for a gun store in Indianola—Stonewall's, in fact—and crate of Sharps rifles going to McCulloch's Hardware in Indianola. Kegs of powder were going to Stuart's Hardware in Indianola, and Hampton's Mercantile appeared to be getting ammunition and two boxes of Colt's revolving pistols, .44-40 caliber, so the slugs would fit the Winchester repeating rifles heading to Lee's Mercantile or Pickett's Hardware & Sundries.

Lee . . . Pickett . . . Stonewall . . . McCulloch . . . Stuart . . . Hampton. Names of generals who had fought for the Confederacy. Of course, in a state like Texas, or Arkansas, or other Southern states, a visitor could find a lot of businesses named after those heroes of the Lost Cause. But how many hardware stores and gun shops could a town like Indianola, all but wiped out by a pair of devastating hurricanes in the 1870s and 1880s, support? Fallon didn't think, from what he remembered reading, that Indianola could support even a newspaper. It was a damned ghost town.

But some gun salesman in on the eastern coast would not know that. He wouldn't likely even give a damn because the commission—if salesmen for these companies earned a commission—on sales of this scale would buy his wife or mistress a lot of jewelry and keep him in quality brandy instead of forty-rod rotgut.

There was also a crate of Sharps carbines bound for the Indianola marshal's office, but the name of the marshal left Fallon uttering a soft curse under his breath: Rufus K. Conley.

It appeared the newspaper editor of the local rag in Indianola also served as the city policeman.

Suddenly, another thought crossed Fallon's mind.

CHAPTER THIRTY-TWO

He wasn't thinking of his dead wife. He wasn't thinking of his murdered baby daughter. He wasn't thinking at all about revenge, which was all that had been driving him since he had gotten that awful news in Joliet a hellish eternity ago.

Hell, he wasn't even thinking about avenging the cowardly assassination of Malcolm Maxwell, attorney general for the state of Texas.

Somehow, this would point to the men or the one man who was responsible for framing Fallon, for ruining his life, for wiping out Fallon's family. Maybe that man was Chris Ehrlander. But right now, Fallon wasn't even thinking about the lawyer from Fort Smith who was now working for Colonel Justice.

He was thinking about the United States of America. He was thinking about all the horrible stories he had heard in Fort Smith bars, in camps out in the Indian Nations, even on those old trail drives and buffalo hunts. He had been born too late to serve in the Civil War. His mother used to tell him that he should thank God every night in his prayers that he had been born too late to *"see that awful elephant,"* his mother would drawl.

As a kid, naturally, Fallon had figured that war was nothing but fun and glory, daring deeds, and waving sabers and winning battles for the good of your country and the medals some general, or maybe even the president himself, would pin on your chest before a grand gathering in the state capital or even Washington City.

Now Fallon knew better. He had seen men with wooden legs or no legs at all. Men with eye patches. With scars. Missing fingers. With hollowed-out looks on their faces. There had been that man in one of the buffalo camps who woke up screaming. Twice he had woken up and found his gun and fired it empty into the stars because he had not seen the Big Dipper but George Custer leading his Michigan cavalry boys in a charge against the skinner's Confederate boys in Virginia.

Fallon had ridden with federal marshals who had fought in the Civil War, some wearing the blue, others fighting for the South, and more than a handful of bushwhackers from Missouri and Red Legs from Kansas. Most of them never talked about the battles. The ones, Fallon learned, who bragged about all they had done during the late war, usually were liars.

War is hell. War was hell. War would always be hell.

So were prisons.

Fallon wanted no part of either.

Things were starting to add up, Fallon thought. Maybe. And if they added up to something, Fallon hadn't quite grasped the final answer.

The voice of American Detective Agency operative Christina Whitney rang through Fallon's mind, drowning out the metallic noise of speeding iron wheels and the creaking of the express cars.

"Say what you're thinking out loud," Christina Whitney had instructed Fallon, *"whether you're bouncing your thoughts off another operative or operatives, or just thinking out loud to hear how it sounds to you."* They had been in Alabama, not far from the piney forests of Spanish Fort, near the site of Fort Blakeley, where some Union general—Canby, if Fallon remembered right—had led his forces against starving Confederates and captured the earthworks, securing Mobile Bay for the Union.

The irony of the battle? The fight had happened just hours after Robert E. Lee had surrendered to General Ulysses S. Grant between seven hundred and eight hundred miles away at Appomattox Court House in Virginia.

"Talking to yourself doesn't mean you're insane," Christina had said with a warm smile. *"It even can help you keep control of your faculties."*

Fallon wet his lips as he studied the crates of weapons and ammunition and kegs of gunpowder.

"The weapons are being stolen from individual stores—not the U.S. Army," he said. "Maybe some of the stores aren't real. The ones in Indianola, for instance. Carson Fork. Wilsonville. Maybe those are real. Probably are real."

He nodded. That sounded just about right. He could see how things might happen after the cargo was hauled off this train and taken, probably south of the border into Mexico.

A businessman in Wilsonville, Texas, complains to Winchester that his order of rifles has been stolen by bandits in Texas. Winchester tells Wilsonville that as soon as it gets its money back from the express company in charge of delivering the cargo safe and sound the Wilsonville store will get its money back. Same with the outfit in Carson Fork, New Mexico Territory. Some pencil pusher with an abacus in Connecticut might take a long time before he figured out just how much money Winchester was out. Steal from the federal army and the secretary of war, and the president would spare no expense to go after the bandits. Winchester would likely hire some private detectives—maybe from the American Detective Agency but the Pinkertons if the Winchester brass had any business sense—to go after the outlaws.

"The Mexican Army won't care a whit about four missing Gatling guns," Fallon said aloud, "because the Mexican Army never ordered those guns. They came from Major Rufus K. Conley of the *Texas Times* in Indianola."

He moved down the aisle again, staring at the shipping labels.

Winchester would be out the most. Colt would be second. The others . . . ? Fallon shook his head.

He spoke again in a quiet but controlled voice. "Remington won't think much about losing three boxes. Same with Marlin, Hopkins & Allen, Sharps. Union Metallic makes cartridges. The gunpowder? These kegs come from various companies. Not enough for anyone other than a pesky detective or maybe a newspaper reporter to think a whole lot about it."

He stared at another box. "Volcanic Repeating Arms," he said aloud. "What the hell is Volcanic Repeating Arms?" Then he remembered. "Didn't they buy out or merge with or something like that with Smith & Wesson?" His head nodded, and he said, "That's it. That's Smith & Wesson. So Smith & Wesson loses two boxes of revolvers, one bound for Julian, California, the other for Prescott, Arizona. They likely won't think a whole lot about that. Probably won't occur to them that they lost both gun boxes on the same train."

But . . . ?

Again he looked at the high stacks of Winchesters and a fair number of boxes from Colt.

"There's no way Colt and Winchester will dismiss losing that many guns," he said. "That's too big a loss for even the most idiotic of an accountant. They'd have to alert the government." Fallon shook his head. "The Texas Rangers? The hard cases that I've known to ride for that group would swim from Indianola to get those guns back and kill anyone who dared try to stop them."

Fallon had reached the far end of the rocking railroad car. The door was barred shut. He tried to remember how many cars were ahead of him. He stupidly had not been paying that much attention, just lying on the ground, listening to the wheels as the train braked to a stop, thinking only—as he and others had been trained—to do his job, and only his job.

Of course, he didn't have to go through the car. He could step onto the platform, climb the iron hand- and footholds, and cross the roof. Leap into the tinder and all that coal—this train wasn't one of those wood-burning locomotives—and . . . and then what? Could he stop the engine?

Another lesson echoed inside his head, but this

one came from Dan MacGregor and not Christina Whitney. *"Know what you're getting into, Fallon. Don't step into a fight without knowing everything—and everything includes a way out."*

He didn't know how many other cars were now filled with men hired by Colonel Justice and, most likely, Major Rufus K. Conley—and who else.

"But," he said, "I know what's happening in this car and the one immediately behind me."

He looked at the lantern before his gaze fell upon the kegs of gunpowder.

"Destroy the guns. Without guns, Justice can't launch his new war."

His stomach turned a little queasy.

This part he didn't want to say out loud.

Blow up this car, and he'd kill everyone on the train, most likely, including himself. Oh, Fallon could toss the lantern from the doorway and then leap over the platform and pray for something soft to land upon. But at this rate, twenty, maybe as much as twenty-five or even thirty miles per hour, Fallon would likely break practically every bone in his body—and that's if he didn't bounce off the embankment and underneath the rails and be disemboweled like Ryker, Drexel, and Hansen might have been a few minutes earlier.

From the lights he had seen when the train was pulling into the water stop, Fallon had figured that this was not just a freight but a freight-and-passenger run. Blow up the train, and more innocent people would die.

He couldn't uncouple the cars—even if that was possible for a man who had ridden trains but never worked them—since the engine was in reverse. Uncouple the car and the engine would still be pushing them.

Unless . . .

Fallon whispered to himself.

"Unless the engine stops. The engine stops, there's a chance these cars keep rolling. Rolling away from the passenger cars. It rolls far enough."

He wet his lips and massaged his right hand.

"Far enough," he said, "and then I can toss a lantern into the kegs of gunpowder. Blow Colonel Justice's arsenal to kingdom come."

He frowned.

"And what about you?" he asked himself. "If you don't break your leg or neck, there's still a probable chance that you get killed by exploding bullets, shrapnel, pieces of the train as they rain down on you."

He cursed and moved toward the open doorway.

"There's one thing you have to be aware of," Christina had told him. *"You can get killed. That's why you don't want to get close to anyone. You don't want to."* She had lifted her eyes and stared at him for a long time. *"Did you think about that as a lawman?"*

"You tried not to," he had told her. *"But I knew . . . my . . . wife . . . thought about it all the time. And . . . it was always there, in the back of my mind."* He had chuckled. *"We always thought just like most of the outlaws we were hunting thought. They had a creed, too. We followed theirs."*

* * *

Fallon stepped onto the platform, his feet sticking against the drying blood, and went into the express car.

He spoke the creed of outlaws in the Indian Nations and deputy federal marshals in Judge Parker's court aloud.

"If you got to die, die game."

CHAPTER THIRTY-THREE

Colonel Justice wasn't just promising his new recruits a new Confederate States of America, he had also been offering them wealth. That's where the money was meant to go, because Fallon didn't believe most of the recruits were that interested in avenging perceived Yankee atrocities or reinstituting slavery. Not after almost thirty years. No, Fallon had been a federal lawman long enough and had spent more than enough time in various prisons with various criminals to know that most of them wanted only one thing.

Money.

Here in sacks scattered about the floor of the express car that was beginning to reek of death lay one of Colonel Josiah Jonathan Justice's payrolls.

He knelt beside the unconscious guard, shoved him, harder, slapped his face. Nothing. He checked to make sure the man was still alive and felt breath on the back of his hand. But the guard remained out cold—and even had Fallon been able to rouse him, the man wouldn't have been able to help at all.

"Enjoy your rest," he said, and sighed and moved toward the safe.

Fallon strained to lift the heavy sack, gave up, and dragged the money-filled canvas bag across the floor, around the corpses, grunting. He wasn't weak, and he doubted if the sack weighed more than seventy pounds, but a doctor employed by the American Detective Agency had warned him, and other operatives, that the human body can tolerate a finite amount of stress. Muscles can freeze up. The brain can practically go to sleep. Emotions can go in opposite extremes. Fallon's muscles did not want to cooperate, and that right hand of his had started throbbing again.

It didn't matter.

He wasn't going to collapse on the floor. He would neither burst into tears nor drop into a heap and fall asleep. He couldn't black out, either, for he had too much to do. Fallon glanced at the regulator clock on the wall, noted the time, and backed out of the express car onto the platform. Once the sack lay on the hard floor, Fallon pushed it to the southern side. Southern, he told himself, providing that they were traveling west. He glanced at the sky, but clouds covered the stars and the moon, if there was a moon tonight.

Now Fallon squatted, pushed open the gate that allowed passengers to disembark from the car off the platform, and he shoved the sack into the darkness.

How much money had he just thrown into the darkness, into the rough land? What would the express agency have to say about that? What would Sean MacGregor say when he learned what Fallon had done?

Fallon didn't give a tinker's damn.

He might not win any medals. He might be sued, fired, or thrown back into Joliet to finish his original sentence with a few years tacked on. But, by thunder, Colonel Justice wouldn't be using this money to start another Civil War. He wouldn't be able to pay men to kill hardworking, honest attorney generals.

His back hurt. His thigh muscles tightened. Fallon ignored the pain and his body's revolt and he returned into the express car.

Another bag filled with stolen money waited. Hell, there were a lot of bags. He made note, if only mentally, of the time, and lifted another sack. This one was much lighter, for it carried only paper currency. Fallon grabbed at another sack, but missed, almost tumbled to his knees and against the cabinet of cubbyholes. He couldn't risk falling.

If he hit the floor, he might not be able to get back up. He found himself weaving toward the open door, and not because of the train's wobbly movement. He was falling apart. Weariness was taking its toll, but Fallon made it out into the darkness again. He hoped the wind would revive him. Instead, it left him shivering. Fallon sucked in a deep breath, exhaled, and tightened the open end of this sack. He tightened it as best he could, knowing that wind could carry the money to Houston, Beaumont, into the Gulf of Mexico, to Louisiana, or parts unknown. He dropped it over the side and into the darkness, then without taking time to think again about all that he was doing, he stepped back into the express car.

He remained cold and kept right on shivering. The wind did cool down the temperature outside, but this was Texas, and not just Texas but the southern part of Texas. In the late part of spring, and people knew there rarely was anything that resembled true spring in this part of the state. There was summer. There was late summer. There was Indian summer. There was no fall, not much of a winter, and spring might last a week or two before summer started again. In short, Texas was hell. But Fallon kept on trembling, feeling cold as he had felt that time in the Nations in February when the blue norther came upon him without warning and he had spent two days and three nights in a miserable cave that barely held him and maybe two thirds of his horse.

Fallon grabbed another sack and thanked the Lord that this one was as light as the last one he had tossed off the train. He looked at the clock again, had to strain his eyes to make certain of the time. His eyes burned, and he opened his mouth and tasted salt on his tongue.

"Damn," he said. "I'm sweating."

Sick. Malaria? He'd never had that before. A bad fever? Or was this part of the body's reaction to extreme stress?

It didn't matter. Fallon wiped his brow, aware of the dampness that started at his armpits and soaked both sides of his shirt down to his hips. His heart pounded. He found it difficult to get his lungs to suck in enough air.

But he kept right on working. Doing his job. Foiling, at least temporarily, Colonel Josiah Jonathan Justice and his nefarious operation.

He was outside again, freezing in the biting wind. He smelled smoke, saw cinders in the distance from the smokestack of the locomotive. He headed toward the railing, stopped, and turned.

"You damned fool," he said. "The other side. Toss the sacks on the southern side. The right side, if this isn't south. *Right* meaning to my right when I come out of the door toward the engine that's in reverse."

Would he remember that?

He came to the edge and pitched the bag into the darkness.

After wiping sweat again, fighting back a cough, and turning around, he needed to grip the exterior wall with his left hand to help him make it back into the express car.

Fallon looked at the clock again, took five steps toward the bags filled with money, and stopped. He had already forgotten what time it was.

Write it down, he thought, but shook his head.

How do you explain that if Justice or Drexel or Chris Ehrlander find those times in your pocket? Just remember what time it was. And what time it was when this scheme of getting rid of the money started.

He moved, stopped, and cursed himself again.

Drexel? You don't have to explain anything to Drexel. Drexel's miles to the east. Coyotes and other critters of the night are feasting on his guts.

He bent, took a firm grip on another sack, and heaved. The bag did not budge but almost pulled him onto the floor. Wouldn't that have been a hell of a thing? Fallon thought.

The whistle screamed, startling Fallon.

He knew about signals engineers used, but he couldn't remember what they were. Or what this signal might have meant since, unless some of Justice's men had developed a conscience, the engineer and the fire-man who had started this run were back near the trellis lying dead beside the tracks.

Which also got Fallon thinking.

They had blown up the bridge. No eastbound trains would be coming through until that trellis was rebuilt. No westbound engines, either. Work crews would be taking trains or handcarts, and anyone traveling from the west would be certain to notice the money sacks along the railroad company's right-of-way. So ideally Fallon would need to have someone find that money first, someone with an honest streak. About the only person to come to mind was Christina Whitney, and Fallon had no idea where she was. Yet that was the least of his problems. If some poor Irish refugee happened upon a sack containing tens of thousands of U.S. script, or a few hundred bucks in Morgan dollars, or a tremendous amount of wealth in double eagle gold coins, so be it. This was, after all, America.

For the time being.

He saw the rolling cart against the wall for the first time, and cursed himself for his blindness and his failure to think everything through. Had he seen that pushcart earlier . . .

Well, that was spilt milk. He staggered across the weaving car to the wall, grabbed the cart, and guided it and its squeaking wheels to the piles of bags filled with money. Fallon lifted those onto the cart, and now his muscles did not seem to rebel. Once he had the remaining few bags loaded, he had to summon just about his last ounce of strength to pull himself off the floor. But at least he had the cart's handles to lean on, and though it was hard to push, he managed to get the cart to the wall next to the open door.

From here, it would be a lot easier to get those bags thrown over the edge.

He picked the heaviest one first, and that practically left him numb and exhausted. But he refused to quit. He couldn't quit.

He dragged the next bag to the edge, and then that damn whistle screamed again.

It had to be a signal, but Fallon's trainers, and more important, Josiah Jonathan Justice, had decided that men on the train with their own jobs to do had no need to learn what any whistle blasts meant. Fallon could guess. He guessed that they had to be getting close to the end of this train ride.

They weren't heading to San Antonio or Corpus Christi—not unless those two cities had followed Colonel Justice's insane plan and had withdrawn from Texas and the Union.

Indianola? The thought caused Fallon to straighten. He found more strength and got the last bags tossed off into the night. Now, all Fallon had to do was unhook the coupler and separate the last of the cars with the train. Then he could blow the ammunition and arsenal to oblivion.

He pushed the cart away from the wall and the door, and his feet felt the stickiness of the dried blood on the platform.

"Plan ahead," Dan MacGregor had often told him. "Think what might happen. Think about anything that could happen."

Christina Whitney had added: "And have an answer for

everything in case something doesn't work out exactly how you had planned."

If he survived. If the arsenal wasn't destroyed. If and if and if and if. Fallon shoved the cart farther, and then he saw the two dead guards. Well, those men were beyond caring, and if they were looking down upon Fallon from the hereafter, maybe they wouldn't mind at all having their bodies to help with the cause. But what about the man knocked cold? He was still alive and likely didn't want to die.

Maybe if I put him outside, on another platform . . . Fallon swore. *If he doesn't just roll off onto the tracks and under the wheels.* His head shook. *Hell, let me see if I can get the cars uncoupled first.*

Remembering a crowbar over by the cabinets, Fallon walked there, bent, grabbed it, and started for the other car, the one with the gunpowder and arms that Justice planned on using for his new Southern states.

Separate the cars. When the train stops, the momentum will carry the rest of the train forward. Fallon would turn up a lantern and toss it against the kegs of gunpowder. Then he'd pray that he could figure out how to stay alive.

That was what kept running through Fallon's head as he moved toward the door. That was the last thing he remembered except for the whistle of the engine blaring one more time, the jarring sound of the brakes, and the floor rushing up to meet Fallon as he fell hard and the train began its screaming way to a sudden stop somewhere in the predawn hours and somewhere in the southern part of Texas.

CHAPTER THIRTY-FOUR

The savage slap across his right cheek brought Fallon around. His eyes opened, but he saw nothing but colorful shapes. His face burned from the powerful hand. The back of his head hurt. Hell, his entire body ached.

The hand came around, a backhand this time, and the knuckles dug into Fallon's face, brushed past his nose.

"Wake up, you dumb horse's ass," a voice Fallon recognized spoke, and Fallon felt the spittle from the man's mouth showering his face.

The hand lowered to the one gripping Fallon's shirt, and both hands shook Fallon like a playful dog with a sock. "Wake up." Fallon felt himself bouncing around, his neck snapping one way, then the other, before the earthquake ceased, and the right hand grabbed Fallon's hair and pulled.

"Are you going to wake up or do I cut your throat?"

Fallon still couldn't see clearly, but his voice was firm. "You lay another hand on me, Holderman, and you'll be choking on your own blood."

Now Fallon saw Aaron Holderman, ex-convict,

first-class lout, and operative for the American Detective Agency, drawing back his left hand as Fallon balled his own two fists.

"That's enough, Holderman," another voice said. Fallon recognized it, as well. His head turned, and Aaron Holderman let go of his grip on Fallon's hair.

Fallon spit out blood. He could use a drink of water, but he knew better than to ask for that.

The maniac of several Southern and Texas plantations, Colonel Josiah Jonathan Justice knelt in the express car, dressed in the resplendent uniform of a Confederate cavalry officer. Only if Fallon remembered the insignia right, this wasn't a colonel but a general. And the uniform's frock coat did not smell of mothballs, nor did it look thirty years old. It was made by a tailor, and quite recently. Justice wore a plumed hat, the purple ostrich feather stuck in the right side, which was pinned up with a large golden Texas star.

"Where the hell is the money, Private Alexander?" Justice demanded.

Fallon squinted, shook his head, pretending to be groggier than he really was, hoping to buy some time, stalling to come up with a decent answer. He had failed at his mission to blow the weapons up, but at least Justice didn't have all that money.

"Damn it, mister, what happened to the money?"

Fallon rubbed his head.

Footsteps sounded, and another pair of gray pants with yellow stripes came into Fallon's view. A Texas drawl said, "No sign of Drexel, Gen'ral Justice. No sign of Ryker and Hansen, neither, suh."

Fallon's head rose to stare up at the newcomer. "Well, suh," the madman said, "if you'd taken care of

Ryker in Austin as you were ordered, maybe I wouldn't have had to use him."

It hurt to raise his head, but Fallon made himself get a look at the tall, lean man wearing the Confederate uniform of a major. He had a gray mustache and goatee and wore a big, black Texas sombrero, with a pair of Colts, butt forward, belted across his waist.

"Yes, suh," the man said, though those cold blue eyes burned with hatred.

"See if you can get what I need to know from this silent fellow, Captain Bennett," Justice said as he pushed himself to his feet. "It is not befitting that a general and a man of property like myself be reduced to such vile, low interrogations."

As the cotton king rose, the leathery Texan came down to his knees. His eyes were hard.

"My name's Fred Bennett," he said, slowly drawing the Colt on his left hip. "I'll ask you once. If you don't answer, I'll scatter your brains across this car. You savvy?"

Oh, Fallon savvied, all right. This was the Texas Ranger he had read about, the hero who had tried, according to that Dallas newspaper, to prevent the cold-blooded murder of Texas Attorney General Malcolm Maxwell. He was the man who had killed two of the assassins and must have recognized the third, Josh Ryker. It made sense now. What were the chances that a Texas Ranger would recognize a two-bit thief and thug like Ryker? Or would happen to be outside Humphreys's Hotel in Austin when the murder took place? Bennett had been there for another reason. It often played out this way, Fallon figured. The first rule to pull off an assassination is to kill the assassins. Ryker had foiled the play by escaping—and forced Justice to use him in the train robbery. Ryker would probably have been killed had he lived through the holdup, but Fallon had foiled that plan by killing Ryker himself.

Bennett's presence also meant something else. The late Malcolm Maxwell had been right. This conspiracy went all the way to at least one of the Texas Rangers. The attorney general had been wise in bringing in an outside detective agency, and not the Texas Rangers.

"Drexel . . ." Fallon began, still shaking his head. "Ryker." He lifted one hand to his head as if trying to clear his addled brain. "Double cross."

Colonel—make that *General*—Justice knelt back down.

"What?" the magnate exclaimed.

"We got the safe open," Fallon said, nodding at the wreckage. "I remember seeing the door open. Ryker came in. Then Drexel—he was right behind me—I saw a movement, the flash of gunmetal." He sighed and gently touched the knot on his head. "That was it. The lights went out."

"And Major Hansen?" Justice asked.

"I don't know, sir. Never saw him."

"Why didn't they kill ya?" the Texas Ranger asked.

Fallon turned and glared. "Feel the size of this knot, Bennett. Drexel damn sure tried."

It was Aaron Holderman who stepped behind Fallon, grabbed Fallon's wrist, and flung it away from the back of Fallon's skull. Then Holderman put his own meaty fingers over the bloody, sticky, swollen lump. Fallon cringed, ground his teeth, and somehow managed to stifle a curse. Holderman's fingers felt like brass knuckles.

"It's legit," Holderman said. "But he might could have done it hisself. You know. When the train stops, he grabs that timber yonder, or uses his own gun, knocks hisself out. So we don't hang him as a traitor?"

"Knocks himself out?" Fred Bennett rolled his eyes. "Don't be an idiot." The former Ranger looked again at Fallon. "So what do you think, buster?"

Fallon didn't bother trying out a theory. What a man like Fred Bennett was looking for was to get Fallon to trip himself up, but Fallon wouldn't take that bait.

"Mister . . ." he started.

"It's Capt'n, buster," Bennett corrected. "Capt'n Bennett. Don't forget that." He waved the long barrel under Fallon's nose.

"Captain," Fallon said, though no trace of respect could be found in the tone. "I told you all I know. The safe was open. I started pulling money out. I saw Ryker . . ."

"And how did you know Ryker?"

"We were in The Walls together."

Bennett glanced at Holderman. "They was there," the big detective said. "Didn't like each other."

The Ranger stared again at Fallon. "Then what?"

"Then Drexel tried to stove in my head," Fallon said bitterly.

"And you didn't think something was up when Ryker come in from the car where he was supposed to be getting the guns ready?"

"I didn't know a damn thing about what was in the other car. I still don't know. That's not how we were trained. And besides, I didn't have a whole lot of time to think anything. I saw Ryker. Drexel. I caught a glimpse of a pistol. And that's all."

Josiah Jonathan Justice's secretive—or nontrusting—way of training suddenly made sense to Fallon. If the outlaws hijacking the engine knew about a fortune in gold, silver, and currency in the express car, greed might enter their minds. Same with the car filled with a fortune in weapons and ammunition. Justice ruled not as a compassionate general like Robert E. Lee. He had the mind of a thief and outlaw, like Jesse James or Bob Dalton.

"When did they get off with the money?" Justice demanded.

Fallon let out a faint chuckle that lacked any humor. "I wouldn't know, but my guess is it happened right after they knocked me out. As soon as they could. Toss the sacks out, then leap. Before . . . where the hell are we?"

The turncoat Ranger and the insane leader stared at each other. Neither bothered to answer Fallon's question.

"That bridge we blew is forty-two miles from here," Bennett said.

"Tell me something useful, Capt'n," General Justice belted back. "I know the distance to the gorge, an' I know that it's useless—for now—to do anything but get our arms to safety. Other Rangers, men with integrity, will be heading this way quickly."

"We cut the telegraph lines," Aaron Holderman said. "Blew the bridge."

Justice turned to the detective. "I do not recall asking you to join this conversation, Private."

Stepping back, Holderman dropped his head.

"What about the money, suh?" Bennett asked.

"Hang the money. Ryker, Drexel, and Hansen will learn that their mistake of double-crossing me was a fatal, and a painfully fatal, mistake. But for the moment, we must take what victory we can. The law will hang us if we tarry, suh. Get the guns—especially the Gatlings—and everything we can salvage onto the wagons. Pronto."

"And what about him?" Fred Bennett still held one of his .45 caliber Colt revolvers.

General Justice slowly climbed to his feet. He studied Fallon for a long time.

"Put him to work in the other car. We need every capable hand. But if he is not capable . . ." The mad fool grinned. "Muster him out of the New Confederate Army for Justice."

CHAPTER THIRTY-FIVE

The New Confederate Army *for Justice*. It certainly fit, Fallon thought, because this war was not for justice, it was all for Josiah Jonathan Justice, cotton magnate, Confederate soldier, thief, murderer, and madman.

Fallon walked ahead of Holderman, onto the platform, into the car with the Gatling guns and other weapons. Too bad, Fallon thought, that he hadn't had time to blow this cargo to kingdom come, but as long as he remained alive, he'd get another chance.

"Get to work," Holderman said, shoving Fallon toward the stacks of crates filled with Winchester repeating rifles.

"Don't just watch, Fatty!" the Ranger growled from behind. "You help him."

Fred Bennett raised his voice. "All of you. Quit yer damned lollygaggin'. If the Rangers or the army catches us, we'll all be jerked to Jesus by a hangman's rope."

Fallon took one end of a crate, and Holderman, scowling but with brains enough to keep his mouth shut, took the other. Fallon backed toward the open

side, the double doors slid wide, and a heavy farm
wagon backed up to the tracks. Only a handful of
crates had been unloaded, and other wagons were
waiting to back up. That told Fallon that he hadn't
been unconscious for too long. This ragtag army was
just getting started to the business at hand. The business was robbery.

What Fallon noticed was that none of the bandits—
the privates in Justice's army—wore any kind of uniform. He saw worn-out hats of various colors, faded
denim jeans or striped woolen britches, some chaps,
high-heeled boots, ratty bandannas, and a wide range
of leather and iron. In fact, Fallon saw no gray uniforms, not even butternut, and no one had unfurled
a Confederate national flag, not even a battle jack.

Fallon laid his end of the wooden box atop another, and once Holderman had placed his side
down, they slid the heavy crate until it butted against
the pine box next to it and against the front of the
wagon's box. Both men turned and stopped to let two
other enlisted men in the New Confederate Army for
Justice step out of the box car with their load. Fallon
glanced up at the car, saw just a few initials and
smaller writing that told him nothing, but then
glanced toward the engine and tender. The tender,
black and greasy, had writing in cursive gold letters.

Houston–Victoria–Laredo Rail Road
ESTABLISHED 1885

Well, they weren't near Houston. Fallon knew that
much. The terrain was drier, and the trees had all but
quit growing. Fallon had never been to Victoria, but
he didn't think they were near that South Texas burg,

either. He had thought, given Major Rufus K. Conley's apparent hand in this treasonous affair, that they would have departed by ship from Indianola. But Fallon knew they were nowhere near the Gulf of Mexico and the Texas coast. No salt on the air. No seagulls. Not the way the sky was supposed to shine when you got near the coast.

Laredo.

Laredo made more sense. The land was flat and dry, and the wind was dry. The humidity that had weighed on them like heavy bricks had all but vanished. After that first camp and training period, they had moved, two hundred—Fallon could only guess—miles, south and west. Spent some more training there, then moved a hard day's trip southwest, and finally another twenty miles or so to the railroad tracks where they waited for the train to stop at the water station.

So . . . maybe three hundred miles, if that . . . where would that take them?

Laredo. Fallon had no map to look at, but it made as much sense as anyplace else. Laredo was right on the Texas border. All Justice had to do was get his cargo across the Rio Grande.

Fallon went back inside, Holderman right behind him, and they let another pair of workers carry a box of rifles to the wagon. Outside, the voice of General Justice rattled the planks of the railroad's rolling stock.

"The Gatling guns, men! The Gatlings should be our first priority."

It took more men to get the four boxes of Gatlings into the wagon. After that, they went back to bringing Sharpses, Remingtons, and Colts out.

The sun rose. They sweated. Splinters dug into their palms and fingers, while Justice, Bennett, and the woman-knifing Merle barked orders from underneath the shade of their canvas-covered wagon.

"The money?" Fallon heard Aaron whisper.

They had found a new, faster way of unloading the car of its plunder. Fallon and Holderman stayed in the wagon, and others brought the boxes of weapons, gunpowder, and ammunition to them. Fallon grabbed a box of .45-70 cartridges, likely for the Sharpses. He moved past the big detective without answering, then had to help Holderman find a solid place to put a smaller box that likely carried Smith & Wesson revolvers.

"Ryker wouldn't have double-crossed that fathead." Holderman, sounding like he had a brain, nodded toward the General. "Drexel, maybe, but Ryker loved the Southern cause more than whiskey or God. I didn't know Hansen."

Fallon studied the brute. Holderman had betrayed Fallon at every opportunity, and Holderman had been Fallon's enemy since long before Fallon had been freed from Joliet. Freed? Not hardly. Paroled, but paroled into the hands of a vindictive bastard named Sean MacGregor.

"I gave you that derringer, Fal—" Holderman stopped himself from using Fallon's real name.

Fallon nodded at the boxcar. "A crate of something heavy's waiting for us."

They pulled the Marlins into the wagon and set the box down nearby, then two more rifle boxes, after which Fallon waved his hand and said, "This one's full. Bring us another."

"How many more?" Justice yelled.

Fallon looked at one of the sweat-soaked workers

in the car. The man looked at a bigger man, and he gave Fallon an estimate.

"This should be the last load, General!" Fallon shouted back, hating to call a raving madman any rank. He moved to the canteen hooked on a hand-hold at the side of the car. After drinking, he passed the container to Holderman while a driver brought around another heavy farm wagon.

Holderman drank.

"Save some for the boys in that furnace," Fallon told him, and nodded at the open door.

"The money," Holderman whispered.

"I think this is our biggest concern," Fallon said, and tilted his hat toward the approaching wagon.

"If they find that money—or the bodies of them three you killed—you're dead, I'm dead, and this operation is dead."

"How do you know they're dead?" Fallon reached up, took the canteen, and brushed past Holderman toward the open doorway.

"Because you ain't," Holderman answered.

Fallon handed the canteen to the smallest of the men inside the car. He turned around and guided the wagon back until it almost touched the car. He looked up at the bone-tired men up in the car.

"Two of y'all want to switch?" Fallon asked.

To his surprise, the men shook their heads to a man.

"We got this handled," one of them said in a Scottish brogue. "And you two are good at loading that wagon."

Fallon shook his head in amazement. "If you say so," he said, and wearily climbed into the back of the wagon.

"Get inside and help them, Ace!" Justice yelled at

the driver, who immediately obeyed. The driver had been at that stagecoach station when Merle and the others had murdered the crew—and one of Justice's volunteers who had opened his big mouth.

Fallon and Holderman took the first two boxes, hardly even looking at each other. But Fallon kept thinking that Holderman had a point. This cargo could still be destroyed. Maybe Holderman wanted the money for the reward the express office would put up. Maybe he wanted it for himself. But he was right about one thing. At some point, either railroad officials, Texas Rangers, random passersby, or some of Justice's mercenaries would discover the awful remains of Hansen, Drexel, and Ryker—and the money Fallon had pitched off the side. Once word of that reached the leader of the New Confederate Army for Justice, Fallon's life would be over.

He tried to remember the time on the clock when he had started pitching the money into the dark night. If the train was making twenty miles an hour, they'd cover a mile in about three minutes or so.

He didn't trust Holderman, but Holderman had slipped him that derringer that had come in mighty handy when those thugs ambushed the burial party at Peckerwood Hill. Holderman did seem incredibly loyal to Sean MacGregor, another greedy, untrustworthy villain. Fallon didn't know how much money he had tossed off the train, but banks, companies expecting payrolls, remittance men expecting money from abroad, and other assorted individuals, some of them hardworking and many of them honest, would want a chance at getting that loot back.

"Seven miles," he whispered, "maybe six. No more than eight." He made it seem harder to load the case of Colt revolvers atop a box of rifles. "That's when it started. Last sack was dropped maybe a mile, could be two. That's the last drop."

"How many sacks?" Holderman asked.

They moved back to the end of the wagon to take one more load.

Fallon laughed. "I honestly don't have a clue."

CHAPTER THIRTY-SIX

When the wagons were pointed south on the other side of the tracks, General Justice ordered that the locomotive be fired up and sent to Laredo with a full throttle. "In case," Justice said with a laugh, "they have somehow received word and are sending a posse on the next eastbound."

Fallon was about to climb into the seat of the wagon hauling the Gatling guns when Justice called out his name. Fallon dropped back to the ground and saw that General Justice had moved off the covered wagon and into an expensive-looking phaeton, pulled by a matched set of fine horses. The horses, to no surprise, were gray.

"You'll do me the honor of riding with me, suh," Justice called out, and Fallon found his hat and limped over to the buggy.

"I'll drive," the lunatic said with a glint in his eye. "I cannot say that you have earned my trust to hand you a whip."

"I'd prefer that you drive, too," Fallon said as he walked around the black phaeton and climbed into the passenger's side. "Since you know where we're bound, General."

After leaning back into the comfortable leather seat, Fallon swallowed and glanced at the backseat. Some traveling cases, maps, books, and a case of brandy. On Justice's lap lay a LeMat revolver, one of those nine-shot pistols that, by adjusting the striking mechanism, could also fire a large shotgun bore. A handful of cavalry officers had favored that weapon during the war, but Fallon had rarely come across one during his career as a deputy federal marshal in the Indian Nations.

"Move out!" Justice ordered. "Mr. Merle. Lead the way."

Merle pulled out ahead, leading a posse of cavalrymen—or at least outlaws in the formation of a cavalry unit. A few outriders took off ahead, and the wagons fell into a line behind Justice's buggy. Fallon noticed the last of the horse soldiers following the last wagon, and each wagon had at least four armed guards—three in the back and one next to the driver.

But other wagons, loaded with sandstone, moved off toward Laredo, or north, and east. So did several horsemen.

"A diversion," Justice said with a slight chuckle. "The lawmen leading the posse will be confused. They'll have to send some of its posse in the other three directions. Brilliant strategy on my part, don't you think?"

Fallon nodded his approval. Brilliant? Not quite. With the Mexican border maybe a mile from the railroad tracks, no lawman in his right mind would think the bandits would flee anywhere but the Rio Grande—

especially with a set of tracks—more wagons, more horses—pointed south. Fallon wondered if any of Justice's junior officers had argued with his plan. He doubted it. On the other hand, two men on each wagon, five riders on horseback with each party, that was twenty-one men Justice didn't have with him.

Reduces the odds for me, Fallon thought, and grinned, but it did not last for long.

"What are you thinking?" Justice asked.

"That the law could catch those men," Fallon lied. His mind was preoccupied with the thought about the wagons and riders riding east.

"They won't talk," Justice said. "Word has gotten around about what happens to men who talk. You were there. Have you forgotten?"

The image of the woman being stabbed through her heart sickened Fallon.

"But they could be held in jail," Fallon said.

"Habeas corpus, my friend," Justice said.

"Which often gets ignored by frontier lawmen," Fallon said. "I have firsthand experience on that matter, General." Of course, Fallon's experience came from being a deputy marshal and not an outlaw.

"I am not worried. What's twenty men to me?"

Fallon did a quick count of heads. No, he decided. Justice wouldn't be stupid enough to attack the great state of Texas and the sovereign ground of the United States of America with a force this size. There had to be more, many more, soldiers waiting for them on the other side of the Rio Grande. Maybe Justice was sacrificing those twenty-one. Or maybe they were off to murder more men like Malcolm Maxwell.

But that patrol riding along the rails to the east presented a big problem to Fallon's future. In about a mile or so, they'd undoubtedly come across the last bags of money Fallon had pitched out of the express car. Which they might keep for themselves, or they might tell their commander. They could miss it, but if they did not turn north or south, they'd soon discover more money—and eventually, by now, the vultures would be circling over some dead men.

"How's your head?" General Justice had to shout out over the noise of hooves, wheels, and heavy cargo traveling across the hard, sunbaked sandstone.

"It hurts," Fallon said.

"Then reach behind me and open one of those bottles."

Fallon obeyed, and read the label: COURVOISIER & CURLIER FRÈRES. It was a cognac, and the vintage was 1851. The bottle, and the brandy inside, were older than Harry Fallon.

"Open it," the General ordered.

"I don't drink," Fallon reminded him.

"But I do," the man said in that thick Southern drawl. "You'll find a corkscrew in the kit at your feet."

"Glasses?" Fallon asked after he had the bottle opened.

"There's no manservant to wash the dishes, my boy," Justice said, pushed the reins into his left hand, and held out his right.

Fallon handed him the bottle and watched the madman gulp down a few swallows. Then Justice offered Fallon a swig.

"No thanks," Fallon said, and remembered to add: "General."

Fallon studied the country. Flat. Hot. He saw several birds, but this was spring, practically summer. Doves and warblers he recognized. A few others, he had never seen the likes of before. The jays down here were green, not blue. It was too hot by then to see many four-legged critters, though Fallon caught glimpses of a few jackrabbits in the shade trees. Not that there were many trees here, for this would be what old cowhands had called the Texas brush country. Prickly pear lined the sides of the road, but what Fallon saw mostly were thornscrub, some mesquite, and soap brush. Stuff that would stick you if you weren't careful.

"That's a shame about Drexel," Justice said.

Trying to trip me up, Fallon figured, *catch me in a lie. Give himself a reason to empty the canister in that shotgun barrel on his pistol.*

"I'll meet up with him one of these days if I'm lucky," Fallon said without looking at Justice. "And he won't be so lucky."

"That was a lot of money," Justice said.

Fallon shrugged. "Two bucks is a lot of money to me, General."

Justice again offered the bottle of old cognac to Fallon, who shook his head. Smiling, the cotton and sugarcane king again took a swing and set the bottle between his legs, near the big pistol, and used both hands now on the reins.

"What did you think of Drexel?"

Fallon shrugged. "I wasn't inside The Walls to learn enough about him, other than he was a low-down swine."

"You would not trust him?"

Now it was Fallon's turn to smile. "He was a guard, General. I was a convict."

"And Major Hansen?"

"I never met him, sir."

"How about Ryker?"

Fallon shrugged. "We didn't see eye to eye."

"Yes. From what I understand, you two clashed the day you got to prison."

Now Fallon felt uncomfortable, but he hid those emotions. Ryker had been out of The Walls, allegedly transferred to the prison in Rusk, but had escaped. Fallon knew how much work Justice put into training his men, and Ryker had been trained well enough to murder Malcolm Maxwell in the center of the capital city of Texas, and get away. Get away when another employee of Justice had also been trained and sent to Austin to kill the assassins after they had murdered their target. But how much had Ryker told Justice about Fallon? Anything?

"We got into a tussle," Fallon said.

"Over any particular reason?"

Fallon shrugged. "I never got a chance to ask him. Drexel put me in the sweatbox right after the fight."

The General grabbed the whip and lashed out above the far-side gray horse's ear. The buggy picked up a bit of speed and turned off the road.

"But I still used Ryker, Mr. Alexander," Justice said. "I figured if he proved himself good enough to escape the situation in Austin—and make it back to where he had been instructed to return—well, then maybe he was a man to be trusted after all."

Fallon smiled. "And where did that get you, General?"

He saw the face pale, the eyes flame in anger, and Justice's knuckles turn white as his hand gripped the handle of the whip tightly. But Justice made no other move, no comment, and the LeMat still bounced along his lap, but somehow never clanged against the neck of the bottle of 1851 cognac. The buggy dipped between more mesquite, and Fallon saw the murky waters of the Rio Grande. He leaned back in the seat.

"You are impressed, Mr. Alexander," Justice said as the grin returned and his composure moved from anger to pleasure.

"This is what they called a pontoon bridge," Fallon guessed. "Isn't that what it is, General?" It had taken him a moment to recover and remember to add the rank the crazy leader appreciated. "I heard some men talk about using them in the war."

"Indeed," Justice said. "Cumberland pontoons, as they were called, helped those damned Yankees win the war. Rosecrans used them first, and then General Thomas, commanding the Army of the Cumberland, took Rosecrans's idea and improved on it. Sherman, that fire-crazy demon, laid them across the Etowah River and marched to the sea, the devil.

"But this is not a Yankee invention, suh. The first pontoon bridge dates to the eleventh century B.C., in China. If you were to read Herodotus, you would know that the Greeks used them, as did the Persians. And now they will allow the New Confederate Army for Justice to escape."

Men lined both sides of the banks, and the wooden bridge looked anything but steady.

"Don't fear you will drown, Mr. Alexander," Justice said. "They are lightweight, but the Yankees designed a fine bridge. Strong enough to support artillery pulled by horses and wagons loaded for a four-month winter campaign. They are easy to build, easy to transport, and get us across the river safely and in a timely manner."

The men were saluting as the horses touched the wooden bridge first.

"It beats getting wet, doesn't it, Mr. Alexander?" The madman lashed out with the whip, and moments later, the phaeton was on Mexican soil. "Getting across the bridge in Laredo would have been a battle that would have done my army no good," Justice said. "We would have won, of course, but the cost would have been high. We'd have to fight through the Yankees and the lawmen in that miserable patch of filth, and once we were in Mexico, the damned dictator Porfirio Díaz would have tried to kick us out. His army is commanded by lunatics and morons fill its ranks, but I wish to avoid violence at all costs."

Fallon felt the gall rising in his mouth. He remembered the dead man at the sugarcane field being carted off to be dumped in the swamp. The woman the butcher named Merle had killed, along with several other innocent people—and even one of Justice's own men simply for asking an innocent question. And all those dead men on that train.

"The Texas Rangers and the Mexican Army will be watching every river crossing they know of, Harry." So he was Harry now. Pretty soon Fallon would be Hank. *Only my friends call me Hank.*

"None is here," he said as he pulled hard on the reins to stop the buggy, and then set the brake and turned around to watch his army, his plunderers, cross the portable folding bridge from Texas to Mexico. It was, Fallon had to concede, one impressive sight.

"The river here is usually impassable," Justice said. "Quicksand. Deep pits. But our only concern is getting poked by mesquite. There is a canyon three miles ahead. We will camp there, let our men recover, rest, then light out before the moon rises. We will be guided to our camp. And then begin preparations for our next mission. The invasion of Texas." He found the cognac and drank greedily.

"You have to be guided . . . ?" Fallon started.

"I detest this wretched country, Harry." Justice wiped his lips. "But it is easy to find friends in Texas, especially since I hang my hat, mostly, in Louisiana. These greasers hate Texans. So I have promised them they can have their country back, at least to the Nueces River, once I have reclaimed what is rightfully mine."

Fallon sat back in his seat. The more General Justice talked, the madder he sounded. A stark raving lunatic.

"Ah, I admire promptness in a man." He pointed the bottle of 1851 cognac ahead, and Fallon turned to see a burly Mexican loping over the ridge on a pinto pony. The rider came into view, and Fallon felt his stomach twist some more.

"*Bueno. Amigo.* It *es muy grande* to see you again."

Juanito Gomez reined in his horse and stuck out a beefy paw. Fallon made himself smile and accepted the firm grip.

"It's good to see you, too, Juanito," Fallon said. "I haven't seen you since we buried you at Peckerwood Hill."

CHAPTER THIRTY-SEVEN

Juanito Gomez let out a throaty roar of approval as he pulled away his hand and offered a weak salute at General Justice. He fired out words in Spanish, too fast, too accented for Fallon to understand any of it, but Josiah Justice wasn't anywhere close to being fluent. Fallon quickly realized that Gomez was speaking Spanish just to annoy the General.

"That is an old Mexican greeting," Gomez said. "You have done well with your mission, I see."

"Well enough," Justice said.

"And the money?"

Justice lifted the cognac to Fallon. "Pass this to your friend, Private Alexander," he said, dropping the friendliness now that others were in earshot. "Señor Gomez, I trust you to lead us to our sanctuary. We will discuss payment upon arrival."

"*Bueno,*" Gomez said. "*Vámanos, muchachos.*"

Juanito Gomez had chosen an excellent hiding spot. The path was so hard, it would take an Apache to follow the trail, and mesquite covered the entranceway into the canyon—only the thorny mesquite brush could be moved, and was being moved, by men who emerged from the canyon after Merle rode up, dismounted, slipped through the brush, and found the others.

With heavy gloves and heavy coats, a dozen men pulled up the trees that had been chopped, and the wagons and horses proceeded into the canyon.

"Always do the unexpected," Justice told Fallon. "The mesquite will deter most investigations, whilst those who know this country will remember that Saqueo Cañon is a box canyon. Only a fool would camp there when he is being pursued." He nodded at the corkscrew and Fallon lifted it off the floor and found another bottle of 1851 cognac.

"Or a genius," Justice concluded.

When the last of the men made it into the canyon, the diggers replanted the mesquite, which fit in with the clumps of that thorny brush that climbed up the canyon walls. Probably the mesquite would eventually have grown to cover the path, or maybe it had, and that was what Justice's men had cut down. Anyway, it would look natural enough if Texas Rangers or lawmen who did not know the area disobeyed international law and crossed the river in pursuit. None would expect wagons to have made it through that thorny forest. The Mexican officials wouldn't likely want to rip their sleeves and their skin looking for weapons and money that had been stolen from *norteamericanos*.

The cut mesquite eventually would wither and die, but by then, Justice's army would be moving to another camp.

To no one's surprise, the camp that night was cold.

No fires. No hot food. No liquor. Just water and guards on double duty. Fallon was a servant, opening bottles of cognac for Justice, Merle, Bennett, and Juanito Gomez. He studied the canyon walls, but knew he had no chance of escape. The next day, after lounging around the canyon until dusk, Fallon hitched the grays to the buggy and again served as Justice's driver. The General was in a foul mood, but six bottles of thirty-plus-year-old cognac with a supper of tinned caviar and cans of peaches and tomatoes likely produced a wicked, wicked hangover.

At night, Juanito Gomez and a handful of Mexican bandits guided the wagon train across the Mexican desert. They rode east for two days, keeping a steady but not backbreaking pace.

"How are you doing, amigo?" Juanito Gomez asked as Fallon once again hitched the gray horses to the phaeton.

Fallon looked at the burly Mexican and shrugged.

"The General, he wastes your talents, my friend. You are a fighter. Not a chauffeur."

Fallon nodded at the buggy's roof. "I'm out of the sun," he said.

After a hearty laugh, the bandit slapped Fallon's shoulder. "It will take more than a roof, I fear, to keep a bullet out of your head." He made the sign of the cross. "Out of all our heads."

"Rurales?" Fallon asked.

"No. Bandidos." Gomez looked into the distance. "We enter the land of the worst of my race. Killers. Young and old." His head shook with a genuine sadness.

"They butcher their own villages, terrorize their own people. They are evil. Me? I am just a thief. Sometimes a killer. But usually just a thief. I do not make war on my own people. I rob gringos, mostly Tejanos. I am not like those . . ." His last word was in Spanish, and Fallon did not know its meaning, but he had a pretty good guess.

"Do you plan on robbing us?" Fallon asked, and smiled, though he was dead serious.

"It was considered, amigo. But I think it is better that I collect my money from the General—if we live that long—and send him off to Texas to fight his war and die gloriously. You would do well to ride with me, amigo. You. Me. We would be like your Frank and Jesse James. For we are brothers."

"Which one are you?" Fallon asked. "Frank or Jesse?"

The Mexican's laugh felt genuine. "Which one is still alive, my friend? He would be my choice."

He started to walk away, laughing, but turned around, and his eyes and voice turned serious again.

"If we are attacked," Gomez said. "Do not show mercy. These"—he spit instead of cursed—"are heartless butchers. Kill them. Send them all to hell, for surely they will do that to us all if they are given a chance."

On the third morning, in a camp in an arroyo so that travelers would be unlikely to spot them from the trails, one man did bring up the matter of money.

"General!" he called out. "You promised us fifty dollars."

Fallon watched the man, a lean, swarthy Texan with

a black beard and a pair of revolvers holstered on two gun rigs that hung low on what little hips he had. Fallon also looked at the men standing behind him, now moving away in case their general decided to start blasting with his big LeMat.

Since arriving in Mexico, Fallon had observed the men riding with this army. He had yet to see Aaron Holderman, which was good. Maybe Holderman had been sent with the party that rode east along the railroad tracks. Holderman certainly had motivation to go there, for the money that he knew Fallon had tossed out of the moving train. Those chances, however, were slim. But having even a modicum of hope made Fallon feel a little better.

"Me and the boys," the Texan drawled, "want to get paid, boss."

"When we return to Texas, Private," the General replied.

"You said as soon as we got to Mexico. I give you a few days to live up to your word."

Fallon stirred the cold beans in his plate.

Justice turned to Merle. "Shoot that blowhard, Captain," he whispered. "Shoot him now. That will serve as a lesson to these other rapscallions with mercenary hearts."

"It will serve as a reason to riot, sir," Merle answered.

"He's right," the Ranger Bennett agreed.

Well, Fallon thought, at least the men didn't obey every order their psychotic leader issued.

"I want my money!" the blowhard demanded.

"And you shall get it, and a double eagle as a bonus, my friends," he said. "But not now. The money, our payroll, is on its way to our Lexington and Concord, our Fort Sumter—where we launch our glorious campaign."

Which, Fallon knew, would not appease men with mercenary hearts.

Justice must have known that, too, for he added: "But I have five bottles of cognac left. Excellent vintage." He nodded at the buggy. "You may help yourselves, but if there are any fisticuffs, any loud voices, any act that might compromise our mission, our destiny, and you will be put to the sword."

It wasn't exactly the kind of speech that Grant, Lee, or Washington likely would have given, but it did the job.

"What do you think, Harry?" Justice asked.

"You're out of cognac," Fallon replied.

The man laughed. "You have a fine wit, suh. Do you know why I continue to allow you to drive my phaeton?"

Fallon shrugged.

"I have lost Barney Drexel," he said. "He was my captain. I have need for a captain. Oh, I know, Bennett and Merle are captains, but you have leadership abilities and you have been fighting the late war, the war we never should have lost, in your own way."

Fallon remained quiet.

"You are also brave."

Fallon shrugged again.

"Would you like to be a captain in the New Confederate Army for Justice?"

"What about Gomez?"

"A greaser?" The man chortled. "Surely you jest, suh. The greaser will get some pesos, and, once victory is obtained, maybe that land south of the Nueces River. For the love of God, I never understood why Texas wanted it so badly in the first place. It's just a bunch of desert, befitting only scorpions, rattlesnakes, and tarantulas."

"What do I have to do?" Fallon asked.

"Kill, suh. You have to kill. You have to kill, kill, kill, kill, kill. Learn to hate. Hate with all your heart. And then kill the men you hate. And kill the men you have to in order to stay alive."

Fallon gave the General a quick nod. "I'm getting pretty good at that," he said. The sad part, Fallon understood, was that he had not lied. He was damned good at killing. He had killed more men in the past months since he had joined the American Detective Agency than he had during his entire career as a deputy marshal. And since Joliet, he had learned to hate. There were still some men that he had to kill, not to stay alive, but because he hated them.

"Good. You will be a captain. In due time. I still want to get to know you a little better. But once we reach our final camp, I will introduce you to my other captain. Then we will toast our upcoming glory. Our new nation. Our independence. And our wealth."

"I look forward to meeting him, sir," Fallon said, "and serving ably under your command."

Justice slapped Fallon's leg. "Bully for you, suh. You shall like Captain Ehrlander. He isn't the fighter you are. But Chris has brains. He has tenfold the brains of most men, and is slippery as a wet eel."

Chris Ehrlander. Now Fallon knew for sure. Ehrlander was in that deep with Justice.

"I look forward to meeting Captain Ehrlander, sir," Fallon said again, and he thought:

And then sending him to hell because I hate his guts.

* * *

They resumed their march the next evening. When they turned south a few days later, they began traveling in the daylight. Long days. Days that drained the strength of the men and the horses. And they were out of 1851 cognac.

It was moving south that troubled Fallon.

He figured they would be heading back to Texas, perhaps crossing the Rio Grande around Brownsville, but now they traveled deeper into Mexico. He tried to remember those maps he had seen.

It was late in the next day, with dust blowing in his eyes, and General Justice as irritable as the tired horses pulling the buggy, that Fallon understood where Justice was taking his men. And why.

Then a bullet blew out the left gray horse's brains.

CHAPTER THIRTY-EIGHT

The horse dropped in a heap, stopping the buggy suddenly and pitching Josiah Jonathan Justice to the ground while spilling the LeMat onto the phaeton's floor. Fallon dropped the reins, set the brake, and dived as bullets riddled the leather seats and splintered the box in the back that once had held many bottles of vintage cognac.

Hooves thundered. Guns roared. Men shouted. Other men screamed. Above that, Fallon could make out the shouts and curses in rapid-fire Spanish. Chaos and carnage surrounded him. The other gray horse was killed. A horse shot past the phaeton, dragging its rider, one boot caught in the stirrup, behind him until a barrage of gunfire killed that horse.

Fallon grabbed the LeMat. He heard a horse slide to a stop. Rolling over, Fallon thumbed back the hammer of the heavy French weapon. A bullet slammed into the wooden floor inches from Fallon's face, sending slivers of wood into his cheek.

The man was Mexican, sitting atop a clay bank, with a giant sugar-loaf sombrero on his big head. He was dark-skinned, dark-eyed, and wore a suit of black suede. The pistol he carried had to be one of those relics from the War Between the States, maybe a Walker, probably a Dragoon, but it was being cocked and if that man didn't kill Fallon, the one behind him—thinner, clean-shaven, but a Mexican bandit who held a repeating rifle—most certainly would.

Fallon squeezed the trigger, and the roar of the LeMat deafened him, the flash of flame and smoke blinded him, and the kick of the big pistol just about tore his right hand from his arm.

He somersaulted off the buggy, landed on his stomach, jarring his ribs but not knocking the breath out of him. Beside him, General Justice had risen to a seated position and was unbuttoning his Confederate frock coat, cursing as he fumbled with the myriad brass buttons.

"Confound it," the General roared, likely dazed. A bullet clipped the purple ostrich plume from Justice's hat, which somehow had remained on the man's big white head. "Confound it. I must find my .36."

Fallon brought the LeMat up, found the lever at the end of the hammer, and flipped it into the standard position. Justice had set the striker up, so that it would fire the smoothbore center barrel. Fallon came up, aiming the LeMat at the two bandits. Quickly, he saw enough and dropped back down. He stared at the gun in his hand, knowing now why the LeMat was called the "grapeshot" revolver. The blast from the twenty-gauge barrel had killed both bandits, wounded the first one's horse, and sent the other horse loping and kicking its way toward the nearest hills.

Another rider swung around the buggy, struggling to turn the horse and get a clear aim with the Winchester Yellow Boy—or a cheap Mexican copy of the .44 caliber carbine. Fallon raised the LeMat and sent a .40 caliber ball into the man's brisket. He groaned and dropped out of the saddle, and his horse galloped toward the Gulf of Mexico.

Fallon had fired twice, one from the cylinder, the other from the shotgun barrel. He had eight shots left.

A man, more like a boy, wearing the white cotton clothes of a peon, sandals and a beaten straw hat, ran around the other side. He held an old Enfield rifle, bigger than he was, but was bringing the stock to his shoulder when something popped to Fallon's left and just behind him. A geyser of crimson sprayed from the center of the kid's chest, and the crucifix the boy wore flew upward, then back onto his dead body when the kid hit the ground.

"Vermin!" Justice shouted, and rose to his feet. "Scum of the earth. Dirty, rotten, low-down, thieving greasers! You will get no part of Texas when I have conquered it. For when I am finished with President Grant, I shall take Mexico for my own—just because I can."

Holding a Navy Colt in his right hand, Justice marched to the dead boy and put another bullet into the corpse's chest.

Grant? Fallon wet his lips, tried to see through the dust. Ulysses S. Grant hadn't been president in years. Hell, Grant had been dead for more than five years.

Two riders galloped out of the blinding dust. Fallon raised the LeMat again, then stopped. He stared at General Josiah Jonathan Justice, who walked toward the approaching bandits, the Navy .36 pistol hanging at his side as he strode. The wind drove dust into Fallon's eyes, and he had to lower himself behind the rear wheel of the buggy. He spit out sand, wiped his face, and saw the cotton and sugarcane king walking fearlessly. A bullet tore a hole in the crown of his Hardee hat. Another whined off a rock at his left foot. The riders bore down. The General kept walking.

Suddenly a bullet ricocheted off the iron rim of the wheel. Fallon spun, dropped, raised the LeMat, and put a bullet into a gunman's stomach. The man dropped his pistol, clutched his belly, and fell to his knees. He pitched forward, pushed himself off, and staggered off to the south. Fallon raised the LeMat, stopped, and spun around. That man had a bullet in his gut. He was dead, just didn't know it, and soon would wish he could just die.

Fallon raised the LeMat again.

He needed Justice alive. He needed Justice to get back to his camp. If the General got killed in this ambush, Fallon might never be able to catch up with Chris Ehrlander—and kill him for murdering Fallon's wife and daughter.

Fallon pulled back the hammer, but instantly General Justice brought the Navy up in speed that did not match the maniac's age and ability. Yet Fallon saw the blasts from the Navy's barrel and heard two distinctive reports, and both riders pitched backward off their horses.

"Scoundrels!" Justice yelled. "Have you no decency? You ambush us instead of meet us head-to-head in proper battle! How dare you? I shall exterminate your miserable race!"

Fallon ran to the General and grabbed the thick woolen sleeve of the man's new gray coat.

"Unhand me, suh," Justice wailed as he turned

around and started to bring up the pistol. "Or we shall meet on the field of honor."

"General!" Fallon said. "It's me, sir. Harry." He pushed the General down and brought up the LeMat again. A bullet knocked off Fallon's hat. The big revolver spoke again and a man spun around, staggered to his right, made the sign of the cross, and fell, spread-eagled, on his back.

All Harry Fallon thought about was how to stay alive and somehow keep Josiah Justice alive. Mexican renegades were attacking American renegades—a renegade army that had, if you looked at it one way, invaded Mexico. The New Confederate Army for Justice was fighting its first major battle with one objective:

Stay alive!

The Mexicans were fighting for reasons of their own. Weapons that could help them overthrow Porfirio Díaz. Wagons. Money (if they could find much).

It seemed a stupid reason for men to fight.

Justice's Colt rang out again. Fallon didn't know if the General's aim had been true, for Justice was firing over Fallon's shoulder, and now Fallon was pushing Justice hard to the ground. Again, he brought up the LeMat to kill or wound some other enemy charging him, but this time, Fallon wasn't quite quick enough.

He never heard the shot—for the country was filled with gunfire and echoes, and screams and thundering hooves—or even saw the muzzle flash from the revolver as the bandido fanned the hammer.

Fallon felt the punch in his left shoulder, felt the fire, and tasted the blood. He dropped to the ground, still clutching the LeMat and trying to fire it, but he

couldn't see. The dust and pain blinded him, and his
shoulder burned like blazes. He had trouble breathing, but, damn it, he told himself: "You aren't dying.
You aren't dying. Not yet."

He didn't realize he was speaking the words. He
just wanted to find that low-down snake who had put
a slug in his shoulder.

A shadow crossed Fallon's face, but after blinking
away sweat, all he could make out was a dim figure. A
figure in gray. And hair that seemed to be as white as
snow.

Something latched on to Fallon's right wrist. Fallon
fought, but that just wasted what little energy and
strength he had left. The LeMat was wrenched from
Fallon's grip. He heard three quick blasts.

His right hand, no longer holding the heavy revolver, came up, found the shoulder, and pressed
down as tightly as he could against the bleeding, burning hole.

"Captain Alexander!" General Josiah Jonathan Justice shouted. "Captain Alexander, do you hear me?
Open your eyes, mister, that is a direct order! Open
your eyes!"

Fallon thought his eyes were open. He tried again.
And this time he saw the grim face of the General, his
facial hair and skin blackened in spots by gunpowder,
whitened in places by alkali dust.

"We are not retreating, Captain," Fallon thought he
heard Justice say. "We are regrouping, suh, and victory shall be gained. On your feet, Captain. Let us fall
back, but we march in order, suh. We march in order."

When Fallon did not move, Justice reached down,

shoving the LeMat into his waistband beside the Navy Colt, and jerked Fallon to his feet.

Fallon almost blacked out. The world spun around and around, and his stomach turned over.

"You shall pay my laundress, Captain," Justice said, "for removing your vomit. I paid two hundred dollars in New Orleans, suh, for this uniform."

The General was stark raving mad, but he seemed to understand that if he let go, Fallon would be falling flat on his face. He wasn't marching anywhere.

A Mexican ran toward them, lifting a machete. Holding onto Fallon with his left arm, Justice drew the Navy with his right, thumbed back the hammer, squeezed the trigger, and when it snapped on an empty chamber, he reversed the grip and threw the revolver. The butt caught the enemy in the forehead and sent him to the ground. As the killer rose, shaking his head, while fumbling around the ground for the machete, Justice found the LeMat and blew out the bandit's brains.

Now he started toward what appeared to be a fort. A fort? No, Fallon realized, it was one of the wagons. The wagons had been rounded into not exactly a circle, but some kind of a redoubt. That's where General Justice planned to regroup.

Regroup. Fallon shook his head. Like Custer at the Little Big Horn.

"General! General! General!" Fallon's eyes barely opened. "Let me help."

Juanito Gomez came into view, shoving a smoking Remington revolver into his holster. Fallon wasn't sure how far they had come, but the fort, the wagons filled with guns and ammunition, did appear somewhat closer. He still heard shouts and gunfire. He smelled death and dust. And his shoulder hurt like hell.

Gomez slid to a stop. He raised both hands. *"¿Qué eres . . . ?"* the Mexican began.

A splotch of crimson appeared high in Gomez's shirt, and he twisted and turned and dropped to his knees.

The outlaw looked confused. Blood seeped from one corner of his mouth. *"¿Por qué razón hizo . . . ?"*

"Do not speak Mexican to me, you scoundrel!" Justice yelled, and continued to help Fallon along, toward the dying bandit. "You undoubtedly led us into this ambush."

The man raised his left hand. His right tried to find the revolver he had dropped. *"Para Dios . . ."* he began, but never finished his prayer. The LeMat spoke again, and the bullet ripped through Juanito Gomez's hand and blew out the man's right eye.

"Onward, lads," the madman said, dropping the LeMat and now lifting Fallon over his shoulder. Fallon felt himself being carried through the dust, past the bloodied corpse of Juanito Gomez, toward the fort of wagons and horses, and . . . maybe . . . some more men.

As he carried Fallon, Josiah Jonathan Justice bellowed a familiar song out of his forceful lungs. It was the last thing Fallon remembered before the dark void swallowed him whole.

I wish I was in the land of cotton,
Old times there are not forgotten;
Look away! Look away! Look away! Dixie Land.
In Dixie's Land where I was born in,

Early on one frosty morning,
Look away! Look away! Look away! Dixie Land.

I wish I was in Dixie. Hooray! Hooray!
In Dixie's Land I'll take my stand
to live and die in Dixie.
Away, away, away down south in Dixie.
Away, away, away down south in Dixie.

CHAPTER THIRTY-NINE

Cold water revived him. Actually, the water was lukewarm and had been emptied from a coffee cup onto his face. He turned to his left, a mistake, because the pain in his shoulder left him yelling out, and moved to his right, coughing, spitting out water, and wiping the water off his face.

"You ain't dead, not yet, nohow, and that bullet's out of your arm," a Texan drawled. "Get to your post, Alexander. At least you can die like a man."

Fallon's vision came into focus. The murderer named Merle came into focus, and the man spit tobacco juice onto Fallon's right boot as his left thumb and forefinger reached inside a vest pocket. He brought out a flattened piece of lead. "Thirty-two caliber," Merle drawled. "I've been hurt worser with a slingshot." He tossed the bullet that had slammed into Fallon's shoulder onto Fallon's chest.

"Get up. We need ever' gunhand we got."

The bandaging job wasn't a work of beauty, but the rags Merle—or someone—had used looked relatively clean, and didn't tear the wound open when Fallon sat up. He wet his lips, then hit the back of his head, which had just started feeling back to normal a few days before the ambush, against a wagon wheel.

Fallon wiped his face. Merle reached behind his back and pulled out a long-barreled Smith & Wesson. "Figure you ain't much good with a long gun. You got six beans in the wheel here. Make 'em count. Them greasers will likely charge directly."

The right arm lifted, to Fallon's surprise, without tormenting the left shoulder. He opened his hand, and Merle, grinning without humor, laid the cold walnut butt of the .44 Russian on Fallon's palm. His fingers and thumbs clasped the grip, and despite the fact that the .44 felt like a howitzer, Fallon didn't drop it. He lowered his arm, came to his knees, shoved the revolver into his waistband, and got a grip on the spokes of the wheel. Only then could Fallon pull himself to his feet.

"All right," Merle said. "So you're tough enough to stand on yer own two feet. Let's see if you can walk ten yards to the Gen'ral." Merle turned his back and walked away.

It would be easy to shoot him in the back, Fallon thought, but he left the Smith & Wesson in his waistband and used the wagon's side to make his way toward the command post of the New Confederate Army for Justice. Which was Merle, Fred Bennett, and General Josiah Jonathan Justice, standing behind a freight wagon, covered in dust and filth. Sweating men who had shunned their frock coats or shell jackets. Bennett had a dirty bandage wrapped around his head, no hat, and blood had dried to an ugly black, except for the dust coating it now, that ran from his temple, past his right eye, and down his beard-stubbled cheek.

Justice fanned himself with his hat, the LeMat still shoved in his waistband. Winchester rifles, brand-new and just out of the box, leaned against the wagon's side. Fallon saw the other wagons, with the surviving men huddled behind the wheels and inside the backs. They didn't look like soldiers for the New Confederate Army for Justice. They didn't even look like outlaws. They resembled frightened children and young men, weary, battered, and coming to accept the fact that death was close at hand.

"Captain Alexander." Justice stopped waving his hat and placed it back on his head. His eyes brightened and he even smiled. "It is grand to see you on your feet, suh. You look sharp. You look like a man ready to fight."

Fallon knew that he looked like hell. And that he felt awful.

Yet he tried to salute, and said, "At your service, sir."

"Do not despair, men!" the General shouted, and stepped away from the wagon, looking down the line of wagons both ways. The wagons had been formed into a loose circle, and the horses and mules—those that had not been shot dead in their traces—were tethered behind the biggest wagon.

"Help is on the way," Justice said in a feeble attempt to rally what men he still had left. "Victory is at hand. The New Confederate Army for Justice shall not be defeated!"

"Go to hell, you dingleberry!" someone answered.

Justice appeared not to have heard.

A voice shouted from the hills. It was Spanish. Fallon could make out only a few words, and he moved to the back of the wagon and looked through the space separating this freight wagon with the next one in line. Bodies littered the field. Bodies of horses and men, already bloating in the heat. Vultures had begun circling the sky, and the wind had stopped blowing. It was enough to make a man sick, but Fallon had nothing in his gut to throw up. He had left that on the sleeve of Justice's frock coat. Fallon saw the coat. The General had used it to cover a dying man, a boy who lay shivering on the ground underneath the wagon.

Sometimes Fallon didn't know what to make out of Josiah Justice—other than he was stark raving mad.

"They want our gold, sir," Captain Bennett translated. "Again."

Merle was honing the blade of his savage bowie knife on the iron rim of the front tire. "Don't we all," he said in a mirthless tone.

"They don't know . . ." Fallon whispered.

Justice whirled. "Alexander, what are you talking about? They don't know what? Confound it, man, you will explain your meaning."

Fallon's head shook. "They think we're carrying gold."

"Which we was supposed to be doin'," Merle said, still honing his blade.

"That is obvious," the General wailed, "since that is what they demand we give them. Gold." He laughed. "United States script. Money we do not have thanks to traitors."

"Gomez . . ." Fallon started, but stopped when Justice gripped the butt of his LeMat.

"We do not speak the names of scoundrels, cowards, and traitors at this command post, Mr. Alexander. Never! Do so and you shall find yourself in front of a firing squad. Or . . ." He laughed. "We'll just send you out there running to those dirty little Mexicans. Give you a choice. Get killed by us. Or butchered by them."

Fallon touched his left shoulder, shuddered slightly, and swallowed down what little moisture he could summon up in his mouth.

"He told them about the gold," Fallon said. "But not the weapons."

Merle stopped sharpening the blade of the bowie. Bennett turned from staring at the hills, and the enemy, and looked Fallon directly in the eye. Justice rubbed his fingers across his sweaty, white head.

Actually, Fallon didn't think Juanito Gomez told the Mexicans anything. Gomez had come to help Fallon and the General. Justice had been out of his head and had killed the bandit. But the look on Gomez's face, and the words Fallon recalled him uttering, suggested that he was no traitor. At least, he had not betrayed General Justice. Besides, Fallon remembered that conversation he had with Gomez days before this ambush. Gomez wasn't part of this group. He hated them almost as much as he despised Texans. The big Mexican's words echoed inside Fallon's head: *"Kill them. Send them all to hell, for surely they will do that to us all if they are given a chance."*

"What do you mean?" Justice demanded.

"They're asking for gold," Fallon said. "Not weapons, bullets, and gold. Just gold. *Dinero.*" Fallon knew that much Spanish. "Money."

It made sense. By now news of the robbery had spread across the United States and her territories, likely north to Canada, and definitely into Mexico. But the United States government wouldn't want a turbulent country like Mexico, with a dictator in charge and revolutionaries popping up like weeds after a wet spring, to know that a veritable arsenal had disappeared south of the Rio Grande. They just reported that money had been stolen from the express car.

Bennett shook his head. "So what do you want us to do, Alexander? Give them the money we have? You think that'd stop them from killing us? You think they'd let us go for what probably wouldn't add up to fifty dollars?"

"I propose that we surrender," Fallon said. "And then we send them all to hell."

CHAPTER FORTY

"This is a foolish enterprise," General Josiah Jonathan Justice said as he fanned himself with his hat. "You will waste precious lead that we might need when we drive the Yankee vermin out of Laredo, then Gonzalez, then San Antonio, then Austin . . . Waco . . . Dallas . . ." He shook his head and pointed toward the coast. "Reinforcements will be arriving directly. There is no need for us to do anything but wait."

"You've been mentioning those reinforcements since they attacked us yesterday, General," Merle said as he studied the diagram and directions in front of him.

That caused Fallon to stop feeding the new .30 caliber Army cartridges into the hopper. He had not realized how long he must have been out. But, of course, now it was so obvious. He had been shot yesterday afternoon. Merle had dug the slug out of his shoulder, and Fallon had slept through the rest of the day and into the next morning.

At least he had been able to sleep. Most of these mercenaries had been awake for more than thirty-three hours. Others were sleeping an eternal sleep. Fallon sighed and fingered another cartridge. That was about all Fallon could handle with his bum left shoulder. Two other soldiers sat in the back of the wagon, feeding cartridges into more hoppers. On the wagon behind them, another crew worked at assembling one of the two Gatling guns.

Justice refused to allow more than two of his new, stolen army trophies of war to be used against greasers.

"This is ridiculous," the General started, and the Mexicans began shouting again.

"They might have a spyglass," Bennett said, softer this time. "And see what we're doing."

"If that were the case," Fallon said, "they'd be asking for the guns, too."

Bennett nodded. "Maybe. I hope so."

The voice from the hills died down.

"What did that mongrel say?" Justice asked.

Merle put a finger in his ear, twisted it, as if that could help, and pulled it out. He said, "This is our last chance. Either we surrender now. Or we will be put to the death. Kinda like the Alamo." He chuckled.

"If only Davy Crockett had a Gatling gun," said Bennett as he tightened a bolt. "I think," he said, "this one's ready. Once we put it on the tripod."

Fallon looked over the tailgate at the next wagon. A bald man, shirtless, sweating, muscles bulging, nodded. "Ours is ready, but we ain't sure how you fire it."

"Put both hoppers in the slots," Bennett said, staring at the directions. "Turn the crank."

The Gatlings used what the directions and diagrams called a Bruce-style feed system. When the first hopper was emptied, it could be removed while the second hopper fed the .30 caliber cartridges into individual chambers. Fallon filled the twentieth cartridge into another hopper. He handed it to Bennett.

"Four-man crews per gun," Bennett said. "Everybody knows what he's doing?"

No one did. But they all nodded.

"Four hundred rounds per minute." Someone whistled.

"Just turn the crank slowly," Fallon said. "These guns have a tendency to jam."

"And aim low," Merle said.

Fallon, Bennett, and two men would be working the gun in Fallon's wagon. Merle crossed over to the wagon with the bare-chested bald man and two other tired soldiers of fortune.

General Justice yelled: "All right! Wave the white flag. Wave it high. Walk with dignity, men, and listen to my command."

Reluctantly, what was left of Justice's New Confederate Army for Justice began walking or limping out of the circle of wagons, toward the hills, handguns stuck behind their backs. Most of them raised their hands high over their heads. Leading the way was General Josiah Jonathan Justice. Beside him, his sergeant waved a flag of truce.

Lying down next to the Gatling gun, keeping his head behind the wagon's side, Fallon saw all of this through a knothole in the pine plank. What these men were doing showed bravery. What Fallon was about to do almost made him sick to his stomach.

"I've killed scores of greasers," Fred Bennett whispered. "Plenty of white outlaws, too. And a few Yankees years and years ago. But I don't reckon I ever done nothing this low."

"Me, neither," Fallon said.

"I don't see nothing wrong with this," said one of the loaders. "They plan on cutting us down."

"I know," Fallon said. "But it doesn't rest any better in my gut."

Clouds of dust formed behind the top of the hill. Fallon found his throat parched, like the land he was on. He wiped his clammy hands on his trousers. His shoulder no longer bothered him, maybe because of how scared he was, and how sick he felt.

"A flag of truce . . ." Bennett spit in disgust. "Killing men while waving a flag of truce. Well, at least I'm getting paid a ton of money . . . Or damned well better be."

"They'll be trying to kill men waving a flag of truce," Fallon said, and the first riders appeared at the top of the hill. "Here they come."

He held up a hand, keeping his three gunnery mates down and out of view. He tried to wet his lips, but did nothing. The Mexicans could be heard now, yelling curses in Spanish and drawing their revolvers or cocking their rifles. Yes, these butchers had no intention of recognizing that white flag. But it still didn't make Fallon feel much better.

"NOW!"

Bennett and the biggest of the men lifted the round cylinder, locked it into place, and Bennett moved behind the gun. Fallon slammed one hopper into place. The remaining outlaw did the second.

"Hit the dirt!" Fallon yelled, and watched as the men who had been pretending to surrender fell belly-first onto the ground. All but one. General Josiah Jonathan Justice stood in front of his command, tall, rigid, a virtual wall, and he drew the LeMat revolver and fired the first bullet of the battle.

The roar from the Gatling was deafening—Fallon couldn't even hear the Gatling in the next wagon bed—and the smoke blinding, plus the wagon bounced

around. The clip emptied, and Fallon withdrew it as
Bennett kept turning the crank. Each barrel roared
as Fallon ducked and handed it to the man in charge
of reloading. He already had another empty hopper
filled, and once he handed it to Fallon, Fallon rose
back into the smoke, ready to take the second hopper
after he replaced his.

Down he went again, taking the warm hopper from
the sweating, wild-eyed outlaw. Fallon saw that General
Justice remained standing, daring some Mexican to kill
him, and the mercenaries on the ground were firing
from prone positions with their revolvers. Horses
reared, throwing off dead men, or dying themselves.

"This is a slaughter," Fallon said, though only he
could hear his own voice over the din of battle. "And
I am its designer." He turned to spit, and brought up
another container of .30 caliber shells to rain upon
the marauders.

As he slammed the hopper into place and lifted his
hand for the next empty one, his eyes teared from the
smoke. Fred Bennett, murderer, traitor, and former
Texas Ranger, was grinning with malevolent pleasure
as he turned that crank, causing a steady *pop-pop-pop*.
The gun could not continue at this rate. Already the
mechanism was slowing, and sometimes a chamber
refused to fire. Gunpowder would foul the Gatling,
render it useless. But these men were too desperate
to stop.

Suddenly Fred Bennett jerked the crank, straightened, and his eyes glazed over. Fallon saw the massive
hole just beneath his rib cage, and he knew what had
happened. A bullet had entered at the small of the
killer's back and blown an apple-sized hole in his upper
abdomen. Blood gushed from Bennett's mouth, and

he tried to say something, but choked on the pool of crimson, and as Fallon reached for him, Bennett twisted to one side and fell forward, pushing the barrel down, twisting the crank, and riddling the floor and side of the wagon with bullets from the Gatling gun.

Fred Bennett was dead when he hit the wagon bed.

The soldier of fortune handling the hopper turned and caught a bullet in his forehead that blew off the top of his skull.

"Behind us!" Fallon yelled. He stepped toward the gun and awkwardly spun the weapon around.

The Mexican bandits had some sense. They had sent only part of their band to meet and slaughter the surrendering members of the wagon train. The rest had circled around. General Justice had not suspected the bandits smart enough to try such a simple, and what should have been predictable, move. Hell, neither had Fallon.

He gripped the crank, pointed the barrel down just a tad, and turned the handle.

Pop-pop-pop! The .30 caliber gun spit out lead, although the smoke was so thick, Fallon could not see if he had hit anything. Suddenly, the machine gun stopped firing. Fallon could not even turn the crank.

He leaped, ducked, drew one of the Colts from Bennett's holsters, and hurdled over the side. Two men had made it underneath one of the wagons. Fallon saw horses and dust beyond that. He squeezed the trigger, and the bullet caught the first killer as he tried to push himself to his feet. The man dropped his revolver and clasped his head with both hands. Blood seeped between his fingers as the man fell onto his side, shuddered, and breathed his last. Fallon dived to his right as the second man brought up his Winchester and fired. Fallon aimed from his side and touched the trigger. He missed. The man stepped forward. The last gunner in Fallon's wagon fell over the side, hit the wheel, and slid into the dust, his feet and fingers twitching.

Fallon glanced at the second wagon, but couldn't see any movement, as he fired the pistol again. The bullet went wide. The Mexican fired, but he rushed his shot. Fallon steadied his aim, and his breathing, and touched the trigger again just a split second after the Mexican pulled his trigger. But the Mexican was out of bullets. The revolver Fallon held had one more cartridge, and the chunk of lead hit the man plumb center.

Another bandit leaped his palomino stallion through a gap between wagons. He was shot off his horse by Merle, who had given up on his Gatling gun, as well.

Fallon punched out shells from his pistol. Merle came over. "We're finished!" he yelled. "We're . . ."

He stopped, turned to the north. His eyes became more focused. "Did you . . ." he started. Fallon finished the sentence. "Hear that?"

It wasn't faint—not if they could hear it over the roar of battle and their own ears numbed from the pandemonium of war. But it was a bugle. Sounding: *Charge!*

Maybe the Mexican army had a charge call, but it certainly couldn't sound like this one. Because echoing behind the bugle was a full band playing "Dixie's Land."

Fallon lowered his revolver. He wiped his face. His shoulder was bleeding again, and his legs started to lose strength. He dropped the revolver and gripped a wagon tongue for support. Facing west, he saw General Justice moving forward, putting bullets in the heads of wounded Mexicans as they crawled over the blood-soaked desert sand. Men littered the desert.

Fallon turned around, sat on an empty crate of ammunition, and saw the flash of sabers on the other side of their makeshift redoubt. The battle had turned. The New Confederate Army for Justice would win the day.

Then Fallon was on his back, breathing air, feeling that dreaded void approach him—maybe for the last time. Suddenly a hand lifted him up, brought him to rest on another human, and gentle hands pushed the sweat-soaked bangs off his forehead.

"Hank . . ." He must have dreamed it.

He must be dead.

For he was certain that he was looking into the beautiful eyes of Christina Whitney.

CHAPTER FORTY-ONE

Only Christina had grown a brown mustache. Her hair was brown and short. And she wore the uniform of a Confederate soldier.

"Hang on, honey," the soldier whispered. The soldier sounded a hell of a lot like Christina Whitney, too.

"I'm . . . dead . . ." Fallon said, and his eyes closed.

"Listen to me, you picklebrain," she said in a rasping voice. "Open your damned eyes. You're not dying on me."

"I'm not dying," he said, though he couldn't be certain of that, and he kept his eyes closed. He didn't think he had enough strength to open them. Fallon managed to add: "Yet."

"Open your eyes and look at me," Christina demanded.

He sucked in a deep breath, holding it, and finally let it out slowly. His eyes opened. Christina's face softened.

"What the hell . . . are you . . . doing . . . here?"

"My name's White," she said. "Chris White. We partnered together in a Missouri jail four years ago. Liberty. Thirty days for disturbing the peace. Remember that."

His brain began to fog over.

"What?" he managed to say.

"Remember. Liberty's jail. Thirty days. Four years ago."

She must have felt the presence of someone or heard footsteps because she pressed down harder on the bullet wound in his shoulder, hard enough for Fallon to cry out in pain. That closed his eyes, and when they opened, he recognized the towering figure of General Josiah Jonathan Justice standing just behind Christina Whitney . . . Chris White.

"How bad is he, soldier?" Justice said as he wiped his face with a silk handkerchief.

Christina turned to stare up at the General, and her voice lowered. "Don't rightly know certain-sure, Gen'ral." She turned her head, spit between her teeth. "Dis shoulder of his'n be a-bleedin' like a stuck hawg hangin' from a cedar branch." She started tearing off her bandanna, wadding it into a ball. Then she pulled out a pewter flask from her back pocket—trousers.

She's wearing pants, Fallon thought. *My God . . . Wait . . . yes . . . she's . . . a man . . . pretending to be . . .*

"Chris White . . ." Fallon said.

"That's right, pard," Christina said as she unscrewed the lid and poured clear liquid onto her checked piece of cotton. "You ain't forgot Missouri, I reckon."

"Is that ardent spirits there . . . Private White?" The name came out as more of a question, more of an uncertainty, than the query as to what Christina's flask contained.

"Bona fide corn liquor, Gen'ral," she said, and

held up the flask in her left hand while bringing the bandanna, soaked with booze, toward Fallon's bloody shoulder. "Pap's very own recipe. Folks come clear from down in Pulaski County jes' to sip some of Pap's Cass County brew."

When Fallon had finished screaming, and when the blinding tears finally left his eyes, he saw and heard General Justice coughing savagely while holding the flask he had sampled as far away from his body as a person could.

"Good . . . Gawd . . ." Justice shook his head, coughed again, and studied the flask. "You actually drink this filth?"

Christina squeezed more of the liquor into the hole in Fallon's shoulder, but now he couldn't feel anything. It was like the rotgut had burned away every nerve in Fallon's shoulder. Still, Christina took the flask Justice was handing back to her and swallowed down a swig. Fallon saw that. He tried to shake his head in amazement because Christina simply wiped her mouth and set the container down on a flat rock.

"Ya gots to've growed up with it, I reckons, sir," she said in her thickened accent.

"I see." Justice stepped around. He pointed at Fallon, but held his gaze on Christina. "You know this man, my captain, Harry Alexander?"

"Ain't got nary a clue as to what name he be usin' these days, sir, but I knowed him for a spell up Liberty, Missouri, way. We both got into some tussles. Not ag'in each other. I don't know who he was a-fightin', but I was a-havin' me a high ol' time at a barn dance on Holtzclaw Creek." She snorted, spat again, and peeled back the bandanna to look at the wound.

"That be some spell back, though, Gen'ral. Two years. Nah. Longer'n that. Must be nigh four. Don't rightly reckon it was five, though." She laughed. "Too much of Pa's corn liquor between that stay and today."

"I don't think I know you . . . Private . . ."

"White." She turned and offered a lame salute. "Chris White. Cass County, Missouri. Pa rode with Quantrill. I wasn't old enough to fit 'em damn Yankees back then, but I's sure glad you's givin' me the chance to avenge Pa. He got kilt whilst he were a-ridin' with Howell's Renegades when they tried a-robbin' that bank in St. Joe back in '79. Deke Hollister tol' me 'bout what you was a-doin', so I tracked yer outfit down as soon as word reached me. Chris Ehrlander signed me up. That's how come I knowed where to find ya."

Fallon's fingers balled into fists at the mention of Ehrlander's name. He tried to sit up, but Christina pushed him down.

"Set still, ol' hoss," she said. Her eyes remained firm. "And drink some of Pa's toddy."

She started bringing the flask toward his lips.

Justice stared at the back of her head, then at Fallon before Christina blocked Fallon's view. He heard the General say, "Take care of him, White. He's too good of a fighting man to miss our next campaign." Justice walked away.

Fallon's lips tightened, but Christina said, "You do need to drink this. Might not cure you, but it'll stop the hurt. In your shoulder, that is."

She lifted his head, and he took more of the rotgut than he wanted, coughed about a dozen times after swallowing the first mouthful, then Christina brought the flask back to his lips and made him swallow even more.

"From the carvin'," she began, still using the phony accent, "around that hole there, I reckon they gots the lead out. That's good. Maybe you won't die from blood p'is'in. You jes' sleep, ol' hoss, and let Chris White take good care of you. Like the Gen'ral says. You's too good a fightin' man to miss our next campaign."

He did feel better. Well, he felt . . . tired . . . too exhausted to hurt. She lowered his head onto something soft, and he saw General Justice standing over another wounded man, a wounded soldier of the New Confederate Army for Justice.

"This man is gut-shot," Justice told the man tending the wounded man. Then Justice stared down at the man. "You served your country well, sir. You fought valiantly. But we cannot leave you behind. Just know that we are grateful for your service, and that your kin will know that you died nobly in battle." The LeMat was in the General's hand, and the last thing Fallon heard was the report of the giant weapon.

He woke to a rocking that was neither rhythmic nor rocking. His shoulder hurt, but no longer throbbed or burned, and he breathed in scents of what smelled like rotting fish and salt. A lot of salt. Wherever he was, it was dark, but he knew he no longer was lying on the ground somewhere in Mexico.

"Welcome back," Christina Whitney said, and she sounded like Christina Whitney, not a Missouri ruffian and son of a bushwhacker, although when Fallon's eyes finally focused, after Christina lighted a match and brought it to the wick of a candle, she still looked like Chris White—only dirtier now.

He tried to remember everything that had happened. He tried to speak, but his lips, tongue, and throat did not work. She was setting the candle into a holder and putting that on a box. Next she found a canteen, which she uncorked. Once again, she started to lift his head, but he pulled away from her.

"Let me," he managed to say. "See if . . . I . . . can . . . sit . . ."

He made it. No dizziness sent him tumbling back into the purgatory of oblivion. The shoulder hurt no more—but no less, either. And he could breathe better, even smell better, but the latter only made him groan and gag. Wherever he was stank like the guts of a catfish.

Now he took the canteen.

"You are one hard rock," Christina said.

He drank. Drank again.

"Not too much," she warned.

At least he could talk now without sounding like a dying frog. "Where are we?"

"Aboard the C.S.S. *Justice*," she said.

She went on to explain. The survivors of the ambush—there were no Mexican survivors, Christina said—had regrouped with the main force on the coastline, which was where the frigate *Justice* lay anchored in water deep enough to support it and the weight it was about to carry. The Gatling guns that had been used had been cleaned and disassembled, returned to the boxes. Weapons had been issued to all soldiers for the New Confederate Army for Justice. The men did not seem overly thrilled that they would not be paid yet, but there wasn't much they could do. Before long, some of Porfirio Díaz's rurales would come this way—the buzzards were sure to invite investigation—so General Justice had given them a choice. They could stay here or sail away to Texas. All of them decided not to be mustered out of Justice's army. Besides, they had seen just how Justice mustered out his soldiers.

"How long have we been at sea?"

She told him.

He started to ask another question, but quickly put it aside. Instead, he drank more water, then handed her the canteen so he wouldn't be tempted to drink again. "How the hell did you find us?"

She grinned. Even with that mustache glued on her lips, even with the dirt, and grime, and the fact she had been in this ship's hold, sweating profusely, she looked beautiful. Maybe that was Fallon's imagination. Or the fact that the candle lit up only so much.

"I am a detective, Hank," she told him. "A pretty damn good one, too."

"I never doubted that."

"We had operatives near Justice's operations, from Florida's Panhandle to southern Texas. When no one reported you at Hell on the Brazos, we knew you had to be somewhere else. Didn't take long before we got word that you were in Louisiana. And when the superintendent at The Walls reported that you had died, we knew, most likely, that the operation was starting up. When we found out for certain . . ."

"But how did you get here . . . I mean . . . to Mexico?"

"Chris Ehrlander. I thought you knew that."

CHAPTER FORTY-TWO

Fallon stiffened. Hatred filled his heart.

"I wasn't lying, Hank," Christina told him. "Not to Justice. Chris got me here. Well, he told me where to go. Chris gave me my cover."

"*Chris?*" Immediately, he regretted his tone. It sounded petty, or rather like he was jealous. Then it struck Fallon that was how he felt. It wasn't the hatred he felt for Chris Ehrlander. He was jealous of the man because Christina was on such familiar terms with him.

She took his hand and squeezed it. "Hank. Chris has been working for the American Detective Agency since before this operation. He's the one who told Sean MacGregor and Dan all about you. He said that he had been trying to prove your innocence all these years, that he wanted to avenge the murder of your wife and daughter."

Fallon's eyes closed. He pulled his hand away, but she brought it right back and squeezed tightly. And he was too weak to put up much of a fight.

"He set me up," he told her. "He killed Renee and Rachel."

"No." The voice was but a whisper, but it came with a force. Fallon had to open his eyes. "Barney Drexel killed your family. Had your family killed, I mean. I thought you knew that."

"Drexel?"

"Yes, Hank. He was a guard at the Missouri State Penitentiary before he came to Texas. He helped set up the operation there, at least from all that Chris—Chris Ehrlander—and Dan MacGregor found out. Well, Chris told Mr. MacGregor. I'm not sure when exactly Dan learned everything. I didn't know—but I didn't even know you until we started the operation—until Chris told me."

"Chris Ehrlander?" It hurt Fallon just to say the words.

"He's your friend, Hank. He's been your friend for years."

He felt sick.

"I'm a lousy detective," he said. "I had it all wrong."

She looked up, and, satisfied that all remained safe, came down and kissed him gently on his lips.

"It's all right, honey." Lifting her head, she said, "Where is Drexel?"

"Dead," Fallon said. Hell, he had gotten his revenge—and hadn't even realized it.

"Dead?"

Fallon explained what had happened on the train, and as he did, a strange feeling came over him. He had killed Barney Drexel while performing his duty . . . in self-defense . . . not out of the bloodlust of vengeance. And this knowledge left him feeling whole.

Maybe he wasn't as cold-blooded as prisons had made him out to be.

But something else struck him.

"I was sent to Huntsville . . . The MacGregors, Holderman, Chris Ehrlander knew Drexel was there. Which meant they knew he might recognize me." The fury started returning. Maybe he wasn't so whole after all. "Hell, it's only a miracle that Drexel didn't remember me sooner than he did."

Christina leaned back. "Drexel was at Rusk, not The Walls."

Fallon stared at the woman. He knew she was a great actress, but she couldn't have been that good.

"He was at The Walls," Fallon said.

Her shoulders slumped.

"Why would MacGregor have sent me to Huntsville if the operation was based out of Rusk?" Fallon said. "Drexel was there, at The Walls."

"I don't know," Christina said after a long silence.

"And why did I get sent to Yuma first? Jeff City I can understand. The Mole was there. But Yuma?" He shook his head.

"Listen, Hank," she said, her voice firm. "I don't have those answers. I just don't know. Remember, I didn't meet you—except for a passing nod at the elevator in Chicago—until we started planning for this. This is the case I'm working on. And you're working on it with me. And there's one important thing here. We need to get out of here alive."

He sighed. "Yeah. I know."

"Where's the money?" she asked.

Fallon looked at her again. "From the train. The reports we have said you made off with more than two hundred thousand dollars. That's a lot of money. That can finance . . ."

He finished the sentence for her. "A war." His head shook. "You haven't heard from Holderman?"

She shook her head.

Well, that had been a long shot. Fallon told her how he had tossed the money—all of it, or at least most of it—out of the express car along the side of the Houston-Victoria-Laredo Railroad. But he had told Holderman what he had done. It wasn't what he had wanted to do, and it certainly wasn't how he thought things would play out, but he didn't have much of a choice.

"Holderman wasn't part of our convoy," he said. "Justice sent some riders with wagons in the opposite directions. I have to guess that Holderman was with one of those groups."

"Maybe with the party that went east?"

He shrugged. "Maybe, but I wouldn't count on it. And even if he did, he would have been outnumbered."

"Even if he did," Christina said, "he'd still be Aaron Holderman."

Which, to Fallon's surprise, caused him not only to grin, but to laugh.

"I've been down here since just after the train job," she told him. "So there's a chance that Holderman did get the money."

He remained quiet. She kept on talking.

"Without the money, Justice can't fund a war. I was in camp long enough to know these men aren't revolutionaries. They're thieves, killers, and rogues—no better, no worse than those bandits that attacked you. If they don't get paid, they'll leave Justice in droves. This new Civil War will die before it ever truly begins."

He frowned. "It already began," he told her. "You know about Attorney General Maxwell."

Christina's head dropped. "Yes," she said, barely audible. "I guess . . . I didn't . . . think . . . But . . ."

"I know. But Josiah Justice is a raving lunatic. He'll do something. Something crazy. Even if he has only a dozen zealots with him, he'll . . . and with four Gatling guns. With all the weapons and gunpowder he has on this ship. It's just not going to be pretty when he gets to shore. Besides, for all we know, that money—all two hundred thousand dollars—is waiting for him when this bucket lands."

She said, "And we don't even know where he's landing. Even Chris Ehrlander said he had no clue."

"Yes," Fallon said, "we do."

She studied him.

"Indianola."

Her head shook. "That's a ghost town, Hank. Two hurricanes wiped it off the face of . . ." Which is when she understood. "I'm a lousy detective."

Fallon made himself grin.

"I should have seen it. We all should have seen it," Christina said, angry with herself. "Of course. Indianola. No one would think about Indianola. People moved out of there by the scores after that last hurricane nigh ten years ago."

"And Rufus K. Conley has a newspaper office there," Fallon said.

"Preaching his propaganda," Christina said. "I figured he was there because . . . well . . . he hated people. I mean, if you read what he writes."

"He doesn't hate all people. Just Northerners. And Conley didn't just print news about the Southern Confederacy. Apparently for a town with very few people, it has a lot of gun shops and hardware stores. Rufus Conley ran some of those, too."

Her head shook again. "I am a lousy detective."

"No," he said. "But we've solved the crime. How do we stop a war?"

Christina lifted the candle. Her face showed doubt. She wet her lips.

"Hank . . ."

He waited. He knew what she was going to say. He didn't want to hear it from her, but before he started to say something, she pressed her fingers against his lips. "We're in the cargo hold," she said, soft but firm, and resolve slowly showed in her pretty eyes. "Your favorite general put you down here. He figured you'd likely die. He wanted to keep the men, those he had left, up on the decks or in the cabins there." She raised the candle toward Fallon's feet. "The kegs of powder. The ammunition. It's all . . . here."

"One spark." She had to catch her breath. "Could save a lot of lives."

One spark would also take a lot of lives, Fallon knew, including Christina's. Yet before either could say anything, find an alternative to sacrificing themselves for their country, or agree to blow up themselves, the C.S.S. *Justice*, and General Josiah Jonathan Justice and his killers for hire, the door to the hold opened from above.

Instantly, Christina blew out the candle.

Sunlight bathed them through the opening, causing both to shield their eyes and turn their heads. By the time they had recovered, General Justice and Captain Merle were standing next to them.

"A candle?" Merle said. "Are you trying to blow us to hell?"

Christina's head shook, though she still looked away from the two newcomers. "Capt'n, I knows where nots to put no match, sir. Burned me down a passel of buildin's back up in Cass County when I was but a babe. A-hopin' I might be like Mrs. O'Leary's cow."

"Huh?" Merle said.

"Never mind," the General said. "How is our patient, Private White?"

"I was about to see if he could make it up dem thar stairs, Gen'ral. Not just fer him, though. Dis place stinks somethin' awful."

"Indeed." Justice appeared to be grinning. "You do seem better than you were after our encounter at what history will call the Battle of Mexicali Bay."

"Ready for duty, sir," Fallon said. "After I get something to eat."

"Bully, Captain Alexander. Bully. We land directly. The war starts anew, but this one will not drag on for four long years."

"Of course, sir."

"Help him up, Private," Justice ordered.

Christina adjusted the butternut shell jacket she was wearing, hiding her breasts, which she had strapped down with cotton wrappings. She pulled her hat down lower, complained about the sun after being stuck in that dungeon since last night, and studied the gulls flying over the ship's masts.

Fallon leaned against her for support, which was also more of an attempt to protect her should something go amiss.

The waves were rough for the Gulf of Mexico, and Fallon saw the Texas coast.

"Are we that close to home, sir?" he asked.

Justice laughed. "In good time, Captain. In good time. This is the path many fishing vessels take. If we sailed farther out in the Gulf, then steered for Matagorda Bay, it might arouse suspicion. For this moment, we are merely catching fish to feed the masses in Galveston . . . Houston . . . Corpus Christi."

Behind them, Merle whispered, "Maybe you'd like to feed the masses on this ship something other than gruel."

"Captain Merle," Justice said, shaking his head. "Look around you."

Justice stopped, and pointed. Fallon saw men huddled around the edge of the ship on both starboard and port sides. Over the pounding waves and squawking gulls, he could hear their violent retching.

"Do you think these soldiers would rather be dining on steak and fried eggs right now?"

It wasn't an appealing sight to see on the way to eat supper.

Fallon looked up at the mast, turned, and stared toward the stern. The Bonnie Blue Flag flew from the rear, which might not get the attention of a Confederate flag.

Merle went to eat elsewhere, leaving Justice alone with the cook, two other mercenaries, and Fallon and Christina. They ate in the captain's dining room, grits and some sort of fish, fried in grease, with apples that they had to eat carefully to avoid biting into any worms, and drank coffee that was just awful. Fallon wondered if he would soon join those unfortunate men as they puked their guts out into the sea.

Justice told them little, merely recapped all that Fallon had missed, bragged about the great victory won at Mexicali Bay, and after everyone passed on dessert, he walked with the two mercenaries back to the hold. By then it was dark, and one of the guards held a lantern. They stopped by the opening to the hold.

"Captain Alexander," Justice said.

Something was wrong here. Fallon could feel it. He stared into the grinning face of the General.

"How long have you known Private White?"

Fallon remembered. "Four years. Five. Something like that. We did some time together in a jail up in Missouri."

"Yes. Yes. That's it. How was Private White's beard back then?"

"Sir?"

Justice's right hand shot out, grabbed the end of Christina's mustache and ripped it off. "Because," Justice yelled as Christina brought both hands to her upper lip and shrieked.

"For a man with such a fine mustache," Justice said, reaching for his LeMat, "I suddenly wondered why there's no beard stubble on her face!"

CHAPTER FORTY-THREE

Christina dropped to her knees, eyes tearing from the pain. Fallon started toward Justice, but the deadly bore of the massive gun stopped him.

"We are bound for Matagorda Bay," Justice said. "I thought about waiting to execute the both of you at Indianola. But it just struck me that I'd much rather have the two of you walk the plank." He tilted his head back and let out a maniacal laugh.

Which was all Fallon needed.

He brought his right leg up and the foot of his boot caught Justice full in the crotch. The smoothbore barrel sent a blinding flame that scorched the bottom of Fallon's left forearm as he reached for Justice, but the buckshot that filled that barrel never touched Fallon.

It hit somebody else, though. Fallon heard the sharp scream as he lunged at Justice, missing the chance to grab the arm that held the big LeMat. Justice tumbled onto the deck, and Fallon went over his back. He slid a ways on the deck, wet with water from the rocking Gulf of Mexico, rolled over, and saw gray trouser legs running past him. Fallon came to his knees. Justice had forgotten about the revolver he held in his right hand, and for a man who had just received a mean kick in the privates, he was moving very, very fast. Fallon rolled over. His eyes widened.

"My God! My God! My God!" shouted one of Justice's men accompanying the prisoners. Fallon couldn't hear him well because the mercenary who had been carrying the lantern was gone. But a glow could be seen from inside the cargo hold.

The man turned and ran, past Fallon, after Justice. Christina Whitney had recovered from the pain of having the fake mustache ripped off her upper lip and had stepped onto the stairs that led into the hold.

Suddenly, Fallon knew what had happened. Justice's LeMat's grapeshot barrel had sent its load into the man carrying the lantern, and both man and lantern had dropped inside the cargo hold.

Fallon leaped to his feet, suddenly aware of the commotion of some of the seasick soldiers—and shouts from those not puking over the sides or into buckets. Reaching the steps, Fallon's eyes shied away from the intensity of the flames. The lantern had exploded on the floor, the kerosene carrying flames toward the crates of ammunition and the kegs of gunpowder. The man who had been carrying the lantern lay spread-eagled on the floor, a cavernous, bloody hole in the center of his chest.

Christina was removing her shell jacket in an attempt to beat out the flames.

Fallon grabbed her arm before she took another step down.

"Forget it!" he shouted.

"But—"

He didn't let her argue. She wouldn't be able to

stop that fire. Flames already leaped at a box of shells for Winchester .44-40s. Moving back up the steps, he jerked her savagely. He moved as fast as he could, dragging her up the few steps she had managed to climb down, and then flinging her in front of him once they reached the deck.

A gagging, weaving man rushed by him, stared into the opening, and ran down the steps.

"Don't . . ." he started, and reached for the man, but missed. Another soldier of fortune slid to a stop, peered down, screamed, "Mother of God, we're all gonna die!" and bolted for the side of the ship, disappearing into the night. Fallon never heard the splash after the man dived overboard.

Christina was up by then, and Fallon moved toward her, turned her around, and pushed her in the direction he had seen General Justice running.

"Hurry!" he yelled.

"But . . ." she tried.

He turned her around as the first pop of an ignited Winchester cartridge echoed from the smoking hold.

Fifteen steps later, the pops sounded like a Gatling gun being cranked. Ten steps later, the explosion lifted the ship partway out of the sea and sent flaming debris out of the hold and scattering across the decks. Fallon went one way, sliding toward the edge as the ship listed toward its starboard side. He didn't know where Christina went. He grasped at everything and anything, bottles, ropes, canvas sails, and finally stopped himself by slamming his boots against a trunk. The ship settled back, but that violent movement sent several other seasick individuals waving their arms frantically, then falling backward, into the night, into the Gulf of Mexico.

Fallon rose. Someone pushed him aside and ran toward the stern. Fallon looked up. Flames lighted the night sky. Smoke churned out of the cargo hold's opening. Fire spread across the ship, and another one shot up the mainsail. Ashes already started raining down.

"Jesus help us all," he said, and started for Christina Whitney. He found her, sitting up, staring with widening eyes at the orange flames. He grabbed her hand just as the next explosion rocked the ship sideways, up and down, and sent them rolling toward the bow. Only the bottom post of the mainsail stopped them from continuing down, but the ship's bow leaped out of the water, and they rolled away.

Again the ship steadied, though listing now to the port side, and the stern beginning to sink.

Another keg of powder or crate of cartridges exploded as one, but did little to disturb the doomed C.S.S. *Justice.* Fallon pulled Christina to her feet. She blinked.

A man rushed past them, screaming in terror and pain, his chest aflame, his hair burning. He bolted toward the starboard side. Fallon made out a figure standing at the rails, holding out his hands, yelling something that Fallon couldn't make out. Apparently, he was trying to stop the burning man from diving overboard. Instead, the man on fire dived and took that one trying to stop him off the ship. Both disappeared into the Gulf.

Fallon swore. He stared at Christina, whose mouth moved, "Oh . . . my . . . heavens."

Turning her around, Fallon guided her toward the lifeboats on the port side.

They found General Josiah Jonathan Justice in

one boat, holding that big LeMat, yelling, cursing, demanding that they lower him down first.

"This is the officers' boat, you blasted fools! Officers first. Get me down now or, by thunder, you'll all drown or burn! Trooper, sound 'Officer's Call'! You, work that crank. Get this boat down first, you fools, then all sailors, all enlisted men, all good men and true shall join us." He fired over one man's head. "Our camp is just there! Just there! They will send help. But you must get this ship down first!"

Although the C.S.S. *Justice* appeared to be sinking fast, the men obeyed, either out of misplaced loyalty and duty, or fear. Fallon pulled Christina toward the boat. The LeMat trained on Fallon's chest.

"Stop!"

"I'm an officer, sir," Fallon said. "Remember."

He saw the debate going on in Justice's eyes. Justice hesitated, but also saw those men. It was exactly what Fallon had hoped he would see, and figure out. Turn down Fallon's request, and the men would storm the lifeboat, probably throw Justice and the LeMat overboard. The LeMat held only nine bullets—eight after that warning shot, and maybe fewer. Fallon didn't know how many rounds Justice had fired just to get himself inside the lifeboat and have crewmen start to lower it into the sea.

Fallon helped Christina into the boat, but Justice waved the revolver, screaming, "No, no, no, no! Only officers!"

"Sir," Fallon said, "you need someone to row for you. Don't you, General?"

The zealot's eyes were wide with insanity, but he nodded and waved Christina aboard. Fallon found another man, the youngest, and pulled him toward the boat.

Justice's brow knotted.

"The other oar, General," Fallon explained, and eased the teary-eyed youngster into the boat.

Another explosion rocked the ship.

"Get in!" Justice ordered as Fallon looked around for someone else he might be able to save.

"Sir . . . I'm . . ." Fallon started, but a gray-bearded man with a crooked nose pushed Fallon toward the lifeboat.

"Get in there, blast ye," he said. "The sooner we get this boat down, the quicker we get the next one into the sea."

A moment later, Fallon found himself at the ship's bow, staring at Justice and the big LeMat.

They started down. The ship rocked from another explosion. A voice above, on the deck, called down, "Wait! Damn you, Justice, you ain't leavin' me up here!"

Fallon's head lifted to see Merle. The man moved toward one of the ropes. "I'm an officer, too, you ignoramous." Merle grabbed the rope.

"Don't you know that the captain goes down with his ship?" Justice called out, adding with a sinister laugh: *"Captain!"* The LeMat roared, a pink mist sprayed from the back of Merle's head as he fell out of view on the listing, burning, ruined deck of the ship.

That also broke the hold Justice wielded over the crew and the soldiers of fortune. Instead of being lowered at a safe, deliberate rate, they must have either cut the lines or simply let the crank turn relentlessly. The lifeboat dropped into the water, almost capsizing, spraying them with water and slamming them against the hard, salt-soaked wood. Yet somehow, the boat stayed right side up, and it even began drifting away from the sinking, burning ship.

Fallon started toward the stern, but Justice grabbed the pistol he had dropped, which was cocked, and aimed it first at the boy on the starboard side, then at Christina on the port.

"Sit down, you traitor. Or I'll send this wench to hell."

Fallon sat. Justice wasn't completely crazy. He remembered that Christina was a woman.

"Work the rudder, Seaman Alexander," Justice ordered.

They rowed away, the Gulf of Mexico or Matagorda Bay or wherever they were, reflecting the increasingly violent flames that quickly spread across the C.S.S. *Justice.*

Looking behind him, Fallon saw another lifeboat in the water, one on the starboard side of the doomed vessel. Another, on the port side, was filling with men. The oars worked, water rippled, and another explosion sent flames and embers into the sky like fireworks on Independence Day. Flaming chunks of wood rained down into the choppy waves, and the hisses sounded like the sighs of demons in the night.

There other sounds, too.

"God have mercy," said the boy working the oars with Christina.

Yes, Fallon thought, as another man screamed somewhere in the water.

It hadn't taken long. Sharks . . . and maybe barracudas—had come to feast on the dead and dying.

By the time the lifeboat struck bottom, the moon was rising, bringing light to the skies now that the burning frigate was slipping beneath the waves. The boy rowing the boat leaped over the side and splashed through the shallows toward the coastline. General Justice did not even send a bullet after the kid, but merely stood, pulled down his hat, and stepped into the water. He took a few steps before remembering the other passengers, crew, whatever you wanted to call them, still in the lifeboat.

"Come," he said happily. "The war begins tonight. Port Justice is just over there."

He pointed the LeMat's barrel toward the northwest—at the exact moment explosions and flashes of light erupted from that direction.

CHAPTER FORTY-FOUR

When Fallon and Christina reached dry land, the sounds of battle intensified. General Justice stood several yards ahead, where the pebbly sand ended and brush and grass began. Distance muffled the pops of pistols and rifles and the faint calls from bugles as Justice yelled out:

"What is the meaning of this? I gave no order to attack. I have not sounded a retreat."

Feet splashed in the bay, and Fallon looked back. One of the lifeboats had reached the Texas shore, and men were running down the beach, away from General Justice. Two . . . no, three . . . other boats were making their way, but two pointed farther toward the east, farther from the raving lunatic who had thought he could start and win another Civil War. The third was steering off to the southwest, also moving as far away from General Josiah Jonathan Justice as feasible.

The flames from the ship were almost out. Then they were. And the Gulf of Mexico took the C.S.S. *Justice* to the bottom.

Fallon knelt beside Christina Whitney, who sat staring at the sea.

"Are you all right?" he asked softly.

Her head nodded ever so slightly.

General Josiah Jonathan Justice marched back and forth, one hand holding the LeMat, the other scratching his head. His hat had blown across the beach. He muttered and mumbled as he walked, little that Fallon could understand, little that made any sense. Waves broke and splashed gently on the shore, and the moon rose higher, brighter now. The gunfire to the northwest and the sounds of bugles, of shouts, slowly died.

Fallon felt Christina Whitney standing beside him.

"I guess," she whispered, "Dan found the camp."

"Indianola?" Fallon asked.

She shrugged. "I've never been there, but it makes sense. It has to be."

So the American Detective Agency had managed to foil General Justice and his treason. Sean MacGregor would be proud of his son. No, that wasn't right. Sean MacGregor would be happy that he had finally topped the Pinkertons. Sean MacGregor would take credit for everything and might not even mention Dan MacGregor—and certainly not Christina Whitney or Harry Fallon—to all the newspaper reporters.

"What's he doing?" Christina nodded at Justice.

"I don't know. I doubt if he does."

"Do we stop him?"

"Let him walk," Fallon said, shaking his head. "He's not going anywhere. But he still has that big grapeshot revolver. And we don't have any guns."

So they settled on the beach, listened to the waves, watched the stars, and kept their eyes on General Josiah Jonathan Justice as he marched back and forth, back and forth, until finally dawn broke, and Justice sat in the sand, buried his head in his hands, and sobbed like a child.

Justice stopped and made a beeline for the water. Fallon nudged Christina awake. They had been sitting, backs against a mound of sand. Fallon likely had fallen asleep, too, but he was wide awake as the insane fiend moved past them, didn't even notice them. Briefly, Fallon thought Justice planned to walk into the Gulf and start swimming, planning to drown himself after his far-fetched dreams of a new Confederacy had been destroyed.

Now he knew that wasn't the General's intention—yet.

"On your feet, lads!" Justice snapped as waves, now gentle, splashed across his boots and trousers. "The war is not lost. I dare say that we have it won. On your feet. We march. We march in fifteen minutes. We march to VICTORY!"

"My . . . God . . ." Christina whispered.

"Trooper, find my horse. You will follow me. Hurrah, boys! Hurrah for Dixie! Hurrah for the Confederacy! Down with Yankee tyranny!"

He kept addressing soldiers . . . and the sight sickened both Fallon and Christina. The soldiers, the remnants of Justice's New Confederate Army for Justice, would not be following the General anywhere. The Gulf of Mexico had washed them from the sunken C.S.S. *Justice* to the shores near what once had been a thriving port town called Indianola.

Fallon could tell that at least one of the bodies had been ravaged by sharks. Only his upper torso had made it to the beach, yet Justice saluted him, and said, "Lieutenant. Find your sergeant, mister, and have your company fall in."

Whirling, he spun around, came out of the water, and had taken about a dozen steps on the rough sand when the gunshot roared just behind Fallon and to his right. Justice twisted, and he tried to raise the LeMat when another bullet slammed into his abdomen and sent him flying back in the sand.

Fallon spun at the first shot, saw the smoke and flame spit from the barrel of a Colt, and he took a quick step, then stopped. The Colt was aimed at him now, the hammer had been eared back, and the finger was on the trigger.

Chris Ehrlander grinned. "Hank," he said. "Christina. Good to see you."

Fallon said nothing, but Christina said questioningly, "Chris?"

"Don't take another step, sweetheart," Ehrlander said. He looked back at Fallon and shook his head. "You're a tough man to kill, Hank."

Only my friends call me Hank.

"I'm still alive," Fallon said.

"For a moment."

Fallon's head bobbed. "You never told Dan, Christina, or anyone else that Barney Drexel rode with Parker's court at the same time I did." It all made sense now. "You figured he'd recognize me."

"My mistake. I forgot just how stupid and blind Barney was."

Fallon felt that rage returning. He had it figured out, but Christina had convinced him that he was wrong. Not that Fallon could blame her. Hell, Fallon hadn't seen it back when he should have—before he even set foot in Joliet. Now he could picture how the attorney looked at Fallon's wife. It was Chris Ehrlander who had set Fallon up, maybe with Drexel's help, but probably not. It didn't matter. Ehrlander figured with Fallon locked up in prison, Renee would eventually fall for a moneymaking, handsome solicitor. And when he realized that she'd never let Fallon go . . .

The hands turned into fists. Chris Ehrlander wasn't stupid enough to talk too much. The soldiers, Rangers, detectives who had wiped out Justice's Texas base camp would be coming soon, to investigate those shots. Fallon and Christina should be dead now, but Ehrlander hadn't pulled the trigger.

"The money," the crooked lawyer said.

"Money?" Fallon asked.

"Don't stall, Hank. You know what I mean. Two hundred thousand dollars being transported in the Houston-Victoria-Laredo train. You were in the express car, and since Drexel's remains were found stretched out for about a mile along the tracks, he didn't get it. Neither did Ryker. Or that asshole Hansen. That leaves you."

"Or Holderman," Fallon said.

Those eyes revealed doubt now. If Holderman had taken part in the raid on the Indianola camp, Ehrlander would have known Fallon was lying. The look told Fallon that Aaron Holderman wasn't around.

"You're lying," Ehrlander said, and trained the Colt's long barrel on Christina's chest. "Tell me. Or she dies."

"You tell me," Fallon said. "How and why you had my wife killed. My child. And how you set everything up with Sean MacGregor."

Ehrlander shook his head. "I don't have time," he said.

He was right. He just didn't know it. The shot rang

out, and Chris Ehrlander spun around, discharging the Colt that spit up sand against his legs as he dropped to his knees, clutching his stomach, trying to straighten, and then falling to his back.

Fallon swung around, looked down the beach to see General Josiah Jonathan Justice sitting up, legs spread out in front of him, holding the smoking LeMat with both hands. The big pistol fell between his legs, and he tried to rise, but fell back. Blood trickled from his mouth, and his eyes found Christina Whitney.

"*Sic semper tyrannis!*" Justice shouted. "The South is avenged." He toppled back onto the beach, dead.

A moment later, Christina Whitney and Harry Fallon knelt beside Chris Ehrlander. His face was already pale, and his eyes began glassing over. He wouldn't be telling Fallon anything now, so Fallon spoke to him.

"I might not know everything right, but here's what I think. You contacted Sean MacGregor as soon as you heard I was being paroled," Fallon said. Christina looked away from the dying lawyer and murderer and locked her pretty eyes on Fallon. "Because you knew I'd come looking, and eventually, I'd come to see you. I don't think you'd be stupid enough to tell MacGregor that you were a woman-and-child murderer. He—or his detectives—might have figured that out. Anyway, they sent me to Yuma. You figured I'd get killed there. But I didn't.

"But then I wound up in Jefferson City. And I met The Mole. The Mole killed Rachel and Renee. And that makes sense, too. You arranged for those hired assassins to kill my family—because you knew you could never have Renee for your own. The chances of me coming out of that operation weren't good, either, but I fooled you and Sean MacGregor." He let out a mirthless laugh. "I think Sean MacGregor had more faith in me than you did. Or even I did. I should've given him more credit. But by then the Texas attorney general had approached MacGregor's company, and this was a case too big. You worked with MacGregor, still hoping I'd get killed. But Drexel didn't recognize me. Ryker got transferred to Rusk. What I can't figure out is why you just didn't tell Justice that I was an operative for a Chicago detective agency."

"How would he have known that?" Christina said. "That would have aroused Justice's suspicion of him." She nodded at the dying man. "He wanted the money. He wanted you dead, Hank. But the money would get him out of the country. Away from a hangman's rope."

"Right. The money. That's why he told you where to find us in Mexico. He might get you killed, but he had to have Justice's army destroyed somehow."

She shook her head. "I'm sorry, Hank. He had me fooled."

"No," Fallon said. "He was just too close. To you. To me. I should've seen him for what he was, a skunk, all those years ago."

Dan MacGregor and others began coming out of the brush. MacGregor and a cavalry officer barked orders, and several men moved toward the body of Justice and the drowned and mutilated corpses on the beach.

Ehrlander tried to say something, but began choking, spitting out blood, and fear registered in his eyes. Fallon stood and pulled Christina to her feet.

"Come on," he told her, and led her away, toward

Dan MacGregor, letting Chris Ehrlander choke to death on his own blood.

Dan MacGregor was walking toward them. A bullet had grazed the left side of his head, which had been wrapped with a strip of cotton, now bloodstained. He looked completely exhausted. "Ehrlander?"

"Dying," Fallon said. "Probably dead by now."

"You?" MacGregor asked, staring hard at Fallon.

Christina shook her head. "Justice."

The detective looked back at the General's body, then sighed and faced Fallon and Christina again. "What happened to the guns?"

Fallon nodded at the Gulf. "Blown to pieces and sunk."

MacGregor sighed.

"Rufus Conley?" Fallon asked.

"As dead as Indianola," MacGregor said. "Along with, by our first count, thirty-two others, fifteen arrested, most of those wounded. The rest running for Mexico. We lost five dead, ten wounded."

"What the hell happened? The ship? Justice? Ehrlander? What . . . ?"

Fallon raised his hand to stop the detective. He had a question of his own.

"Have you seen Aaron Holderman?"

CHAPTER FORTY-FIVE

Walter Wilkinson, superintendent at The Walls, stepped back in total shock when Harry Fallon came through the double doors and into the Texas State Penitentiary at Huntsville. His jaw dropped agape and he looked for his guards to come to his protection. Dan MacGregor, Christina Whitney, and two Texas Rangers followed him.

Fallon walked by the petrified man, tipped his hat, said, "Good afternoon, Warden," and walked toward the prison infirmary.

He found Dr. Abel Crouch sitting in his office, staring at a framed photograph. He looked up at Fallon and smiled.

"Mr. Fallon," he said. Not Alexander. Fallon.

"Doc."

"Solve your case, Detective?"

Fallon shrugged. "Juanito Gomez solved it for me."

The old man's head bobbed. He went back to studying the photograph.

"We had the warden pegged," Fallon said.

"Superintendent," Doc Crouch corrected.

"The warden had managed the operation in Jefferson City. We just went with the theory that Wilkinson would've been in charge here, too." Fallon sighed. "But you had to sign the death certificates. Hansen's. And Gomez's. You also had to sign off on any inmate to be sent to a work camp. And Christina Whitney did some checking. Years ago, you were the doctor at the Missouri State Penitentiary in Jefferson City. Under another name, of course."

"Gene Wadsworth," Doc Crouch said. "My mother's maiden name. Only it was Eugena."

"Which made it easier to identify you."

"My purpose all along, Fallon." The doctor looked up again, grinned, and let his gaze fall again to the picture he caressed.

"So when you came here," Fallon said, "you just scrapped the murder-for-hire scheme used in Missouri and saw the chance to start the Civil War again with Justice."

"For which I was to be well paid."

"It didn't work out."

Crouch shrugged. "It didn't work out for me in the Second Mississippi, either. More than thirty years ago."

"Will you walk down these steps with me, Doc?" Fallon asked. "I left some Texas Rangers by the gate."

Youth shone in the old man's eyes. He nodded appreciatively at Fallon, pushed himself from his chair, and handed the photograph to Fallon. "Do you recognize him, Mr. Fallon?"

Fallon looked at the photograph of an Indian, a fairly big Indian, wearing the striped uniform of an inmate in The Walls. Fallon shook his head.

"His name was Satanta. A Kiowa chief. Convicted, if you can believe this, of murder—murder committed against teamsters in a raid up in the northwestern counties of the Lone Star State. Probably before you were born. He was up here, on this floor, when he was told that he would never get out of prison alive. Unlike Juanito Gomez, Cole Hansen, and a few others, he is actually buried on Peckerwood Hill. After dying a death befitting a warrior."

With that, the old man ran. Fallon reached for him, missed, turned, and watched Dr. Able Crouch, alias Dr. Gene Wadsworth, dive through the window.

Fallon moved slowly, pulled out a curtain from the broken edges of glass, and stared down as the blood pooled around the dead man's body. Guards and a few inmates had rushed to the old man. A few looked up. One of the guards said, "He must've pushed ol' Doc. Murdered him!"

But an inmate said, "Don't be a blasted fool, George. The old reprobate killed himself. Like ol' Satanta!" The inmate, John Wesley Hardin, raised his head. "You want me?" he called up.

Fallon shook his head. There had been too many deaths already. Hell, maybe Hardin would get paroled. Texas could use a good lawyer.

After offering a lame salute, Hardin turned, plucked a cigarette from one of the guards' fingers, and moved toward his wall, where court was about to be called to order.

On the top floor of the flatiron building in Chicago, Illinois, the little man in the extremely large—and very brown—office opened a drawer, withdrew a sheet of paper, and slid it across the desk.

Fallon leaned forward and looked at it.

"I didn't realize that you had the power to grant full pardons," Fallon said, sliding the sheet back toward Sean MacGregor.

"It will be signed," the old Scot said. "You've done a good job for me, and a fine service to your country."

The ringleaders in Texas were all dead or out of the country. A prison board member, with strong connections to the governor, had killed himself. A parole board member had bought a ticket on a steamer for some country Fallon had never heard of.

"I did three jobs for you," Fallon corrected.

"I will see that you are well paid."

Fallon laughed. "With what?"

"I can afford to be generous, Fallon. The U.S. government will be paying me quite handsomely. We prevented a terrible war. We put a stop to traitors."

"Yeah." Fallon stood.

The little man glared. "You forget your place, Fallon. I got you out of Joliet."

"You damned near got me killed more times than I can count. You almost got Christina Whitney killed. You wouldn't have cared had your own son died." Fallon shook his head and walked toward the curtains. "I didn't trust Dan for a while. He even went a little crazy in Missouri, but, hell, we all go a little crazy. Prisons do that to people. But Dan's a good egg. He'll do a nice job running the American Detective Agency while you're in prison."

"Prison! Sir, I'll—"

Fallon jerked open the shades, and light—brilliant summer Chicago sunlight—bathed the office of Sean MacGregor for the first time in eons. Fallon saw dust motes filling the room like snow. The man screamed, turned, and shielded his eyes.

The doors opened, and Aaron Holderman staggered inside, the chains around his wrists and ankles clattering on the office's brown, ugly floor. Dan MacGregor followed. So did Christina Whitney. And several deputy U.S. marshals, a handful of Chicago newspapermen, and—at Fallon's insistence, just for spite—three Pinkerton detectives.

"Sean MacGregor," one of the marshals said as he withdrew a writ from his coat pocket. "You are under arrest for the robbery of the Houston-Victoria-Laredo Railroad, for defrauding the United States government, for . . ."

"Holderman!" The tiny man looked even smaller. "You damned fool."

"Boss . . ." the brute began, "they jumped me. I . . ."

Fallon felt a little sorry for the ex-convict. After all, Holderman had slipped Fallon that pocket pistol before he went out to Peckerwood Hill in Huntsville. Aaron Holderman couldn't help it that he had mush for brains, and no sound judgment, and that he was likely just following Sean MacGregor's orders when he back-shot those other Justice men and took a wagon filled with money north to San Antonio, where he bought a ticket to Chicago to deliver roughly two hundred thousand dollars to the president of the American Detective Agency.

He had paid for the ticket with a freshly minted double eagle. That's what had led the Pinkertons— Fallon couldn't wait to hear that at MacGregor's trial—to Chicago. It hadn't taken much pressure for Holderman to talk.

The little man kept screaming even as the marshals led him away.

Dressed in a new suit—and not the kind they give you when you walk out of Joliet—Harry Fallon sat on the bench at the train station. His shoulder didn't hurt much these days, and the autumn breeze felt really good. Over the past few months, he had slept well at the boardinghouse where he was supposed to have been living for several months. He had shared nice suppers with the wheelwright who was supposed to have been his boss. Now it was time to leave Chicago.

He looked up to find Christina Whitney walking toward him. Beside her strode Dan MacGregor. Fallon stood, removed his new hat, and waited.

MacGregor shook Fallon's hand.

"Congratulations," the new president of the American Detective Agency said.

"Thanks, Dan."

"I need to thank you," MacGregor said.

Fallon shrugged. "Just run a legal operation." He pulled back his coat, revealing the badge pinned on the lapel of his vest. "Otherwise, I might have to pay you a visit."

Dan MacGregor laughed and handed a few business cards to Fallon. "In case," he said, "you need a good detective agency to help you out West. Take care, Harry."

"Call me Hank," Fallon said, and shook the young man's hand again.

MacGregor laughed as he walked away. He called out to Christina, "Are you coming?" But he did not stop to hear her answer. She didn't answer. She didn't have to.

Christina moved closer to Fallon and looked at the badge.

"United States marshal," she whispered. "Not deputy."

Fallon shrugged. "It's a political appointment. Republicans get back in office, I'll likely be out of a job."

"But impressive . . . for an ex-convict."

"I've been pardoned," Fallon said with a smile.

He motioned at the bench. She sat. Fallon slid his grip out of the way and found a place next to her.

"What's Cheyenne like?" she asked.

"I wouldn't know," Fallon said. "I've never been to Wyoming."

"It probably gets cold."

"So does Illinois. And after Yuma, Jeff City, and Texas, cold sounds nice."

She laughed.

"Got any interesting cases going on?" Fallon asked.

"I resigned," she said.

"Too bad. Dan lost a good operative." He realized he still held MacGregor's business cards, so he slipped them inside his coat pocket.

A woman walked by, pushing a baby in a stroller.

Christina stared after it for a long time.

"I hear women can vote in Wyoming," she said.

Fallon nodded. "I hear that, too."

A man in a striped suit and scuffed gaiters, carrying two grips, stumbled down the steps and slid to a stop in front of their bench. Panting, his face flushed, hair plastered on his forehead, he gasped, "Excuse . . . me . . . Has the . . . four-oh-nine . . . left yet? Westbound. Headin' . . ."

"No," both Fallon and Christina answered simultaneously.

"It's late," Fallon said.

"Won't be here for another twenty minutes," Christina added.

"Oh, wonderful . . . what a relief." Stress left the man's face. "Thought for sure . . . I'd miss it . . . want to . . . see my family . . . in . . . Omaha." He adjusted his straw hat, thanked them again, and carried his baggage toward a man selling peanuts at the corner.

Fallon reached inside his coat pocket and withdrew his ticket. Christina opened her purse and looked at hers.

"Four-oh-nine?" Fallon asked.

"Four-oh-nine," Christina said.

"Runs all the way to Sacramento," Fallon said.

"I'm not going that far," Christina said.

Fallon returned his ticket, and Christina slipped hers back into the purse.

He wet his lips, closed his eyes, and saw Renee. She was holding Rachel and nodding at him. She looked so beautiful, so understanding. Her lips parted, and he could hear her say, *It's all right, Hank. It's all right. You're not in prison anymore, darling. Open your heart, dear, and live your life. Everything will be fine. We'll always love you.*

His eyes still closed, Fallon said, "I'm glad."

A moment later, he felt Christina's slender fingers come into his hand, which he closed around hers.

NATIONAL BESTSELLING AUTHORS
WILLIAM W. JOHNSTONE
and J. A. JOHNSTONE

SHOTGUN JOHNNY

NO ONE MESSES WITH SHOTGUN JOHNNY.

It takes a brave man to ride shotgun for the
Reverend's Temptation Gold Mine in the Sierra
Nevada Mountains. It takes an even braver man to
try to rob a coach of bullion when the shotgun rider
is Johnny Greenway. Armed with his weapons of
choice—two sawed-off double-barreled shotguns in
custom-made holsters for pistol-quick draws—
Shotgun Johnny ain't stopping for no one . . .

NOT UNLESS THEY WANT TO DIE.

Johnny Greenway was once a family man. A well-
respected marshal who always played fair. Then
his wife and son were killed by cutthroats. Johnny
killed the killers. And hung up his badge—and
picked up a bottle. Now a shadow of his former self,
he has nothing much to live for. But when he
singlehandedly stops a bank robbery, he catches
the eye of the banker's daughter. She's impressed
by Johnny's gun skills and offers him a job riding
shotgun. First he'll have to stop drinking and clean
up his act. But that's not all that needs cleaning.
The mountain trail to the mine hides
the filthiest, dirtiest gang in the territory.
They're gunning for the gold.
But Shotgun Johnny will be
gunning for them . . .

Look for Shotgun Johnny, on sale now.

"Ouch!" said "Rocky Mountain" Vernon Wade.

"What'd you do?" asked his partner, Pete Devries, with a snort of laughter.

"Burned myself." Wade winced as he shifted his hot coffee cup in his hands. "Think it's funny?"

Devries shrugged and sipped from his own hot cup. "Yeah, I guess so."

"Why is my burning my hand so funny to you, Pete?" Wade asked, glaring across a corner of their low fire at his partner, Devries.

"Oh, hell, I don't know," Devries said. He was tall and sandy-haired, and the brim of his Boss of the Plains Stetson was pulled low over his gray-blue eyes. "I reckon it was funny cause you otherwise act so tough. Forget it, Vernon. Stand down. I just chuckled at somethin' I thought was funny, that's all. I didn't mean to give offense."

"You did give offense."

"Well, then, for that I apologize."

"I am tough, Pete." Wade glared darkly. "And don't you forget it."

"Okay, I won't forget it." Devries looked off into the darkness of the Sierra Nevada mountain night.

"There you go again, laughin'."

Devries looked back at Wade, who was dark and solidly built with a thick beard he hardly ever washed and certainly never ran a comb through. On a previous bullion run he'd pulled a tick out of it the size of a sewing thimble but only because Devries had noticed it and mentioned it. Otherwise, it might still be there, sucking blood out of the humorless killer's cheek.

"What'd you laugh at that time, Pete?" Wade wanted to know.

"Oh, hell, Vernon!"

"Stop callin' me Vernon, Pete. Folks call me Rocky Mountain or nothin' at all. Folks call me Vernon only when they want to disrespect me, an' you don't want to do that, Pete. You really don't want to do that!"

"All right, all right, Vern . . . er, I mean, *Rocky Mountain.* I apologize for callin' you Vernon and for any and all other sundry ways I might have given offense during our time workin' together!"

"In case you're at all interested in anything except snickerin' like some twin-braided schoolgirl, I jerked with a start because I got distracted by a sound I heard out there." Wade pointed his chin to indicate the heavy darkness beyond the flickering orange light of the fire. "And, while I was silently opinin' on the source of the sound and the possible nature of the threat, if the sound's origin is in fact a threat, I let the cup tip a little too far to one side. So I was, in fact, reactin' as much to the sound as to the hot coffee washin' onto my fingers."

"Well, now that we got *that* all straightened out,"

Devries said, trying very hard not to give another wry snort, "what sound did you hear or think you heard?"

"I heard it, all right." Wade set his cup on a rock ringing the fire. He grabbed his Henry repeating rifle, rose from where he'd been sitting back against the wooly underside of his saddle, and walked over to stand by a tall fir tree at the edge of the encampment. One of the three horses, tied to a picket line nearby, gave a low whicker. "I got the hearin' of a desert jackrabbit, an' I heard somethin', all right. I'm just not sure what it was."

"Why don't you take a guess?"

Again, Wade turned a dull, hateful stare at his partner. "You don't believe me? Or you think I'm just actin' like some fearful old widder woman, hearin' things?"

Devries looked at the Henry. Wade held the sixteen-shot repeater in his right hand, partly aimed, threateningly, in Devries' direction. That was no accident. Wade wanted Devries to feel the threat. Devries knew that it was entirely likely that Rocky Mountain Vernon Wade would kill him for no more reason than because he felt Devries had insulted him, which Devries supposed he had though he'd mostly just been funning around.

Before they'd started working together, hauling bullion down out of the mountains from the Reverend's Temptation Gold Mine to the bank in Hallelujah Junction, Devries had heard that Wade was thin-skinned and hot-tempered. He'd also heard that Wade had killed men for little more reason than he'd taken offense at how they'd glanced at him, or for something someone had said in passing likely not even meant as an insult.

Now Devries realized those stories were true, and he made a mental note to tread a little more cautiously from here on . . .

"No, no, Vern . . . er, I mean, Rocky Mountain!" Devries said. "Will you please get your shorts out of the twist they seem to be in? I do not think you were acting like no widder woman. I believe that you in fact heard something, and I was just thinking that if you can't pinpoint exactly what that something was, maybe you could just opine aloud on it."

Wade studied him skeptically from over his shoulder.

Devries heart quickened. Jesus, he did not need this. Life was too short to be guarding gold with some sorehead with a hair trigger. And as loco as an owl in a lightning storm to boot!

Wade turned his head forward suddenly, sucking a sharp, shallow breath. "There it was again."

Devries pricked his ears. All he could hear was the snapping and crackling of their low fire and the infrequent stomps and shifts of the two horses and pack mule picketed twenty feet away. "I didn't hear anything."

"Well, I heard it."

Devries set down his coffee and rose from the log he'd been sitting on. He grabbed his Winchester and walked over to stand near Wade. Devries stared out into the darkness beyond their camp here in Henry's Hollow, not far from the South Fork of the Avalanche River and Grizzly Falls. He held his breath as he listened, squinting into the darkness, blinking, waiting for his eyes to adjust to the lack of light over here.

Normally, only fools and tinhorns would build a fire when they thought there was a chance they were being stalked. But neither Devries nor Wade had thought anyone would be fool enough to shadow them—two gunmen of significant reputations in this neck of California and Nevada. No man was fool enough to think they could swipe the bullion out from under Pete Devries and Rocky Mountain Vernon Wade.

Devries had thought so before, and, not hearing anything except the hooting of a distant owl and the soft scuttles of some burrowing creatures, he still thought so.

Maybe Wade was not only crazy. Maybe he was like some fearful old "widder" woman—hearing things.

Best not allude to the possibility, Devries silently admonished himself. Or at least do so in a round-about way . . .

"Hard to believe anyone would fool with us, Rocky Mountain," he said softly, staring into the darkness. "I mean you alone carry one hell of a reputation on them broad shoulders of yours. How many men have you killed, anyway?"

"I stopped countin' when I was twelve."

Devries snapped a disbelieving look at the big man standing to his right.

Wade felt it was his turn to snort. He turned to Devries with a crooked smile inside his black beard. "Just foolin' with ya, Peter. I think I stopped countin' when I was thirteen and a half." His smile grew wider.

Devries smiled then, too, thinking it was all right since Wade had made a joke.

Was it a joke?

Not that Devries was all that impressed or afraid of Vernon Wade. Devries had been a gunslinger and regulator of some renown for half a dozen years, before he'd ended up in the Texas pen for killing a barman in Nacogdoches. His attorney had gotten him out early when he'd discovered that the prosecutor had bought guilty verdict votes from three jury members. Devries hadn't been out of the pen for more than two days before he'd broken into the prosecutor's home one night and slit the man's throat while the man had been sound asleep beside his wife, who'd woken up screaming when she'd heard her husband choking on his own blood.

In other words, Devries' past was as impressive as Vernon Wade's. Pete just wasn't the blowhard Vernon was. Yes, *Vernon.* Devries might call the man "Rocky Mountain" to his face, just to keep things civil between them, but in his own mind he'd forever know him as *Vernon.* Or maybe even Vern*ie*. The only reason Pete didn't put a bullet through the blowhard's left ear right here and now was because this bullion run they were on, from the Reverend's Temptation to Hallelujah Junction, was one of the most perilous runs in all the Sierra Nevadas. The Temptation was a rich mine, and every owlhoot in California and Nevada knew it. There might be a handful just stupid enough to make a play for the gold, maybe not knowing who was guarding it.

The way Devries saw it, four eyes were better than two. Best to keep the peace.

Besides, Devries didn't want to ruffle the feathers of his comely employer, Miss Sheila Bonner, the young lady who'd taken over the Bank & Trust in Hallelujah Junction from her father, who'd also owned the Reverend's Temptation Mine. Miss Bonner was quite the looker, maybe the prettiest woman Devries had ever laid eyes on. She filled out her fine, if overly conservative, frocks just the way a dress was meant to be filled out. Pete was figuring to make a play for the woman. Not to marry, of course. Devries was not the apron-strings sort. But he purely would like to see what Miss Bonner looked like under all them fancy trappings, and, most of all, how she'd treat a fella after the lamps were turned down in her deceased father's stylish digs on a nice shady lot in Hallelujah Junction.

Devries didn't want to do anything that might spoil his prospects for a conquest. Shooting his partner, he supposed, might do just that. He'd put up with only so much, however. He could always shoot dim-witted Vern*ie*, and blame it on a bushwhacking owlhoot making a play for the bullion.

He stifled a laugh then jumped with a little start when Wade leaned toward him and said quietly, "I'm gonna wander on over this way. What I heard came from over there. You head that way. We'll circle around, check it out."

Devries' hackles rose a little at being given orders by one so cow-stupid not to mention ugly and with the hygiene of a hyena, but what the hell? "All right," he said, rolling his eyes. He still hadn't heard anything and was beginning to believe his partner really was as jumpy as that "widder" woman.

Vernie strode into the darkness to Devries' right. Devries stood looking around and listening a while longer. When he still hadn't heard a damn thing except the soft crunch of Vernie's boot in the dead leaves and pine needles, he indulged in another acidic snort then moved out into the darkness to his left.

"Big dummy," he muttered under his breath, and chuckled.

He stepped over a log, pushed through some shrubs, and stopped to look around and listen again.

Nothing.

He turned to his left and headed along the camp's eastern periphery, maybe ten feet beyond the reach of the fire's dwindling umber glow. When he was off the camp's northeastern corner, exactly opposite from where he and Vernie had separated, he stopped and listened again.

Not a damn thing. Hell, even the owl had stopped hooting.

Pete yawned, raked a hand down his face. They'd had a long day on the trail in the high-altitude wind and burning sunshine. He was tired, wind- and sun-burned, and he was ready to roll into his soogan. They'd rig up the horses and pack mule and set out again on the trail that led down out of the mountains soon after first light.

He turned to look back over his left shoulder, across the encampment toward where Vernie must be stumbling around in the darkness, chasing the shadows of ghosts. Pete had just opened his mouth to call out to his partner, when Wade himself yelled suddenly, "Stop! Stop! I see you, dammit! Stop or I'll shoot!"

Wade's Henry thundered—a loud booming report that made Devries leap with a start, his heels coming up off the ground.

He jerked again when the Henry spoke again . . . again . . . and again.

The sound of running footsteps sounded on the far side of the camp, maybe two hundred feet away, beyond the horses that were nickering and prancing around in fear, the mule doing the same, braying softly, all three tugging on their picket line.

"What is it?" Devries yelled, his heart pounding. "What do you see, Vern . . . I mean, *Rocky Mountain?*"

The running footsteps stopped suddenly.

Wade said something too softly, or maybe he was too far away, for Devries to hear.

Pete did hear the sudden gasp, however. It was loud as gasps go and it was followed by what sounded like a strangling sigh. The sigh was followed by a shrill, "Ahh . . . ohhh . . . ohhhh, *gawd!* Oh, you dirty, low-down . . ."

There was a light thump.

"What is it, Wade?"

Devries ran toward the sound of the commotion. He sprinted through the weak light thrown by the fire and then out of the light again and into the darkness near the whickering, skitter-hopping horses and mule. A deadfall pulled his right foot out from under him, and he hit the ground hard.

He lifted his head, sweating, his heart thundering in his ears. "What is it, Rocky Mountain?"

He stared into the darkness, breathing hard from the short run and the fear that verged on panic.

Footsteps rose on his left. Devries whipped his head in that direction. Someone was moving toward him, taking heavy, lunging strides. He saw the man's thick shadow.

"Wade?" he called. "Rocky Mountain, that you?"

No reply except for the heavy, lunging steps. The thick man's shadow moved through the forest, crouched slightly forward.

"Wade?" he called again, panic a living beast inside of him.

He looked around quickly, not hearing anything but the big man's approach. Still, he had the sense that he was surrounded and that men were tightening their positions around him.

He turned again toward the camp. The light from the fire began to reach the approaching man. Devries swung around from the darkness and, squeezing his cocked Winchester in both hands, hurried back into the camp just as the thick figure stepped up to the fire on the camp's opposite side.

Devries stopped.

"Rocky Mountain?"

Vernon Wade stood with his knees bent. He was crouched forward, chin dipped toward his chest, his arms crossed on his belly. Slowly, Wade lifted his head. He wasn't wearing his hat. His shaggy, unwashed hair hung in his eyes, which flashed in the fire's umber light. His gaze found Devries gaping at him from the other side of the fire.

"Th-they're . . . they're . . . here," Wade said in a strangled voice.

Devries sucked a breath when he saw what appeared to be blood—what else could it be?—oozing out from between his partner's crossed arms. Blood and Vernon Wade's innards.

Devries shuddered as though racked with a violent chill. Cold sweat pasted his shirt under his leather jacket against his back.

"Who's here, Rocky Mountain?"

"Oh . . . oh, *gawd*!" Wade sobbed, dropping to his knees. He lifted his head and stretched his lips back from his teeth. "*They killed me!*"

His arms fell to his sides. As they did, the guts he was trying to hold inside him plopped onto the ground before him. He fell face forward and lay across his bowels, shuddering as he died.

Devries stared down at the big, dark lump of his dead partner. "Who killed you, Rocky Mountain?" he whispered, rolling his eyes around, trying to peer around to all sides at once.

He glanced toward where he and Wade had placed the panniers filled with bullion from the Reverend's Temptation, between their two saddles, one on each side of the fire. Devries blinked his eyes as if to clear them.

The panniers were gone.

Again, his poor abused heart gave a violent kick against the backside of his sternum.

Someone laughed behind him. It was a high, devilish squeal. It was followed by the crunching of running feet.

Devries whipped around, raised his Winchester, and fired.

"Who are you?" he shouted, ejecting the spent shell from the Winchester's breech and seating a fresh one in the action.

He fired again. Again. The rocketing blasts shattered the night's heavy silence and made his ears ring.

More squealing laughter, like the laughter of a devilish boy pulling a prank, rose on his right. It mingled with the laughter of what sounded like a woman.

Devries slid the rifle in that direction, cocking it, the spent shell pinging onto the ground behind him. The rifle leaped and roared in his hands, flames stabbing from the barrel.

More laughter—this time on Devries' left.

Pete fired.

He fired until he had no more cartridges left in the Winchester's magazine. He winced when he heard the ping of the hammer dropping benignly against the firing pin.

He stared through his wafting powder smoke into the darkness around him.

No more laughter now. No more running footsteps. No more sounds of any kind. Not even the breeze.

The horses and mule must have pulled free of their picket line and hightailed it, for he did not see their bulky silhouettes on his left, though in his anxious shooting he hadn't heard them bolt.

The empty rifle shook in Devries' hands.

He dropped it as though it were a hot potato. It plopped onto the ground at his feet.

He reached across his belly with his right hand and pulled the big, top-break Russian .44 positioned for the cross-draw on his left hip. His hand was shaking so badly that he had trouble unsnapping the keeper thong from over the hammer, raising the heavy pistol, and cocking it.

"Show yourselves!" he screamed. "Show yourselves, you devils!"

His own echo washed over him, further chilling him. It sounded like the echoing cry of a terrified old widder woman.

A man's voice said casually behind him, "You boys sure can cook a good pot of coffee."

Devries whipped around so quickly that he almost fell.

He swung the big Russian around, as well, and aimed toward the fire. The blaze had been built up a little so that the light shone on the face of the man crouched over the opposite side of it. The man held a smoking tin cup in his gloved hands.

Devries moved slowly toward the fire. His heart was like a giant metronome in his chest, the pendulum assaulting his heart like a sharpened steel blade.

Devries stopped about ten feet away from the fire, staring aghast at the man hunkered there on the other side of the flames, on his haunches. He had a devil's grinning face with high, tapering cheeks obscured beneath a thick, sandy beard, and wicked slits for eyes. Coarse, sandy blond hair poked out from beneath the battered Stetson stuffed down on his head. He wore a buckskin coat with a fox fur collar. A Colt's revolving rifle leaned against the log to his right, within an easy reach.

The man smiled his devil's smile at Devries. He raised his coffee to his lips, blew on it, and sipped. Swallowing, he straightened to his full height, which was maybe six feet, if that. He was not a tall man. But, then, Harry Seville had never needed to be.

What Seville lacked for in height, he made up for in pure cunning and black-hearted meanness and storied savagery.

Footsteps sounded around Devries. Squeezing the big Russian in his hands, he swung the pistol from right to left then back again, that metronome in his chest fairly shredding his heart. Men stepped into the firelight around him by ones and two and threes and fours . . . until well over a dozen men aiming rifles or pistols at him surrounded him, grinning beneath the brims of their battered hats.

Make that over a dozen men and one woman, a big one who looked very much like a man except she wore a long, black skirt. She was laughing beneath the round, wide crown of her man's felt hat.

"Ah," Devries heard himself say in a small, defeated voice. "Ah . . . hell . . ."

The big man laughed heartily, his devil's eyes slitting so much that they were nearly closed. The other men laughed as well. They laughed and elbowed each other and pointed out the object of their mockery. They snorted and brushed fists across their noses and poked their hat brims back off their foreheads.

Devries had just begun to feel warm water trickling down his leg before a hand slugged his hat from his head from behind then grabbed a fistful of his hair. Pete cried out as the brusque hand pulled his head back by his hair until he found himself staring up at a big, dark man towering over him from behind. Devries tried to raise the barrel of the Russian, but then he felt an icy line drawn across his throat, and all strength left him at once.

He sank to the ground, gasping, lifting his hands to his neck to try to remove the cold noose that had been drawn taut around him. His fingers touched only the oily slickness of blood.

There was no noose. His throat had been cut.

Lying on his back, Devries stared up from the ground at the man who'd killed him. He was a tall, broad-shouldered gent in a bearskin coat and a bullet-shaped black hat from beneath which twin black braids trailed down over the front of his broad shoulders.

Seville.and his half-breed Sioux partner, Louis Raised-By-Wolves. He knew their dastardly reputations.

Devries had done some lousy things on this earth,

but he didn't believe he'd ever committed an atrocity horrible enough to warrant the last thing he saw on this side of the sod be Louis Raised-By-Wolves staring down at him, chuckling at him and licking Devries' own blood from the blade of his bowie knife as though it were the sweetest nectar he'd ever tasted.